FORTS:
Liars and Thieves

Steven Novak

Published in the United States of America by Quiet Corner Press in cooperation with The Literary Underground, Yucaipa, California 92399
www.litunderground.com

Cover design and interior illustrations by Steven Novak

www.novakillustration.com

ISBN: 0615480098
ISBN-13: 9780615480091 (Quiet Corner Press)

DEDICATION

This one is for Pete, Laura, Cecelia, Morgan, Heather, Lia and Celes.

ACKNOWLEDGMENTS

First and foremost let me thank my wife for sticking with me even when she shouldn't have. A great many thanks to my entire family as well. It's been a rough few years for some of us. Through it all each and every one of you has been there for me when I needed you. Since there's no way I could ever hope to truly pay you back, I'm giving you an acknowledgement in my crummy little book.

Guess that makes us even, Steven?

I should also throw some thanks in the direction of my pals at the Literary Underground and especially to, MJ Heiser for having the guts to weed through my sloppy writing and make some sense of it, and of course Mary Ann Bernal for doing some last minute clean up. I love you guys. We're making lemonade out of lemons and we're having fun doing it.

Lastly, a hearty huzzah to everyone out there that forked over their hard earned cash for this thing. You didn't have to. You could have spent that money on a couple sandwiches, or maybe even a trip to the theater. Instead you bought this.

I tried my best to write you something worthwhile.

Hopefully I didn't let you down.

-Steve

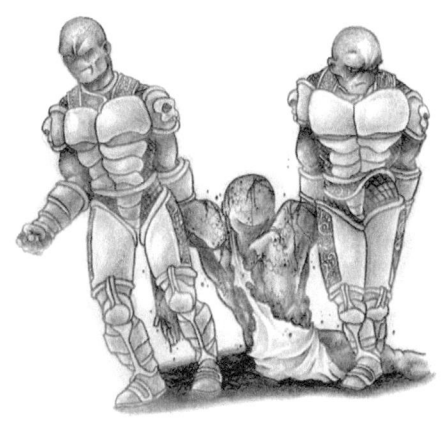

1. TRAITOR TO THE CAUSE

For him, time ceased to have meaning long ago. How many days had he spent shackled in the king's dungeon? Could it be weeks? Months even? Long enough that the heavy chains around his ankles sliced into his skin, merging with the muscle underneath and forcing the flesh to heal grotesquely around them. How often was he dragged from his cell and beaten? How many times had he teetered through a wobbly haze, barely conscious on the razor-thin line between life and death? Two hundred? Three hundred? Maybe four? His body no longer resembled the one he'd spent a lifetime becoming familiar with. Quite adept in the dealing of punishment, the guard's fists had changed him into something else. Like a reflection in a broken mirror, he was shattered, distorted, and barely recognizable. Busted numerous times, his jaw dangled from his face, useless. All but a few of his teeth had been removed — some ripped out during hour-long torture sessions, others knocked loose during any one of the regular beatings. His skin, once a healthy dark green, had become a disgusting, blotchy mess of purples, blues, and deep grayish-blacks. Even the most minute of movements on his part brought forth worlds of agony. The gentle breeze from a window nearby instantly reduced him to tears. His limbs had long since ceased functioning, devolving his form a million years and making upright movement impossible. Having suffered through things no creature should ever be forced to feel, he found himself crumpled in a garish heap at the feet of the massive, stone-faced tyrant king of Ocha. A small part of him wondered if he'd made the right choice. This pain could have been avoided. He brought this on himself.

Gently nudging the broken, tangled body of the creature sprawled before him, the massive king sighed deeply. "How sad it is to see you like this, Krystoph. I had such high hopes for you. You were so very talented in the art of killing … so frighteningly, wonderfully talented. There was a time, not too long ago, when my opinion of you approached admiration."

Shaking his head while flashing a disgusted look at the broken lump, the king turned swiftly, pacing back to his throne before reclining with yet another heavy sigh. "I gave you everything, and what did you offer in return — deceit, lies, and thievery? You've shamed your king. You've shamed your country and all those calling it home. You've shamed yourself."

His ears smashed and barely of use, the broken lump of flesh that once answered to the name Krystoph was able only to make out half the king's words, and even they seemed distant and jumbled. Despite this fact, his clouded brain managed to put the pieces together well enough to get a general idea of the point the ruler of Ocha was trying to make. Doing his best to ignore the unbelievable amount of pain shooting through every centimeter of his body, Krystoph lifted his weary, half-conscious face with a shaky defiance to the creature he once admired beyond all others.

While using a hand consisting mostly of broken fingers to hold his jaw in place, he grumbled, "Y-you … ki-killed m-my … my … family."

Quietly the tyrant King Kragamel chuckled. "You are mistaken old friend. Long ago you gave your life to me, and in return I allowed you the privilege of serving as a general in the greatest army the world has ever known and will ever know. In doing so, your family became my family. You see, unlike what you've stolen from me, their lives were mine to do with as I pleased. They were mine to kill."

In direct response to the words, Krystoph's distorted excuse for a body lurched forward angrily. His broken legs awkwardly thrust the mass of wrecked bones and torn muscles in the king's direction. Something more a guttural noise than a fully imagined word rose up from his belly, exploding from his mouth like searing magma. Despite the fact that his fingers had been shattered beyond the point of usefulness, Krystoph reached for the king's foot, clawing at his thick leather boot. The rabid, snarling growl did little to frighten Kragamel though. His expression remained stoic. Many times in the past Krystoph had proven the most capable, the most willing, and the most vicious soldier his army ever produced. The snarling, sniveling mass of bloody flesh kneeling before him now – this was not Krystoph. Nothing remained of Ocha's most feared general, and the revolting thing he'd become was of no threat. Placing his foot on top of Krystoph's head, the king easily shoved the broken lump of flesh away as two beefy guards rushed in, pulling Krystoph further still from Ocha's benevolent leader. The flow of adrenaline having passed, Krystoph began at last to feel the result of his outburst. His body was in no shape for such an act. Now he found himself struggling not only to reclaim his escaping breath but also to deal with the flashes of deep, searing pain tearing him apart from within.

"I will give you one more chance old friend." The king offered sternly from atop his throne. "Tell me where you've hidden it. End this nonsense. You know I will locate it eventually; you will have suffered for nothing. Why take your misguided hatred for me out on the Ochan race? Should this great nation suffer because of your random loss of common sense? Tell me where it is … tell me where it is and this all comes to an end. Tell me where it is, and I assure you I will make your death quick and painless."

Though one of his lungs was punctured months ago, Krystoph breathed in deeply, managing to momentarily gain control of the pain pouring over him like molten steel. His brain was on fire, his head on the brink of an explosion. Grimacing through eyes drowning in blood, he attempted for the first time in weeks to pull his twisted, mangled body upright. Seeing this, the two guards hovering nearby immediately moved close and shoved him back to the floor. With a flip of his wrist and a slight gesture of his fingers, King Kragamel ordered them to stand down. Managing successfully to maneuver himself to one knee, Krystoph bit down on his lower lip with the few reaming teeth in his mouth and grunted deeply, eventually hoisting his tattered, starved, frail body upward. Teetering atop wobbly, useless legs, he raised his shaky head, staring defiantly into the eyes of Ocha's most feared king.

With a voice of whispered rage he choked out a single word, "No."

Overcome with the undeniable urge to rip the head from his former general's shoulders and place it on a pike in the center of the castle courtyard for all to see, the king instead shoved his emotions down, successfully centering his rapidly expanding rage.

Krystoph would have loved nothing more than to see him frazzled, and because of this, frazzled was by no means an option. Calmly looking past Krystoph's unsteady form, Kragamel called out to the back of the room: "Gragor!"

From the opposite side of the massive throne room, the then newly-appointed, still young, fresh, and anxious to please general of the king's armies moved across the floor in long, determined strides. Stopping alongside Krystoph, the massive Ochan dropped to a knee, bowing his head in reverence of his king. "Yes sire?"

"We could torture this traitor until the end of our days, and it is unlikely he will ever tell us what we need to know; he has been trained too well. He has outworn his usefulness. I shall waste no more time on him. I want you personally to take him to the fire caves, open his throat, and watch the life bleed from his sad excuse for a body. Do not burn his corpse though ... let the combustion beetles make a meal of him instead. This fool is undeserving of a proper torching."

Though barely noticeable to most in the room, Gragor grinned ever so slightly. "Of course sire. Consider it done."

Still wobbling, his body shaking violently as a jolt of pain traveled up his spine, Krystoph managed to remain standing, his steely gaze never once moving from the king. Even after hearing the words from Kragamel's mouth, at no point would his expression falter.

The king would have loved nothing more than to see him weakened and because of this weakness was simply not an option.

Gragor locked his muscular arms around Krystoph's torso, tugging his busted, useless form backward across the cold stone floor. From his throne the tyrant king of Ocha watched intently until his former general was pulled from sight. He allowed himself only a moment to dwell on his choice before moving to the next order of business. The king had ordered many to die during his tenure. Krystoph was no different than any of the others.

Once dead they are gone and once gone they never come back – this was the way of things.

2. FAMILY VISITS

"Boys?" Edna Williamson called out from the bottom of the stairs. "Your father and the chaperone should be here soon! Why don't you come downstairs?"

Both Tommy Jarvis and his younger brother Nicky clearly heard her words, yet neither made a movement toward the bedroom door. It had been months since either boy had been in the same room with their father. The abuse allegations, and subsequent investigation proving them to be true, resulted in their removal from his care and placement with a foster family. For almost half a year they lived with a couple of retirees named Ed and Edna Williamson. In spite of their comically similar first names, the Williamsons proved to be decent, caring people — not perfect people by any means, but good people — the kind of people Tommy and Nicky barely believed existed anymore. Neither boy had forgotten about their father, yet at the same time they were only now beginning to settle in to their new life with the Williamsons. Things were easier for them here, quieter and certainly a lot less painful. The truth of the matter was that neither boy found the idea of introducing their father back into their lives even remotely appetizing. A week and a half before, a social worker for the state sat the pair down, telling them that Chris had been attending his meetings, that he was sober, and remorseful, that he was making great strides, and was anxious to see them again. Of the two, Nicky was slightly more open to the idea of reuniting with their father, but then Nicky's past experiences with the old man were quite different from Tommy's.

The memories – the awful, stinging memories –just recently began melting away for the fourteen year old Tommy Jarvis. What would happen now though? What would happen, when after all these months, Tommy came face to face with his father? Would the very old, very thick anger boil up from wherever he'd managed to shove it down deep inside his belly? Would the pain attached to those memories like a nasty parasite feeding off a half-starved host prove too much to bear? There were some questions in life for which one simply didn't want answers. For Tommy Jarvis, these were those very questions.

"Boys? Come on now, don't dawdle . . .get your behinds down here." Edna yelled out a bit more forcefully from downstairs.

Propped up on his elbows, Nicky reluctantly slid his feet over the side of his bed, sighing deeply. Across the room Tommy remained on his back, staring blankly up at the ceiling. His eyes were closed, his chest rising and sinking patiently with each breath. Tommy didn't want to forgive his father, and he couldn't understand why everyone seemed to expect him to. Even if the old man had changed – even if he never again laid a hand on him, or screamed at his little brother – so what? The damage had been done.

Some things, once done, can never be undone. It was as simple as that.

Things were by no means perfect with the Williamsons, but they were certainly better than anything the Jarvis brothers had experienced in a very long time. Tommy understood completely that he and Nicky's time with Ed and Edna was limited - a temporary solution at best. Temporary or not, it was something he wasn't ready to let go of. Nicky was speaking again and doing better in school. Last week Tommy spotted his little brother talking to another boy outside the building after school ended. Nicky had a friend - a real, living and breathing friend. Things were getting better. For the first time in years, happiness - even on the tiniest of levels - seemed attainable. It could all go away with the snap of the fingers — or the stinging crack of a backhand across the face if they were forced to move back in with their father. Only recently, Tommy had experienced, for the very first time, the wonderful sensation of going to bed without a welt on his leg, a scratch on his arm, or a fractured bone inside his chest. Lately his sleep had been deep and comfortable and warm, his dreams non-existent. How utterly amazing it had been to simply sleep, free of nightmares and without worry. It was luxury he had forgotten existed. What did a life with his father have to offer? Why did he deserve a second chance? He didn't.

"Are you coming down?" Nicky asked Tommy while standing next to his bed, and staring at his older brother from across the room.

Tommy breathed deeply, turning his head slightly in Nicky's direction. "No...and neither should you."

"We have to."

"We don't have to do anything Nicky...especially not for him." Twisting his body sideways while pulling his knees to his chest and curling into a half-fetal position, Tommy turned away from the confused face of his little brother and toward the opposite wall.

At the bottom of the stairs, Edna Williamson was a moment away from calling to the boys again when she noticed Nicky slowly making his way toward her. Tommy, though, was nowhere to be found.

"Where's your brother?" She asked the youngest Jarvis boy as he passed her on his way into the kitchen.

"He doesn't want to come down," Nicky responded softly, never turning in her direction.

From the opposite end of the room, Ed Williamson sighed with a deep, noticeable frustration while tugging his aching body up from a very comfortable position on the couch.

"I'll go have a talk with him," he grumbled, slowly beginning the long journey up the stairs.

"Don't you go flying off the handle, Ed . . .this isn't easy on the boy."

"I know Edna, I know. Give me a little credit will you. I'm just going to have a little chat with him, that's all."

"If he's not ready to come down, the social worker said we shouldn't push too hard . . .especially not for the first meeting."

Ed was near the top of the stairs now, his chest straining, his aged knees aching from the journey.

Stopping momentarily to catch his breath he looked down at his wife of so many years while rolling his eyes, "I remember what she said . . .I remember. If there's anyone in this house that knows what he's going through, it's me. Relax. I'm not going to push the boy, trust me."

The wrinkled, slightly more crooked than it was twenty years ago smile on her husband's face instantly reassured Edna Williamson. She loved Ed. She loved him as much as the day they were married, though for entirely different reasons. Love is funny like that, having the uncanny ability to morph into something completely foreign while still holding onto the things that made it so unique, wonderful, and safe in the first place. The sixty-three year old Edward Williamson was a good deal different from the twenty-four year old version. In his heart though, despite the changes brought on by age and experience, he was still the same man she fell in love with and still a comfortably perfect fit for her.

Reaching the door to the boy's bedroom, Ed stopped for a moment to collect his thoughts. Rubbing his hand across his balding head covered sparsely with stringy gray hair, he sighed deeply. His mind wandered back many, many years to his own father, to the unresolved issues he allowed to remain unresolved until the day his father died. As frustrated as young Tommy Jarvis had occasionally made him over the last six months, he cared about the boy. In fact, he cared about the boy so deeply that it surprised him. When Edna suggested they become a foster family, the one thing Ed never counted on was forming any real, serious feelings for the children sent to live with them. After his own son's untimely death so many years ago, he simply didn't think he was capable of such a thing anymore. Having loved a child so deeply only to have that love taken away – he always believed it left him hollow and incapable of reaching that peak again.

The appearance of the Jarvis boys had proved him wrong.

After mustering up a bit of courage, he pushed the bedroom door open gently, "Hey pal, why don't you . . ." Ed's voice quickly trailed off.

The room was empty. Tommy was gone. The window on the opposite wall was wide open, loose drapes flapping softly in the fall breeze.

Shaking his head, Ed calmly called out to his wife from the top of the stairs, "I think Tommy is going to sit this one out, dear."

3. LIFE AND TIMES OF A LOCAL BULLY

"Hey loser…wake up."

Donald Rondage slowly opened his eyes, the blurry world around him folding clumsily into focus.

"I said wake up! Come on, move your pudge!"

Not fully aware of what was happening, Donald was shoved in the square of his back and rolled awkwardly off the couch on which, until that very moment, he was sleeping quite soundly. With a heavy thud, his oversized body collapsed to the floor, colliding with the legs of a nearby table. The smack of thick wood into soft flesh instantly sent a sharp pain across the muscles in his shoulder and down the right side of his body. Wincing while trying to get his bearings, he looked back at the dusty lime green couch. Silhouetted by the light of a nearby lamp like pair of angry shadows were his two older brothers. Behind them, three local boys of whom he was only slightly familiar cackled at his situation like a pack of wild hyenas.

"Get your fat ass out of here, Roundy . . .the adults have got some business to take care of," his oldest brother, Alex, stated gruffly while delivering a stiff kick to Donald's side. "Go hang out in your room and play dress up with your dollies — I don't really care. You can't stay here, though."

The group of boys instantly converged on the empty couch. Alex pulled a sandwich bag filled with a light green substance from his jacket pocket. "Alright you losers, this is the good stuff I've got for you today, so I'm expecting top dollar. If you're looking for the cheap crap, the door's right over there — don't let it hit you in the ass on your way out."

Despite being filled with an overwhelming urge to leap onto Alex's chest, push him to the floor and smack him around, Donald instead pulled himself to his feet and shuffled toward his bedroom. While Donald Rondage might have been considered large when compared to the average fourteen-year old, Alex and Will were large for average seventeen- and eighteen-year olds, respectively. He wouldn't have stood a chance against one of them, let alone the pair *and* their drug addict friends as well. Over the years Donald had found it easier to simply keep his mouth shut and go his own way. Standing up to his brothers in the past had proven to be an extremely painful experience. Neither Alex nor Will had ever given Donald the slightest bit of respect – after all, he was only their half-brother – barely a brother at all, really, at least in their eyes.

Donald had never met his father. The few times that he tried to ask his mother about him, her response was always the same, *"He was a loser, Donny . . .a mistake. Trust me, you're better off forgetting he even exists."*

While it sounded simple enough in theory – just to forget about him — Donald had spent the majority of his young life wondering about the father he'd never met. What did he look like? What kind of man was he? Why did he leave? What would he think of his son if they ever came face-to-face? He hated his father, which he found strange. To be filled with such incredible hatred toward a person while at the same time longing so very badly to meet them was a contradiction he'd wrestled with for years. At this point, though, he had resigned himself to the fact that he would more than likely never find the answers to his questions concerning the man partially responsible for his creation. It's because of this that, long ago, he made the decision that simply not having questions in the first place was the only truly viable solution. In order to move on, he had to accept the unknown and the unknowable. The invisible man would forever remain invisible.

Arriving at his bedroom, Donald stomped inside, slamming the door behind him with the vague hope it might silence the sounds of his brothers' voices. His bedroom was sparsely decorated, little more than a twin bed with a dresser. His clothes, strewn haphazardly across the floor, were dirty and wrinkled, as if they hadn't been washed in months — which was exactly the case. The Rondage family had never had much money, and what little they'd managed to scrape together was almost never spent on Donald — or even his brothers, for that matter. His mother Victoria was a single parent raising three boys with little to no help from any of their fathers. Every few months a new boyfriend moved in, burned through what little funds she might have managed to scrape together, then got into a screaming match with her, broke a piece of furniture, and was instantly sent on his merry way. So many men had come through the doors over the years that Donald could scarcely recall even half their names. There was Dale, Roger, Mark, Walter, another Mark, a Marcus, Edgar, Bo, Bob, Bill, and who could forget the guy with the tattoo covering his bald head that wanted Donald to call him the Mash Man?

Yep, his mother sure knew how to pick them.

Coming from what was essentially the "wrong side of the tracks," Donald had spent his life feeling like an outsider at school. It didn't take long for this feeling of inadequacy to transform into jealousy. Not long after that the jealousy turned to anger - as jealousy has a tendency to do. He'd chosen to spend his formative years locked inside this wall of anger.

Falling face first onto a pile of clothes scattered across his bed, Donald ground his teeth together while silently cursing his mother and brothers under his breath. Why couldn't his family be like everyone else's? Why were things always so much harder for him than the rest of the kids at school? Those jerks didn't deserve what they had – not a single one of them. It wasn't fair. None of it. Inhaling the disgusting, sweaty butt-stink from the seat of a dirty pair of jeans snuggled against his nose, Donald's mind wandered from his frustrating excuse of a life to the mysterious land of Fillagrou and his experiences there. As frightening as it was – stumbling into another world, fighting muscled lizard men and seeing so much death firsthand – as terrifying and painful an experience as it proved to be, he missed it. In Fillagrou, he had powers. In Fillagrou, a house weighed no more than a rock, and a rock could be crushed to dust between his fingers. In Fillagrou he was something, he was somebody – unlike what he was here, which was nothing.

The annoying, screeching cackle of his brothers and their friends in the other room had grown louder. Every high-pitched shriek stabbed him in the ears. The awful smell of their smoke was slowly creeping under his door, sinking into the fibers of his clothes and sheets where it would undoubtedly linger for days. A sharp pain in his head pressed against his temples, further feeding his hungry annoyance. Rolling off his bed, Donald grabbed a sweatshirt from the floor and pulled it over his head. He didn't want to be here anymore. This house and the people living in it were the cause of every single one of his problems. He saw no point in spending more time in their company than necessary.

He needed to get away. It didn't matter where he went – anywhere was better than here.

Opening the broken window in his bedroom took some work, as it was sloppily painted shut some years ago. Immediately after prying it loose, Donald pulled himself through and ended up in the backyard. The sky above him was gray, heavy with cloud cover. A chilly fall breeze hit him square in the face, immediately reddening his nose, cheeks and ears. Inside the house Donald could still hear the excited squeals of his brothers and their annoying friends. Pulling the hood of his sweatshirt over his head, he began walking in the opposite direction with his shoulders slumped deeply. Eventually the laughter faded away, swallowed up by the soft rustle of the dead, falling leaves. The direction in which he headed was of no real importance. All that mattered was that it led away from home. His mother was working the late shift and wouldn't be home for hours. There was no rush. He had all night.

4. TEARFUL REUNION

Chris Jarvis showed up at the Williamson's home at ten 'til five. The state appointed social worker had yet to arrive. After shutting off the engine, Chris leaned back in the seat of his car, taking the opportunity to breathe deeply. Still gripping the wheel, he noticed his hands were shaking ever so slightly, sliding back and forth across the worn, tightly drawn leather. It had been so long since he'd seen either of his children, since he'd gazed into their eyes. It was even longer since he'd seen either of them smile.

Chris was only now beginning to understand how badly he had failed his boys. Three months sober had brought a variety of previously blurry moments over the past few years into crystal-clear focus – some of which he wished he could forget again. The enormity of his wrongs was staggering. Not only had he failed his children, but he had failed himself as well. The question now became: Would Tommy or Nicky ever find it in their hearts to forgive him? Could they? Did he even deserve their forgiveness? Could he forgive himself? *Should* he forgive himself?

In the rearview mirror, Chris watched as the car belonging to the social worker pulled into the driveway behind him. Instantly the thump of his heart quickened. He mashed his sweaty hands together, his fingers twitching and twiddling and tightly intertwined. Ahead of him the home of Ed and Edna Williamson loomed like a massive black question mark across the darkening mid-afternoon sky. Within its walls lay his past, his present and his future. Behind the cheap vinyl siding rested something not everyone is fortunate enough to receive in their lives – inside lay a second chance.

From his thinning hairline dripped a worried, panicky sweat. Months of counseling, hour upon hour of baring the deepest, darkest, most shameful recesses of his soul to people he barely knew, had led him to this single moment. He couldn't fail. He wouldn't fail, not again. Chris retrieved his wedding ring from his jacket pocket. The modest gold band was stained with bluish-green spots, scratched and old, grimy looking by even the oldest of wedding band standards. He thought he'd lost it after Megan's death – another victim of one of his many drunken stupors. While cleaning three weeks ago he discovered it wedged beneath some old boxes in the garage. It was chipped, it was filthy — yet it could be made clean. He knew that much like this ring, anything could be polished if given the proper time and care. Making a fist, he squeezed the tiny band of gold so tightly it left an imprint on the skin of his palm. If ever in his life there had been a moment he needed Megan beside him, this was it.

Hearing the doorbell ring, Edna Williamson quickly crossed the distance between the kitchen and the front door. After checking her hair in a nearby mirror, she took a deep breath and opened it. On her front porch, an awkward, slightly shameful smile spread across his face, stood Chris Jarvis. Having spent months wondering exactly what the man would look like, Edna found herself slightly disappointed with the reality. Hearing what the Jarvis boys had been put through, she half expected the boogeyman, something terrifying and evil, something less a human being than a force of nature. The person standing shyly on her porch, though, was no creature of darkness - this was just a man. Despite his six foot, two hundred-or-so pound frame, Chris Jarvis looked significantly more sad than imposing. Like a child caught with his hands in the cookie jar, he seemed ashamed of himself, so much so that he could barely look her in the eye. Surprisingly, rather than feeling anger toward him, Edna Williamson suddenly realized she was overcome with pity.

"Mr. Jarvis," She stated simply, slightly nodding and doing her best to keep things proper, cordial and businesslike.

"Hello, Mrs. Williamson," Chris responded softly, uncomfortably digging the tip of his shoe into the concrete beneath his feet.

"Mrs. Williamson?" A somewhat high-pitched feminine voice squeaked out from behind Chris. "Hi! Mrs. Williamson, I'm Amber Frye, Child Social Services."

A smallish woman with long blonde hair pulled tightly back into a ponytail stepped out from behind Chris, extending her hand forward. Edna quickly made note of the fact that the girl couldn't possibly be more than twenty-five or twenty-six years of age, if that. Suddenly she felt very old. Suddenly she cursed herself for not spending more time fixing her hair.

"Nice to meet you, Ms. Frye." Edna answered politely, shaking the young woman's delicate hand while admiring the luxurious length of her eyelashes. "Please, both of you, come in."

Immediately after stepping into the Williamson's home, Chris caught sight of Nicky standing at the end of a hallway leading to the kitchen. Behind his son, a hand resting gently on the boy's left shoulder, was a stone-faced Ed Williamson.

Unlike his wife, Ed felt absolutely no sympathy for Chris Jarvis and doubted he ever would. The man had done terrible things –to his own children, no less. The very idea confused and disgusted him in a way that brought new meaning to the words. Chris Jarvis deserved no sympathy. For some things there are no excuses, no reasoning that instantly makes them acceptable or understandable, and this was one of those things. Ed's grip on Nicky's shoulder tightened a bit, his fingers pressing protectively into the boy's flesh.

A fatherly instinct he long thought buried rushed up from his chest and into his hands – quite suddenly he didn't want to let the boy slide from his grasp.

Standing in front of his youngest son after such a very long time, Chris Jarvis found himself overcome with a mixture of excitement, happiness, incredible shame, and awful fear. Emotions too large and complicated to fully comprehend scattered wildly in every direction inside his brain. Every time he managed to grab hold of one, another buzzed past, causing him to lose his grip and forcing him to start over.

With no idea what to say, Chris chose to mumble the obvious. "Hi, Nicky."

It was stupid, simple, and meaningless. It did nothing to capture the magnitude of the moment, yet it was all he could manage.

Neither son nor father made a move. The air in the foyer of the Williamsons' home quickly grew silent, thick and gooey, like a jar of extra sticky molasses. For nearly a minute, not a single word was muttered. Feeling the urge to move closer to his son, Chris glanced in the direction of the diminutive Amber Frye for confirmation.

After nodding to him, Amber found herself absent-mindedly averting her gaze, unable to fully deal with the awkwardness of the situation. Technically this was her first time in the field. Having only been hired earlier this year, most of that time had been spent behind a desk filing, documenting, copying, and doing everything else generally referred to as paperwork. Despite having trained for situations such as this, she quickly realized that it in no way prepared her for the starkness the reality of the moment would carry with it. She felt like a voyeur, as if the moment were something she shouldn't be seeing – even if it happened to be her job.

Taking two steps in the direction of his son Chris whispered with some caution, "It's good to see you again buddy . . .you - you look good . . .your hair's gotten longer."

Extending his finger, Chris pointed toward his son's shaggy, brown locks. They had grown a bit over the last few months, coming perilously close to covering his eyes and making the boy look a bit like a spindly, dark haired sheep dog. Not sure what to say next, Chris let his body decide for him. Slowly lifting his arms and opening them wide, he awkwardly invited his son to give him a hug. It was an enormous step – moving from zero to sixty in less than a second — but it was a step he felt he had to take.

Even with everything that had happened in the past, with everything he'd seen the old man do to his brother and everything that was done to him — quite unexpectedly Nicky Jarvis found himself filled with the overwhelming desire to be close to his father once again. Swallowing deep, he wiggled himself from Ed's grip, leaping forward as if his legs were spring-loaded, and melted into Chris' outstretched arms.

Tears welling up in the corners of his eyes, Chris Jarvis enveloped his son completely, pulling him tight to his chest while squeezing with every last muscle in his upper body. His hand reached forward to cup the back of Nicky's head, his fingers intertwining with the boy's thick hair.

In a half-there, shaky on-the-border-of-tipping voice, he choked, "I missed you Nicky. I missed you so much. I'm so sorry."

A lump in Nicky's throat made it impossible to answer back. Instead of trying, the teary-eyed boy tightened his grip on his father's waist, pressing his head harder against the man's torso. Half-happy and half-sad, the tears in Chris' eyes responded in a way mere words could never do justice.

Simultaneously frightening and heart-warming, the inherent strangeness of the moment was not lost on Nicky Jarvis, or anyone else in the room for that matter. Trying his best to not think of what had happened in the past, or what might happen in the future, Nicky instead let the safety of his father's hug fill him with much-needed warmth for the first time in a very long time. A part of him believed that this moment might never come again – making it even more important that he enjoy it while it lasted.

In spite of her best efforts to not get caught up in the moment, Edna Williamson could feel her cheeks warming, an unwanted moisture building up behind her eyes. With a tissue retrieved from the pocket of her pants, she dabbed away the tears before they caused her makeup to run and smiled kindly at the father-son reunion, praying it would be the first of many.

Near the end of the hallway, Ed Williamson turned his back.

5. MY ENEMY, MY FRIEND

The trip across town to the tree fort took some time, and when Tommy finally arrived the sun had already begun its slow descent into night. Fall had stripped the tree branches bare, its dead brown leaves lying scattered across the ground below. No longer hidden behind thick foliage, the haphazardly constructed tree fort seemed less impressive than he remembered it. Every crooked, rain-warped board and bent nail was exposed for all to see. What seemed astoundingly well constructed in the summer suddenly looked sloppy - obviously the work of a child. The icy weather of the coming winter had begun to freeze small sections of the stream near the tree's base; thick chunks of smooth, dirty ice now sprouted sporadically from the water's edge. Underneath the water and the ice was the doorway to Fillagrou. Now more than ever Tommy wished he could go back. Having tried unsuccessfully on numerous occasions since returning six months ago, he came to the realization long ago that it simply wasn't possible. Something Zanell said to him before saying goodbye for the last time scratched at the back of his brain like an unwelcome visitor: *"The door lets through who needs to be let through, when they need to be let through."* It was cryptic, it was stupid, and it was apparently true. This was no simple doorway, and unfortunately for Tommy Jarvis it seemed off limits — for the moment, anyway.

"Don't bother trying, weirdo. It ain't gonna work."

The deep voice came from somewhere behind Tommy. Quickly rotating in place, he glanced upward toward the tree fort. Leaning halfway out of the crudely constructed window near the front with an annoyed smirk on his face was the burly-bodied Donald Rondage.

"I've tried going back at least twenty times. All it got me was soaking wet," Donald grumbled, cautiously making his way down the rickety boards nailed to the tree's trunk. "I even stole an old snorkel from my brother's room and searched every inch of that damn stream bottom with my bare hands. Guess what I found? Zero. Nothing. For a while, I started thinking that maybe I dreamt the whole damn thing. I guess you showing up here proves that's not the case."

Much had changed in the relationship between Tommy and Donald over the last six months. Since the third grade it seemed to Tommy that Donald's sole purpose in life was to make his a living hell. During school, after school, on the weekends, and during breaks the torment would come at any time and any place. Fillagrou changed that. Since returning, Donald had not only stopped bullying Tommy, but everyone else as well. He'd withdrawn into himself and transformed from a loud obnoxious bruiser to a silent brooding bruiser. Though the two boys had never really spoken at length about what happened, they had occasionally exchanged a knowing glance in the halls at school. Over time Tommy had slowly come to the rather shocking realization that he had more in common with Donald Rondage than he ever believed possible. This, of course, terrified him.

Leaping off the last rung of the ladder, Donald waddled in Tommy's direction, a smarmy look stretched across his pudgy face. "I'm not telling you anything you don't already know though, am I, weirdo?"

Tommy didn't answer. He didn't need to — the look on his face had given him away.

"Ha! I knew it! How many times have you dived in there? Fifteen? Twenty? Twenty-five? I bet you've been shoulder deep in that muddy crap fifty times, haven't you weirdo? Ha!"

Laughing to himself, Donald picked up a rock from the chilly-stiff ground and whipped it full force into the water while grumbling to himself, "Goddamn doorway."

Standing at the water's edge, the pair of boys stared down into the chilly darkness of the barely moving water. Somewhere behind the murky, greenish drink were worlds inhabited by creatures they once believed could only exist in movies and storybooks— a completely different universe, filled with an endless array of possibilities unlike anything they had known before. So achingly close – so very unreachable.

Sighing deeply while speedily growing tired of staring at something he couldn't have, Donald turned away from the stream and quickly changed the subject. "So how's life with the foster parents?"

Tommy didn't respond. His attention remained on the mysteries hidden beneath the water, and he wasn't quite ready to turn away.

"They aren't smacking you around too, are they?"

Almost instantly Donald regretted having said it.

The details of what happened to Tommy and his brother spread quickly around school after the boys were removed from their home. Passing from student to student, the news made its way from one end of the school to the other in a matter of hours – the way news such as this tended to do. Initially the information caught Donald off guard, and though he would never admit it, a part of him suddenly felt guilty for treating Tommy the way he had for so many years.

Turning from the water, Tommy stared at Donald sternly.

"What? What? Come on, it was a legitimate question . . ." Donald quickly added, his mouth continuing to mutter stupid things independent of the common sense in his brain. Tommy's steely gaze remained unwavering.

"Alright, alright. Look, I'm sorry, whatever, I didn't mean it. Relax, it was just a joke. Geez, what's the matter? Can't you take a joke, weirdo?"

Sighing deeply while shaking his head, Tommy again turned his attention to the water.

For a few minutes there was silence. The only noise for at least a mile in every direction was the gentle movement of the unfrozen water and the soft sway of the trees in the breeze. Wiping a small glop of leakage from his cold nose, Donald scanned the area around him to see if anyone else was within earshot and finding none.

"Look, I didn't mean it, okay?"

His tone was apologetic, even shamed, carrying with it an honesty that Tommy hadn't thought he was capable of. This was not the same Donald Rondage he'd grown up with. This was not the same Donald Rondage that beat him up on the way home from detention. This was not the same Donald Rondage that knocked his tray over at lunch or tripped him in the hallway or gouged the tires on his little brother's bicycle. No, this Donald Rondage seemed almost human — or at least as close to it as he'd likely ever come.

Never turning his attention away from the stream, Tommy answered back softly, "Don't worry about it."

Again came the quiet as both boys attempted to come to terms with what might be the start of a budding friendship between two of the most unlikely participants a friendship could ever hope to find.

Overcome with an urgent need to break the wholly uncomfortable silence, Donald chuckled, "Hey, if it makes you feel any better, my old man is probably a piece of crap too. I'm starting to think it's a requirement for the job or something."

An awkward, slightly sad laugh crept up from Tommy's stomach, splitting his lips. It caught the breeze and floated away, infecting Donald. Within minutes the pair were laughing, their giggles rattling what few leaves remained attached to the trees around them. Shared laughter between lifelong enemies is similar to a force of nature; like it or not, change can hit you when you least expect it.

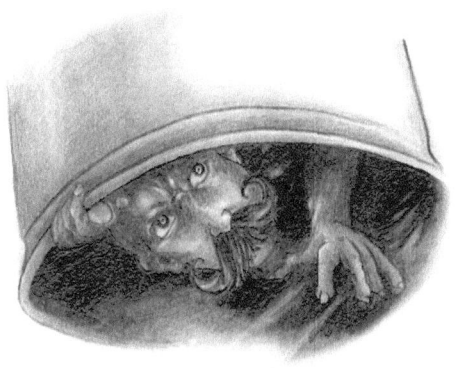

6. LATE NIGHT VISITOR

"Hey kid! Come on, wake up . . .move it . . .get up. I aint' got all night, putz . . ."

Half a whisper, half a command, the gruff-gravelly voice snaked its way into the dreams of the sleeping Owen Little, instantly conjuring up memories of adventures in a faraway world.

"Come on you little schmuck! I don't believe this crap . . .wake up!"

Stiffly something jabbed him in the shoulder – then again, this time a smidge harder. Intent on continuing his sleep, Owen rolled away from the voice and the pokes, pulling his blanket underneath his chin while mumbling angrily through lips slick with drool.

"Okay, fine. That's how you want to play? Fine…I tried doing this the easy way, boyo, but if you insist on making things difficult, then I guess that's just the way it's gonna hafta be."

Half asleep Owen was only vaguely aware of the feeling of tiny feet walking up his back and across his neck before coming to a stop on either side of his exposed ear. Barely recognizable was the sensation of an equally miniscule pair of hands touching the side of his face, of tiny-warm breath perilously close to his ear canal. He would however become completely and totally aware of all these things in a matter of moments. "I said wake up!"

The voice was so loud that it felt as if it were somehow screamed from inside his ear rather than out. The flesh covering the soft cartilage vibrated, the dangly underside swinging back and forth like a pendulum. Yelping loudly, Owen leapt to a sitting position before rolling awkwardly off of his bed and onto the floor. With his right hand he reached up and cupped his ear as a sharp ringing mashed against the inside of his skull and down the side of his neck. Unsure of what was happening, he began frantically scooting across the carpet of his bedroom trying to get away from the awful buzzing. His eyes hadn't yet adjusted to the low light levels and because of this he spotted what seemed to be little more than a blurry red shape shoot up from his bed and come to a hovering stop three feet from his face. Even in his darkened bedroom with limited visibility, Owen could tell instantly that whatever it was, it wasn't human. Hands shaking, ears ringing, and overcome with fear, the boy's body reacted before his mind had time to weigh the options.

With a pitch high enough to shatter glass he screamed, "Da —"

Before he could fully get the word out, a tiny arm wedged itself over his mouth. The tiny arm was attached to an equally tiny body, which belonged to none other than tiny Roustaf.

"Exactly what do you think you're doing, kid? Relax! It's just me. You start screaming and you're gonna put us both in a pretty major pickle," Roustaf sternly stated while trying his best to keep his voice just above a whisper. He wedged his entire torso over Owen's lips in order to keep the child from waking every living thing in the neighborhood.

Content that he'd successfully squashed Owen's idea of calling for help, Roustaf rotated in mid-air while keeping his bare foot pressed firmly against the boy's mouth. "It's just me, your old buddy Roustaf. Remember me, goober?"

Still shaking, his heart pounding, Owen nodded his head slowly. His eyes having adjusted to the light, he could now clearly make out the tiny winged, red-skinned man hovering just inches from the tip of his nose. It had been months since he'd seen him, but a six-inch tall flying man dressed in filthy blue overalls with little horns and a handlebar mustache couldn't be mistaken for anyone else.

"Alright then...glad to hear that we're on the same page," Roustaf added, cautiously pulling his foot from Owen's dry lips.

Slowly the tiny man floated backward and above the boy's bed, landing softly on the sheets, and stated quite sarcastically, "Oh, by the way, it's nice to see you again too. Geez, kids got no manners anymore."

The strangeness of seeing Roustaf standing on his bed twiddling with his bushy mustache was almost too weird for words. It had been half a year since Owen followed Donald Rondage and his goons to the Jarvis brothers' tree fort. Almost six months since he ended up caught in the middle of a war on a world filled with castles and dinosaurs and lizard men built like professional wrestlers. As wildly insane as it was, after a while seeing Roustaf in Fillagrou started making perfect sense. When you're riding on the back of a giant turtle named Walcott, a six-inch tall devil simply wasn't that weird anymore. Now though, staring at the miniature man in his bedroom standing on his Star Trek bedspread next to the stuffed animal his mother gave him when he was a baby – well, this was another thing entirely.

The pounding in his chest beginning at last to slow, completely unsure of what to say, Owen stammered, "Wha-wha-what are you d-doing here?"

"Oh, I was just in the neighborhood, thought I would stop in and shoot the breeze. What do you think I'm doing here, kid?"

Roustaf answered in the lovingly sarcastic way only he could pull off. Floating over to the dresser on the right of Owen's bed, his expression briefly turned stone serious. "Look . . .I need your help."

"No, no, no, no, I'm through helping you guys! I nearly got killed fighting in your stupid war! You can count me out, forget it, find someone else. You need to get out of here! The last thing I need is my dad strolling in here and finding you."

Roustaf was only barely aware of Owen's protests as he poked inquisitively at the buttons on a remote control half buried under a stack of magazines on the boy's dresser. Immediately after touching the power button, a television on the opposite end of the room lit up, bathing the entire area in flashes of color. The loud, repetitive sounds of Hollywood gunfire created by an early morning movie blasted from the television's speakers, instantly threatening to wake everyone in the house. Frantically Owen scrambled across the floor to shut it off. Tripping over his own feet, he stumbled forward and crashed into the nearby dresser, sending magazines, books, and a half-filled glass of soda tumbling to the carpet.

Now covered in sticky cola, he immediately hustled to clean everything up. "Oh crap, oh crap, oh crap, now you've done it, look what you've done!"

"Calm down kid, let me give you a hand…"

"No!" Owen responded with a worried snarl while using his right hand to swat at the hovering Roustaf as if he were a fly. "You stay away! You get out of here! I don't want your help! You're going to get me in so much trouble! Go back —"

He halted in mid-sentence. The unmistakable sound of heavy feet making their way down the hallway leading to his room managed to sneak into his ears during a lull in the sounds of gunfire on the television. His father was awake.

Glancing up at Roustaf with eyes as wide as saucers, he whispered, "Hide. Hide right now."

"What?"

"Hide. Hide right now. Hide quickly."

Roustaf could now hear the footsteps as well, getting closer. "Where do you want me to go kid?" he mumbled while spinning in circles mid-air, trying to find something to climb under and use for cover.

Hearing his father's hand turning the doorknob, Owen grabbed the empty cup of soda, put it over Roustaf's head, and slammed it upside down onto the dresser. He trapped the tiny red man underneath it a mere moment before the door to his bedroom swung open violently.

Immediately after entering the bedroom the half-asleep, half-awake, fully enraged Mack Little spotted his only son curled up at the foot of his bed sitting in what looked to be a puddle of spilled soda and soaked magazines, with his television blaring in the background. Mack could do little more than shake his head in disbelief.

"Owen, what the hell are you doing in here?" He moaned with a deep sigh. "Do you know what time it is? I've got work tomorrow morning, and you're watching action movies and throwing soda all over the place? Seriously?"

Glancing at his father sheepishly, Owen shrugged his shoulders. Mack had just about reached his wit's end concerning his son. Six months ago, after Owen disappeared for nearly a week only to return with an idiotic story about being sucked into another world, he tried his best to be patient with the boy. Various counselors told him eventually Owen would come clean about where he'd been and what happened. They claimed all that the boy needed was time – so time is exactly what Mack gave him. Six months later and still Owen had the same story – falling through a doorway at the bottom of a stream, becoming invisible, watching a castle explode — not a single, solitary deviation. School counselors hadn't helped; significantly more expensive outside therapists hadn't done much more. Mack Little was tired and out of options. There was simply no way around it. He tried to deny it for years, but he couldn't lie to himself anymore: His son was a weirdo, plain and simple. Rolling his eyes, he reminded himself once more that it must come from his mother's side of the family. Strangely this made him feel a little better.

Rubbing the sleep out of his eyes, too tired to yell, Mack instead simply sighed and turned back toward the hallway. "Just . . .just shut off the television and get back to bed, Owen. We'll talk about this in the morning."

"Okay dad. I'm sorry."

"It's alright, it's not your fault."

"I love you dad," Owen added while shutting off the television.

"Love you too buddy . . .love you too."

A moment later his father left the room, closing the door behind him and bathing it once more in a deep darkness.

Lifting the glass ever so slightly, Roustaf peeked out and asked, "Pssst! Hey kid . . .is the coast clear?"

"Yes, it's clear," Owen huffed as he crawled back into bed, pulled his blanket up to his chin, and turned away from Roustaf.

Squirming out from his hiding place, the tiny red man fluttered over to Owen, landing softly on his shoulder. "Alright, now we can get back to why I'm here."

Owen quickly interrupted. "Go away."

"What? Look kid, do you have any idea how long I've been wandering around this place trying to find one of you? Let's just say that Zanell may know everything there is to possibly know, but she has a lot of work to do when it comes to giving directions. I've hid in sewers, peeked in windows, been chased by about a million annoying, loud furry things with jagged teeth and breath like Megalot poop! I need your help, and I can't go away un—"

"Look, I'm not going to help you! I'm sorry, I just can't. I'm not your savior! I'm not who you think I am, I'm just a kid and I just want to be left alone. My dad already thinks I'm a lunatic. I just — I can't. I'm sorry. Just go away . . .please."

Pulling the blanket underneath his nose, Owen squeezed his eyes shut tightly, trying his best to keep from crying. It wasn't that he didn't care about Fillagrou or the people he met while there, because there was no denying that he did on some level. He cared about them a lot, actually, but his presence there in the first place was an accident, a mistake – not some stupid fulfillment of a prophecy. Though the situation ended well, and despite the fact that there were exciting moments scattered throughout, there was simply no way he could envision willingly putting himself into the situation again. He wasn't strong enough and doubted he ever would be.

Realizing there was no way he could force the boy to come with him and knowing he was short on time, Roustaf relented. "Okay kid, whatever you say."

Fluttering his tiny wings, the little man lifted himself off of the bed, hovering toward the slightly open window he used to enter the room in the first place. As much as he knew beyond a shadow of a doubt that he needed Owen's help, a part of him understood exactly what the boy was going through. After all, Owen was just that – a boy. So much responsibility hoisted onto the shoulders of one so young – it was a lot to ask. Maybe too much.

Coming to a stop at the window, the moonlight dancing off the curves in his nearly transparent wings, he turned briefly toward Owen's motionless form. "You've gotta do what you've gotta do kid. I can respect that, even if I don't agree with it. Before I go though, do you happen to know where any of the other twerps live? If I can avoid spending the next few weeks trying to keep from ending up as a red splatter on the front of those big metal boxes with wheels, that would be absolutely fantastic."

7. LATE NIGHT ADVICE

Tommy Jarvis opened the patio door leading into the Williamson's house just enough for him to tiptoe through. The door had a tendency to squeak if opened too far and a squeaking door was the last thing he needed while sneaking into the house at one in the morning. Tommy had spent at least two hours sitting alongside the bank of the stream with Donald Rondage, recalling snippets from their adventures in Fillagrou and laughing like old friends. Admittedly, at first it seemed a little weird. Being so close to Donald while not the least bit worried about getting beaten to a pulp proved a unique experience to say the least – unique in a strangely good way Tommy wasn't completely sure he was ready to accept.

Having successfully navigated his way quietly through the darkened kitchen and into the living room, Tommy was abruptly frozen in his place when the sternly deep voice of Ed Williamson cut through the darkness. "Welcome home, bud."

A lamp in the corner of the room suddenly clicked on, bringing everything into a blurry focus. Seated in an old chair underneath it, dressed in a pair of very old-timey striped pajamas and a long blue robe with a weary look stretched across his wrinkled face, was Ed.

"Don't worry, I covered for you with your dad, Edna, and the girl from social services. I convinced them you just weren't ready to come down."

Not sure what to say and more than a bit confused by the situation, Tommy responded with a simple "Thanks."

Using both arms to brace himself, Ed pushed himself into a standing position with an obvious wince. "I guess I could ask you where you were tonight but I have a sinking feeling that you might think it's none of my business, so I won't bother." Slowly he moved toward Tommy, one hand pressed firmly against his sore lower back. "I know it's hard forgiving your dad, believe me. I understand what you're going through more than you might think I do, bud." Less than three feet from Tommy, Ed reached out with one hand and placed it firmly on the boy's shoulder. His boney old fingers tugged softly at Tommy's flesh for a moment before patting it three times gently. "You can't hold on to the anger forever, trust me. It'll mess you up if you do, eat you up inside. It'll change the way you look at things and change the way things look at you. Once that happens, there's no coming back."

Tommy lowered his head, looking away from Ed and to the floor. The single lamp in the room was casting long, deep shadows underneath his eyes as his hair hung loosely in his face. Ed was unsure if anything he said would get through to the boy – unsure if he was even listening. Like most men of his generation, Ed Williamson's father was never completely at home with the concept of affection. It made him uncomfortable. He found it to be strange, awkward and ultimately pointless. Carl Williamson's idea of disciple was simple; the back of his hand or a whack from his belt - both seemed to get the job done well enough. A bit of a troublemaker, little Eddie Williamson spent his most formative years becoming all too familiar with both. In Tommy, Ed could see a bit of himself. It was all there: the anger, the resentment, the silence and the shadows – the similarities were undeniable. Though age had erased many of Ed's earliest memories, like microscopic particles of blood left at a crime scene, there were some things even the years couldn't dispose of. Maybe the words wouldn't mean much to Tommy now, but eventually they might sink in.

Despite the general perception of most, definitions are by no means constants. What means one thing today might mean something entirely different the next. The truth is that words are as varied and unique as snowflakes - ultimately a matter of perspective.

Glancing at the antique grandfather clock in the opposite corner of the room, Ed took note for the first time of just how late it was. For the life of him, he couldn't recall the last time he was awake at this hour. The undeniable, unrelenting urge to sleep instantly began crawling into the space behind his eyes, making them heavier than a pair of sandbags covered in concrete. With a deep yawn, he turned from Tommy, tossing a half-smile and a heavy sigh in the boy's direction before heading toward the stairs leading to his bedroom.

"Try to get some sleep kiddo," he added with a subtle gesture of his wrinkly hand as he approached the base of the stairs.

Surprised by the lack of annoyance in Ed's voice, Tommy allowed himself a moment to breathe. He had expected the old man to yell or at the very least give him that "disappointed grandfatherly" look that he'd shot Tommy's way on numerous occasions since coming to live with the Williamsons. In the end, what he got was the exact opposite.

Noticing the old man was almost halfway up the stairs, Tommy called out to him with a half whisper: "Ed?"

Stopping, Ed turned in the direction of the boy, taking advantage of the opportunity to let the joints in his knees rest. "Yeah? What do you need bud?"

"Why were you waiting? Down here I mean. Why were you waiting for me?"

Ed paused for a moment, his eyes drifting to his bare feet. His toes were chilly. Edna purchased him a pair of slippers years ago;

he'd never worn them though, believing they looked entirely too much like exactly something an old man would wear.

With a wrinkled grin, he turned again to Tommy who was now standing at the base of the stairs with his hands buried deep in the pockets of his jeans. "Just making sure you made it home alright." A moment later Ed Williamson resumed the long trek upward. "See you at breakfast, bud."

For ten minutes after Ed disappeared from view, Tommy sat silently at the foot of the stairs with his knees pulled close to his chest. Through a window to the right of the front door he stared at the bluish-gray moon, lit up like a low wattage bulb across the pitch-black sky. Unlike most other nights, there were almost no visible stars – only an endless blanket of blackness stretching outward for eternity. So much nothingness. A void so deep that no one could ever hope to see its bottom – the occasional, sporadic light representing an eternity of possibilities floating among a vacant pool of perpetuity. It was quite scary and quite beautiful.

Grabbing a flashlight from a drawer in the kitchen, he slowly made his way upstairs and into his bedroom, taking care not to wake Nicky. From a tote bag crammed underneath his bed he retrieved his sketchpad. Lying on his stomach, he pulled the covers over his head and clicked on the flashlight. He would spend the next three hours sketching in silence before eventually falling asleep. It had been weeks since he'd drawn anything.

It felt good.

8. A CALL TO ARMS

Owen's directions proved astoundingly accurate. It took Roustaf a little more than ten minutes to make the trip across town under the cover of darkness. During the day, while doing his best to stay out of sight, he was forced to move slowly — most of the time feeling as if he was spending more time ducking in and out of bushes than making any real progress. Zanell's awful directions hadn't helped matters any, leading him to believe that maybe she didn't see things quite as clearly as she claimed.

"No matter what happens, no matter how long it takes, make sure you stay out of sight."

That's what she said to him before leaving. Roustaf followed her instructions to the letter and spent twelve days sneaking around in this weird new world because of it. The time spent wandering around aimlessly searching while living off the strange fruit growing from the occasional tree wouldn't have bothered him so much if he hadn't been in such a hurry. Time was not on his side. He needed to find the children. He needed to bring them back to

New Tipoloo safely and he needed to do it quickly. Everyone was counting on him.

Donald Rondage's dwelling looked smaller than the ones on either side of it, just as Owen said it would. The grassy area in front was mostly dead, and the wood making up the outer walls looked old and worn. Cutting through the air, Roustaf quickly made his way over the broken metal fencing toward the rear of the home. He pressed his face against the glass of the second window from the left and peered inside, but saw no one. Owen specifically said the second window from the left, and this was the second window from the left. Donald should've been there. So why wasn't he? A feeling of annoyance bubbled up from Roustaf's stomach. Reaching up with one hand he began gently stroking his mustache, trying his best to remain calm. The food on this world wasn't agreeing with him. Two days ago he ripped open a discarded bag containing a very thin, remarkably salty and extremely crunchy circular chip-like thing. By God it tasted good — completely and totally unlike anything that had ever passed through his lips. At the same time though, it left him with a seriously awful case of heartburn and messy runs the likes of which he didn't ever want to think about again. Why would anyone mass-produce a food that resulted in such nasty leakage? It did taste delicious though – there was no getting around that.

Roustaf was quickly growing weary of this place. The creatures here were weird in a way that made weird sound like a bad thing. They came in so many varied shapes and sizes and colors, each of them dressed in clownish garments, and a select few with terrifying bits of technology attached to their bodies or sticking out of their ears. He wanted to find the children and go home. He needed to find the children and go home. Thankfully, after a day and a half of surveillance at the big building where large groups of youth seemed to gather for periods of time every day, he spotted Owen. After failing to convince the boy to return with him to New Tipoloo, he managed to locate the dwelling of Donald Rondage. Unfortunately, the pudgy-bodied bully was nowhere to be found.

Long story short, his mission was going horribly.

"Holy crap . . .you've got to be kidding me."

The instantly recognizable voice came from behind Roustaf. Spinning in mid-air, the tiny red man turned quickly in its direction. Standing a few feet away, the soft blue moonlight glowing from behind and casting him in a dark silhouette, was none other than Donald Rondage.

"Seriously? Is it really you? What are you doing here, Squirt?" Donald chuckled, taking a step toward the little winged man. "How the hell did you manage to find me?"

Ecstatic over the fact that he managed to locate Donald, yet a bit annoyed that the boy seemed as cocky as ever, Roustaf moved closer to him, coming to a stop twelve or so inches from his face. "Why is it that you kids seem intent on asking me the same stupid question? I'm here because I need your help, Slick. I need you to come back to Fillagrou with me."

Donald's smile disappeared. He'd dreamed of this moment – dreamed of the time he could return to Fillagrou, dreamed of having powers, and dreamed of being able to pick up giant boulders and knock down trees with his pointer finger again. Of course, a very large part of him always assumed that the opportunity would never actually present itself. With it suddenly staring him in the face, Donald couldn't help but feel as if his dream were instead a nightmare.

"What do you mean go back? Like, right now? Like — go back with you right now? Why do you need me to go back?"

"Yes, like right now. Like right now, right at this very moment," Roustaf responded, moving a few inches closer to the boy and staring directly into his eyes. "Something has happened. Things went wrong. There's a new player in the game. Let me just save us both a heap of time and say that we need help from you — all of you. We've needed your help for days now, but trying to hunt down you damn kids has been a much larger pain in my patoot than I thought it would be. By the way, if anyone asks, it was Zanell's fault."

Upon hearing Zanell's name, Donald suddenly perked up, "Zanell? How is she — wait — what? All of us? Tommy? Have you talked to Tommy yet?"

"No, actually I was hoping that you could help me out with that kid. Owen told me that he wasn't sure where ol' Tommy and his brother were holed up these days . . .said that you might be able to point me in the right direction."

Donald's breathing began to slow, yet remained noticeably awkward as he began to find it more and more difficult to inhale deeply with the pace of his heart slowly quickening. "Yeah . . .the, umm, Williamsons . . .wait, you've talked to that little dork Owen? Where is he?"

Sighing with annoyance, Roustaf ran his hand over the top of his bald head, letting his fingers trace the shape of the tiny protruding horns. "Look kid, I'd love to fill you in on the all the details, but how's about I do it on the way to Tommy's place? I've already wasted way more time in your world than I've got to spare. We need to get crackin' if we're gonna have any chance of getting done what we need to get done in the time it needs to get done. So what do you say? You wanna come along or what?"

Donald paused for a moment, a sudden gust of wind whacking his hair against the side of his face and spinning Roustaf's miniscule body in mid-air. Suddenly the reality of returning to Fillagrou, of putting his life on the line, of getting shot with an arrow through the shoulder again — or worse — terrified him to the core. Was this really something he wanted? After all, none of this had anything to do with him. These monsters weren't his family and this most assuredly wasn't his war — was it?

"What - what's the rush? I mean, why-why are you in such a hurry?" Donald added sheepishly as another gust of wind threatened to knock Roustaf to the ground.

Struggling to steady himself, Roustaf replied sternly, "They got Walcott, kid. They got Walcott."

9. THE JARVIS BOYS

Pencil still gripped between his fingers, blanket still over his head and flashlight still in the On position, Tommy Jarvis finally succumb to the alluring siren call of sleep. It had been only a matter of minutes, but his eyelids were too heavy to hold open any longer. His weighty head flopped to the bed, providing a moment of much needed rest for the aching muscles in his neck. The boy's sleep proved short lived, however, as the sound of a pebble bouncing off glass abruptly jolted him again to the waking world. A second similar yet more substantial clank of stone on glass caused him to toss off his covers, his weary eyes glancing across the dark, empty room and toward the moonlit window. Snatching the flashlight, he pointed it in the direction of the sounds just in time to see another rock smack against the glass. *What in the world? Who was throwing rocks at his window in the middle of the night? Maybe Staci?* No, sneaking around at one-thirty in the morning was never Staci's style. Sure, she had recently begun going to the tree fort every couple of weeks to sit and talk with Tommy without her parent's permission, but she never stayed out late enough to arouse suspicion. Tommy was still off limits as far as the Alexanders were concerned. Launching pebbles at the side of his foster parents' house in the wee hours of the morning is a chance she simply wouldn't take – no matter the reason. Nicky remained sound asleep in his bed on the opposite end of the room as Tommy quietly made his way to the window. Carefully opening it up, he poked his head halfway out.   His eyes traveled down to the dimly lit backyard. Barely noticeable in the dark, arms waving wildly in his direction with a cocky smile across his face, Tommy spotted the undeniable outline of Donald Rondage.

"Hey weirdo, get your ass up." Donald called out, his voice two-thirds a whisper, one-third a yell.

Worried that the burly bodied, naturally deep-voiced Donald was going to wake the Williamsons, Tommy responded with more than a hint of annoyance. "What are you doing? Get out of here."

Instead of answering back, Donald pointed to Tommy's right. Before Tommy could fully turn his head to see what his tormentor-turned-acquaintance was motioning toward, something buzzed past his ear, causing him to stumble backward into the bedroom and land hard on his rear.

The sound of his body crashing to the floor instantly woke Nicky. "Tommy? What are—" The youngest Jarvis boy was stopped mid-sentence when a reddish blur zoomed past his face, causing his dark hair to scatter wildly in every direction. Making a loop in the air just above Nicky's head, the blur that was Roustaf came to an immediate stop on top of the headboard behind him. Though the room was still quite dark, the nightlight Edna plugged into the wall for Nicky provided just enough illumination for Tommy to recognize the tiny man.

"Roustaf?" He whispered, eyes staring blankly over his little brother's shoulder.

"Roustaf? What're you — huh?" Nicky questioned, more than a bit frazzled, unsure of exactly what was going on.

Noticing the direction in which Tommy's eyes were staring, Nicky slowly twisted his body, turning his head to look behind him.

Standing on the headboard, arms resting on his thin hips, the ends of his mustache curled into perfect bushy loops, was the familiar face of tiny Roustaf.

Instantly Nicky's fear dissipated, replaced by an overflow of excitement. "Roustaf!" He yelped louder than he should, his voice cracking noticeably.

Tommy quickly moved to his brother's side. "Nicky, keep it down; you'll wake Ed and Edna, dope."

Nicky smacked his hand over his mouth and mumbled "Oops, sorry," through his fingers apologetically.

Crawling onto the bed alongside his brother, his legs hanging over the edge, Tommy now spoke in questioning whispers: "Roustaf, what are you — what are you doing here?"

The tiny red man groaned deeply. "I swear, the next person that asks me that question is going to get a swift kick to wherever it is that they stash their reproductive organs." Shaking his head, Roustaf lifted himself off of the headboard, his tiny wings carrying him across the room, then set down beside Nicky's nightlight.

"What's the point of this thing?" he asked with noticeable confusion, cautiously poking it with one finger, half expecting it to be scorching hot.

The proximity of the little man to the nightlight exposed every wrinkle on his miniature face, making him look much older than Tommy remembered. Quickly losing interest in the bizarre wall torch, Roustaf returned his attention to the Jarvis brothers, who were now staring at him from the bed four feet away.

They looked so young. Their pale faces, messy hair and blotchy skin only added to the overall effect. For a moment he almost felt bad about being there, about having to ask them to do what he knew he had to ask them to do. To drag creatures so young into such danger . . .there was something inherently wrong about this, something he hadn't yet made his peace with.

"Look kids, I'm going to make this short because we don't have a whole lot of time to waste. As much as I'd love to say that I'm here to take a nice long nap on that incredibly soft looking mattress of yours, the truth is that I was sent to bring you back to New Tipoloo."

"Why?" Nicky interrupted, his eyes wide and his jaw hanging low.

Glancing at his brother, Tommy instantly recognized the look on his face – part excitement, part fear. He understood the emotion Nicky was feeling quite well, because he was feeling it too.

Again lifting himself into the air, Roustaf fluttered to Tommy's side, bouncing to a gentle stop on the bedspread. "The war was going alright for the most part. Walcott may not look like much, but that tubby-shelled schmoe knows his way around a battlefield, there's no denying that. We were bobbing and weaving with the best of them, catching the Ochans off guard and scoring some small but significant victories — that is, until the dope and Pleebs went and got themselves captured."

As if a switch somewhere inside his head had been suddenly thrown, Tommy's hesitance and fear transformed to anger. "Pleebo? What happened to Pleebo?"

Of all the creatures Tommy met in Fillagrou, it was Pleebo he remembered most fondly. It was Pleebo he first met. It was Pleebo who was there when he first experienced his powers in the dusty tunnels of Tipoloo. It was Pleebo who was there for him in the tower when he came face to face with Prince Valkea. It was Pleebo's face he last saw when saying goodbye.

Taking note of the worried, angry expression on the boy's face, Roustaf tried his best to quell his fears. "Relax kid. We think they're both still alive, we just don't know for how much longer."

Fifteen minutes ago, Roustaf would have severely doubted there was anyone in the entire world more anxious to rescue his friend Pleebo than he was. Staring at the expression on Tommy

Jarvis' face, though, he understood this had been an incorrect assumption.

After taking a moment to collect his emotions, the little man continued, "Some new information has recently come our way. King Kragamel has located something — something that puts a lot more people in danger than just Pleebs and Walcott — something that could cause a bucket load of problems for everyone, everywhere . . .including here."

Leaning in closer to the little red man, Tommy asked, "What do you mean here?"

"I mean right here, Slick, as in this place you're living with that weird little glowing thing you got on the wall over there, and the plastic bags filled with chips that give you terrible diarrhea, as in everyone in this town — everyone in your world."

While Tommy stared at the little red man with an expression of anger and worry, Nicky's voice chirped from nearby. "Diarrhea?"

10. ONE MORE STOP

It took less than fifteen minutes after hearing of Pleebo and Walcott's situation for the Jarvis brothers to dress in the dark, pack a few essentials into their packs, climb out their window, and repel down the side of the Williamsons' house with the aid of a rusty gutter. Tommy spent the first five of those fifteen minutes making it perfectly clear to his younger brother that he didn't think the boy should come along. The first trip to Fillagrou had proved violent and exceedingly dangerous. Tommy was punched, kicked, tossed across a room, and very nearly choked to death. Donald had been shot with an arrow, and Nicky and Staci were thrown into a dungeon, dragged across the floor by their clothes, and hung out a window like clothes on a line. The group as a whole bore witness to the real life brutalities of war, just barely escaping with their lives. There was simply no way Tommy was going to allow his brother to be put in such danger again.

If something were to happen to Nicky – if he were to get injured, or worse – Tommy didn't imagine he could live with himself.

Nicky, however, fought him every step of the way, ignoring his older brother's comments entirely while stuffing his backpack with anything he believed might come in handy. The younger of the Jarvis children then abruptly put an end to the conversation by reminding Tommy that it was he who saved them from Prince Valkea, not the other way around. As much as Tommy didn't want to let his brother go along, Nicky had no interest in letting Tommy go without him. Eventually Tommy relented. He had to. He couldn't tie Nicky to the bed or knock him out and leave him in the room. Even if he did, what would stop him from following in their footsteps an hour later? In the end, there seemed no point in arguing. Instead, Tommy decided he would simply keep his brother very close the entire time, and in doing so, hopefully keep him safe.

After leaving the Williamsons' the foursome quickly made their way across town. There was one more person to pick up before heading to the tree fort.

For Staci Alexander, sleep came relatively quickly. The day had proven uneventful; it had been full of the things of your basic fourteen-year old, not quite an adult, yet no longer a child. Angela Duncan got into a shouting match with Kaity Nelson at lunch after hearing a rumor that she was spreading a rumor that Scott Drake got her pregnant. Mrs. Sanderson broke it up immediately, sending both girls to the principal's office. Parents were called and detentions were promptly handed out. When Social Studies ended, Jessica Walker told Staci that Megan told Alexis that Brett Baker told her that he thought she was cute – it was all very complicated. Finding out that Brett could possibly, maybe, if the rumors were true, think she was cute surprised Staci. Despite the fact that Brett was widely regarded as the schools resident hottie, and dating him would surely raise her social status a few notches, Staci had no real interest in him. Sure, he was handsome and funny and outgoing and popular and played forward on the basketball team and worked on the yearbook. What he wasn't, however, was Tommy Jarvis. Since returning from Fillagrou, Staci's parents had instructed her repeatedly to stay away from Tommy. Though it was quite out of character, she had chosen to ignore them. Instead, she took full advantage of every opportunity to sneak to the tree fort and spend time with the elder Jarvis boy. In the halls at school the pair often exchanged glances, half-smiles and subtle looks. Staci quickly began to realize that she had an uncanny ability to bring a smile to Tommy's normally frowny face with even the simplest of gestures. She liked this, and understood that it was not something to be taken lightly. Unlike with other people, a smile on Tommy's face meant something; it was similar to the act of creating a diamond from a piece of coal. More and more, Staci had found herself counting the hours until the next time they could sneak off together, until the next time she could hear his voice, see those cute dimples in his cheeks, stare into his soft blue eyes, or feel the warmth of his hand in hers. Though she hadn't yet fully made sense of these newfound feelings and mostly foreign sensations, she was enjoying them all the same, and she didn't want them to go away.

Arriving outside Staci's house, the group of children and Roustaf ducked behind a row of neatly trimmed bushes at the foot of the driveway. As much as Tommy was finding it nearly impossible take his eyes from Staci's residence, and more specifically her half-open bedroom window, directly parallel to it was his old home. Looming like a great dark cloud across an even darker sky, the mere sight of the place instantly made the hair on his arms stand at attention and the tips of his fingers tingle. Many things had taken place behind its blackened windows, moments he'd tried hard to forget, moments clinging like cancerous lesions to the inner walls of his brain. Ever since moving in with the Williamsons, Tommy had avoided this place, avoided dealing with the emotions it would undoubtedly stir to the surface.

Kneeling beside him, Nicky noticed the expression on his older brother's face, fully understanding what he was going through. Though the meeting with their father earlier in the day had proven more good than bad, it hadn't prepared Nicky for the sight of his childhood home again. His stomach twisted into itself uncomfortably and settled deep and heavy in his torso, suddenly tied into an excruciatingly undoable knot. With a cautious hand Nicky reached across the grass, his fingers coming to a stop on Tommy's closed fist. In the still autumn air the brothers exchanged a knowing glace, their silence speaking louder than words could.

"Alright, you guys stay here. I'll fly up, get the girl, and we can get this show on the road," Roustaf stated gruffly, his wings fluttering as he lifted off the blades of grass currently reaching his midsection.

"Wait," Tommy interrupted. He snatched one of Roustaf's tiny red legs between two fingers. "I'm going with you."

"No offense kid, but I can make it up the side of that house a lot quicker and a heck of a lot quieter than you can."

Tommy's expression remained steadfast and determined. "I'm going with you," he said again, more a statement of fact than a request.

Realizing there was no time to argue, Roustaf relented. "Alright, Slick," he said, and wiggled free from the boy's grasp. "Let's see if you can keep up."

A moment later the tiny red man lifted over the bushes, cutting through the air and quickly closing the distance between himself and the second floor window of Staci Alexander. Not far behind him Tommy sped across the grass. Doing his best to avoid any sort of eye contact with his father's home, he kept his eyes trained on Staci's house, and specifically on Staci's bedroom. Quickly making his way into the backyard, he leapt onto a tree near the patio. He had climbed this tree often in his youth. As children he and Staci could be found perched on one of its branches, collecting leaves or poking with youthful innocence around a fully stocked bird's nest. Leaping from one of the longer branches, Tommy deposited himself as quietly as possible onto the second floor overhang. Even moving with great care, the entire trip from bushes to house took him less than five minutes. Arriving outside Staci's window, he found Roustaf spread out on the windowsill pretending to be asleep.

"What took you so long, Blondie?" The tiny red man said with a smile, sarcastically miming a yawn.

Just as Tommy knew it would be, Staci's window was partially open. She always had a weird fear of suffocating at night if fresh air wasn't allowed into the room. It made no sense when she was nine years old and it made even less sense at fourteen. By the time she turned thirty it would seem absolutely bonkers. Wedging his fingers underneath the window, Tommy pushed it open slowly. A gust of wind flowing into the room caused the drapes to scatter and flap. With Roustaf right behind him, Tommy crawled headfirst through the opening. Carefully moving across the dresser placed underneath, he stepped lightly onto the carpet. Though it was difficult to make out details in the darkness, the overall layout of the room felt familiar. In the corner, Staci was coiled up in a mass of blankets like a caterpillar in a cocoon, her hair pulled back into a very tight ponytail. His heart skipped a beat, and Tommy pressed his hand to his chest. Underneath his palm he could feel it move, sense the warmth created as it spread copious amounts of blood across his torso. Tommy's feet suddenly felt like concrete, too heavy to move, as if somehow bolted to the floor.

"Well, what are you waiting for kid? Wake her up," Roustaf whispered as he came to a soft landing on Tommy's shoulder.

"I'm going to, I just . . .I don't want to freak her out or anything. She's a wimp. She's scared of spiders. If she starts screaming and wakes up her parents, we're screwed."

"I hear ya, kid, but if you don't wake her up before daybreak we're pretty well screwed anyway."

Breathing deeply, Tommy took a single step forward, his entire body shaking. The closer he moved to Staci, the more details came into focus: the heavy quilt rising and falling with each breath, one of her tiny, well manicured feet sticking out from underneath near the base of the bed.

Again Tommy halted his forward movement. "Why does she need to come along anyway? What if she gets hurt? We should just let her sleep."

"No way, Slick. I'm already coming back without one of you; there's no way I'm showing up with two missing. Look, if you're not going to at least give her the option, I sure as hell am."

With a subtle flutter of his wings, Roustaf lifted off Tommy's shoulder, moving toward the slumbering girl.

Again Tommy reached out and snatched one of the tiny man's legs. "Alright, alright, calm down, it was just an idea. I'll wake her up. Go wait by the window or something."

Roustaf shook his head and sighed deeply. "Fine, make it quick . . .and don't ever grab my leg again. I've let it slide twice now, but I ain't gonna let it go again."

By the time Roustaf had returned to the open window, Tommy was kneeling beside Staci's bed. His heart pounding, his breathing ragged, he reached out with one hand until it was hovering over her blanketed form. Swallowing deep, he gulped down the uncomfortable lump in his throat, softly tapping his index finger against her shoulder.

His voice was barely a whisper. "Staci? Stace, wake up . . ."

Half asleep and not quite sure of where she was, who she was or what was happening, Staci rolled in his direction and pulled the covers closer to her face. "Mmmm . . .who? Tommy?" Her eyes remain closed as she smiled in his direction dreamily, only half awake. "Oh, hi Tommy. What're you doing here?"

Tommy slowly pulled his hand away and placed it stiffly at his side. Still on his knees, he scooted across the carpet away from her bed. His mouth hanging low and his eyes like saucers, his lips began to move, but no sound escaped. A slightly goofy grin stretched across Staci's face as she yawned deeply, wiping tiny bits of crust from the corners of her eyes. Slowly becoming more and more aware of her surroundings, her eyes fluttered gently as her arms stretched high above her head, loosening her stiff muscles. Upon seeing Tommy Jarvis kneeling at the foot of her bed and maybe for the first time realizing it was, in fact, not a dream, her muscles tightened and her body began to shudder.

A very deep, very real guttural scream formed in the pit of her stomach before racing upward at an incredible speed. "Aigh!"

Leaping at her, Tommy placed his hand over her mouth. "No, no, no, don't scream, don't scream! It's just me!"

Though terrified by the fact that Tommy Jarvis was sitting next to her bed in her darkened bedroom with his hand over her mouth, Staci's breathing began to slowly relax. The smell of his hand was familiar and warm. Part of her was happy to see him, while a much larger part was horrified by the fact that he seemed to have snuck into her bedroom in the middle of the night for unknown reasons. Reaching up, she grabbed his wrist, trying to pull his sweaty hand from her mouth.

"Are you okay? Are you going to be quiet? You aren't going to freak out, are you?" Tommy asked, keeping his hand pressed firmly against her lips.

Awash with confusion, Staci shook her head from side to side, tugging at his stiff wrist once more.

"Okay, just don't freak out. I can explain all of this, just don't freak out." Sliding his hand off her face, Tommy cautiously backed away and slipped off her bed and onto the floor.

For a moment there was only silence between the two, neither having any idea whatsoever of what to say next, their unblinking eyes staring at one another from across the darkened room. Releasing the vice-like grip on her quilt, Staci swallowed deep and watched as Tommy raised himself into a standing position.

Brushing a clump of hair from her eyes, she finally mustered the courage to speak. "Tommy . . .Tommy, what are you doing here?"

Before he could answer, the miniscule reddish blur of an airborne Roustaf zoomed up from the windowsill and over Tommy's shoulder, landing near her painted pink toenails at the end of the bed. "*We're* here because we need your help, girlie."

Staci responded by swallowing something the size of a golf ball lodged in the back of her throat.

11. **RUNAWAYS**

Sometime around two-thirty in the morning, a series of heavy thumps woke Janet Alexander from a fairly deep sleep and a rather funny little dream. Her muscles tensed and her eyes darted from side to side. Reaching across the bed with one hand she shook husband awake. "Dale . . .Dale, wake up. Wake up, Dale!"

"What? What is it?" her husband of fifteen years asked, though only barely awake himself. He was groggy and quite annoyed.

"I think I just heard something coming from Staci's room. Get up."

"What?"

"Get up and see if your daughter is alright, Dale. I swear I just heard a noise coming from the other room . . .go see what it is."

Propping himself up on an elbow, Dale rubbed his eyes with his free hand and shook his head in confusion. "Are you serious?"

"Yes, I'm serious! I heard something! Go make sure Staci is all right . . .go now!"

Though only half aware of what was going on, Dale had lived with his wife long enough to understand arguing with her would likely get him nowhere. It was better to keep his mouth shut, better to relent and do what she asked. Pulling himself out of bed and checking on his daughter, who was probably fine, would save him not only a lot of time, but a good deal of headache as well. Throwing the covers off, he swung his legs over the side of the bed. The hardwood floor was cold against his bare feet, sending shivers up through his legs and into his lower spine. With a heavy yawn he stood, grabbed his robe from a nearby dresser, and threw it on. Sliding his feet into a pair of slippers, he began moving toward the bedroom door.

A blanket pulled up to her face, his concerned wife whispered from behind him, "Be careful."

Dale mumbled his annoyance underneath his breath.

He exited the bedroom and moved slowly down the hall in the direction of his daughter's room, still shocked by the fact that his wife was actually making him do this. There was a very big, very important sales meeting he needed to attend only a few hours from now. If he showed up tired or haggard or in any way whatsoever not on the top of his game, it could have dire consequences for the company. Dire consequences for the company would in turn result in dire consequences for his paycheck, and dire consequences for his paycheck was not a good thing.

Reaching Staci's room, Dale knocked softly three times on her door. "Stace?"

While waiting for an answer, he ran his hand through his messy-stiff bed hair. Years ago he could have entered his daughter's room whenever he liked. In fact, in those days her door was rarely, if ever, closed. She was getting older now. Age had brought with it many changes, one of which was the desire for privacy. As is the case with most in his situation, Dale was finding the realities of parenting a teenager difficult to come to terms with.

Growing up meant going away, and going away is often a hard pill for a parent to swallow.

Fifteen seconds passed without a response, and he knocked again. "Stace hunny, it's daddy. Are you alright in there?" Still there was no answer.

Then, out of the blue, he heard it: A bang, maybe a shuffle, something falling to the floor followed by a pair of barely audible whispers. Dale's muscles went tight, and his body pulled straight and rigid. Despite being half asleep only a moment ago, his senses instantly sharpened.

Grabbing the handle, he violently shoved the door open. "Staci? Are you alri—"

Immediately focusing on Staci's bed in the corner of the room, he noted the fact that it was empty. Through his peripheral vision he spotted the shape of someone with a head full of long, flowing brown hair climbing out the window onto the second story overhang. Before his brain even had time to consider a course of action, his body lunged in the direction of the bobbing ponytail. Shoving the dresser underneath the window out of the way with one hand and knocking it to the floor, he stuck his head angrily into the chilly night air. To his left, making her way carefully down the tree in the back yard, he caught a glimpse of his only daughter. Below her, already on the ground looking up at her, was the all-too-familiar Tommy Jarvis.

With his entire upper body leaning out the window, Dale screamed at the top of his lungs "STACI, WHAT THE HELL DO YOU THINK YOU'RE DOING!? GET BACK HERE! Staci, what the hell do you think you're doing? Get back here!"

His voice was booming so loud it could be heard a block away. Tommy Jarvis immediately looked up in the direction of the earsplitting sound. Despite the darkness, he could clearly make out Dale Alexander's shape, the glare of the moonlight reflecting off the whites of his eyes.

"Staci Lynne Alexander! You get back here right now!"

Moments after Dale's head disappeared back inside the house, Tommy could hear the stomping of the large man's feet as he ran through the interior of the home and down the stairs leading to the backdoor. Looking up, Tommy noticed that Staci had stopped climbing halfway down the trunk of the tree, her body frozen in fear, no doubt wondering if she'd made the right choice in deciding to follow Tommy Jarvis and the little red man out her window and into the night. The sound of the Alexanders' patio door slamming open cut through the mostly quiet night like the report of cannon fire. The porch light flickered on. The heavy thump of Dale Alexander's feet on the aged, water damaged deck echoed off the surrounding houses in the neighborhood, waking neighbors three doors down. All down the block, windows that were black moments prior turned a warm yellow-white. Sleepy residents pulled their blinds open, hoping to catch a glimpse what was causing the commotion.

His heart racing, Tommy looked up at the petrified girl above him and screamed, "Hurry!"

12. RETURN TO FILLAGROU

With every stride, the frightening screams of Dale Alexander faded further away. Running at full speed, chests heaving, sweat pouring from their brows, the group of children quickly made their way through the space between the Parkers' and the Thompsons' houses and into the tree line adjoining their back yards. Once inside the forest, they were forced to slow just a bit. The surrounding trees were thick, clumped much too closely for anyone to move easily between them, especially in the middle of the night. The ground beneath their feet was uneven, cluttered with fallen debris not uncommon during the fall season. What little moonlight they had relied on until this point was now blocked by the partially leafy treetops. Visibility beyond even a few feet quickly became impossible. A significantly denser darkness folded around them, pulled them in, and turned them around, erasing all sense of direction. Hurriedly moving to the head of the group, Nicky reached into his backpack, where he retrieved a flashlight and clicked it on. He and his brother had traveled through these woods on their way to the tree fort more times than he could count. He knew every tree, every hole in the ground, every pile of leaves, and even every broken twig like the back of his hand. If anyone could get them through the forest quickly, it was he.

Turning to face the rest of the group with a somewhat excited smile on his face, he stated confidently, "Follow me."

Bringing up the rear of the pack, a terrified and confused Staci Alexander was being pulled forward by Tommy. After Roustaf initially told her what was happening in Fillagrou, who had been captured, and what was at stake, she was anxious to help — maybe even a bit excited. As utterly horrifying as her initial trip to the strange Red Forest had been, a large part of her wanted very badly to see it again - to see her friends and hear their voices, not to mention hug Fellow Undergotten once more. She couldn't explain why, but since her return from Fillagrou, the urge to go back had been gnawing at the inside of her brain like an unreachable itch she needed badly to scratch. Now faced with the reality of what it would take in order for her to step foot on the strange alien world again, she couldn't help but wonder if she was making the right decision. Around her the air felt thick, wet, and heavy, cluttered with the sounds of crumpling leaves, snapping twigs and the breathy pants of her traveling companions. From somewhere behind, something bright and wobbly emerged: a beam of light created by a flashlight flickered across the scattered trees, lighting up their tattered aged trunks. The voice of her father, though weak and faraway, could still faintly be heard in the distance. What would her parents think? How mad would they be? Staci had always prided herself in the fact that she was never what some might call a "problem child." Studious in her schoolwork, she always had high grades, wasn't known for being overly emotional or prone to flights of fancy, or backtalk of any sort. For all intents and purposes, her parents couldn't have asked for a better daughter. Running away in the middle of the night and ignoring her father's enraged screams was unlike her. Would they ever forgive her? Would they be able to look at her the same way again? Why was she doing this? It didn't make any sense. She shouldn't be doing this and she knew it.

Her mind awash with a million different thoughts, Staci's attention was drawn away from the ground momentarily. Stepping awkwardly on a loose twig, her ankle twisted in a direction ankles aren't meant to twist. The ground rushed up quickly to meet her face. A pair of arms wedged themselves underneath her armpits, stopping the forward movement of her body a mere moment before it collided with the dirt.

"Whoa! I've got you, I've got you. Are you okay?" The voice was tender yet deep, frightened yet controlled. The voice belonged to Tommy Jarvis.

As Tommy pulled her to a fully upright position, she turned toward him, their faces so close that they could feel the heat of each other's breath on their chilled skin. The reflections from Nicky's flashlight cascaded across Tommy's eyes, bobbing back and forth hypnotically like partially translucent fish behind the glass of a bowl.

"I'm fine . . .I-I'm fine," Staci stammered, overcome with the sensation of momentary weightlessness in his arms.

In this one instant she understood why she agreed to come along so willingly. If she were to be truthful with herself, she realized that it wasn't for Tipoloo or Fillagrou or the war or Fellow Undergotten or Roustaf or Nicky — though they had played some small part. It was for him. It was for Tommy.

The realization was both wonderful and horrifying.

Like fingernails across a chalk board, the deep, grating voice of Donald Rondage quickly dragged her from her dreamy stare and back to reality. "Hey losers, if we don't keep moving, little Miss Staci's old man is going to catch up to us! The dude might be half naked and wearing a pair of slippers, but he's moving pretty fast. Come on!"

Five or so minutes later the group exited the trees and made their way up and over a large grassy field and into yet another line of trees at the bottom of the hill. The glow of Dale Alexander's flashlight had disappeared by the time they reached the Jarvis brothers' tree fort. Standing next to the stream hiding the doorway to Fillagrou, the group as a whole stopped to catch their breath.

High above them, the poorly constructed tree fort achingly creaked, wobbling ever so slightly as a result of a particularly stalwart gust of wind.

Hovering four feet above the surface of the half-frozen black water, an anxious Roustaf turned to the children, his fluttering wings invisible against the night sky. "Well, is everyone ready?"

He received no response.

Moving his flashlight over the stream, Nicky breathed in deeply and held it, trying his best to slow his racing heart. The barely moving liquid looked darker than he remembered — darker, deeper, and a million times more ominous. It seemed so clear to him earlier, so simple. Returning to Fillagrou and helping his friends — there was never a moment's hesitation. Now, though, staring down at the doorway, everything seemed far hazier. At last he exhaled, turned his head, and glanced in the direction of his older brother.

Standing five feet away, Tommy could see the hesitation in his little brother's eyes and hear the fear in his uneven breathing. A large part of him secretly hoped that Nicky would back out, prayed that he might take his flashlight and walk home to the Williamsons' where he should have remained in the first place. At least there Tommy could be sure he was safe. On paper, the idea of returning to the strange world that very nearly killed them six months ago made no sense whatsoever to Tommy. Even with their incredible powers, even with the prophecy and the help of Nestor, Walcott, Pleebo and the citizens of New Tipoloo, it made no sense. They were just children after all, Donald, Nicky, Staci, and himself — every last one of them, just children. They were children doing things children had no business doing. They were children in situations in which children had no right being involved. A feeling, cold, icy, and impossibly thick inside Tommy's stomach, told him this was a bad idea. This wasn't a game, it wasn't a storybook or a fantasy film; this was real life. In real life things didn't always end well. In real life, the good guys didn't always win. In fact, more often than not, in real life there was no such thing as the good guys. Real life is gray and unending. Real life is a question with no answer.

His eyes glued to the silent group of children, Roustaf could only shake his head. Dragging four children onto the frontline of a war felt plain wrong on every level. Had he been asked to do the same thing a year ago, his answer would have been a resounding no. They didn't belong there and they shouldn't be a part of this. Things had changed since a year ago, though, and changed drastically. After seeing firsthand what the children were capable of, he discovered an odd, confusing, and slightly nonsensical faith in the prophecy of the Fillagrou elder. Maybe, somehow, despite the odds against them, these children could fix everything. Even if they couldn't, even if the prophecy was little more than the pointless ramblings of a mad Fillagrou elder pushed to the absolute limits of his sanity, they were without a doubt capable of magic on a level he never believed possible. He had witnessed firsthand how Tommy wiped out an entire Ochan regiment with the subtle twist of his wrist. It was remarkable, something he could never forget, even if he wanted to. If the children couldn't put an end to the war, maybe, just maybe, at the very least they could save Pleebo and Walcott. Despite his reservations, it is for this reason alone that Roustaf resigned himself to the reality that he had to at least try. Over the course of the war, many times he'd been asked to do things that he didn't completely agree with, but such is the nature of combat. This was simply another of those instances.

"Wait a minute," Donald interrupted, moving slowly from the back of the group to the water's edge. "How do we know this thing will even take us back? I've tried it more than a couple times since returning and ended up having to walk all the damn way home dripping wet."

"I don't know kid," Roustaf responded with honesty, looking up from the stream while lifting himself a few feet higher into the air. "All I can tell you is that Zanell guaranteed me it'll work, and while she might suck at directions, she's fairly spot on with her predictions these days."

"Yeah, yeah, yeah, I forgot. It lets through who it needs to let through when they need to be let through . . .I remember her crazy spiel." Donald sighed deeply, running his fingers through his greasy hair and rolling his eyes.

Turning briefly, he looked behind him in the direction of his house. For Donald the choice had already been made — in fact, it was remarkably simple. He didn't want to go back home. There was nothing to go back to really — nothing worthwhile anyway. Rolling his eyes and shaking his head, he dipped one foot into the water. The ice-cold liquid instantly seeped through the fabric of his worn and beaten gym shoe, soaking the dirty sock within. Turning toward the rest of the group, he scanned their faces, eventually stopping on Tommy Jarvis's.

A crooked smile slowly spread across his lips. "Screw it. Let's go for it."

Not fully realizing he was doing it, Tommy smiled back.

13. THROUGH THE TUNNELS

The undeniably familiar yet wholly unique experience of traveling from one world to the next washed over Tommy's body less than a second after dropping feet first into the greenish-black stream water. In an instant, everything that once was washed away. Concepts of form and shape no longer existed. The universe swallowed him completely, tugging him into the strange in-between where direction no longer had meaning and gravity became merely an abstract. Up folded into down and left transformed to right; back and forth came together at last, morphing into a bizarrely cohesive hybrid of the two. In the passageway between the place he knew as Earth and the strange world referred to by the locals as Fillagrou, sound and thought and idea were without meaning. In this strange nothing there existed only space — or, more appropriately, a vague reflection of the concept of space, an unproven hypothesis of an idea not fully fleshed out. These sensations terrified Tommy the first time he experienced them after falling into the stream with Donald Rondage six months ago. Something was different now. The silence, the emptiness, and the sensation of non-sensation felt oddly comforting and weirdly fulfilling. More than the Fillagrou forest, more than the

Williamsons' house, more than with his father or in the town he was born, the void felt like home. If only it could have lasted longer.

From the darkness, the moist, slightly chilly feeling of water swept in from underneath him. Again his fingers could feel; again his body had shape. Fully submerged in an extremely familiar liquid, he began swimming toward a bit of blue light above him and broke the surface of the water a moment later. While he was gasping for air, two sets of hands pawed at various parts of his upper body, grabbing the fabric of his shirt and lifting him from the dark liquid. Just as before, what was a stream ten to fifteen feet wide and miles long in his world was now barely more than a puddle, barely large enough to hold the entirety of his body. After awkwardly dragging him onto solid ground, Nicky and Staci helped Tommy to his feet. Both were dripping wet, Staci's petite body shivering uncontrollably in the nippy air of the Fillagrou night.

"Exactly how you remembered it, huh?" she chirped with a half-smile as she rubbed her hands up and down along her arms in an ultimately ineffective attempt to raise her lowered body temperature.

Tommy smiled back at her and laughed slightly. He was beginning to feel the cold himself, but tried his best to ignore it. Around him the Red Forest was pitch black, the only bit of light coming from a rather large, hauntingly blue moon peeking through the breaks in the dense foliage of the trees. As it had been night in his world, so it was here. Whizzing past Tommy's head, Roustaf came to a hovering stop a few feet from the boy's face in the center of the group.

"We better get moving," The tiny man injected, wringing water from the pants leg of his overalls. "I'm thinking we can make it to New Tipoloo before daybreak, as long as we don't move like a pack of one-legged Lazigorns."

The children stared back at him with confused expressions; none of them had any idea what in the world a one-legged Lazigorn might be. Whatever it was though, it did indeed sound slow.

The next three hours were spent hiking quietly through the darkened forest with Roustaf leading the way. Before beginning, the little mustached man had instructed the group to keep the chatter to a minimum, or more specifically to "shut your yaps." In the six months since the children laid waste to the Ochan fortress, decimated its army, and murdered its prince, patrols of the Red Forest had tapered off somewhat. Tapered off, however, by no means meant they had ceased completely. The forest remained quite dangerous — the less of a ruckus created, the safer for all involved.

Two of Fillagrou's three suns were slowly making their way up and over the horizon when the group at last arrived at the hidden passageway leading to New Tipoloo. One by one they dropped through a trapdoor in the grayish-brown soil that was camouflaged by a pair of densely covered bushes. From here they made their way through a maze of stuffy, pitch-black underground tunnels with enough twists and turns to confuse anyone not wholly familiar with their layout. No less than ten minutes into the trek, Donald Rondage began to wonder how in the world Roustaf knew where he was going — if, in fact, he did at all. Though the entire trip had taken barely more than thirty minutes, the sweltering heat and dust, coupled with an awful wet clay smell, made it seem a good deal longer. Donald's feet were sore, his calves on fire. A large, throbbing pain in his head had begun pressing against the interior of his temples. Moments away from reaching his physical breaking point, Donald glared upward just in time to see Roustaf come to a stop in front of an enormous stone blocking their path, thus putting an abrupt end to their forward movement.

Turning in the direction of the children, salty sweat pouring down his shiny face, Roustaf muttered with just a smidge of sarcasm "Well, we're here. That wasn't so bad, now, was it?"

Not a single one of the group answered, instead choosing to let the frowns on their weary faces do the talking for them.

"Hey kid," Roustaf added, pointing in Donald's direction, "Do me a solid and knock three times, pause, then knock again. I'd do it myself, but my entire fist is barely the size of your fingernail, so they're a bit more likely to hear you."

Donald sighed and, slumping his shoulders while pressing past Nicky, he moved toward the stone.

After brushing away some caked dirt from the surface, he turned briefly to the little red man hovering behind him. "What happened to the little locking thingies? You know, like you guys had at the other place?"

"Hey, gimme a break slick. You do understand that this place was built in kind of a rush, right? Excuse me if we're not completely up to code quite yet."

Donald responded by shaking his head annoyingly, then doing as instructed — three knocks, a pause, and then another. Ten or so seconds afterward the tunnel began to shake, thick clumps of wet dirt and hazy dust falling onto the children's heads. Staci let out a high-pitched yelp as a rather large chunk smashed into her scalp, exploding to pieces. Lurching to the side, the massive, unwieldy rock rolled into the wall to the right, eventually disappearing completely and at last exposing the previously hidden city of New Tipoloo. It took a mere moment for both Tommy and Donald to recognize it, but the recognition resulted in a pair of soft smiles.

Much of the original city was destroyed, and its inhabitants gruesomely slaughtered, during a raid by the Ochan army. After they finished their killing, the Ochan soldiers collapsed the ground above into the city, forever burying it and all those who called it home. In a matter of hours they had successfully put an end to what had taken years of painstaking labor to create. Destroying a city and obliterating all hope. It seemed so frighteningly simple a task. Even the very thorough, very dangerous Ochans, however, were not perfect. A nearly endless array of tunnels branched out for miles upon miles in every direction. Finding and destroying them all proved an impossible task even for Ocha's most ruthless and dedicated. Following the destruction of Prince Valkea's fortress, the freed slaves located these untouched tunnels, expanded upon them, and built themselves a new home, a new safe haven, a place to begin the fight anew.

At the foot of the now open doorway, anxious smiles spread across their bizarre faces, stood an enormous crowd of creatures. Every face, every body, was totally unique from the last. This was a wild array of creatures from ninety-nine separate worlds, each giddy with anticipation, each anxious for a brief look at the children of the prophecy.

For Staci Alexander, the sight was quite simply overwhelming. In direct response to the enormous crowd, her feet absent-mindedly began to shuffle backward, her body eventually coming to a stop after smacking into Tommy's chest. Quickly turning to face him, she could only shake her head back and forth, indicating without doubt that she now wanted to return home. This was too much for her, all of this — it was simply too much to take. She never should have agreed to come along. She didn't belong here. Putting his hands on her shoulders, Tommy smiled, trying his best not to laugh at the slightly comical look of terror etched on her face.

Attempting to calm her, he whispered softly, "It'll be okay."

While the gesture didn't douse her fears completely, it did strangely manage to relax her.

Led by Roustaf, the group hesitantly moved from the tunnel into the dimly lit, slightly less stuffy city. The moment they stepped into the light, a boisterous, joyful cheer rose up from the crowd. So very loud was their excited roar that it shook the walls of the city, creating a subtle tremor beneath the children's feet. To the citizens of New Tipoloo, these were not simply children; these were the creatures that rescued them from certain death. These were the beings that single handedly destroyed an Ochan castle and murdered the son of the tyrant king. These were the creatures that saved their lives. These were their saviors. To the war torn masses, the children were seen as great and powerful beings that would eventually bring an end to the unending suffering that had become the whole of their existence.

No, these were not children. These were gods.

Tommy's grip on Staci's shoulders tightened significantly, the deafening sounds of the citizens of New Tipoloo's jubilant, hopeful shouts ringing in his ears and rattling the brain inside his skull. Having been smacked in the face so abruptly by the sight in front of him, it suddenly seemed so clear; Staci was right in wanting to leave. This was too much.

This was too much and this was going to end badly.

14. PROBLEMATIC REUNION

His heart steadily pounding, Nicky Jarvis lifted himself onto the tips of his toes while scanning the massive crowd for a single familiar face. He found none. A few feet in front him, Roustaf hovered in mid-air, his barely six inch long body the only thing standing between the children and a mass of excited creatures extending throughout the city.

"Settle down, ya bums!" Roustaf's gravelly voice bellowed, his arms waiving back and forth wildly. "Settle down and make some room unless you're looking to get your jaws boxed!"

While Roustaf's voice proved surprisingly deep for one of such diminutive stature, it was easily drowned out by the substantial horde of feverish Tipoloo citizens. The great living wall of multi-colored flesh, fur and slime began slowly moving in the direction of the children. Noticing that things were very quickly getting out of hand, Tommy made his way to the front of the group. Pushing past Roustaf and his brother, he shoved the remaining children back through the doorway they originally used to enter the city. Ever since Roustaf left New Tipoloo on his mission to retrieve the children and bring them back to Fillagrou, the anticipation of his return had been building. With the tiny mustached man having been gone for some time, anxiousness was given ample time to stew. Slowly brought to a boil, it had transformed into pure, unadulterated, undeniable exhilaration. Having been brought back to life by the warm glow from Staci's fingertips, many among the crowd very literally owed their existence to these strange creatures that bled the color of the forest. Pressing forward, their arms raised in happiness, their voices echoing throughout the city walls, they wanted simply to be near their saviors, to touch them and give thanks for everything they had already done and the things yet to be accomplished. Indeed this was a mob, but it was a mob with the absolute best of intentions. Pressing past Roustaf, the mass of creatures advanced further toward the children, forcing them to retreat deeper into the dark tunnel.

Peeking out from behind his brother's back, his hands shaking, unsure of what was going on, Nicky spotted the top of a very familiar looking bluish-green head cutting through the mass of rainbow colored alien flesh. Covered in thick scales, with a subtle striped pattern running along the surface, the bald head bobbed up and down swiftly through the screaming masses, moving with expert precision. Standing directly behind Nicky, sandwiched between the youngest Jarvis boy and the hulking form of Donald Rondage, Staci noticed the head as well and recognized it immediately as belonging to none other than Fellow Undergotten.

"Come on! Move it! Settle down, will you! Settle down!" Determined to move forward, Fellow shoved aside a group of ecstatic teenage Ricardians and ducked under the thick, fur covered arm of a seven foot tall Garzabull.

Through the slim openings in the crowd, he could just barely make out the shape of the four children huddled tightly together in the entranceway. He was moving much too slowly, though. Navigating the sea of exhilarated citizens was akin to attempting to ride choppy waters in a raft with a hole in the bottom; it was eating up too much time. The crowd would reach the children long before he did, and in their excited state, anything could happen. The children might be hurt, or worse. Clumsily twisting his body between flailing arms, Fellow turned to look behind him. No more than ten feet away, Nestor Rockshell and a select group of his best soldiers were struggling with the horde as well.

"We're not going to make it in time!" Fellow screamed loud enough for Nestor to hear over the wails of the crowd. "We need to get a handle on this now!"

The words were like music to the Tycarian soldier's ears.

Annoyance had slowly been building inside Nestor. Carefully pushing his oversized body, covered in its even more oversized shell, through the mass of Tipoloo citizens was, for him, an exercise in the limits of his patience — an exercise he'd grown weary of. This needed to stop, and it needed to stop now. Turning his head, he nodded to the Tycarian soldier behind him, who turned and nodded to the one behind him, and so on. One by one, the massive turtle men removed the bladed weapons from the sheaths attached to their sides and lifted them into the air angrily.

Breathing in deeply, weapon drawn and muscles tightened, Nestor screamed louder than he'd screamed in quite some time, "Calm down and back away from the children! Now!"

As quickly as the excitement began, it ended.

Over the last six months, the citizens of New Tipoloo had come to know the voice of Nestor Rockshell well. In many ways, he and the King of the Tycarian people, Walcott Shellamennes, along with Pleebo, Zanell and, to a lesser extent, Fellow Undergotten, had become the leaders of the new revolution. When Nestor spoke, it was time to listen, and listen they would. A moment before Nestor's annoyed yelp, the city was so loud one could scarcely hear the sound of their own voice. Now a single pin drop could be easily recognized. Having settled down, the crowd parted to the sides of the street, opening a tight yet passable path for Fellow, Nestor, and the soldiers.

Still crouched behind his older brother, peeking through a space between Tommy's arm and torso, Nicky watched the mass of bodies open up, at last bringing Fellow into view. Upon seeing his friend for the first time in six months, Nicky smiled brighter than he had smiled in years. Ducking under his brother's arm, he charged full speed from the tunnel and leapt happily into the fish man's outstretched arms. Fellow hugged the little boy tightly, pulling Nicky's head against the fabric of his dusty shirt. An uncommon warmth flushed Fellow's naturally chilly cheeks, transforming them into a soft baby blue.

Smiling brightly, he said with a chuckle in his voice, "Whoa, whoa, whoa. It's good to see you too, kiddo . . .it's good to see you too."

Not far behind Nicky came an equally blissful Staci Alexander, her body colliding into both of them full force, her arms not only wrapping around Fellow but the youngest Jarvis boy as well. During their initial trip to Fillagrou, more than anyone else it had been Fellow Undergotten who helped the both of them. Fellow Undergotten made it his personal mission to keep them alive, to ensure their safety and maintain their sanity. Of all the creatures they met, it was Fellow Undergotten they had missed the most. His cheeks having now turned white, Fellow grinned a mile wide while trying his best to keep from crying. The war had taken everything from him, leaving Nicky and Staci the closest things he had to family. To see them alive and well, with such happiness in their voices, was conjuring up emotions he hadn't felt in years — indescribable emotions— emotions he didn't want to let go of.

"It's good to see you guys too," he muttered again through thin, shaky lips, while patting Staci gently on the back of her head.

From behind Fellow, the massive-bodied Nestor Rockshell moved toward Tommy and Donald, who were still standing in the tunnel leading to the city. Sliding his broad sword into the sheath strapped to his massive shell, the six foot tall turtle man came to a stop directly in front of the boys.

Nodding his head, he smiled slightly with a stone-seriousness befitting a warrior. "Let me be the first to formally welcome you to New Tipoloo, lads. I must apologize for the exuberance of our citizens; they have been awaiting your arrival with much anticipation."

Still a bit frightened, though trying his best to disguise it, Donald moved in front of Tommy. "N-no worries, right? It's good to be back. I like what you've done with the place . . .lots of . . .dirt."

Nestor grinned slyly at the boy's joke, but the slight smile on his face evaporated just as quickly, and his tone turned deadly serious. "I apologize that I must now cut our reunion a bit short. Time is not on our side, lads, and we must move briskly."

"Nestor, don't go scaring them just yet." The soft, familiar feminine voice came from behind the turtle man, though his massive form obscured its speaker.

In one smooth movement, the lanky, waif thin form of Zanell stepped into view of both Tommy and Donald. Brushing the impossibly thin, astoundingly white hair from her face, she flashed a pleased grin in Tommy's direction. Her sunken, oversized eyes, with their watermelon-sized red pupils, never left his face as she moved to within a foot of him.

Reaching forward, she brushed the back of her bony hand against his cheek. "It's good to see you again, Tommy Jarvis." Turning her attention to Donald, she did the same, causing the young boy's pudgy cheeks turn a deep red in direct response to her touch. "And you as well, Donald."

This was a very different Zanell than the children met when they arrived in Fillagrou for the first time. In their absence, Zanell had taken the mantle of spiritual elder with amazing ease. Inheriting her grandfather's position upon his death, and being given the sight beyond sight, had changed her dramatically. For Zanell, the universe was a very different place than it had been only six months ago. In the lives of every creature there are unknowns — mysteries and certain things about the past, the present and the future — that one is simply not meant to know; this, however, was no longer the case for Zanell. To her, the universe had become an open book, the lives of every single living thing since its creation barely more than a few sentences. From her perspective, everything had already happened; the stories had reached their conclusions a million times and would do so a million more. There was an undeniable confidence in her movements, the kind of confidence that could only result from one knowing all there was to know.

Turning her attention back to Tommy, she sighed deeply, images of what was about to happen to the young boy flashing across the vast, jumbled landscape that had become her mind. "While Nestor's approach was gruff to say the least, he is not incorrect when he says that time is not on our side. If we are to save the universe, we will need your help."

Tommy noticed an ever so brief yet painfully obvious expression of sadness creeping its way into the deep wrinkles on her face. Zanell noticed his awareness and quickly looked away. The gesture sent a chill down Tommy's spine.

Zanell glanced now in the direction of Fellow, Nicky, Staci and Nestor, then across the sea of wide-eyed New Tipoloo citizens. From this moment on, everything would change. The trials lying ahead would test the limits of every living being currently huddled around her. While some would emerge physically unscathed, the vast majority would be forever emotionally scarred. By the time the dust of war cleared, most would be dead.

Sighing deeply, she feigned a smile, then said to the children, "Come, there is someone I need you to meet . . .after all, he's the reason you're here, and he's been anxiously awaiting your arrival."

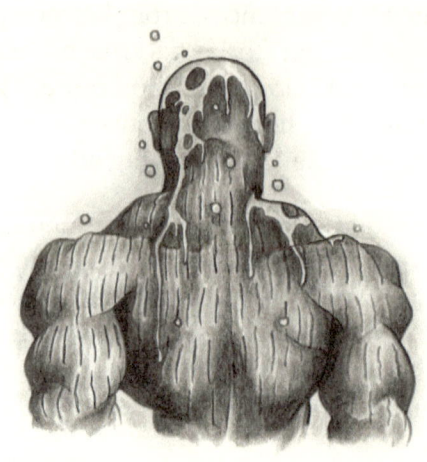

15. TRAITOR TO THE CAUSE

Pleasantries having been exchanged, Zanell led the group
through the crowded New Tipoloo streets, excited onlookers
watching with wide-eyed interest as they passed by. Walking
directly behind Zanell, Tommy took note of the fact that this
Tipoloo was very different from the original city. There were
similarities of course — the construction, for instance. Both had a
very hand-made feeling, seeming to not only have been dug by the
strength of fingers and whatever tools might have been available,
but dug quickly. This new incarnation, however, was stocked with
food, weapons and other such amenities that were no doubt
scavenged from the remains of Prince Valkea's fortress. For the
most part, the citizens seemed fairly well fed and surprisingly
hopeful, and this was the most remarkable difference of all. The
original Tipoloo had been little more than a death camp, a dreary
pit stop between life and a drawn out, excruciating death. New
Tipoloo was different. This city didn't seem to be simply a place to
survive as much as it was a place to live. The idea that the smiles on
the faces of its inhabitants might be directly related to him
frightened Tommy. It seemed unreal, maybe even a bit wrong. To
his left he saw a large group of staunchly stoic creatures with dull

orange flesh, square heads and wide facial features, bent at the knees, silently bowing in his direction. Unable to look them squarely in the eyes, Tommy turned his head; he didn't deserve this sort of reaction. No one did.

Bringing up the rear of the group, strolling with his chest puffed out and a smile a mile wide stretched across his face, Donald Rondage was having a very different reaction to the situation. Every bow, handshake or strange alien gesture of thanks directed toward him was met with a smug, toothy grin. Donald had missed this; he was somebody again, suddenly he mattered. When an odd looking, rail-thin creature with a floppy nose at least two feet in length, yet very human in overall shape, dropped to the ground in front of him and kissed the dirt at his feet, the boy could barely contain his smile. This is where he was meant to be; this is who he was meant to be. A sense of pride unlike anything he had ever felt swelled inside him, blowing his head up like a balloon and filling it with wonderfully hot air. Standing behind Donald, Nestor rolled his eyes before gently nudging the boy and his rapidly expanding ego forward with his massive flat paw.

A trip that should have taken ten minutes ended up being closer to fifteen, mostly due to the crowds. Zanell at last came to a stop in front of a modest dwelling dug into one of the city's walls. Gently pushing aside a rickety, oddly shaped and poorly constructed wooden door, she motioned for the children to enter without saying a word. One by one, the group stepped into the tiny, dimly lit room, huddling close together and filling it to capacity. Standing at the opposite end of the barely ten foot wide dwelling, cast in deep black shadows with his massively muscled back to the door, stood a figure of enormous stature. His skin was a dark grayish-green, covered in an endless amount of scars drawn tightly over a mountain of muscles hidden underneath. With nearly perfect spacing between them, the scars didn't resemble anything the massive figure might have received in battle. Instead they looked almost intentional, bearing a close resemblance to hash marks.

The thick, sharp scales, the green skin, the overly muscled body; Tommy immediately recognized this giant creature's species. He was Ochan.

Lifting a small clay bowl above him, the shadowy lizard man trickled the clear liquid inside over the top of his bald head. "Unbearably humid down here," he grumbled in a morose tone, never turning from the wall. "Hate the humidity."

Tilting his head to the side, he glanced over the massive muscle of his shoulder, inhaling deep while grinding his sharp teeth together and showing just the slightest bit of annoyance. "Thought there would be five?"

Hovering in mid-air, Roustaf carefully moved over the tightly packed crowd to the front of the group and alongside Tommy and Nicky.

"Yeah, well, here's the thing. I couldn't convince the other one come. I tried, but the kid wasn't having any of it. I wasn't about to carry him back kicking and screaming, so this'll have to do," he stated almost apologetically.

The massive Ochan turned back to the wall, half growling under his breath. From a modest, ancient-looking table next to him, the creature retrieved a heavy-looking armored chest plate. He lifted it over his head and rested it on his sturdy shoulders. The armor was covered in dings, slices and noticeable dents, parts of it looking like it had been welded and repaired numerous times. It was painfully obvious that this Ochan had seen battle, and lots of it. The already stale air around him grew weightier still as he strapped the armor in at the sides, pulling it so tight against his flesh that it almost resembled a second skin.

"Will four be enough, gypsy?" he mumbled to no one in particular while lifting a massive sheathed sword from the shadowy floor and strapping it to his back.

From the now closed doorway came Zanell's soft response. "Four will suffice."

Again the Ochan mumbled underneath his breath, clearly annoyed. "Magic. I despise magic . . .needlessly complicated and unpredictable . . .troublesome. Nothing good has ever come from it."

Grumbling, he began to slide five smaller, yet equally dangerous looking, weapons into various leather straps hanging off his thick belt. Turning slowly, he stepped from the shadows and into the light of a nearby candle resting on a shelf built into the wall. His face looked aged, yet by no means old. It was also the only part of his exposed flesh not covered in the strange scars. Drops of transparent liquid continued to drip down the side of his face, over his mouth and across the nape of his neck. Hidden under a heavy protruding brow, his black pupils scanned the group of children huddled together at the opposite end of the diminutive dwelling. Lingering for a moment on Staci and Nicky, his dark eyes at last came to an unblinking, unmoving halt on Tommy Jarvis.

The silence in the room was deafening.

Only the breathing of those inside and the soft flicker of two candles could be heard. Eventually the enormous Ochan began to speak. "Hurm. I knew you were young, heard the stories . . .never imagined."

His voice was deep, echoing against the walls and quickly bouncing back. Every breath he took shook the ground underneath the children's feet. Without realizing it, Nicky backed away slowly, behind his brother and toward Nestor near the rear of the room. Her heart racing as memories of Prince Valkea flooded her mind, Staci followed suit. Glancing at Tommy, she noticed that the boy was stone-faced, his eyes locked onto those of the burly green monster. Independent of thought, Tommy's hands pulled tightly into fists. While he might not have been aware of what he was doing, the massive Ochan instantly took note of the gesture, smiling slightly before locking eyes again with boy.

"Perhaps introductions are in order," Zanell added, stepping between the two, feeling the unquestionable tension in the room. "Children, this is Krystoph. Believe it or not, he has come to help us save your world."

16. THE TERRIBLY MISERABLE TALE OF KRYSTOPH

Complete and total belief in any one thing can prove wonderfully freeing in its simplicity. Such explains the life of a young Ochan named Krystoph. The eldest of ten children, he came from earnest and humble, yet entirely honorable beginnings. Working as one of King Calador's blacksmiths, his father was able to provide safety for his family by giving them a home within one of the king's many fortresses. In a world as accustomed to war as Ocha, safety was often a difficult to find and highly sought after commodity. As was the case with most male Ochan youths, the child Krystoph joined his king's army immediately upon reaching the age of maturity. At this period in Ochan history, seven kings ruled the whole of the planet. Spread out across its five continents, it was these seven that held the lives of the entire Ochan race in their hands. Each king hated the next with a passion, and the ultimate goal of all was exactly the same: to conquer the land of the others and take the land and people for their own. The citizens living under the rule of each king remained staunchly faithful to his ideals. Like his father, Krystoph believed King Calador was the center of the universe, the keeper of his wellbeing and the shining example of Ochan greatness. To question one's king was unheard of, as his word was truth and his truth was the word.

King Calador's army proved a perfect fit for the young Krystoph. Smart, athletic and quick to learn, the child was found to be quite adept in the concepts of war, not to mention surprisingly at home with the idea of killing. To murder in the name of your king was considered honorable — to die in the preservation of his power more so.

Years spent in unwavering, exceptional service of King Calador resulted in Krystoph's quick ascension in the military's ranks. When Krystoph's father finally met his death, he did so of old age, a rarity among Ochan males. Krystoph took pride in this fact, believing beyond a doubt that Calador's might and the protection of his armies were the direct cause. Not long into his service, murder ceased to have meaning for Krystoph, as if it were somehow a separate entity from war. The dead became statistics; the larger the number, the greater the success.

A month after Krystoph was promoted to General, King Calador died quite unexpectedly in his chambers with only his son, Prince Kragamel, at his side. Calador's death was never fully explained; some attributed it to the Groun, a rare disease the king had dealt with his entire life. Others, though, believed it to be a random occurrence, or some other manner of unexplainable illness. Fewer still settled on the most simple of concepts, old age. While none proved to be a wholly satisfying explanation, not a single one among the king's devout opted to delve further. When hushed whispers in shadowed backrooms rose to the possibility of the newly appointed King's involvement, his loyal soldiers squashed them immediately.

To question the honor of a king — such an act was punishable by death.

While there were indeed similarities between the new King Kragamel and his deceased father Calador, the heir to the throne seemed impossibly intent on expansion and obsessed with the ideals of power. Not simply content with existing or protecting, the new king not only wanted more, but believed it to be his destiny. Whether it was to spite his father, or in the spirit of competition, or possibly even in search of respect, the young Kragamel dedicated himself to expanding the reach of his influence with a fever no Ochan before him had ever shown.

Stumbling onto the doorway leading to Fillagrou proved to be the first step toward accomplishing his lofty goals.

At the outset of the Great War, Krystoph who led the charge. It was Krystoph who planned the initial invasion of Fillagrou, he who discovered the doorway to Dearagorn, Hackenstat, Chintaran, Grilgamorph and countless others. In the name of his king, Krystoph ordered the deaths of millions and the slavery of millions more. This was his role, and this became his sole reason for existing. Much like his new king, this was his destiny. In the service of his people, General Krystoph soon found himself filled with contentment, pride and happiness mere words alone could never hope to express.

As is often the case with power, in order for one to achieve it, another must be squashed. The higher the corpses stack, the higher into the clouds one can reach. The bodies of the fallen make a superb ladder.

Everything in General Krystoph's life changed for the worse with the invasion of Tycaria. The forty-forth world discovered hidden in the Red Forest was populated with sturdy, well-trained, battle-ready creatures lead by a king referring to himself as Walcott Shellamennes, who proved surprisingly resourceful. Filled with a vigorous fighting spirit rivaling even that of the Ochans themselves, the Tycarians became the very first species to respond to their invading aggressors in accordance of the laws of motion themselves: *for every reaction there is an equal and opposite reaction.* When the divisions under Krystoph's control began suffering setbacks, Kragamel's patience with the well-decorated general appointed under his father's reign began to wear thin. The initial invasion, expected to take mere days, stretched to weeks and the weeks into months with still no significant progress made. Feeling the need to remind his general of the importance of his duties,

Kragamel ordered Krystoph's family murdered — his wife, his child, his brothers, his sister and their offspring, every last Ochan with an ounce of his family's blood coursing through their veins was murdered in the name of expansion and country and war.

The reaction was of course extreme, even for an Ochan king.

As stated before, complete and total belief in any one thing can prove wonderfully freeing in its simplicity. That is, until the moment arrives when the pillars on which that belief stands crack and crumble. The veil lifted, the chinks in the finely constructed, beautifully polished armor that had protected him his entire life exposed, Krystoph suddenly found himself left with nothing.

What is an Ochan who no longer has faith in the very things that made him Ochan?

He was alone, no king, no family and none of the things in which he found solace or happiness. Instead there existed only disillusionment coupled with confusion. The implosion of the ideals he held most dear stirred a sweltering anger inside him. Like a pot boiling over, Krystoph's hatred for Kragamel poured from his mouth, its thick, vile, foamy froth rolling across his flesh, seeping into his pores and transforming him from the inside out. The concept of vengeance had always played an important role in Ochan life, nearly as prominent a role as family, safety or king. If he were to be denied three, Krystoph would ensure he savored the fourth to the best of his ability.

The success of the Ochan military when traveling from one strange new world to the next could be attributed to much more than simply superior strategy, size and experience. Unbeknownst to those not associated with the highest of military rank, what more often than not turned the tide in their favor was in fact the thing Ochans in general felt most uncomfortable with: magic, a deep, dangerous and powerful magic unlike anything mastered by the Ochan race before, a magic created by a mysterious artifact birthed into the universe by an ancient race of blind, deformed Ochans called the Conjurers. While many kings before Kragamel occasionally relied on the Conjurers and their peculiar powers as a source of counsel, none before him embraced their ideas with such earnest interest. Behind closed doors, away from the pervasive distaste for magic felt by the commoners, the king gave large groups of Conjurers safety, home and nourishment. Kragamel freed them from poverty, hunger and suffering, thus providing them with a purpose greater than any they had ever known. In return for his uncommon kindness, the Conjurers bestowed on the new king the Rongstag — a talisman with greater power than the Conjurers had ever mastered. One half of the Rongstag gave he who wielded it the ability to render useless an entire world's technology, while the other half negated all magic. Without the aid of magic or superior weaponry, no world could hope to stand against the bladed, hard-knuckled, close-quarter warfare the Ochan race spent centuries mastering and held so dear. Due in no small part to this fantastic new artifact, ninety-nine worlds fell like dominos.

In retaliation for the murder of his family, Krystoph struck at the heart of the Ochan nation's hidden power. Masterfully stealing one half of the Rongstag, he hid it in a place he believed it would never be found, and it is there that it has remained. For this act of treachery against his people, Krystoph paid with his life — or so it was believed.

What the tyrant king Kragamel failed to realize was that Krystoph died long before the newly appointed General Gragor dragged his hapless, broken shell of a body to the fire caves and slit his throat, allowing the combustion beetles free reign at this insides. What was left to rot among the sweltering awfulness of Ocha's turbulent underground that day was little more than a shell, an empty vessel that once housed an unwavering belief in people and king. The mass of improperly healed bones, exposed wounds and gangrenous limbs that crawled from the caves into the chilly night air three weeks later had already begun to fill itself with a different cause entirely. Stumbling into the darkness, the thing that once thought itself a proud Ochan set forth on a new mission, the murder of a king. Vengeance is the most dangerous beast one is likely to encounter; once it has you in its grasp, more often than not it is there you will spend the remainder of your days.

The hunger of vengeance is unrelenting and it will not be denied.

17. LIARS

Every breath was like a knife stabbing the twelve year old Tommy Jarvis in the chest. Even the most simple of movements sent a torrent of unrelenting pain flashing throughout the entirety of his body. Outside the cold window pressed against his shoulder, the darkened world passed by in flashes. Streetlights soared like shooting stars, dragging behind them ghostly trails that wagged across the blackness like the latent images of never-there monster tails. In desperate need of a tune-up, the car underneath him clanked and creaked, its engine struggling to maintain even the most average of speeds for any significant amount of time. Across from Tommy, only half awake and hunched over the steering wheel, was his father. The eyes of Chris Jarvis were wide, the stubble on his face at least two days old. Since the funeral for his wife earlier in the week, Chris spent his days fading in and out of reality. This was due in no small part to the endless stream of mind altering, wonderfully numbing liquid consistently making its way down his gullet and back up again into his brain. Problems were easier dealt with when one had the help of friends, and Chris found his friends in bottles. Faced with a red light, Chris slammed on the breaks, bringing the car to a screeching halt. Briefly glancing to his right, he watched with the slightest bit of worry as his eldest son

86

clutched at his chest, a strained grimace stretched across his boyish features.

Gripping tightly on the leather of the steering wheel, he looked away, his breaths coming in more rapid succession with every passing moment. "We'll be there in a minute."

The hospital was still six blocks away, but it was not the time or even the amount of pain his son was in that worried Chris at the moment. There were much larger things at stake, things involving his personal well being and things involving the truth. The sweat pouring down his forehead seeped into the crack of his lips, salty and warm. He awkwardly swallowed it down. From two feet away, Tommy groaned deeply. The boy's breaths seemed labored and anguished, and a barely there wheeze escaped his lips. Chris asked himself *How did this happen?* Sifting through the blurry memories scattered across his mind like debris from an explosion, he found few answers. How could he do this? How could he do this to his own son? Worse yet, what if someone found out?

Before he even realized what he was saying, the words were leaving his mouth. "It was an accident Tommy; you got in a fight at school. You didn't tell me until just now. It was an accident."

Tommy could only barely hear his father. Stretching his neck upward, he twisted his nose toward the fresh, moist air pouring through the half-opened window next to him. The dewy smell of early morning entered his nose and traveled down his chest, caressing his injured ribs from the inside. The momentarily relief carried with it an all too brief moment of clarity, making it possible to once again put his other senses to use.

Again came his father's voice, clearer this time, more insistent now with the hospital only a few blocks away. "Do you hear me Tommy? It was an accident, right? Look at me and tell me it was an accident."

Reluctantly Tommy turned his head to his father, the pain in his chest moving outward once again, pouring over him like molten lava and scorching his insides. The person sitting across from him bore little resemblance to the man he'd known for the entirety of his young life. His father had changed. Whether by situations beyond his control or on account of a weak will, the father Tommy once knew and once loved was gone. In his place sat a drooling, wide-eyed, frightened and confused monster, an only partially existent thing that had lost control of everything in its life, including itself. Pulling into the hospital, the rusty car at last came to a stop and the engine puttered off.

Again Chris turned to his son. "I'm not going to ask you again Tommy. Look at me and tell me it was an accident, tell me you got in a fight at school."

His voice barely a strained whisper, Tommy Jarvis at last relented. "I . . .got into a fight . . ."

"Into a fight where?"

"At - at school."

"And you didn't tell me about it until this morning."

"No, I didn't."

"Didn't what?"

"Tell - tell you about it until this morning."

"It was an accident."

"It-it . . .was . . .an accident."

While escaping Tommy's cracked lips, the words stung far more than the pain in his chest.

X-rays were performed in the hospital, showing beyond a doubt that the boy had not one but two broken ribs. While being pumped full of wonderful pain relieving fluids, the doctor asked him how such a thing occurred. Tommy recited his father's story verbatim. The doctor was surprised the boy lasted as long as he did without telling anyone; while glaring at Chris questioningly for a moment, choosing for whatever reason not to voice his concerns, he said the pain must have been unbearable. As if reading from cue cards or recalling a well-rehearsed speech, Tommy again fed the young doctor the story; again he lied. He didn't know why he did it really — realizing that it made no sense whatsoever — and yet, the words came. Traveling from his brain, they exited his mouth and were given form, becoming an independent part of the universe. Like the mad scientist's monster, they were now alive, hungry and dangerous. This was only the first time Tommy would lie for his father. There would be others, many in fact. With every one, the boy's resentment grew. With every false truth, the pile of rancid, slimy blackness building in his gut expanded, pressing against his interior like a great cancerous tumor. Much the same as a virus, Chris Jarvis' disease infected his son, twisting the boy into a distorted, grotesque funhouse reflection of himself. Eventually the day arrived when the lies came easier for Tommy, when he didn't bat an eye or offer even a second thought. It was on this day that Tommy at last determined the price for years spent wading through lies, for time spent covering up his father's misdeeds — forgiveness.

Perhaps not so strangely, he found some semblance of peace in this decision.

18. CONTEMPLATIVE TRAJECTORY

After speaking with Krystoph, it was determined that the group would set out on their journey the following day. Their mission was to retrieve the half of the Rongstag Krystoph had hidden away years prior. Apparently, according to the former Ochan general, the King's army had been rapidly closing in on its position for some time. If recovered, Kragamel would again have the ability to render any magic useless, even the magic wielded by the strange children of the prophecy. Adding to the problem was the fact that Pleebo and Walcott had been captured. Though most of the rebels seemed to believe neither had given up the location of the doorway leading to the children's home world, many thought it only a matter of time before they relented. The Ochan methods of information retrieval were legendary, honed to a finely tipped, deadly dangerous point through years of practiced warfare. Even those with the strongest of wills couldn't hope to hold out forever against the unrelenting mental and physical torture to which they would undoubtedly be subjected. Some, like Roustaf, believed both Pleebo and Walcott would sooner die than give in to Kragamel. Others, such as Krystoph, found Roustaf's idea to be idiotic in its idealized simplicity. Any creature could be broken down, no matter how staunch their defiance. Like most Ochans, Krystoph believed it better to be proactive, to make your fate, instead of allowing it to make you. Victory was a pleasure rarely enjoyed by the meek. The Rongstag needed to be recovered and it needed to be recovered quickly. When the meeting at last came to its conclusion, Zanell informed the group that the citizens of New Tipoloo had invited the children of the prophecy to attend a feast in their honor before setting off on their journey. Donald, Staci and Nicky cordially accepted the invitation. Feeling anything but celebratory, Tommy chose to stay behind.

With the rest of the group having left for the excitement in the Southern Passage, Tommy found himself lying on his back in Zanell's dimly lit dwelling. To celebrate anything seemed fraudulent, strange and just plain wrong. Nothing about the situation they had willingly strolled into seemed worthy of merriment. He was worried about the safety of his little brother and Staci, wishing he could have convinced them to stay home and cursing himself for not trying harder. At least there they would have been safe — for the time being anyway. Closing his eyes, Tommy breathed in the stuffy, stale-warm air around him. Off in the distance he could hear the soft echo of an exuberant cheer created by the citizens of the underground city. Clearly these creatures truly believed, beyond a shadow of a doubt, that he and the others were saviors, that they could somehow change their lives for the better. Despite the vivid memories of the things he accomplished during his first trip to Fillagrou, the idea still felt ludicrous to Tommy. After all, he was still just a boy, a boy who barely had control over what occurred in his day-to-day life. To believe he held the fate of so many in the palms of his hands simply made no sense. On top of it all, the idea of being led anywhere by the likes of Krystoph felt, on the surface at least, like a mistake of monumental proportions. The Ochan was clearly insane, mad with a lust for revenge. There was no viable reason for actually believing anything he'd said. Tommy wondered how it was that no one else could see it.

The mission, the rebellion, and Fillagrou were all doomed.

"Hello Tommy." The soft voice belonging to Zanell wafted up from the half opened doorway.

Lazily Tommy opened his eyes, then sighed deeply as he scooted into a sitting position with his back against the dirt wall near the rear of the tiny room. Zanell closed the distance between them with just a few strides of her long, bony legs. With her back to the wall, she dropped to her rear alongside Tommy, bringing her thin, sharply edged knees close to her chest and wrapping her even thinner arms around them. Tommy took note of the fact that she smelled like trees, like a cool fall day, and found it to be an oddly comforting aroma. Pleebo smelled the same way. Never looking in Tommy's direction, Zanell instead stared at the open doorway on the opposite end of the room and sighed deeply, her massive eyelids slowly closing before opening once again.

Very matter-of-factly, she sympathetically stated, "You're troubled."

Tommy paused for a moment before answering, collecting his thoughts, unsure of an appropriate response. "I don't get it. I mean, why us?" He turned his head to Zanell, his eyes partially hidden behind his stringy blond hair. "You're supposed to know everything that's going to happen, right? It seems to me like that has got to be as big an advantage as you can get. So why do you need us? I mean, you know what the Ochan's are going to do, so just do it before them."

Underneath her breath, Zanell chuckled quietly enough to ensure Tommy didn't take notice. "There was a time, Tommy, when I can remember saying the very same thing to my grandfather. You know what he told me? He pinched my cheek, ran his fingers through my hair, and said it's not as simple as that."

Rolling his eyes, Tommy looked away. Digging the tip of his dirty shoe into the ground, he kicked up a small mound of dirt, making sure that his annoyance with her cryptic answer was clearly visible.

"It's a difficult sensation to explain, Tommy, the kind of thing that needs to be experienced in order to be fully understood. You see, our fates remain our fates, no matter what. Believe me when I tell you that you, or I, or even those who chose to set them in motion to begin with, can't alter them in any way. That being said, they are also quite alive, evolving and constantly changing." Noticing immediately that her answer did very little to make the boy feel any better, Zanell attempted to word it differently. "Look at it this way. There are many roads down which we can choose to walk; at some point though, each one curves back to a single point when the walking has reached its end. The finale of all things is the absolute; everything in the universe, including the universe itself, has a well-defined end. No matter how that ending is reached, this is something that simply cannot be changed."

Annoyed, Tommy rose to his feet and moved to the other end of the room with a huff. Coming to a stop in the shadows, he leaned against a wall and rolled his eyes. He was sick of Zanell's double-speak, tired of things that didn't make sense. Though only fourteen years old, Tommy didn't particularly like the finality of her statement; a large part of him wanted not to believe it. If she was correct, if there really was no control, what was the point?

Wiping the hair from his eyes, he turned toward her again, mumbling through tight, angry lips: "That still doesn't explain why me, why any of us? No offense, but if I had to go looking for saviors, my little brother and Staci wouldn't exactly be high on the list. I mean, come on . . .Nicky still wears underwear with Spider Man on them."

Slowly rising, Zanell moved toward the boy. She understood what he was feeling and could relate to his frustration. She knew more about him than he could ever hope to understand or likely feel comfortable with.

Gently resting her hands on his shoulders, she twisted his body so it was facing hers. "Now that is one question, Tommy Jarvis, that I even don't have an answer for. Why you? Why Donald? Why me? Why my brother or Roustaf or King Kragamel or anyone? I don't know. The universe is a grand, fantastic story, made up of trillions of smaller stories told from trillions upon trillions upon trillions of vastly different perspectives, each of them with their very own leading character. To say it's complicated simply doesn't do it any justice. Yet, in the whole of things, there are roles we're meant to play, things we're meant to do…whether we choose to or not. You're more special than you can imagine, Tommy Jarvis. You have a strength inside you, an ability to observe and understand and create in a way so few are blessed."

Tommy pushed her bony hands off him and again moved away, quickly running out of places in the tiny dwelling to escape. With a heavy sigh, Zanell's shoulders slumped, her eyelids half closed and her expression mournful. In her heart she knew he couldn't yet understand, but recognized with pristine clarity the instant not too long from this in which this would change.

White hot flashes of Tommy's life, both past and future, exploded into existence in the blackness of her mind like stars reaching their eventual supernova. "I know everything you've been through Tommy. I know how hard it was." Before continuing, she made the specific choice to keep her distance from the boy in order to let him have the space he seemed to feel he desperately needed. "I know you don't see it yet, but there is beauty to be found in even the most awful of situations, and much strength to be gained through forgiveness. Every living thing has the inherent ability to exceed the sum of its parts. Think what a sad, sad world it would be if the whole of our existence were defined by simply the physical. Thankfully, I can guarantee you this is not the case."

Again a chorus of cheers echoed throughout New Tipoloo's stuffy, underground streets, rising up from the Eastern Passage and drawing the momentary attention of both Tommy and Zanell.

Realizing she was better served simply allowing Tommy his time alone, Zanell began moving slowly toward the open doorway. "Well, I suppose I should join the festivities. I don't know how my grandfather did it — all the pomp and circumstance that comes with being an elder — life would be so much simpler without it. Ah well. Feel free to stop by if you like. The citizens of Tipoloo have opted to use much of the remaining Ochan rations in order to better honor the return of the five — or four as the case may be. I haven't been to a festival of any kind since I was very little, younger than you even. I almost forgot how wonderful they can be. I am no fan of the Ochans, mind you, but they sure do know how to eat. If you'd rather stay here though, no worries. I'll cover for you."

With a wink and a grin, Zanell at last exited the dwelling, closing the door behind her and bathing Tommy in near total darkness. Again the sound of faraway laughter bounced off the walls, sneaking through the cracks in the doorway and invading his ears. Plopping back down into a sitting position, Tommy scooted his body again against the wall and closed his eyes. In the sticky quiet air of the darkened room, his mind wandered to his father and his mother. These thoughts intermixed with Zanell's enigmatic words before blending together like a vast mushy, confusing gruel. For an ever so brief moment, Tommy considered joining the revelry in the Southern Passage — but it was only a moment.

19. CAPTIVE FRIENDS

Every muscle in his body ached, every fiber enflamed and burning. His stomach felt heavy despite its emptiness; his eyelids drooped as if made of lead, pleading to remain shut. The welts covering his pale, grayish skin pounded in an unyielding, diabolical rhythm. The shackles that kept him standing upright every hour of every day around his freakishly thin ankles and wrists had rubbed the skin underneath bare, slicing through and scraping the bone underneath. Like the desert, his throat felt as if it were filled with sand, thin lips cracked and bleeding. The tiny cell around him was bathed in a deep, frigid blackness. Like all of Ocha at this time of year, the air was painfully cold, a cold so harsh it nibbled at his flesh like the teeth of a million tiny, hungry insects.

To put it simply, Pleebo was in hell.

Through the silent, chilly darkness came the clank of locks, the opening of a ten inch thick piece of steel molded into the shape of a door. Barely mustering the energy to lift his head, Pleebo glanced across from him and through the bars of his cell just in time to witness a pair of burly Ochan soldiers dragging the nearly unconscious body of Walcott Shellamennes across the floor. Opening the cell across from his, they pulled the massive bodied turtle man inside. The Ochans secured his shackles, locking him into an upright position against the back wall. Minutes later they were gone, and again came the silence. Pleebo attempted to open his mouth, trying desperately to coax his vocal chords back to life. What resulted, though, was little more than a jittery lip coupled with a weary, far-away moan. If in fact there was any moisture left in his body, he would have used it to produce tears. How long had he been here? How many beatings had he suffered? How many times had he answered the same question in the same interrogation room, to the same foul-breathed Ochan faces: *"Where is the doorway to the hundredth world?"* How often had he lowered his head, choosing to count the bloodstains on the frigid stone floor instead of answering? How many times had he ached to simply give in? How easy it would've been, and how quickly the pain would've ended. All he had to do was tell them what they wanted to know, and it all would have been over. The act would've proved simple and painless. Again Pleebo tried to call out to Walcott, yearning to hear the Tycarian's voice, needing his friend to give him strength and remind him he was doing the right thing. Again the ragged-raw muscles in his throat failed.

Hidden in the shadows of King Kragamel's dungeon, not more than thirty feet from Pleebo's current position, Walcott Shellamennes was wading neck deep in very similar feelings. Today the guards had seen fit to remove three more teeth from his mouth with little more than a rusty, blood-stained pair of pliers. Afterward, they broke what was left of the unbroken bones in his feet. With nothing being given proper time to heal, he wondered if he would ever walk again. Hacking a sticky warm discharge from his blood-filled mouth, he willed the muscles in his fractured jaw to life. He needed to let Pleebo know that he was all right, or at the very least alive.

"Plll-Pleee-boooo . . ." The Tycarian king's voice was soft, shaky, and faraway, entirely devoid of its once regal nature.

It was deep enough, however, for Pleebo to hear in the vast silence of the dungeon. Upon recognizing Walcott's voice, a half-smile climbed the corners of Pleebo's battered and bruised face. Knowing he was physically unable to answer, Pleebo moved his arms ever so slightly, rattling the heavy chains binding him to stone. Though subtle, the sound proved enough for Walcott to realize his friend was still alive, and he breathed a sigh of relief. Lowering his head, Walcott cursed himself underneath his breath. This was his fault. He should have planned better, should have been ready for anything. He failed Pleebo, failed New Tipoloo, and failed the revolution. In the deepest recesses of his heart, the places he rarely opted to visit, he wondered why he ever agreed to lead them in the first place. Striking down Gragor in Valkea's courtyard had filled him with false confidence. In reality, he was too old and too tired. Like most things, war was better left in the hands of the young and the capable. Ego had been the downfall of many great kings, and apparently he was no exception. After weeks locked away in the dungeon and hour upon hour of torture, Walcott scarcely believed there was anything left in his body to break. At this point, Kragamel no doubt understood that acquiring information concerning the whereabouts of the final doorway from either him or Pleebo was unlikely. There were more subtle methods for retrieving information the king hadn't yet entertained, leading Walcott to believe that this was no longer simply about the children or the doorway — this was about the death of Prince Valkea. This was personal.

As is the case with all things personal in nature, it wasn't likely to end anytime soon, even in death.

Walcott had continually insisted to Pleebo that Nestor was most likely working on a rescue attempt, convincing the people of Fillagrou that all they needed to do was hold on a few more days. Every time the words left his mouth, he understood all too well that they were, in fact, lies. There would be no rescue. The destruction of Valkea's castle with the help of the children was one thing. The Ochans were lazy and unprepared, led by a foolhardy, overconfident Prince. A raid on the war-ready, well-armed castle of King Kragamel in the heart of Ocha would be another thing entirely. Even with the aid of the children and their amazing powers, such a mission would likely prove fruitless, little more than an execution walk. He and Pleebo weren't going anywhere. They were at the mercy of the king, to do with as he saw fit. Whatever little remained of their lives was held firmly in the grasp of his enormous hands.

Lifting his head slightly, Walcott stuttered into the darkness toward Pleebo's cell. "Ju-just a-a little lon-longer . . .he-help on way . . .."

Again he lied, because there was no other choice.

20. UNWANTED VISITORS

The group consisting of Krystoph, Tommy, Staci, Donald, Nicky, Nestor and five of his toughest battle-ready soldiers set off in the wee hours of the morning. Two of Fillagrou's three suns had only just begun to peek over the horizon of its seemingly endless Red Forest. The air smelled thick, clammy and unusually fresh, as if it had only recently sprung from the birth canal of the universe. High above the tops of massive trees that had stood for eons lay an infinite, cloudless sky made up of various shades of red, purple and yellow, colors so breathtakingly amazing that the fourteen year-old Staci Alexander could scarcely pull her eyes from them for even a moment. During her time away, Staci believed she remembered the beauty of this place, but staring at its majesty once again, she realized just how much she had forgotten. When not dragged downward by the chaos of battle, the land called Fillagrou was reminiscent of something from a storybook or a dream; every part of it remaining untouched by war was a revelation awaiting discovery. Housing hidden doorways to a hundred other worlds, in many ways this wonderful, strange place was the center of the universe. Staci could think of no world more worthy of the title.

With Krystoph leading the way, the group steadily trudged through the forest for the better part of the day. Utilizing his extensive knowledge of Ochan patrol routes, the former general managed to keep the travelers a safe distance from potential dangers. At the edge of a vast clearing created by the Ochan army long ago, the group finally stopped to rest. Immediately Nicky dropped to his rear in the dirt, pulled off his shoe, and began massaging the soles of his feet. For at least an hour, they had been bothering him. Not wanting to slow the group, he decided to keep his mouth shut.

From behind him came the voice of his older brother. "Nicky, are you all right?"

Stumbling over his words, Nicky searched for a suitable answer. "I'm fine, just fine. Just airing out my feet . . .sweaty socks . . .should have worn different ones."

It had been his idea to follow Roustaf to Fillagrou in the first place. If he hadn't threatened Tommy the way he did, neither of them would be there. No matter how badly his feet might hurt, there was no way he was going to let Tommy know about it – he couldn't. Besides, what did a couple of sore feet matter when so much was at stake?

From a few feet away, Nestor noticed the conversation between the boys. When Tommy eventually moved away, returning his attention to Staci, the Tycarian patiently approached Nicky. The boy was once again wincing, and resumed the covert massaging of the sensitive muscles on his soles. For Nestor, the decision to send Roustaf to retrieve the children came under much duress. To willingly bring creatures so young into a situation as dangerous as the one they now faced seemed irresponsible at best. Incredible powers or not, Nestor firmly believed in his heart none of them belonged here, despite Zanell's insistence to the contrary.

The war had created many moments, many images, not a single one of which were suitable for the eyes of children.

His enormous body casting an even larger shadow over Nicky Jarvis, Nestor looked down at the boy seriously. "Are you sore, child?"

Slowly Nicky's head turned upward, gazing over the Tycarian's massive shell at the dark green head peering down at him with cold, subterranean eyes.

Swallowing deeply, he stumbled forward while mumbling, "No, no, no, I'm fine, just fine, fine, fine, never better."

Quickly slipping his shoe back on, Nicky stood, only to be shoved back down by the massive three-fingered paw connected to Nestor's right arm.

Nestor kneeled down and leaned in close to the boy, the almost comical differences in the sizes of their bodies more apparent than ever. "There is no shame in admitting discomfort, child. In fact, to keep it a secret could prove more a hindrance to the group in the long run. Fate has seen fit to lump us together, and we are a team. As a team, you must learn to rely on your teammates. Without them, this forest and its hidden dangers will undoubtedly swallow you whole."

Realizing that his mouth was hanging open, Nicky quickly closed it.

"Now tell me honestly, are you injured?"

Staring into Nestor's wrinkled, deep green, scar-covered face, Nicky found himself frozen, unable to move. His mouth was dry and his lip jittered wildly as he attempted to slow the untamed beating of his heart long enough to formulate something resembling a coherent sentence. "My feet . . .my feet are . . .they're just a little sore."

Having spent all of his adult life buried deep within the trenches of war, there had been few opportunities for Nestor Rockshell to smile. Gazing at the innocence in the eyes of the strange alien boy sheepishly spread out before him, he found it difficult not to. Though it seemed so far in the past, he too was once a child; he too remembered fear.

A barely there grin creeping up the side of his face, Nestor glanced briefly from side to side to see if anyone was paying attention to their conversation. "Your secret is safe with me, child. For the next leg of our journey, you'll ride atop my back. It should afford you proper time to heal."

His heartbeat relaxed and the quivering of his lip came to a measured halt. Nicky nodded his head.

The sound of little Roustaf's voice broke the moment shared between the two. "All right, kiddies, this is where we part ways."

Pulling the latch on his dusty overalls tight, the tiny man tossed an even tinier backpack over his shoulder. Fluttering so fast they quickly turned invisible, his tiny wings lifted him off the ground and into the air. The confused heads of the rest of the group turned in his direction one by one.

An annoyed, noticeably angry Krystoph swiftly closed the distance between himself and the miniscule winged man. "Part ways? What are you babbling about?"

Moving closer, Roustaf came to a hovering stop no more than a few inches from the Ochan's massive face. "Don't worry, big guy, the plan isn't changing. You're going to take the group and find your magic amulet thingy. I, on the other hand, am heading to Ocha to break Pleebo and Walcott out of that Ochan death camp you call a jail."

Krystoph smiled slightly. "You're going to Ocha to rescue your friend and the Tycarian king?"

"That's what I said. While you've got a butt-load of muscles, your hearing is just a little crummy, isn't it?"

"Hrmph. Foolish plan — stand no chance — destined for failure."

"Maybe so. I can't just leave them there tough and I wouldn't be much of a friend if I didn't at least give it a shot." Turning from Krystoph, Roustaf began to glide in the opposite direction. "Besides, you've got a good group here, Slick; you aren't going to miss little ol' me that much and I sure as hell ain't gonna miss your witty conversation."

The Ochan held his position, his muscles tight, his brow furrowed deep. "Never should have approached any of you — mistake to believe in the Fillagrou female's magic — unprofessional, the lot of you, unprofessional."

Stopping in mid-air, Roustaf turned again to Krystoph, a sarcastic smile peeking from beneath his bushy mustache. "You're right, it's pretty unprofessional of me; then again, I never claimed to be a professional. I'm just a little guy caught up in a big situation who just happens to sport an impeccable heft of facial hair to boot. Look, lead the rest of the group, find what you have to find. It's important, I know that, I just can't go with you."

Wide-eyed and gap-jawed, Donald Rondage listened intently to the conversation while seated atop a small rock ten feet away. His mind wandered back to Prince Valkea's courtyard, to fending off an army of Ochan soldiers, to an arrow cutting through the flesh of his shoulder — to nearly dying. It was Walcott who saved him. Not the father he'd never met or his absent mother or his annoying brothers, only one person in Donald's fourteen years of life had ever cared enough to do anything for him. As strange as it might have seemed, that person just happened to be a six-foot tall elderly turtle. It was at that moment, in spite of his better judgment, that Donald made a decision: if someone was going to rescue Walcott, he was going along.

"Wait a minute!" Rising from the rock under his rear, Donald moved quickly past Krystoph and toward the tiny red man with the transparent wings. "I'm going with you."

Hovering near Donald, Roustaf pressed his palms against the boy's forehead in a vain attempt to hold him back. "Oh, no, no, no you aren't, kid. You're going with them like you're supposed to, like Zanell said!"

"Oh, yes I am, and you can't stop me," Donald responded defiantly, brushing the tiny man away with one hand.

"You'll just slow me down, kid! No offense, but I can sneak into an Ochan fortress unnoticed a hell of a lot easier by myself! You come along and you'll just muck up the works; besides, I've already got some help lined up, meeting them on the way. You need to stick to the plan!"

"Listen, you little red turd, I'm going. I have to go, whether you want me to or not!"

"Turd? Who are you calling a tu —"

"Shh! Shut up, the both of you!" Krystoph's serious voice cut into the conversation like a cold steel dagger through flesh.

Instantly the group turned toward him, their mouths locked shut. His body hunched behind a relatively thick patch of foliage, the Ochan extended his arm behind him, motioning for the remainder of the group to get down as well.

Kneeling next to Staci, hidden behind the grayish-brown trunk of a tree, Tommy noticed what Krystoph was looking at. From the tree line on the opposite end of the clearing, a pack of seven massive-bodied Megalots had stepped into the open air. Despite being adorned in elaborately decorated saddles, the creatures were without the Ochan riders generally accompanying them. Huffing, the beasts lifted their horned heads into the air, sniffing with simplistic wonder at the mid-day sunlight.

Crawling on his stomach, Nestor moved beside Krystoph, pulled a device vaguely resembling binoculars from his belt, and lifted them to his face. "Where are their masters?"

Scanning the surrounding trees for movement, Krystoph saw none. "These creatures shouldn't be here. Most likely they've escaped — riders will be looking for them and they will not be far behind. This is not good, not good at all. Mindless beasts will lead an Ochan regiment right to us."

"We will stay low, wait for them to leave," Nestor responded, lowering his binoculars.

Hoisting himself to one knee, Krystoph pulled a pair of medium-sized, double-edged blades from either side of his belt. "No, wasted enough time already."

As Krystoph turned to leave, Nestor reached out and grabbed hold of the Ochan's muscled forearm. "Wait...where are you going? We are better served waiting them out."

Krystoph's face was a mask of iron seriousness, his eyes the blackest of possible blacks, and hidden behind them were things that would leave most sane creatures with unrelenting nightmares for the remainder of their lives.

The grip on his weapons tightened as he breathed in deep, grinding his dangerously sharp teeth together. "All of you, stay here, keep down, and remain quiet. I will do what needs to be done."

21. ANGRY ACCUSATIONS

In the last six months, Chris Jarvis had reluctantly learned to forgo the luxury of sleep. Free of the mind-numbing, problem blurring liquids that once clouded the whole of his brain, Chris' perception of the world he inhabited had grown frighteningly sharp. Every memory he thought buried away slowly bubbled to the surface, the shimmer of its reflection proving to be blindingly harsh. Sleep had once been deep and quiet, even uneventful and peaceful; now there were only nightmares. A ghastly jumble of frightening mismatched memories, half-fact, half-fiction, assaulted his senses every time he closed his eyes. Chris made the choice to avoid sleep unless entirely necessary. The first scheduled meeting with his sons the day before proved a bittersweet affair. While hugging his younger son Nicky was an amazing experience, it did little to negate the fact that his elder son Tommy made the conscious decision to avoid him. When it was over and teary goodbyes exchanged, the social service woman, Amber Frye, tried to explain to him that such reactions were quite normal. Reminding him that Tommy would need time to come around, that first and foremost patience should be practiced. Later that evening, during a session with his personal therapist and sponsor, this point was reiterated. If Chris stayed the course, if he continued on the path he set down six months before, forgiveness in some form would eventually come, when truly earned. Though Chris understood this fact going in, a part of him wished it would be easier. For all the work he'd done and for all he'd accomplished, there remained so very much still to do and so far yet to walk. The hole he currently found himself in had been dug by his own hands, and dug deep. The process of climbing out was going to take time. Earning the trust of his first-born son again wasn't going to be easy. In his weakest moments, he often wondered if he would even have the strength.

With the hectic, emotionally draining nature of the day behind him, quite surprisingly for the first time in a very long time, Chris Jarvis met with sleep and became one with it.

So uncommonly deep was his slumber, in fact, that it wasn't until ten o'clock the next morning that he awoke. Were it not for a heavy, insistent knocking on the front door of his house, he might have slept even later. Wearily rolling from his bed and onto the floor, Chris groggily made his way downstairs, the knocking at his door becoming more insistent. Pausing at the full length mirror near the foot of the stairs, he ran his hand through his messy bed hair, smashing it down and trying his best to make it seem mildly presentable. After wiping the final bits of sleep from the corners of his eyes, he opened the door and was greeted by the stern, youthful face of a uniformed police officer. For a brief moment, Chris's heart stopped.

The young, dark-haired officer looked up from beneath the brim of his hat, his eyebrows lifted, his lips down-turned. "Christopher Jarvis?"

Chris hesitated to answer, an unorganized bevy of possibilities flooding his brain, most of which were negative in nature. During the disappearance of his boys with a few other neighborhood kids, not to mention the investigation into his mental health as it pertained to parenting his children, Chris believed that he'd seen enough police officers to last a lifetime. To wake and find one standing on his doorstep for the first time in months could, under no circumstances, be seen as a good thing.

Swallowing deeply, he stuttered, "Yes? What-what's wrong?"

"My name's Sergeant Alvarez. I was wondering if I could ask you a few questions?" the officer quickly responded while pulling a notepad and pen from his breast pocket.

Though he was overcome with an undeniable anxiousness to find out why a police officer was standing on his doorstep so early in the morning, again Chris hesitated to respond, and was notably cautious when he finally did. "Sure. Can I ask though — what is this about?"

"Well, sir, I'm sorry to tell you this, but at about three o'clock this morning, your neighbors reported their daughter and your son Thomas run —"

Sergeant Alvarez was cut off in mid-sentence by the screaming, angry voice of Dale Alexander. "Dammit, Jarvis! This is all your fault!"

Glancing over the sturdy shoulder of the officer, Chris spotted his enraged neighbor bounding full speed in his direction, fists shaking wildly in the air. "I swear to God, if your weird little kid has done anything to my daughter, I'll kill you! You hear me, I'll kill you!"

Tears in her eyes, a frantic Janet Alexander charged from the front door of her home toward her infuriated husband; wrapping him up in her arms, she attempted to keep him at bay. "No! Dale, stop it!"

From a position a bit further down the stone walkway leading to Chris's door, a second uniformed officer quickly made his way to the frantic couple, insisting that they calm down and return to their home.

Wiggling free from his wife's grasp, Dale lunged forward, only to be wrapped even tighter in the arms of the officer. "My little girl, Jarvis! My little girl, you son of a bitch!"

Watching as the police wrestled Dale to the ground, still frothing at the mouth and barking obscenities in his direction, Chris realized his body was frozen in place. Up and down the block, window shades and doors opened. Like moths attracted to a flame, the commotion brought the inquisitive residents of the normally quiet street to the ends of their driveways dressed in their early morning housecoats.

"Mr. Jarvis?"

A second police car pulled in front of the Alexander's house. Two more officers quickly exited and made their way toward the frenzied couple.

"Mr. Jarvis?"

Confused, Chris told himself that this was all supposed to be done with. The healing process had begun— this was all supposed to be over.

"Hello? Mr. Jarvis? Can I get your attention please, sir?"

Pulling his gaze from Dale Alexander, who was only now beginning to settle down, Chris returned his attention to the officer three feet in front of him who had been trying to get his attention for nearly a minute.

Free from his trance, Chris muttered, "Yes, I'm sorry. I'm what?"

More than a bit annoyed, Alvarez breathed deeply, folded his notepad and deposited it back in his pocket. "Look, apparently your son Thomas was seen climbing out of the bedroom window of the Alexanders' daughter around three o'clock this morning. The pair of them, along with two other children that we believe were your other son, Nicholas, and a local boy named Donald Rondage, took off into the forest. Were you here last night?"

"Yes."

"And you heard nothing? Supposedly Mr. Alexander over there was pretty worked up. Some of the neighbors near the end of the block even heard him. Are you telling me you didn't hear a thing?"

As if swallowed by a black hole, sound, light and thought imploded on Chris Jarvis. Tommy and Nicky, his boys. They were gone. Again.

As if rising from the darkness of some subterranean cave, Sergeant Alvarez's voice was now a faraway, distant and echoing thing. "Hello? Mr. Jarvis? Are you telling me you didn't hear anything at all? Nothing?"

Shaking the cobwebs loose in his brain, Chris managed to pull himself back to reality once more. "No. I didn't hear anything. I was sleeping."

Alvarez eyed him up and down, unsure what to make of Chris' reaction. "Well, the boys' foster parents have been made aware of the situation and we have some men searching the woods at the moment. Seeing as this isn't the first time this has happened, more than likely they'll come back when they're good and ready, just like before. Still, I would advise that you don't leave town, just in case we have any more questions."

The seriousness in Alvarez's tone, along with its undeniably accusatory quality, ripped Chris the remainder of the way back to the real world. "Wait, what are you implying? You think—what? Wait, I didn't have anything to do with this."

Rolling his eyes, Alvarez turned to head back toward his car. "Just don't stray too far from home Jarvis. As soon as we have some information, we'll let you know."

After the Alexanders were finally coaxed into their home, the remaining police officers returned to their cars and pulled away. Chris Jarvis never once moved from his stationary position in his doorway. A thick, venomous silence slowly crept across the street, shocked neighbors shooting disgusted glances and silently whispering to one another as they retreated to the safety of their homes. *They think I did it,* Chris told himself. *My sons are missing and they think I did it. My sons are missing* — *again.* It would be another five minutes before he closed the door, and ten after that before he finally sat down.

Sleeping would once again be impossible.

22. TALL TALES OF A MERCILESS KILLER

His movements were such that even the forest underneath his feet remained unaware of his presence. Between the leather clad fingers of his hand, he gripped tightly onto a pair of blades that had served him well for years, blades that violently ended the lives of more living things than he would scarcely endeavor to count. Every breath was carefully regulated, allowing him to inhale the necessary oxygen, while remaining noiseless enough to keep from arousing suspicion. An iron determination etched into the rock-hard features of his face, Krystoph moved through the underbrush of the Fillagrou forest with such expertise that one could easily imagine he'd lived in it his entire life. Keeping parallel to the clearing, his eyes scanned the area surrounding the escaped group of Megalots munching heartily on the deep red foliage. Hearing a faint voice in the distance, the former Ochan general came to a rather sudden stop, his eyes moving instantly in its direction. Less than fifty yards away, a regiment of angry, visibly annoyed Ochan soldiers were slowly making their way on foot in the direction of the grazing beasts. Counting seven of them, Krystoph quickly took inventory of their weapons and general positions, already beginning to formulate a plan of attack. In the years since he crawled from the Fire Caves on Ocha, Krystoph had experienced this exact situation countless times. In his quest for revenge, the Ochan had coldly enacted the murders of so many of his own people — so very many, in fact, that he believed his hands would never truly be free of their blood, his fingers were forever stained. Seeping into his pores, it had now taken residence underneath the thick scales covering his flesh, where it would remain. Despite the fact that he could distinctly remember the looks on each and every one of their faces at the moment they took their last breaths, never once had he second-guessed his quest. Through his veins moved a poisonous, dangerous liquid. As thick as syrup and as cold as ice, his was undeniably Ochan blood. Through him flowed the resolve of a killer, born and bred.

It was vengeance that now gave him purpose. It was vengeance that renewed his life and vengeance he believed would ultimately set him free.

Krystoph tightened his muscles and carefully resumed his forward movement. The forest around him was silent; in the distance the Fillagrou suns had slowly begun their half-day journey of descent. Years ago, when he first set foot in the Red Forest, the former Ochan general abhorred this world. Its stifling hotness, its unending silence, day after day filled with unending torrents of rain, this place was everything Ocha was not, and everything he wanted no part of. Having survived alone, living among the trees for so many years now, Krystoph had learned to not only accept the oddness of this world but also embrace it. Its silence had become his companion, his friend, his witness — and often his accomplice. The silence would never leave him. The silence would never judge him. The silence would never speak of his misdeeds or question his methods. The silence would remain exactly that.

Less than twenty feet from the Ochan regiment, Krystoph positioned himself behind the trunk of a massive, grayish-brown tree. Closing his eyes, he inhaled the familiar tangy-warm scent of the hunt, allowing it to fill his lungs and replenish his resolve. As the group of Ochans moved past him and into the clearing, Krystoph slipped from his hiding place and popped up behind the soldier bringing up the rear of the group. In a single crisp movement, he sliced the creature's neck open with a deadly swiftness belying his massively muscled frame. While precise, quick and fatal, nothing about the attack felt the least bit rehearsed or repeated. This was less a reaction than an action. With his hand over the soldier's mouth, inches away from the blood spraying from his neck, Krystoph pulled the lifeless corpse of the Ochan soldier to the forest floor. At no point did he make even the slightest sound. Moving forward, he repeated the exact same tactic on two more soldiers, each of their bodies swallowed up by the thick forest underbrush with barely a whisper. Buried deep within his chest, Krystoph's heart continued to beat a calculated rage uniquely his own. This was exactly what he had been put here to do. This came naturally. This was his calling.

Stepping cautiously from the tree line into the clearing, the leader of the Ochan regiment moved patiently toward the grazing Megalots. He'd always hated these disgusting creatures, believing them to be far more bothersome than they were worth. The beasts were initially discovered grazing in large numbers by the invading Ochan army on a world called Gleesval. For the most part, despite their size and appearance, the creatures proved harmless and easily trained. The Ochans rounded up the mighty-bodied herbivores and domesticated them, smoothly acclimating them into lives as beasts of burden. If word were to get out that his regiment allowed them to break free from their shackles and escape into the forest, he and any serving under him would likely never live down the disgrace. The creatures had to be recaptured and punished. Less than twenty feet from the nearest Megalot, the Ochan leader extended his hand behind him, motioning for his regiment to follow.

"Step lightly," he whispered at the same time to everyone and no one in particular while removing a thick leather strap from his belt and pulling it into a loop. "On my count . . .."

Never taking his eyes off the steel hook draped atop the rear of the massive creature's thick hide, the regiment leader tiptoed slowly to within five feet of the beast, a smug grin on his face. "One . . .two . . .now!"

Leaping forward, the Ochan latched the looped leather around the hook and tugged backward with all his strength. Frightened by the Ochan's voice, the Megalot thrust forward violently, lifting its nearly eight hundred pound body onto its massively muscled hind legs. With the safety harness firmly attached, the spastic movement succeeded only in pulling the leather strap painfully tight around its neck. The feel of leather against throat was one that had been beaten into the creature since being born into its life of servitude. Without thinking, it settled down, quickly becoming complacent once more.

With the Megalot firmly under his control, the regiment leader smiled brightly, his pointed tongue sliding across his sharp teeth, his head moving from side to side with smug satisfaction. "Oh no! You'll not be going anywhere, you foul beast! I've got you now!"

The Ochan's victory celebration proved short lived, however. Around him the other six Megalots scattered wildly in every direction, barreling full speed toward the trees at the opposite end of the clearing. Much to the Ochan's shock, his entire regiment had apparently failed to gain control over even one of the other rogue creatures.

His smile morphed into an angry scowl as the Ochan screamed at the top of his lungs, "You fools! How have you failed to gain control of your beasts?" Pulling his hands into fists, he turned to look behind him, intent on further admonishing his soldiers. "Is it possible that I have been assigned the most useless of all Ochan warriors? How is it that you fail in even the most simple of tas—"

Where he expected to see an entire regiment, he saw only a single Ochan: Krystoph.

At Krystoph's feet lay the unmoving bodies of two soldiers, their heads submerged in pools of their own blood. Following the trail of blood, the regiment leader spotted yet another corpse sprawled awkwardly in the mud near the tree line. Despite having never seen Krystoph face-to-face, he knew instantly who he was, and he could scarcely believe his eyes. For years, soldiers patrolling the Fillagrou forest had spoken of an Ochan warrior living among the trees, a silent, unstoppable killer with an unrelenting thirst for the blood of his own. Until this very moment though, he believed these stories to be nothing more than tall tales and harmless campfire nonsense created by bored warriors thirsty for battle the likes of which they hadn't drunk in years.

Gripping tighter onto the blood-covered blades in his hands, Krystoph steadied his muscles, preparing himself for the rush of the kill. It was at that moment the regiment leader realized beyond a doubt that what stood before him was no fairy tale. Moving with astounding speed, he reached for the blade dangling from his waist.

His movement was precise and determined, very nearly too quick for the naked eye to capture.

It was, however, not fast enough.

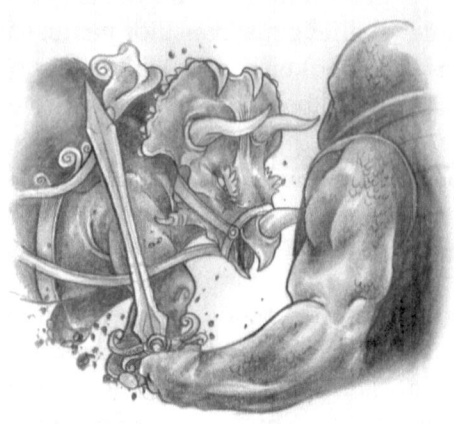

23. STAMPEDING BEASTS

From the moment Staci Alexander stole a glance into the black, cavernous eyes of the Ochan calling himself Krystoph, she knew she disliked him. His every gesture seemed cold and calculated, as if he was making a conscious decision to keep certain things hidden from the group. There was something he wasn't telling them, something he didn't want them to know. Watching his large, muscular body snake its way through the forest away from the group, she swallowed deeply, trying her hardest to ignore the feeling of dread exponentially building inside her stomach.

Staying low to the ground to remain hidden, she crawled on her stomach to Tommy, just a few feet away and tapped him lightly on the shoulder. "I don't like him."

"Who?" Tommy responded in a hushed whisper.

"Him—the green guy, Krystoph."

On this, Tommy could not disagree. There were many things about Krystoph that weren't sitting quite right with him either, though a part of him wondered if this might simply be due to the fact that he was an Ochan. Every member of the Ochan race he had come into contact with had tried to kill him, and there was no denying that this fact could severely impair his judgment. Looking away from Staci briefly, he glanced in the direction Krystoph had scurried, seeing nothing. As if the Red Forest swallowed him whole, the former Ochan general had disappeared without a trace. Not even a single leaf moved in his wake, not a hint of a track left behind. He was simply gone, vanished. Turning his attention back to Staci, Tommy could see the worry on her face; the slight raising of her eyebrows had created a tiny though noticeable wrinkle across her pale, sweaty forehead.

Despite an equally overwhelming uneasiness coursing through his body, Tommy realized he needed to do his best to quell her fears. "Don't worry. It'll be okay."

Reaching forward, he rested his hand tenderly over the top of hers, wrapping his fingers underneath and squeezing gently. Immediately Staci's face turned red, a warmness spreading from her hand, through her arm and finally finding a home in the roundish curves of her cheeks. Despite her worries, despite the ominous, nearly overwhelming fear looming on the horizon like the storm to end all storms — ever so subtlety, she smiled.

The tender, slightly embarrassing moment between the children only lasted an instant.

"SCATTER!" Nestor's shallow voice cut through the silence, quickly garnering the attention of everyone in the group.

Raising herself onto her knees, Staci gazed over the foliage in front of her and toward the clearing. Like a massive wall of sinewy muscles, the pack of six snarling Megalots was suddenly charging in their direction. A cloud of thick, brownish dust rose up from behind them, tossed aloft by the weight of their immense flat feet. Thick spittle with a barely noticeable greenish hint flipped from the corners of their gaping, squealing maws as they snarled violently in confusion and anger. The awesome sight instantly caused Staci's body to freeze in place.

With a noticeable amount of urgency in his voice, Nestor rose to his feet, arms flailing. "Move! Move! Move *now*!" Turning to run, he wrapped his arms around Nicky Jarvis, lifting the boy into the air with ease before sprinting in the opposite direction.

Even with the wall of wild, leather-skinned muscle bearing down on her and threatening to grind her bones into a fine paste, Staci remained still. Much like the expression of terror on her face, her limbs had straightened stiff and unmoving; the horrifying cloud of Megalots shaking the forest floor with every fevered step.

"Staci, come on!" Tommy yelled, tugging her so hard in the opposite direction that her shoulder nearly popped from its socket.

Suddenly running at full speed in no particular direction, Staci was finding it difficult to keep up with the much faster Tommy Jarvis. Her chest was on fire, salty sweat pouring down her face as she tried to scream for him to slow down, but was unable to find the necessary breath. Behind her, the forest exploded as the mass of heavy-bodied creatures slammed headfirst into the tree line. Their sturdy horns easily tore the ages-old gray trees to pieces, the full weight of their bodies knocking more than a few over completely. Coming into contact with a particularly muddy patch of dirt, she lost her grip on Tommy's hand, her feet slipping out from underneath her as the ground rushed toward her face. Though she was able to brace much of her fall with her left arm, the firmness of the Fillagrou soil smacked into the side of her body, knocking what little breath remained from her chest and sending a sharp twinge of pain across her torso. After lifting her head groggily, she spit a chunky wad of mud from between her lips. Her head was swirling, the rumbling in the ground getting more noticeable with every passing second. Less than thirty feet behind, rapidly closing on her position and ready to trample her to bits, was one of the mindless, frustrated Megalots.

With Nicky Jarvis pulled tightly against the underside of his shell as he barreled full speed through the cluttered forest, Nestor could clearly hear at least one massive creature bearing down on him from somewhere behind. Despite being quite spry for a Tycarian, the Megalots were exceedingly faster—deceptively fast in fact, especially considering their gargantuan size. His eyes shut tight, Nicky continued to grip at the grooves in Nestor's shell so firmly that his fingers had gone a nearly translucent white, drained completely of their blood. Taking a moment to glance over his shoulder, Nestor spotted a single howling beast barely more than ten feet away and getting closer. Realizing he had no chance of out-maneuvering the massive creature, the Tycarian soldier altered his plan. Running through the available options, he realized that only one remained; there was only a single choice to be made. Digging his feet in and kicking up clumps of dirt, Nestor's massive body came to a sliding stop.

Prying Nicky from his chest, he pushed the petrified boy to the ground. "No matter what happens, I must insist you do not move an inch, lad!"

Behind him he could hear the approaching monster. Confused, the feral beast was simply running, slamming into everything and anything standing in its path, reducing much of it to little more than splinters. Turning to face the rabid creature, Nestor tightened the muscles in his body. Digging his wide toes into the ground, he further strengthened his position. Breathing deep, he lowered his shoulder and placed his body directly between the tiny boy curled up in the fetal position behind him and the rampaging Megalot charging full bore in their direction. Though a Tycarian's shell is notoriously thick, able to absorb even the stiffest of blows, Nestor couldn't help but wonder whether or not it would withstand the wrecking ball force of the Megalot's body. In the end, however, it did not matter. Even if Nicky Jarvis wasn't a child of the prophecy, he remained a child. For Nestor Rockshell, the decision was simple.

Gritting his teeth, he braced for impact.

Akin to the colliding of two trains, the stampeding Megalot slammed full-force into the sturdy shell of the Tycarian warrior. What resulted was a sound so loud that it reverberated for miles throughout the forest, the percussion blast wobbling one hundred foot tall trees and nearly shaking them loose from the soil. Horn ground into shell, flesh smacked against flesh. The crash sent both Nestor and the Megalot sailing in opposite directions, engulfed in a cloud of scattered leaves and upturned soil. After smashing through one tree, Nestor's body at last came to a stop when it crashed into another, splitting it down the middle as if hit with an axe. Barely conscious, his vision blurring and his body racked with pain, Nestor lifted his face from the dirt and spotted Nicky still curled up on the ground fifteen feet away. With the boy safe, he at last gave in to unconsciousness.

Her body on fire, her mind awash in a tidal wave of confusion, a creature the size of an elephant, with horns as long as she was tall, moments from grinding her to pulp, Staci Alexander shut down. Pulling her legs into her chest, she squeezed her eyes shut so tightly that it instantly gave her a headache. Around her, the forest was shaking with every stomp of the enormous beast, creating vibrations so noticeable that they rattled the fillings recently installed by her dentist. If she could have found the strength to scream, she most certainly would have. Were the Megalot to take one more step, Staci Alexander would indeed have died. That step never came.

An instant before the creature's hoof came into contact with her flesh, a blade four feet in length pierced the thick hide of its neck. Slicing through with ease, the sword split the jugular underneath, which in turn sent a spray of thick, dirty-brown blood in every direction. The Megalot's body stumbled to the side, sliding across the dusty soil before bouncing off of trees and finally coming to a spiraling stop twenty feet behind Staci's still prone body. Her hands shaking, Staci slowly opened her eyes while wiping the sticky blood splatter from her face and fighting the urge to break down in tears. Staring at the odd, gooey substance between her fingers, she gazed through the cloud dust and leaves left in the creature's wake. Standing among the chaos, staring at her with more than a hint of disgust, was the Ochan, Krystoph.

"Should be more careful child. Won't always be around to save you."

24. THE CONJURER COUNCIL

As was usually the case during that time of the afternoon, the corridors of King Kragamel's castle were eerily quiet. All who took up residence inside its walls understood quite well that the king was not to be bothered at this hour. Less of a request than an order, complete silence was expected and obeyed. In the past, the punishment for anything contrary had proven shockingly severe. Descending a staircase hidden in the rear of his personal chambers, Kragamel moved quietly into the lower levels of his castle, beneath even the dungeon and into an area very few of his royal guard were even aware existed. It was here, hidden below the frozen Ochan tundra, that the real cornerstone of the king's empire resided. It was here, bathed in deep shadow and the flicker of a peculiar blue flame that could only be created by magic, that the fate of the Ochan nation had long been decided. It was here, away from the prying eyes of the old-guard Ochan warriors too afraid to confront the realities of the dark arts, that Kragamel housed his very own council of conjurers, an ancient race of disfigured Ochans with a wide array of mystical talents. Reaching the bottom of the staircase, Kragamel continued through a series of dank, stuffy hallways sparsely lit by flickering torches attached to the cold stone walls on either side. The entire journey took nearly ten minutes. At last reaching a massive steel door, the king patiently released a series of locks, each more elaborate in design and function than the last. When done, he pulled open the door with a dusty, aged squeak and stepped into a room darker than the hallways recently journeyed. Light became unnecessary at this point. The tyrant king had made this trek on a daily basis for years and was at this point quite capable of doing so with his eyes closed. Off in the distance, gradually fading from the darkness, came the soft flicker of bluish light. The tyrant king began leisurely moving toward it, the glow getting brighter with every step and slowly bringing into view the bent, garish forms of seven figures seated around it. Each was dressed in a cloak as black as the surrounding room that hung halfway over their faces, bathing the wrinkled guises of the disfigured creatures underneath in murky, intimidating shadow. Lost in concentration, none among the group acknowledged the king's presence. This luxury was afforded to the conjurers and the conjurers only. Were any other Ochan to act the same way, it would have undoubtedly been the final act of their lives. Kragamel came to a stop less than ten feet from the conjurers, his eyes never straying from the haunting blue flame crackling menacingly among the group of mystics.

All at once, in unison, the misshapen things began to speak. "The moment has arrived, my Lord. The endgame has begun."

Upon hearing the words, the black heart of the tyrant king sped. History had taught him time and time again to never question the words of his conjurer council. For as much as his current position of power had been gained through the blood and sweat of his own devices, these mystics had played an undeniably important role as well.

Their blank, milky eyes lost in the hot white-blue flame, the council continued, "Fate has seen fit to return the children to the land of red. As we speak they journey to recapture the Rongstag. If the denizens of fate are to be denied their long harbored vengeance against the Ochan nation, such an act must not be permitted."

"I shall send my ships to intercept immediately," Kragamel quickly responded, his deep voice echoing off the walls of the pitch black room. "The artifact will again take residence on Ochan soil long before they arrive."

All at once the conjurers groaned their disapproval, fearing the measures put in place by their king would not be enough. Unlike the Fillagrou elders, the conjurers were unable to see the future clearly. Blind from birth, the creatures instead relied on feelings coupled with an intuition garnered through a thousand years spent wading through the confusing waters of magic. Where the Fillagrou elders saw pictures, the conjurers felt emotion, hints of things to come. Much to their dismay, what often resulted could be imprecise, like hushed whispers in a darkened room. Suddenly and quite uncharacteristically, the frail form of one among the seven shivered, almost as if absorbing a mild shock. The remaining six questioningly tilted their heads in its direction. This had never happened before, and should not have been happening then.

Through gritted, worn teeth, the single ancient creature began to mumble breathily, "The female child...she is the key. Separate the child from that which is her infatuation. Separate the female and there will be no coming back, no coming back for any of them ."

Though King Kragamel hardly understood the full meaning of the words, he knew well enough to take heed. Many years ago, a Fillagrou elder prophesied the appearance of the children who had, a mere six months ago, murdered his son and only heir to the throne while laying waste to one of his finest castles. In order to ensure that the prophecy made by the Fillagrou named Nelvo never came to fruition, Kragamel understood all too well that he would need the aid of something beyond the sheer brute force of the Ochan nation. He would need the aid of his conjurers.

Again the council began to speak in perfect sync. "You have another request of us mighty king, do you not?"

Kragamel stepped forward, the glow of the haunting blue flame casting deep, frightening shadows in the wrinkles of his face. "Yes."

"Speak then, Lord. We remain in your service."

"The doorway to the hundredth world . . .I need to know where it is."

For a moment the room was silent, the only audible noise was the soft crackle of the rising and falling flame. Hidden beneath their dark cloaks, the ancient wiry heads of the conjurers moved slowly back and forth among themselves, engaged in a voiceless conversation to which only they were privy. Eventually the movements came to a sudden, jarring halt and again they spoke as one. "Two aware of its whereabouts have recently taken residence in your dungeon...a Fillagrou peasant and the Tycarian king."

Upon hearing the far away, strained words, Kragamel instantly perked up.

Weeks of torture having produced no results, he was beginning to doubt whether or not the captured rebels truly had worthwhile information to offer.

All at once the seven heads of the seven conjurers turned in Kragamel's direction, the eerie flicker of the supernatural blue flame reflecting off their blank, glassy eyes. In terrifyingly precise synchronicity they whispered, "Bring the gray one to us. We shall retrieve the information you desire."

25. THOSE LEFT BEHIND

"I still don't understand why I couldn't have gone along. When you consider where they're going, if anybody would've been helpful it's me!" Fellow Undergotten stated firmly, a noticeable amount of annoyance in his voice.

Seated on the opposite end of the tiny dwelling located in the heart of New Tipoloo, Zanell stared back at him with a slight grin on her face.   On some level she could understand Fellow's frustration. The Chintaran builder's affection for the children was no secret. Staci Alexander brought him back to life not once, but twice. Making sure that he repaid her and the other children for what they'd done for him and everyone else locked up in Prince Valkea's dungeon no doubt remained number one on his long list of priorities. When the plan to retrieve the Rongstag was revealed, Fellow was first to offer his services without a moment's hesitation. Zanell, however, had other plans for him. Rising to her feet, she moved slowly in his direction, taking note of the dejected, slightly angry expression on his blue face.

"You're needed here, Fellow," she whispered softly with a reassuring smile while placing her hands on his sturdy shoulders and squeezing gently. "The children will be fine, trust me. Try to keep in mind just who it is that's telling you this, too."

Sighing deep, Fellow rolled his eyes while running his hand over the top of his head. "Yeah, yeah, yeah, I know, you can see the future, fine. I get it. I don't know though; something about sitting around here doing a bunch of useless repairs while those kids are out risking their lives . . .it doesn't feel right."

Never much of a believer in magic, fate or things not easily categorized, Fellow Undergotten had been forced to change the way he looked at the world since his experiences with the "five to save them all." Despite his progress, he hadn't yet come to terms with the strange realities of this new world. As much as he believed in the words of Zanell, an equal part of him didn't particularly like the idea of taking the chance she might be wrong.

At heart this seemed so simple; the children needed help and he should be there to offer it.

Moving away from Zanell, Fellow turned his back to her, gazing out over one of the many quiet, darkened New Tipoloo streets. At this time of night, most of the city's citizens had already retired to their modest, stuffy dwellings, lured in by the sweet siren call of sleep. Their bellies still full from the previous day's festivities, most would no doubt find rest easily, catch it and let it envelop them fully. After everything they had been through, they deserved as much.

"Okay, fine," Fellow responded with some frustration, his annoyance not fully ebbed. "Can you at least tell me what in the world is so important about me being here?"

"You know I can't," Zanell answered with a wry chuckle.

"But why? That makes absolutely no sense, Zanell! You know that, right? I mean, what difference does it make if I know? If the future is the future and can't be changed like you're always telling everyone, then what does it matter if I know? "

Zanell's chuckle grew into full on laughter, serving only to annoy Fellow further.

She wondered how many times she had answered this very question since receiving the power of the elders. How many times had she failed to give a satisfying answer? It didn't take her long to realize that explaining the intricacies of time to one not fully submerged in its warmth was a task that could only be described as impossible. How do you even begin to explain the color red to an unfortunate soul born blind? It simply could not be done. Realizing her laughter was only making matters worse, Zanell took a deep breath and collected herself.

Moving to the other side of the tiny room, she retrieved a half-burned candle from a shelf built into the dirt wall. "Let's stop talking about this. How about a walk? I love Tipoloo at this time of night, don't you? After my parents died, my grandfather would take my brother and me out for walks around this hour. I think he appreciated the silence. It wasn't until I inherited his powers that I truly understood why."

Moving past Fellow, Zanell stepped out the doorway of her dwelling and into the street. The air was sticky-thick, layered heavy and recycled—to most, quite uncomfortable. From her perspective, however, it smelled glorious.

Exhaling deep, Fellow Undergotten at last decided to relent. In his heart, he understood that no answer Zanell could give him would quell the feeling of helplessness in his belly. Though it pained him to admit it, he realized that this was simply too much to ask of her, even with her powers.

Shrugging his shoulders, he stepped into the street behind her. "Alright. Who knows, maybe a walk will do me some good."

Zanell turned to face him, grinning wide once more. "Oh, I'm almost positive it will."

26. AND THEN THERE WERE EIGHT

Not long after the dust of the Megalot stampede had settled, the group of scattered travelers emerged from their hiding places to find that they were suddenly two members short: Roustaf and Donald had vanished.

A brief search of the surrounding area providing no results, Krystoph insisted that the group continue on without them. It was his belief that most likely Roustaf saw the stampede as an opportunity to make a break for Ocha. The pudgy hardheaded Donald most likely followed. Not content with simply leaving without Roustaf and boy, yet understanding that there was precious little time to spare searching for them, Nestor ordered two of his soldiers to track the pair and lead them to the group's intended destination if at all possible. The Tycarian's decision did not sit well with Krystoph.

His group of twelve had dwindled to eight in a matter of hours. This most assuredly was not part of the plan.

The remaining eight trekked on until nightfall, finally deciding to stop for some much needed rest in a tiny cave built into the side of a grassy hill slightly less than a day's hike from their final destination.

"Three hours rest, no more. The night will provide superb cover. Should not waste it," Krystoph gruffly stated, watching as one by one the children dropped to their rears against the walls of the dark, musty cave.

Seeing them rub their eyes, hearing them groan and complain about aching muscles and sore bones, Krystoph wondered if he had made the right decision by approaching the Fillagrou female weeks ago. Of all the great powers these spindly, strange looking little children were rumored to wield, he had seen none. In fact, were it not for his intervention during the Megalot stampede, the young female would be dead. This was a question he had asked himself many times since sneaking into the underground city in search of the Fillagrou elder. It was a question for which, as of yet, he had no answer.

"We shouldn't have left them like that." The soft, diminutive voice coming from the shadows belonged to Staci Alexander. "We shouldn't have just left them."

To the Ochan, her voice sounded frustratingly familiar. Were Krystoph to close his eyes, he could easily mistake it for that of his daughter. So painfully familiar, so achingly familiar. He was rapidly beginning to resent the little girl's voice.

Standing at the entrance to the cave, Krystoph gazed into the darkening forest outside. "The child and the tiny devil have made their choice, little girl. Whether they soak or drown, swim in it they shall."

Her frustration meshed with a nagging, ever-growing fear, Staci angrily lifted herself into a standing position. "That's it? That's all you've got to say?"

Seated next to her, Tommy reached up and grabbed her by the wrist in an attempt to calm her down before the situation got too far out of hand. "Stace—"

Staci brushed his arm away. "No, Tommy! I'm sick of this!" Before she knew what she was doing, ignoring not only common sense but a rather sizable lump of panic settled deep in her gut, Staci found herself stomping in the direction of the massive former Ochan general.

"We just left them! Like they didn't even matter! All because of you!"

Though Krystoph could sense the diminutive female moving in his direction, never once did he avert his gaze from the forest. Despite what the girl might have believed, he had no interest in shouting matches with children. Such was an act left to those with wills weaker than his.

Five feet from Krystoph, Staci finally came to a stop, her face bright red, her chest heaving as she swallowed a nearly overwhelming urge to break down in tears. Cautiously moving behind her, Tommy rested his hand gently on her shoulder. Again she brushed it off.

Images of the snarling, wild Megalot charging in her direction clouding her mind and the feel of its thick blood splatter still caked in the strands of her hair, Staci mumbled through a jittery lip, "Don't you have any feelings? Don't you . . .don't you care about anything?"

Upon hearing this sentence, Krystoph realized he had enough. In a single patient, deliberate movement he turned. Now within a foot of the oval-eyed girl, he leaned forward, his face close enough to feel the warmth of her breath. "The Ochan heart is deeper than you can scarcely contemplate, child. Two things we cherish more than any other: King, and family . . . .." Moving closer still, Krystoph gazed so deeply into Staci's eyes one might imagine he was examining the soul hidden somewhere within. "I no longer have either."

Frozen in place, mere inches from Krystoph's dangerously sharp teeth, her body overcome with terror, Staci chose at last to remain silent. Wrapping his arms around her, Tommy pulled her away from the icy stare of the massive Ochan and back into the shadows of the cave. Krystoph's eyes followed her the entire way, glancing briefly in the direction of Nestor, who had watched the entire exchange with one hand resting on the blade at his side. His frustration waning, Krystoph turned again to the forest. A small drizzle of rain had begun slowly trickling from the thick, dark clouds partially camouflaged by the blackness of the night sky. Always raining . . .it rained so much here. Reaching forward into the open air, he let the droplets gently caress his palm, relishing the simplicity of the transparent, cleansing liquid. There was a time, not too long ago, when Krystoph despised the warm, Fillagrou showers.

Change is an astounding thing.

27. TRAVELING COMPANIONS

"Stop following me, kid! Getting myself into Ocha is going to be enough of a pain in the ass and the last thing I need is something else to worry about!"

Undeterred by the irritated orders of the tiny winged man, Donald Rondage continued following him through the thick foliage of the Red Forest. The boy had no intention of turning around, and even if he wanted to he wouldn't have known where to go. The pair had been moving away from the rest of the group for hours, moments after they realized everyone managed to safely survive the Megalot stampede. Having put significant distance between themselves and the others, Donald sincerely doubted he could find his way back to them. For better or worse, Roustaf was taking him to Ocha, whether the little man liked it or not. Coming to a stop while hovering in mid-air, Roustaf turned to face the boy, an obviously annoyed grimace spread across his dark red face.

Floating a few inches from Donald's nose, Roustaf reached forward with his tiny arm and poked the boy's forehead with an even tinier finger. "Look in my eyes, kid. Look at the seriousness going on here. I'm not going to tell you again to take off. The longer you insist on following me around, the more likely you are to find yourself on the receiving end of a serious beating."

Staring at the face of the little man—barely six inches tall, sporting a bushy mustache curled at both ends—Donald found it difficult not to laugh. Swallowing deeply, he turned his head away in an effort to swallow the giggles rapidly forming in his throat. Despite his best efforts, a half-grunt-half-chuckle managed to escape through a crack in his tight lips.

Roustaf did not appreciate this.

Gritting his teeth, the little man dropped the tiny pack from his back and rolled up the sleeves of his shirt. "Oh, I see how it is. You don't think I can take you, do you? You think your ol' buddy Roustaf is playing around? Think this is some kind of joke?" Pulling his hands into fists, Roustaf posed them in front of his face and began waving them back and forth, similar to an old-fashioned boxer, "Let me tell you something, twerp: I was knocking the blocks off of punks twice your size when you were still floating around in your mother's egg sack!"

With the precision of a hummingbird, the tiny man began zipping around Donald's head, throwing the occasional jab at the air far from the boy's face. "Come on, kiddo, you want to test me? I'll be happy to give you a firsthand demonstration of the kind of damage these meat hooks of mine can do! Put yer dukes up, slick!"

"Look, I don't want to fight you," Donald responded while rolling his eyes and trying desperately to get some semblance of control over his laughter.

"I thought not. Now that you've got an eye-full of these hambones I sometimes call fists, you're beginning to realize what kind of damage they could do, am I right?"

The young boy's voice cracked. Placing his hand over his mouth, Donald keeled over, moments away from being overtaken by an army of giggles. "Not exactly, no . . . .."

"That's it! Congratulations, slappy, you've just succeeded in pushing me over the edge! You really are cruisin' for a bruisin', aren't you? Well, prepare yourself, buddy-boy, because that's exactly what you're gonna get! Here comes the pai—"

Hearing something off in the distance, Roustaf stopped. His body went stiff, his hands instantly dropped to his sides. Darting back and forth quickly, his eyes scanned the surrounding forest.

Breathing deeply, he held it for a moment before whispering to Donald, never once taking his eyes off the surrounding trees, "Shhh—did you hear that?"

"What? Hear what? I don't hear anything," Donald answered back in between a series of chuckles.

Zooming forward, Roustaf placed the palm of his hand on the crest of the boy's lips, his voice suddenly reduced to a stern whisper. "Seriously, kid, shut your pie hole. I heard something, over that way."

Sensing the change in Roustaf's tone, Donald's chuckles evaporated backward into his chest where they were first given life. Very slowly, he twisted his body to look in the direction the tiny red man was staring. What he saw was forest—forest and nothing more. Two of the three Fillagrou suns had already set, the third just barely peeking out over the horizon. Visibility was remarkably limited. After forty or so feet, the various trees, leaves and bushes faded drastically away into a wall of black extending onward into eternity. Sailing in from the west, a soft breeze fluttered the fabric of Donald's shirt, lifting it momentarily off his stomach and tossing his short brown hair gently against his forehead. Very quickly, a deep sense of fear crept underneath his skin and up his back, dragging along the sensitive grooves of his spine.

"I don't—I don't hear anything," The pudgy boy whispered to Roustaf, who was now hovering on transparent wings just a few inches from his face.

The tiny-bodied red man chose not to respond, still unsure if he simply imagined the noise, yet not wanting to take any chances.

"Stay here," He murmured, cautiously hovering forward toward the darkness.

Donald decided to heed the advice, keeping his feet firmly planted in the damp soil underneath. For two full minutes, Roustaf continued to carefully float away from the boy before eventually disappearing from view, swallowed by the darkness. Donald now found himself alone with the silence of the Red Forest. Upon his first visit here he took note of how remarkably quiet this place was; beyond the breeze, and the rustle of leaves, there was no sound. No insects squeaking, no birds chirping, no running water or noises of any kind. It wasn't until this very moment, though, that he realized just how incredibly frightening the absence of sound could be.

After nearly five minutes of unrelenting silence came a noise, faintly pushing its way through the nothingness. Similar to a scream or a yelp, the clamor was far away, yet growing stronger with every passing moment.

Whatever was causing it was rapidly getting closer.

Slowly Donald began to step backward, dead, gray branches crunching underneath the soles of his worn and dirty gym shoes. Coming to a momentary stop, he craned his head forward while twisting his ear in the direction of the noise. Slowly, the subtle noise was morphing into something slightly more recognizable, something that sounded strangely like Roustaf. Refocusing his attentions, Donald could clearly make out the word, "kid" followed by some gibberish and finished off with what sounded like it could possibly be "shrimp" or "twerp" or something similar in nature. It was definitely Roustaf. In a matter of moments, the noise again rose in volume, transforming into a full-on scream and leading Donald to believe that the little man was moving in his direction at an incredible speed. Instantly, he resumed his backward steps. Blasting from the darkness so fast that he was barely visible, tiny Roustaf whizzed past Donald's head, leaving in his wake a blast of wind that caused the boy's hair to scatter wildly.

At the top of his tiny lungs, the little man bellowed, "Run!"

Overcome with fear, Donald watched as Roustaf disappeared once more into the darkness of the trees. From the spot where he originally emerged came a deep, guttural, slimy roar that sounded sort of like a lion attempting to growl while underwater, and somehow succeeding. Meshed with the awful sound of crackling branches and something sounding vaguely like a wet slab of beef being smacked against the side of a tree, the horrifying clatter sent reverberations through the ground beneath the boy's feet, nearly causing him to topple over. The pace of Donald's backward movement sped to a jog, then quickly advanced to a sprint. All at once, the darkened tree line opened up, launching something garish, unpleasant and wholly dangerous from its bosom.

Something was rapidly advancing on the position of the pudgy Donald Rondage at an incredible pace: something looking to end his journey to Ocha before it even began.

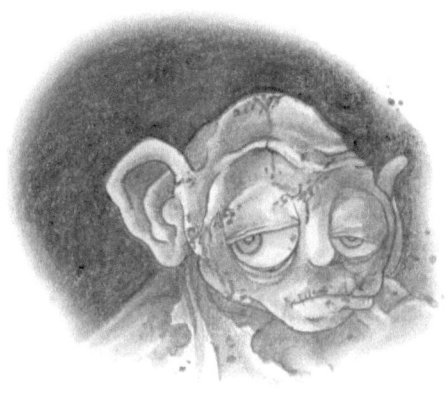

28. BEST KEPT SECRETS

At some point after his last session with the Ochan interrogators, Pleebo faded into unconsciousness. The pain associated with the endless broken bones, welts and cuts now covering the majority of his body simply overloaded his senses and became too much for his brain to process, which instead chose to simply shut down. In a sleep as deep as this, there were no dreams and there was no sound. In this state existed only a funnel of black, extending downward into a nothingness that swallowed whole the ideas of matter, gravity and perception. In this world, Pleebo was weightless and pain-free; in this place nothing could hurt him, because he ceased to exist. How simple it would have been for him to remain here, free of the complexities of war, free of the death and the sadness . . .how wonderfully simple it would have been to at last give up.

Unfortunately for Pleebo, fate abhors simplicity.

Rolling in from the surrounding nothingness came the faint crackle of a woodless flame, coaxing him back to reality. Momentarily fluttering, his sore eyelids at last began to open, despite their best efforts to remain closed. Having not felt a single cooling drop of water in weeks, his cracked lips parted, tiny droplets of blood seeping from the newly ruptured skin. The stone floor pressed against his face was cold and unforgiving. Little by little, his enormous red pupils began to adjust to the darkness of the room around him, focusing on the soft blue light sprouting from the profound black less than ten feet away. At this point, Pleebo realized he was no longer in his cell. The smell of the new surroundings seeped into his senses, stiff, dusty and cavernous, thick like a vat of quicksand. Something grabbed hold of his broken arm, dragging him forward across the stone and toward the blue glow. Too weak to resist, Pleebo allowed his body to go limp. Wherever he was, whoever was tugging at him, he was totally and completely at their mercy. Less than a foot from the soft blue flicker, his broken, horizontal body again came to a stop. Spread out on his back, unable to move his head more than a few inches in either direction, Pleebo stared up at the ceiling, his eyes watching soft blue flickers of light dance playfully on the brick ceiling. One by one, seven cloaked figures converged on his point of view, their faces hidden behind the deep black shadows created by their dusty hoods. Cast in frightening silhouette, the creatures more closely resembled amorphous shapes than actual living, breathing things. These were shadows given dimension, and nothing more.

As a group the seven shadows began to speak. "The doorway, we require the location of the hundredth doorway."

On the inside, under the welts of a thousand blows, Pleebo laughed. For weeks he had been asked this very same question. For weeks he had successfully avoided answering. Surely at this point the Ochans must have begun to realize that they weren't going to get anything from him. Having survived every single implement of torture one could dare dream into reality, Pleebo could scarcely think of anything else they might do to him.

Again came the collected voice of the seven shadows. "The doorway. We require the location of the hundredth doorway."

The unison tone of the shapes was deep, yet far away, almost breathy in its sharpness. "The doorway . . .we require the location of the hundredth doorway."

Closing his eyes, Pleebo forced an awkward, broken smile onto his face. Through a sandy cough, he chuckled, sending sharp pains across his numerous broken ribs. "If I didn't tell — the four-hundred — pound guy with muscles for days anything . . .what — what — what makes you think — I'm going to tell you?"

The shadows ignored his remarks and simply repeated their ghastly credo: "The doorway . . .we require the location of the hundredth doorway."

Without warning, Pleebo's blurry, tired brain began to figure out that the living shadows were the conjurers, and they actually weren't speaking to him at all. In fact, their disgusting lips weren't even moving. Somehow, these things were inside his head.

One after another, from below their filthy robes, the wrinkled, scaly hands of the creatures emerged. Reaching forward, one bony appendage grabbed hold of the one to its immediate left, slowly forming a circle around Pleebo's shattered form.

"The doorway . . .we require the location of the hundredth doorway."

The telepathic chant of the one-group was coming much closer in succession now, the volume rising in sync with the pace. Previously gazing upward, the darkened shadows of their heads now moved toward Pleebo. Glowing eyes like milky glass emerged from the shadows, staring intently at the body of the near dead Fillagrou sprawled across the stone.

"The doorway . . .we require the location of the hundredth doorway."

All at once, an ungodly chill pierced Pleebo's chest, causing his muscles to pull tight while slamming his remaining teeth together like a pair of rigid stones being smacked together. Rapidly, the awful cold began spreading along his organs, instantly freezing them in place. Moving into his neck, the agonizing sensation constricted his air passages, and creeping upward further, it locked his jaw into a ghastly open-mouth position. Firmly intertwined with the dark magic coursing through his body, Pleebo realized that he had failed. These creatures, these hideous shadows with their glowing eyes, would get the information they desired, and he could do nothing to stop them. Moments before the icy blanket enveloped his brain entirely, Pleebo recalled with much sadness the faces of Tommy, Staci, Nicky and his sister Zanell. He'd failed them. Despite his best efforts, despite having been able to withstand more than he ever dreamt possible, he'd failed them. With the disgusting, bitter-cold magic now seeping between the folds in the brownish-gray matter of his brain, a barely noticeable tear leaked from the corner of Pleebo's eye. Almost instantly it froze to his cheek.

29. THE GREAT SNAGGLEWORM ENCOUNTER

His chest on fire as he struggled to catch his breath, Donald Rondage darted through the darkening forest at full speed. Not far behind him, a monster at least twenty feet tall with a segmented body similar to a caterpillar slithered across the forest floor with surprising speed. The bizarre creature growled into the night air through a mouth filled with jagged teeth that were bent grotesquely in every conceivable direction at the tip of its wormlike body. The noise immediately sent a shiver down Donald's spine. Though he could hear the sloshing of the creature's moist flesh as it wiggled through the blackness behind him, never once did he turn to look in its direction; he couldn't. Instead his eyes focused on what lay in front and what rested beneath. Every step on the uneven, debris-covered ground was a potentially dangerous one. Donald was keenly aware that a single misstep could plant him face down in the dirt, leaving him easy pickings for the slimy, snarling worm with the rancid hot breath singeing the hairs on the back of his neck. Again the monster roared hungrily, its massive body smacking into the gray trunks of trees with sickening wet thuds and nearly snapping the thick, ages-old shafts to timbers. While trying to worm its way through a pair of particularly tight trees, the beast became momentarily stuck. Shaking violently from side to side, attempting to work itself free and failing, it could only howl in frustration. Coming to a sliding stop, Donald dropped his hands to his knees and bent over to catch his breath. Glancing briefly behind him, he could see the massive, drooling creature wedged in place, unable to shake itself loose. Its head whipped wildly, thick greenish mucus flipping from its hungry jaws.

"That'll teach you, you ugly bastard," Donald mumbled between heavy breaths, his heart pounding and his limbs sore.

Emerging from the darkness in the opposite direction, Roustaf came to a hovering stop alongside the boy's head, looking noticeably tired himself. "I suggest you stop gloating and keep running, slick."

"What are you talking about?" Donald answered, at last able to stand upright, though his chest remained on fire. "That thing is wedged in there good, aint' going nowhere."

Roustaf sighed deep. "Oh really? You've dealt with Snaggleworms before, have you? Seen this happen a lot? Have a lot of experience in this area?"

Donald shot the tiny man an angry glare. "No, but come on, look at it. I may not know anything about Snagglesquirms—"

"*Worms.* Snaggle*worms.*"

"Whatever. The point is that thing is stuck in there pretty damn good." Reaching down, Donald picked a rock off the forest floor and whipped it at the slimy beast's face. "See? Earthworm Jim isn't going anywhere."

Running his hand over the top of his sweaty head, Roustaf sighed deeply, the sound of the Snaggleworm's wild thrashing growing louder with every passing second, angered further by the rock that had just hit it in the face. Reaching down he snagged a handful of Donald's shirt, trying his best to tug the boy in the opposite direction. Considering the massive size difference between the two, he wasn't having much success.

"Trust me kid, it's in our best interest to skedaddle while we still have a chance," Roustaf stated more sternly, the enormous, slimy creature snarling and snapping at the pair of them from twenty feet away.

Reaching out, Donald snatched the tiny man in a single movement, wrapping him tightly between his fingers. "Listen, you little jerk—I don't know if you noticed, but we don't all have the luxury of flying around without a care in the world like Tinkerbell with a mustache. My legs hurt, I'm tired, and I need to catch my breath!" Pulling Roustaf close to his face, he poked the little man's head with the tip of his finger. "That ugly bastard back there is stuck! It's not going anywhere! Now give me two freakin' seconds to catch my breath and then we'll get the hell out o—"

From behind the pair came the sound of snapping trees, of ancient wood torn to pieces, followed immediately by a mushy, wet growl so loud that it shook loose nearby foliage.

Donald gulped deeply, realizing he was about to eat his words.

By the time he turned his head, the massive Snaggleworm was towering over him. Standing erect on its rear section, the gargantuan monster stretched at least thirty feet into the air. A pair of beady, coal-black eyes shone in the glare of the moonlight. Focusing on the pink skinned child below and the tiny devil clenched between its fingers, the creature clanked its teeth together hungrily. It had been quite some time since it had eaten. The pair would prove a satisfying meal.

"Let go of me, kid!" Roustaf screamed, trying in vain to wiggle himself free from Donald's vice-like grip.

Staring up at the growling monster, Donald was paralyzed with fear and frozen in place. His legs had gone rigid, his jaw hanging open as his lips quivered uncontrollably. A massive drop of drool nearly the size of his head fell from the Snaggleworm's mouth, splashing in the dirt at his feet and drenching his sneakers. Though he was unaware, his hold on Roustaf tightened further still as the sickening liquid seeped through his shoes and onto the socks within. The treacherous looking mouth of the Snaggleworm opened wide, its jagged teeth pointing in every direction at once. In a single movement the creature thrust its open mouth downward, fully intent on chomping its terrified prey to pieces. Moments before swallowing Donald from head to toe, though, an arrow pierced the side of its head. This first arrow was immediately followed by another and another still. The monster wailed in pain, its long body flailing crazily, smashing into nearby trees. Quite confused, and still being crushed by the vice-like grip of Donald Rondage, Roustaf glanced over the boy's shoulder past the great howling worm. Twenty feet away, just barely visible in the darkness, two of Nestor's soldiers continued firing arrows in the direction of the beast. Each arrow connected with its intended target, further infuriating the monster. With at least twelve arrows piercing its slimy flesh, the Snaggleworm turned its attention away from Donald and Roustaf, growling at the pair of Tycarian archers while spitting bucketfuls of slobber in their direction. When arrows began piercing its sensitive eyes, the monster at last relented, retreating into the forest with an annoyed yelp. Long after disappearing into the darkness, the creature's moans could still be heard — frustrated that it would be forced to deal with its hunger pangs for yet another day.

The pair of Tycarian soldiers lowered their bows and slid them back in the harnesses strapped to the rear of their massive shells.

"Are you unharmed?" The nearest soldier asked, moving briskly in the direction of Donald and Roustaf.

The sound of the soldier's deep voice awakened Donald from his trance. With his free hand, he wiped a particularly thick wad of Snaggleworm drool from his hair, flipping it to the ground like sticky molasses. At last his grip on Roustaf loosened and the tiny man wiggled from his grasp immediately.

"Are you unharmed, child?" The Tycarian soldier repeated while reaching out to inspect the boy with his huge, flat paw.

"I'm fine, I'm fine, tot—totally fine . . .." Donald snapped back, brushing the turtle man's hand away and trying his best to pretend nothing was wrong.

"What the hell are you two doing here? Let me guess: Nestor ordered you to track us?" Roustaf asked from behind the boy as he rubbed at his now sore chest.

The muscled Tycarian simply nodded.

"I bet he asked you to bring us back, too, didn't he?"

Again the turtle man nodded. Behind him, his partner continued to scan the surrounding area, ensuring the Snaggleworm had indeed moved on.

"Seeing as how you schmoes just kept us from eventually ending up as steaming piles of worm plop, I suppose it would be in bad form to start complaining about him sending you our way, wouldn't it? As far as going back with you though, it's just not gonna happen. I can't let my friend die in that Ochan hellhole. I just can't. Don't get me wrong, I appreciate the help, but you came all this way for nothing."

Sternly staring into Roustaf's eyes, the Tycarian breathed deeply. Twisting his head, he glanced over his massive shoulder and exchanged a subtle gesture of confirmation with his partner.

Staring at Donald and Roustaf, he responded in a very matter of fact tone, "Then we shall journey with you to the castle."

30. THE SCARS ARE REMINDERS

When at last Tommy Jarvis opened his eyes, he realized that he wasn't sure exactly how long he'd been asleep. Though it felt like only a moment, Nicky and Staci were cuddled up on either side of him, snoring quite loudly . Their arms wrapped around his torso, their chests rising and falling in a steady rhythm, the pair looked like they'd been out for some time. The cave was dark, musty and dank, the air soaked in heavy moisture brought on by the torrential downpour outside. To his left, near the rear of the cave, Nestor and his soldiers were seated around a modest campfire, whispering quietly back and forth while mulling over a map spread out in the middle of them. To his right, at the cave's entrance, stood the silhouetted form of Krystoph. The Ochan didn't seem like he had moved since Tommy last closed his eyes. His head craning slowly back and forth, Krystoph scanned the black forest outside for even the slightest bit of movement. All the while, his muscles remained tense and tightly wound, ready to strike at a moment's notice. Tommy wondered: How long had he been standing in that exact position? How long would he continue to do so? With an unexpected flash of lightning Krystoph's muscled back was momentarily bathed in a blanket of bluish-white. Every muscle, contour and curve was brought into frightening focus, further emphasizing the creature's incredible bulk. Again Tommy couldn't help but take note of the strange scars spread across the entirety of his dark green flesh. What were they? Where did they come from? It was painfully obvious they weren't simply the result of battle: these were something else entirely – something confusing, mysterious, and slightly frightening. After slowly peeling Nicky and Staci's hands from his chest, Tommy carefully rose to his feet, using the chilly stone of the cave behind as leverage. Though he had no idea why he was doing it, less than a moment later he was shuffling quietly toward the motionless Ochan at the foot of the cave. It made no sense, really. If anyone in the group should have been left to their own devices, it was Krystoph. Tommy had no idea what he was going to say, if anything at all, or why he would have wanted to say anything in the first place, yet he didn't turn around. About five feet away from Krystoph, he came to a stop. The heart in his chest was beating double-time. Engorged with blood, it thumped feverishly at the underside of his ribs in tune with his over-hyped pulse.

Krystoph heard the boy shuffling in his direction and could now taste his distinctive scent on the crest of his lips. It was a unique odor, sweet and sour, disgustingly crisp, unlike anything the Ochan had smelled or tasted before. Outside the cave the Fillagrou wind wailed, rattling the trees and kicking up clumps of moist sand. The sound of thunder rumbled angrily from somewhere deep in the belly of the overstuffed clouds.

Never once averting his gaze from the dark, rainy forest, Krystoph mumbled to the quiet child behind, "Leave me be, boy. Return to your slumber. Likely the only opportunity you will have."

His voice was shallow and coarse, instantly causing the hairs on Tommy's arms to stand at attention. Despite Krystoph's insistence, however, he did not move an inch.

"Ochans do not give orders twice, child," Krystoph muttered angrily, flexing the fingers on his right hand and causing the bones underneath to crack and pop.

Though every muscle in his body was telling him to turn around, to crawl between Nicky and Staci and go to sleep, Tommy held his position.

Before he realized it, words formed somewhere deep in the bowels of his stomach were rolling past his lips. "Where did you get the scars?" The moment the question escaped his mouth, he regretted asking it. Why was he doing this? He shouldn't be doing this.

Never turning his body, Krystoph glanced over his heavily muscled shoulder, glaring at Tommy with his cold, black eyes. Perhaps absent-mindedly, perhaps not, his fingers gently traced the contours of the blade hanging loosely from his belt. The feel of familiar steel was soothing and strangely comforting.

Near the rear of the cave, Nestor had been carefully observing the exchange between the two, preparing himself to rush to Tommy's side if things were to get out of hand. Krystoph could sense the Tycarian's glare. Turning his head back to the forest, the former Ochan general breathed deeply, letting the Fillagrou air fill his lungs and cool his nerves. Though every fiber of his being told him to simply ignore the nosey child, he uncharacteristically offered a response, "The scars are reminders."

"Reminders of what?" Tommy asked after a long and quite awkward pause, highlighted by an exceptionally bright flash of lightning.

Extending his forearm to the side, Krystoph opened the back of his hand to the boy's view. Etched deeply into the scaled flesh were a series of freshly cut grooves leaking warm blood across the contours of his skin, underneath and into his palm, where they at last fell to the moist soil below.

"Each represents an Ochan that has perished by my hand." Krystoph added while forming a fist and pulling it from the boy's view.

For a moment, Tommy stopped breathing.

"At first it was difficult, killing my own in the name of vengeance," Krystoph continued as he pulled the bloody hand to his face. "I am not ashamed to say that I openly wept for them at first, questioned whether I had chosen the correct path. In time though, as their numbers grew, it became easier, far too easy in fact. I have since learned that killing your own . . .such an act should never come free of heartache, boy. Eventually the day arrived when I felt nothing at all. No sadness or remorse or regret. Nothing. I found this to be . . .disturbing, inappropriate. The cuts ensure that I shall always feel something. They remind me of what I have done. They make it impossible to forget what I have become, even for a moment."

Turning away from the rain, Krystoph looked down at Tommy with a cold, steely stare, his face an emotionless mask of iron. "Vengeance is both just and disturbing, child. Spending a lifetime wading in a pool of it can distort you beyond recognition, make you view the world differently, make you do things you never dreamt possible. Then again, you know this as well as I, don't you?"

Caught off guard by the comment, Tommy stumbled backward. "What? What are you talking about?"

"We are more alike than you care to admit, boy. Despite their disgusting color, I have seen your eyes before, boy. I know what lurks behind."

Flustered, his heart racing, Tommy again took two steps back, very nearly tripping over a loose rock on the cave floor. What the hell was this green-skinned bastard talking about? Where did he get off saying something like that?

"What? Shut up, we're nothing alike. You're a killer," Tommy growled, wiping a fresh sheen of sweat from his forehead.

Krystoph followed the boy into the cave, leaning close enough to smell the child's breath as it wafted past his cracked lips. "You may be able to fool the Tycarians or the Fillagrou mystic or even yourself. You cannot, however, fool me. I have walked among the corpses at Valkea's castle. If it is true they met their fate at your hand, you are twice the killer I will ever be."

Awkwardly sliding backward, Tommy tripped over his own feet, falling to his rear in the dirt with a heavy thud. Like a living, breathing tower of muscle, Krystoph's dark form now hovered over him, noxious breath escaping through the cracks in his pointed teeth.

From the back of the cave came Nestor's voice. "That is quite enough, Ochan. Step away from the child."

Looking away from Tommy, Krystoph glared at the Tycarian, now a mere ten feet away with his sword drawn. Behind him, weapons at the ready as well, were three more Tycarian warriors, each as dangerous looking as the last. Slowly Krystoph took two steps away from Tommy. Pausing briefly, he scanned the faces of his traveling companions, questioning yet again whether or not he had made the right choice approaching them for help. Making deals with mongrels such as these; was this too high a price to pay? Even for vengeance? He reminded himself, however, that he'd come too far to simply back out. Too many had suffered and died needlessly. Vague remembrances of the faces of his children and the feel of his wife's flesh against his flashed like lightning in the back of his mind. So brief and yet so deadly, so impossible to hold onto . . .too quickly they disappeared, leaving him alone once more. No, to quit now would disgrace their memory. The king must be held accountable.

He had to see this through to its end, no matter the cost.

Turning from Tommy, Krystoph returned to the mouth of the cave and resumed his scan of the forest outside. The rain was slowing. In a matter of hours, Fillagrou's sister suns would again chase away the night, taking their position once more as the protectors of the sky. Every day the battle between night and day raged and every day the result was exactly the same. It was a fruitless war, pointless and without end — a war of which there were no winners or losers.

It was a war Krystoph understood all too well.

31. TALL TALES AND SECOND CHANCES

From the seat of his car, Chris Jarvis carefully scanned the sidewalk on the opposite end of the street. One after another, groups of children strolled by on their way to school. For the most part, those walking alone seemed to have dejected looks on their faces as if marching to their deaths, anxious to be done with a day that had yet to even begin. The children traveling in packs, however, were nothing but smiles, giggling, laughing and whispering, not so much anxious to get down to learning as they were anxious to socialize. Chris had been sitting in this exact position for nearly an hour, carefully examining each child, waiting to spot specific ones among the many. Tommy, Nicky and Staci were still missing, and the police hadn't turned up a single clue. After being threatened by his neighbor and questioned by the local authorities concerning their whereabouts, Chris broke down, coming perilously close to looking for answers in the bottom of the bottle. It would have been so simple, popping the cap, letting the cool, mind numbing liquid slosh around inside his head and blur away yet another in the never-ending problems that had become the whole of his existence.

Which is precisely why he chose not to.

Life isn't meant to be simple. If there is one thing Chris Jarvis had learned over the last six months, it was this very fact. It had taken the loss of his wife, his sons, his job, his reputation, his sanity and very likely his soul for him to figure it out, but figure it out he did; to turn back now would mean to fail and would make it all for nothing. Megan deserved better. His boys deserved better. He deserved better.

Peeking through the partially fogged passenger side window, Chris at last spotted who he'd spent his morning waiting for. On the opposite end of the street, lugging around a backpack thicker than his torso and possibly half his bodyweight, was Mack Little's son, Owen. When the children disappeared for nearly a week six months ago, Owen was with them. When the exact same children disappeared just two days ago, Owen apparently didn't go along. Reaching down, Chris inserted his key in the car's ignition and turned it on. He knew he shouldn't be doing this. Common sense told him that it was an awful idea and should be avoided at any cost. He understood all too well that the police had likely already questioned Owen, thinking that he might have some information to offer. Chris was also keenly aware of the fact that the police already didn't like him, and that stalking Owen wasn't likely to change their opinion for the better. He had to do something, though. For too long, inaction had become Chris Jarvis' first reaction. For too long, he'd been everything but a father to his children. There was no longer a choice. He had to act.

For Owen Little, the morning was proving to be like any other. He was scheduled for a test later in the day, and a difficult one at that, even for someone with grades as solid as his. Last night a pair of police officers showed up at the house, wondering if he might have any information regarding the whereabouts of the Jarvis brothers, Donald Rondage and Staci Alexander. Owen, of course, told them exactly what he's been telling them since "disappearing" the first time: the truth, every word of it. Tommy's tree fort, the doorway at the bottom of the stream, Fillagrou, Roustaf, Walcott, Prince Valkea — the boy recalled every single moment in startling detail. After hearing such a wild tale, as one might imagine, the officers responded simply by shaking their heads, sighing and returning to the station. A frustrated Mack Little immediately sent his son to his room, grounding the boy from television until he agreed to "start telling the truth." Owen didn't particularly care for television anyway and wasn't that upset. In the end, it wasn't the questions that annoyed him, as he'd become rather accustomed to them and the response they generally received. Regaling the rather extensive tale once again to the police, however, unfortunately took a significant hunk out of his study time. As a result, he didn't feel nearly as prepared for today's test as he might have liked. Mrs. Higler's quizzes were notoriously difficult. Going in partially prepared could result in a "B," or, worst-case scenario, even a "B-".

He should have just lifted the cup Roustaf was hiding under that night and exposed the little man to his father. If he'd done so, maybe his dad wouldn't still be looking at him like he was such a lunatic. So why didn't he?

There was a small part of Owen's mind, a miniscule, barely there part that he was trying to ignore and hated to admit existed, that wondered what was happening in Fillagrou. What could have been so urgent that Roustaf saw fit to sneak into his room at night and beg him to return? A much larger part of him, however, didn't want to know. He wasn't who any of the creatures in Fillagrou believed him to be. He was not a savior or the realization of some goofy prophecy. He was just a kid, and he couldn't save them. He never could have. In his heart, Owen believed it was better and easier for everyone if he simply forgot about all of it. It was smarter to shove the entire experience as far back in his mind as he could and bury it forever. Worrying about Mrs. Hilger and her annoyingly tough tests: this was something he understood. This was something he could handle.

The hum of a car engine picked up to Owen's right side, followed by a deep, yet partially whispered adult voice. "Owen Little?"

Readjusting his glasses, Owen glanced up from the sidewalk. A car was creeping alongside him on the street. Its engine was as old as its paint job, clanking and whirring, crying out for a tune-up that had been put off for months or maybe even years. Leaning out the driver side window, sporting somewhat wild early-morning hair and a five o-clock shadow, was Tommy Jarvis's father. Though Owen had never met the man personally, he had seen him from afar and heard any number of wild stories. He'd also been warned on numerous occasions by his own father to keep as far away from Mr. Jarvis as possible. Everyone in town knew what he did to his sons. Secrets such as those tended not to stay secrets for long.

"Owen Little? I'm Tommy Jarvis' father. Look, I was wondering . . .I just want to ask you a couple quick questions."

Lowering his head Owen quickened his pace and mumbled, "Sorry, I can't help you."

"Just a couple questions —"

"I'm not even supposed to be talking to you," Owen answered back quickly, moving from a brisk walk to a light sprint, Chris Jarvis' old car matching his speed precisely.

Frustrated, Chris ran his freehand though his hair. It was crusty, unkempt and a bit wild looking. He suddenly realized he should have cleaned himself up a bit better. He had been in a hurry this morning, and things like shampoo are too often forgotten when in a hurry.

"I won't even get out of the car," Chris added, realizing that they were getting closer to the school with every passing second. In a few minutes he would be forced to turn around and go home. "My sons are missing again, Owen. I just need to know if you have any idea where they might be. If you know anything, anything at all . . .I won't tell anyone, I promise. It's just between you and me. Just tell me and I'll turn this car around and drive home. You'll never hear from me again."

More than a little uncomfortable with the situation, Owen's heart began to pound in his chest. Glancing ahead of him, he noticed that the school was less than five minutes away. If he began running at full speed he could be there in three. Beside him, the engine of Chris Jarvis' car continued to pop, clonk and whir. Owen knew he should stop talking to Tommy's father. The most reasonable reaction to the situation would have been to run as fast as he could to school, jog directly to the principal's office, and let him know exactly what had happened.

Again Chris pleaded, his voice lost and dejected, reduced to a desperate whimper, "Please, Owen. Anything, just tell me anything you might know, anything at all."

Sighing deep, Owen's legs stopped moving. This wasn't what he should be doing. In fact, this was the exact opposite of what he should be doing. It was stupid, it was dumb and it was idiotic, moronic and stupid, yet again. If this were a single question quiz, he'd be getting a big, fat zero.

His father was going to kill him.

"He took them to the fort," Owen muttered, still unable to look Chris directly in the face.

"The fort? The tree fort? Who took them to the tree fort?" Chris asked quickly, stomping on his breaks and leaning further out his window.

Owen shook his head; reaching under his glasses, he rubbed the corners of his eyes with his fingers. Once again, he was going to have to tell this story, and once again the adult listening to him was going to stare back like he was a babbling idiot.

It was a mistake to stop. His father was going to kill him twice.

Staring at the ground, Owen continued, his voice thick with fear and annoyance, "Roustaf took them to the fort. Apparently something is wrong in Fillagrou. He said he needed our help. I told him to find someone else, which—no offense—is exactly what Tommy should have done. I mean, who do these people think we are? How dumb is it to think a bunch of middle school kids can save the universe? It's stupid! It doesn't make any sense!" Realizing he was rambling, Owen breathed deep in order to regain control over his emotions briefly. "That's all I know. Now please leave me alone. My dad will wring my neck if he finds out that I said anything to you."

The look on Chris Jarvis's face was one of complete confusion. The boy standing on the sidewalk across from him had answered with what could only be interpreted as gibberish. What the hell was a Fillagrou or a Roustaf, and why was he sneaking into the bedrooms of a bunch of teenagers in the middle of the night? What in the world did Tommy's tree fort have to do with it? Yet, despite the nonsense of it all, there was something in Owen's voice, something about his accelerated breathing and the way he was shoving his hands so deep into his pockets he threatened to tear through the interior lining while sweat poured from his brow, that made Chris think that, at the very least, the boy believed what he was saying, nonsense or not.

"I really have to get going," Owen added, resuming his walk to school.

For Chris Jarvis, there were no more options. His sons had been taken from him — again — and now they had disappeared — again. So many times since the death of their mother he had failed them. So many awful things he'd put them through. Chris didn't want to be that man anymore. He couldn't be that man anymore.

With what he believed to be the final link to his children walking away from him and ignoring logic, Chris was compelled to speak up. "Owen, wait. I need you to show me exactly where this tree fort is."

32. DECISIONS, DECISIONS

"No! I told you I would show you where the tree fort was and that's it! I shouldn't even be here! I should be sitting in school right now, not getting mixed up in this crap again!"

Moments away from an onslaught of tears, Owen Little buried his head in his hands, his body slumping into the soil directly underneath the Jarvis brothers' fort. He knew he should never have stopped to talk to Tommy's father. He shouldn't have told the man about the stream and the doorway to Fillagrou, and he most definitely shouldn't have agreed to accompany him to the fort. What started out as a relatively average morning for the boy had quickly degenerated into a nightmare. His father was going to ground him, scream at him until his face turned red and that weird vein appeared on his forehead, and then ground him again. After that, he'd kill him for the fifteenth time.

"I never should have come here. I never should have come here. I never should have come here," Owen began to mutter to himself, salty tears streaming down the sides of his face and into the cracks between his fingers.

From the edge of the stream, Chris Jarvis stared into the murky water with a look of absolute confusion. During the short car ride and subsequent trek to the tree fort, Owen regaled him with an outlandish, incredible and utterly impossible tale involving doorways to other worlds, strange creatures, and a number of other things that simply couldn't exist.

The kid had to be lying, right? He had to be lying—lying or insane.

There was absolutely nothing remarkable about the stream water moving slowly below him—nothing odd, or for that matter, even slightly disconcerting. For all intents and purposes, it seemed at first glance little more than a normal, average body of water, likely less than five feet deep. The idea that it could somehow lead to another world seemed idiotic on levels that made the definition of the word idiotic seem pale in comparison. Owen's story made no sense, no sense at all. Turning away from the water momentarily, Chris glanced at the boy slumped over and sobbing behind him. Owen was terrified, his skinny little hands shaking like delicate leaves in the wind and covering his face entirely as he sobbed into his soaking wet palms. No doubt a good deal of this reaction was the direct result of Chris approaching him on the street and convincing him to disobey his father, miss school and to take a strange man he barely knew deep into the woods. There was something about the severity of his reaction though, something that made Chris believe there was more going on here than met the eye. The horror that had overtaken Owen's body was undeniable, and it wasn't directed at Chris so much as it was at the stream.

"Please, I just want to go home. Please let me go home," Owen mumbled through a mouth soaked in his own tears.

Seeing the boy broken down the way he was instantly brought back memories Chris had no interest in reliving. He promised himself many times that he would never again do this to a child, no matter the reason—and yet, here he was.

He'd done enough to this boy—done too much.

Lowering his head in shame, Chris said softly, "Go home, Owen. I'm sorry I brought you here. Thank you for your help."

His lip quivering, Owen lowered his hands, wiping the tears from his face with the sleeve of his shirt. His glasses were foggy, transforming Chris Jarvis, the forest, and the stream into barely more than a blur. Awkwardly, he pulled himself into a standing position and readjusted his backpack. Across from him the blurry Chris Jarvis had turned away, now staring blankly at the stream while rubbing his head.

For Chris, none of what had come from Owen's mouth made sense. It couldn't be possible, not a single, solitary word of it. It just couldn't be. Despite being so sure that it was little more than nonsense and nothing else, Chris leaned forward and dipped the tip of his shoe into the freezing water. Behind him, he could hear Owen shuffling away, the child's tears slightly more under control.

"Owen," Chris added while never turning around, "Before you go, am I supposed to just walk in? How does this work?"

Coming to a stop, Owen turned to face the older man while wiping the remnants of crusty tears from his cheeks. Through slightly less foggy lenses, he watched the grown man again dip the tip of his boot into the water. It had been six months since Owen was here, and the memories of the world hidden beneath the dark waters had come rushing back in all their awful detail. He never wanted to see this place again. He shouldn't be here. He should have been anywhere but here. There was something in the air, something thick, heavy and forbidding, something telling him that he needed to leave as soon as possible.

"Walk in; dive in . . .I don't think it matters," Owens responded with a huff, starting back up the small hill away from the fort, the stream and all of the nastiness accompanying it.

What's the worst that can happen? Chris wondered to himself. If he were to walk into the stream and nothing magical happened, he'd wind up wet and feeling stupid, that was all. On the other hand, what if, despite logic, common sense, and everything he knew about the way the universe worked, Owen was actually telling the truth? Could he afford to take that chance? Could he afford not to? Stepping forward, Chris carefully lowered one of his legs into the water. The liquid was bitterly cold, instantly sending a chill across the entirety of his body and making him shiver slightly from head to toe. After another couple steps, he was almost fully submerged in the muddy-dark drink. Walking forward, he cautiously moved to the center of the stream, the water now up to his waist, the soil beneath his feet loose and slippery. As the moisture began to seep into the fibers of his shirt, it started moving upward, transforming the light colored fabric into something noticeably darker. Standing with his arms outstretched for a moment, he waited for something, for anything to occur. Nothing happened.

Through the trees about twenty feet away, Chris spotted Owen and called out: "It's not working!"

Upon hearing the man's voice, Owen sighed deep. He was halfway up the hill, a tenth of the way back to town. If he moved quickly, he could be back at school in little less than half an hour. After apologizing for being late, he could bury his head in a book or a test and try to forget about the fiasco the morning had turned out to be.

Again came Chris Jarvis' voice: "Owen! Nothing's happening!"

"I don't know! What do you want from me? Try going under!" Owen screamed back angrily, his visible annoyance rising in direct proportion to his distance from the stream.

More than a little frustrated, the boy resumed his eager journey up the hill, his feet stomping with every step. At last reaching the top, he came to a stop once more and turned briefly to look in the direction of the fort. At the base of the hill, everything was silent. From this distance both the stream and Chris Jarvis were hidden from view by a thick line of trees. Did the man go under? Did it work? Was he gone? Was he popping up at this very moment, utterly confused in the red forest of Fillagrou?

Owen had so many questions, yet so few answers.

Shaking his head, he turned to walk away, then, again, stopped. There was still no sound from the base of the hill. Did Tommy's father drown? How could a grown man drown in barely four feet of water? He couldn't—could he? Looking behind him, Owen gazed longingly in the direction of the town, his school, and his house. Turning back again, he glanced toward the fort, the stream, Mr. Jarvis, and the doorway to Fillagrou. The decision of which path to take was so simple and obvious that it seemed barely worth asking. Yet, if this was in fact the case, why was he finding it impossible to decide which way to go? In the most logical recesses of his mind, he understood that he should go home. In fact, he believed he should go home and never come back to this place. Let's take that one step further: that he should go home now, never come back to this place, and try his best to forget that it even existed. Instead, moments later, he was walking back down the hill.

His father was going to kill him.

33. THE EIGHTY-NINTH WORLD

The group had been traveling non-stop for much of the day.
Krystoph allowed the children the exact amount of rest he
promised, and not a minute more. Having become quite
accustomed to traversing long distances on foot over the course of
the long war, the former Ochan general and the Tycarians were
showing not an ounce of wear. Krystoph's even-keeled breathing
hadn't altered in any manner whatsoever. As it was at the outset of
the journey, the Ochan's stride remained confident and strong, his
dead eyes as alert and ready for any possibility as they'd ever been.
For the children, the long, tiring trek had proven significantly more
difficult. Though Tommy was managing for the most part, his legs
were slowly growing sore, and his calves burned. Staci's face was
covered in a thick sheen of salty sweat, helped into existence by the
eternally balmy Fillagrou weather. Occasionally she reached
forward to rest her weary arms on Tommy's shoulders, letting the
boy carry a fraction of her body weight. Tommy didn't mind this at
all, mostly because it was Staci. While Nicky attempted to walk on
his own at first, the sharp pains traversing the soles of his feet
eventually forced him to relent. He had since spent the last two

hours dangling from the rear of Nestor's bulbous shell with the aid of a few conveniently placed leather straps. The ride was bumpy. Bumpy, however, had proven far preferable to the achy-foot alternative.

From the front of the pack, Krystoph raised his arm high enough into the air for the rest of the group to see, his massive deep green hand forming a tight fist. His voice was a deep, yet hushed whisper. "All of you: down."

Immediately the children and the Tycarians dropped to the soil, each holding their breath and awaiting further instruction. Releasing the strap securing Nicky to his back, Nestor let the boy slide to the forest floor, then motioned for him to stay put. With the underside of his shell dragging along the dirt, Nestor crawled quickly to the front of the group alongside Krystoph. Lifting himself momentarily, the Tycarian scanned the area ahead, most of his body hidden behind a particularly thick patch of foliage. Less than a hundred yards away, the forest opened up to an area created when the Ochan army hacked the trees away many years before. Just beyond that, stretching out for at least two miles in every direction, was a vast lake filled with a liquid so deeply brown and impossibly thick that one might easily mistake it for quicksand.

"The doorway to Aquari." Nestor mumbled, more to himself than to the Ochan lying on his belly in the soil beside him.

"Indeed," Krystoph grumbled back, glaring in the direction of the muddy lake with a slightly confused expression on his heavily scaled face.

Pulling binoculars from his pack, Nestor scanned the area ahead carefully. "There are no guards." He whispered with some surprise, "I expected some sort of resistance."

"As did I," Krystoph responded simply.

"What do you think it means?"

"Hurm. Unsure. Many possible explanations. None promising."

Lowering his binoculars, Nestor turned back to the group, briefly glancing at his remaining soldiers and the three children huddled among their massive bodies. Nothing about this mission had gone according to plan. From the Megalot encounter to the desertion of Roustaf and Donald, and now this. None of what had occurred was sitting well with the Tycarian. If there was one thing war had made Nestor keenly aware of, it was that such occurrences were not uncommon in these situations. Like emotions, war was anything if not unpredictable. There was a feeling, however, that he couldn't seem to shake, something nagging at him like a nasty blood-sucking Tycarian swamp tick: an awful feeling of dread he was trying his best to ignore and failing.

"The Ochans are ahead of us, heading to the Rongstag." Krystoph interjected, at last turning his gaze from the pasture. "There can be only one reason to pull so many soldiers from this end of the doorway. They are needed elsewhere. Needed on ships."

In a single fluent movement, the massive Ochan rose to a standing position and removed two swords from the sheaths hanging on his hips. "We can no longer afford patience. Must move now. Move quickly."

Though not completely convinced of Krystoph's assessment of the situation, Nestor nodded in agreement, realizing there was really no other choice. Lifting his stubby arm into the air, he subtly motioned for his soldiers to rise as well. In the end, the decision was quite simple. If the group was to get to Aquari, they would need to traverse the doorway at the bottom of the muddy lake, and there was only one way into the lake: forward. Grasping the broad sword attached to his back, he pulled it from its sheath, the sound of metal dragging across leather cutting through the silence. The steel glistened brightly in the light of Fillagrou's suns; clean and dangerous, it seemed ready to do exactly that for which it was created, honor the name of king and country at any cost.

His face growing sternly serious, Nestor glanced at the group and stated with the confidence of a warrior, "Keep close behind. Keep the formation tight."

Following Krystoph and Nestor, Tommy did exactly that, pulling his little brother and Staci close to his side. Behind them, forming a protective circle around the children, were the remaining battle-ready Tycarians. With his shirt wrapped tightly in her grasp, Staci's body was pressed so closely against him that he could feel the movement of her chest on his back. Her breathing was hurried, her eyes wide and her jaw locked tight. Her delicate fingers pulled the fabric of his shirt even more taut, threatening to tear its fibers apart. To his left, Nicky was tucked in just as close to his older brother, the boy's physical appearance eerily similar to Staci. As the group slowly made its way across the open plain, Tommy wondered once more exactly what they were doing there. This was no place for children, no place for his little brother, no place for Staci and no place for him, for that matter.

He realized that he was slowly beginning to not only dislike Fillagrou, but hate it. As well, he had grown sick of this war, of those engaged in it and the fact that they all seemed to think he needed to be included for some reason. If it ended up hurting any of them, or worse, he didn't know what he might do, what he might be capable of doing.

Much to the surprise of everyone, the group reached the edge of the massive lake without the slightest hint of resistance. Up close, the water looked even thicker and muddier than it had from afar. Its surface was a grainy-brown soup, disgusting and slimy, covered in a thin sheen of clear stickiness that slightly resembled spit. Occasionally a slightly lighter brown bubble the size of a basketball would rise to the surface and explode with an audible pop, sending miniscule grains of sand flying in every direction.

"All of you, in," Krystoph muttered hurriedly, scanning the surrounding area intently, still shocked by the lack of even a single Ochan regiment. "We must reach the ship by nightfall if we hope to recover the artifact before the Ochans."

Upon hearing this, Nicky gazed up from the bubbling glop long enough to mumble, "Ship?"

His enormous flat feet already half submerged in the disgusting liquid, Nestor looked at the boy with an uncharacteristic grin. "Lad, in Aquari, there are no other methods of transportation."

34. EARLY AFTERNOON RENDEZVOUS

"You've gotta be kidding me...how much further is this place?" Donald managed to sputter out despite the fact that he was nearly out of breath and his legs and feet were on fire after hours of non-stop hiking.

"Stop complaining, will ya, kid? In case you've forgotten, no one asked you along for the ride. You made your choice, now deal with it," Roustaf responded with a fair amount of annoyance while running his hand across the perfectly symmetrical lumps along the top of his head.

"Yeah, yeah, yeah, whatever," Donald shot back angrily. "Look, I'm not asking for all that much, just a couple minutes of rest! Gimme ten minutes! Ten stupid little minutes! Wait, wait wait, I'll tell you what, I'll even take five—five lousy minutes! I think the mutant ninja turtles back there would appreciate a break too, wouldn't you, guys?"

Glancing behind him, Donald looked to the pair of Tycarians brining up the rear of the group for confirmation. They stared back sternly, the taller, older of the two rolling his eyes while shaking his massive head.

"Look, slick," Roustaf interrupted, "We're not stopping, not while Pleebs and Walcott are locked up in that hell hole. If the roles were reversed and it was the two of us holed up in there, they'd be doing exactly the same. Besides, I've got a meeting to keep and I ain't missing it. If you can keep that yap of yours shut for another twenty minutes or so, you'll get your break."

Donald sighed deeply, letting his shoulders droop even further. In his heart he knew the little man was right. Walcott wouldn't stop. The Tycarian king proved as much once already when he saved Donald's life. As the memories of that faithful day came rushing back, Donald decided he could last another twenty minutes — or at least attempt to.

"You still haven't told us who we're supposed to be meeting out here," Donald added, trying his best to ignore the fact that his legs were on the brink of turning into wobbly noodles.

Glancing over his winged shoulder, Roustaf cracked a slight smile. "I've been told more than once over the years that I've got a pretty thick head, but I'm not quite as stupid as I look, kid. Believe it or not, I never planned on going into Ocha without some backup."

A mere twenty-three minutes later, Roustaf came to a hovering stop in an area of the forest seemingly no different than any the group of weary travelers had encountered to that point.

"Alright, cool your britches for a minute and take a load off. We're here," The little man muttered while zooming back and forth among the trees, scanning the forest floor from above and searching for something below.

"Here? Stop here?" Donald yelled back, "Here where? Oh, wait — look at that, great job! You found some trees! Trees in a forest! Nicely done, Sherlock, you've cracked another case!"

"Will you please shut your trap, kid, before I come over there and shut it for you?" Roustaf responded without turning to face the boy and twiddling the edge of his beard quizzically, still hovering three feet off the forest floor.

At last the little man came to a stop above a series of large leafy-red bushes surrounded by five smallish trees forming a very rough looking semi-circle. "Exactly where she said it'd be," He muttered to himself moments before darting headfirst into the leafy foliage and disappearing from view.

From five feet away, Donald and the Tycarians watched with interest as the bush began to jitter wildly, loose leaves being tossed about in every direction like a shaggy dog shaking water from its fur. A moment later, the ground under Donald's feet started to shake as if an earthquake were somehow localized in the space directly beneath. Moving backward, he leapt from the vibrating ground onto more stable footing between the stone-faced Tycarian soldiers. Sliding backward into itself, the forest floor eventually opened up, exposing a crudely cut pit in the soil.

Lifting into the air from inside the bush, Roustaf came to a hovering stop directly over the pitch-black opening. "Allrighty, everyone inside. Come on, ya schmucks, let's not stand around scratching ourselves like a bunch of bums with nowhere to go. We ain't got all day."

One by one the group lowered themselves into the darkened opening. A moment after the last of them had descended into the blackness, the trapdoor above closed once again, encasing them in a thick, all-encompassing darkness. Moving cautiously and using the walls on either side of the incredibly tight space to guide them, the group began carefully making their way through a series of underground tunnels not too different from those surrounding the city of New Tipoloo. The mud beneath Donald's feet was thick and sticky — so thick, in fact, that it nearly pulled the shoes from his feet on a number of occasions. The air was stuffy, humid, heavy and suffocating. Donald was finding it difficult to breathe, as it felt almost like he was attempting to snort syrup through his nose and somehow transform it into oxygen.

Quietly he mumbled a few choice four-letter words in Roustaf's direction.

After another ten minutes of walking the tunnel at last began to open up, a dim, yellowish light growing patiently into focus off in the distance. Eventually the tunnel widened enough for the Tycarian soldiers to stand upright, their backs a bit sore from hunching over for so long. Whoever or whatever originally created the Tycarian form never intended for it to easily maneuver through tight places. Much smaller, darker and somehow more crudely constructed than Tipoloo, the new area reminded Donald of an airplane hangar in some ways. There were no dwellings dug into the walls, no stone doorways or families of weird creatures. Just a few sporadically placed torches stuck into the dirt provided the room with its only source of light. At first glance Donald believed the cavern to be empty, though his visibility beyond twenty feet was admittedly limited. Unsure of their new surroundings, the Tycarians tightened their muscles while keeping their flat paws close to the blades strapped to their sides.

"Relax guys. You won't be needing those here," Roustaf added with a grin, motioning to their weapons. "Trust me, this isn't enemy territory."

"It took you long enough."

The voice came from the distance, its speaker hidden somewhere within the shadows. Roustaf turned away from the Tycraians, his tiny grin instantly growing to a full-on smile that curled the edges of his already curly mustache even further. "What the hell are you talking about? I'm right on time, which is a miracle considering all the nonsense I had to go through to get here."

At last the shadows opened up and from them stepped none other than the Grilgamorph slave-turned-revolutionary, Tahnja. The deep black against the bright, almost neon quality of her pink skin proved a revelation in contrasts. With a smile spread across her thin lips, she sauntered on a pair of long wiry legs toward the group, staring directly at Roustaf the entire time. As she moved toward the little man, he, too, progressed toward her. Opening her hand, she extended it outward in Roustaf's direction. Fluttering like a red leaf from one of Fillagrou's trees, the tiny man came to a soft landing on the sleek curves of her pink-skinned palm. The instant his feet were firmly planted, she pulled his little body close to her face and planted a kiss on the whole of his head.

Both touching and more than a little bizarre, Donald tried his best not to chuckle at the sight.

"In any case, I'm glad you finally made it," Tahnja whispered with an obvious lovelorn expression on her drawn face.

"I always keep my promises, toots — especially to a pretty little dame like yourself," Roustaf responded while leaning in close once more to plant a kiss on her lips, which were nearly half the size of his entire body.

Looking past the miniscule man standing proudly in the palm of her hand, Tahnja finally took note of Donald and the burly Tycarian soldiers waiting patiently in the shadows of the tunnel.

"I was only expecting you," She whispered, turning her attention to Roustaf once again and raising the area where her eyebrows would be, if she had any.

"What can I say? Plans change. Is it gonna be a problem?"

"No problem at all," She answered, her ever present grin remaining a constant. "The more, the merrier. Besides, we're going to need all the help we can get."

After planting a quick kiss on her nose, Roustaf lifted himself into the air with the aid of his translucent wings. "Is everyone else ready?"

Extending her now empty hand upward, Tahnja motioned toward the thick, unending shadows directly behind. "Ready, willing, and anxious to crack some Ochan heads."

Donald watched as a group of heavily armored soldiers, each distinctly different in appearance from the last, emerged from the darkness. Their faces sported expressions of readiness and seriousness with just a hint of anxiety. Though each among them belonged to a different race, all had felt the awful sting of war during the course of their lives, and every last one was aching to get their hands on an Ochan, any Ochan. Among those that had survived the horrors of the Dark Army, these were the best of the best, the toughest of the tough, and the hardest of the hard. Though creatures with vastly different backgrounds, they had come together for one reason: the rescue of Pleebo and Walcott.

If a few Ochans happened to get hacked to bits in the process, none among them would likely be upset. For the very first time since following Roustaf into the forest, Donald believed they might actually have a chance.

The foolishness of youth is an astounding thing.

35. BROKEN PROMISES

It had been a little over a month since Megan was diagnosed. In that time, her health had gotten progressively worse. This was a patient disease she found herself grappling with; a disease just now beginning the long process of eating away at her until eventually there would be nothing left. What began as little more than the sniffles and the occasional sleepless night had slowly morphed into something darker and scarier – the kind of something better not spoken of in the company of her two young children. Lately the act of simply pulling herself out of bed in the morning had become a chore for Megan; every movement was a sharp reminder of the dire situation she faced. Seated atop a long wooden bench on the deck, she watched as the sun began its descent, dissolving what had only moments ago been day and turned it into night. She loved the smell of the night air, crisp and deep, with an undeniable, yet so very subtle hint of moisture. The night washed the world clean and left behind its dewy remnants as proof of the transformation. It was the night air, and only the night air, that had proven capable of cooling the ever intensifying fire eating away at her from the inside out. Though the sky hadn't yet been fully enveloped by the darkness,

Megan could already make out the subtle hint of the stars above. Nearly translucent, for the moment they were mere hints, vague ideas of something more bright and beautiful to come later. Before the doctors informed her she had only a few months to live, the moon and the sun and the sky were of little interest to Megan Jarvis. Now though, nose-to-nose with the beginning of the end and realizing a day would soon arrive in which her eyes could never look on such a sight again, the universe seemed an entirely different place. As with everything in the end, it came down to a simple matter of perspective. That which had once been dull and uninteresting had become a revelation.

Unfortunately, as was often the case, it was not until one found themselves faced with the reality of losing something that they learned to appreciate it.

Behind Megan, the front door to the house opened with a squeak, and from it stepped her husband, Chris. The damn squeaky door had bothered her for years and she'd asked him repeatedly to fix it or oil it or whatever he had to do to stop it from making that god-awful noise. Whether due to laziness, forgetfulness or simply because he hadn't found the time, Chris never got around to it. Hearing it now, Megan was strangely glad he hadn't. She wanted to remember the squeak. She needed to remember the squeak exactly as it was and had been for so long. The squeak was important.

"How are you feeling?" Chris asked, leaning beside her while wrapping a blanket over her shoulders and pulling her close to his chest.

Megan took note of how warm his chest felt against the side of her head. Though subtle, she could hear his heart beating deep inside. Like the drum in a well-trained orchestra, the amazingly complicated organ thumped in tune with the heaving of his chest and the rumble of his half-empty stomach. These were the sounds Megan loved — the simple, meaningless background she'd loved since she first heard them.

Closing her eyes, she inhaled deeply, absorbing his odor and holding it in her lungs for a moment before opting to let it settle comfortably across her insides. "I'm alright," she answered with a comfortable grin. "Are the boys asleep?"

"I just put them down," Chris responded, his fingers gently running through her delicate hair and against her scalp.

Pulling the blanket to her neck, Megan leaned in closer to her husband. Opening her eyes ever so briefly, she gazed again at the darkening sky in the distance. Summer would end soon, and before she knew it, fall would come rushing in to take its place. Eventually the bitter cold of winter will have taken over completely, making something as simple as sitting on her porch staring at the stars an almost impossible task. She would miss this. She would miss the stars.

"How are they doing?" she asked with a whisper, closing her eyes again.

For a moment, Chris hesitated. He was beginning to sense the worry in his boys, especially Tommy. While he doubted his elder son was entirely sure of what his mother was going through, it was becoming painfully obvious the boy could sense something was amiss. Every day Tommy got quieter. Every day he retreated further into his crayons and his drawings and the more easily manageable fictional worlds in his head. Every day he was backing further and further away from reality. This, however, was not the kind of thing Chris believed his wife should worry herself with — not now, not when she needed every ounce of strength she had. It was for this reason, and this reason alone, that he opted instead to lie.

"They're fine, doing just fine."

Despite the utilization of his best poker face, Megan could see right through him. The tone of his voice was slightly off kilter. The couple had been married far too long for such a thing to go by unnoticed. Chris was telling her exactly what he thought she needed to hear and nothing more. Over the past few weeks Megan had witnessed firsthand the beginnings of a change in the way her children looked at her, especially her first-born. Tommy knew something was amiss. Much the way one might discern a storm on the horizon simply by the existence of cloud cover, her elder son could sense his mother's distress in the expressions on her face. Pulling the blanket further over her face, Megan used it to wipe the beginnings of a tear pooling in the corner of her eye.

"Chris..." She asked softly, her voice soulful and faraway with a barely there tremble.

"What is it hun? Are you warm enough? Need another blanket?" Chris responded quickly while lifting his rear from the bench, anxious to do anything within his power to make her more comfortable. "What's wrong? Is it too cold? Want to go inside?"

"No, I'm fine, I just . . .there's something I need to ask you."

"What is it? Anything you need, just tell me and I'll get it for you."

Megan shut her eyes tightly, fighting back the oncoming tears with every ounce of strength she could muster and discovering that she was stronger than she ever imagined. Her current situation had proved this beyond a shadow of a doubt. After a breath, followed by a thoughtful pause to corral her wild thoughts, she at last spoke.

"Take care of them . . .when I'm gone. Promise me that you'll take care of them."

"Take care of who? What are you talking about?" Chris answered, with a hint of confusion in his voice.

"The boys. Take care of the boys."

Like a duffel bag full of lead, the comment settled deep in Chris's stomach, further churning his already twisted insides. "What do you mean? Of course I'll take ca—"

"I know, Chris."

"Know what? What're yo—"

Megan shifted her body into an upright position with a slight grimace in order to look her husband directly in the eyes. "I know this isn't exactly what you planned."

"What are you talking about?"

Reaching forward, Megan ran her hand across the side of his face. "It's okay, Chris. I know that this life — — this house, your job — it's not what you planned."

Slightly insulted by her statement, and a bit frightened by the fact that there might possibly be a hint of truth in it, Chris opened his mouth to respond. Reaching up, Megan placed the tip of her finger at the crest of his lips, her weary eyes pleading with him to remain silent a second longer.

"Just promise me you'll never give up on them, no matter what. Promise me — promise me you'll be the man I fell in love with. Be patient. Keep them safe. Try to understand them when you think they don't make any sense, even if they really don't make any sense. Do your best. Just do the best you can. Promise me you'll do that, Chris."

The comment threw Chris for a loop, instantly making him both angry and frightened. The idea that his wife of so many years could question his love, patience for, or dedication to his children infuriated him. Watching her lower lip quiver ever so slightly as she gazed up at him with her tired, achingly beautiful blue eyes, he found himself unable to formulate an appropriate response. He was upset that she would even suggest such a thing, and more upset because he knew exactly why she felt the need to, though he was unwilling to admit it. A soft breeze floated in from the north, flapping Megan's hair wildly and rattling the wind chimes hanging over their porch. While aspects of this life might not have been exactly what he dreamt of, not by a long shot, there was no part of him that regretted a single, solitary moment. The choices he'd made to this point were his and his alone, even those that were unplanned and even those that were thrust upon him. Reaching forward, he placed his hands on either side of Megan's face. She looked tired, the bags under her eyes set deep and worn. Her skin was a blotchy white and red, every day drawing tighter to the skull underneath. She was losing so much weight, slowly transforming into something leathery and worn and just plain different than what she once was. The lone tear cascading down the curve of her cheek proved almost too much for him to bear and he bit his lower lip to keep from crying.

Despite it all, he could think of only one word to describe her: beautiful.

Chris knew that he couldn't be too upset with her, not now, not when she needed him the most, no matter what she might be suggesting. The sickness had tainted her thought process. This could be the only explanation.

Leaning close to her ear, he whispered with a warm, comforting breath, "I promise." Once again, it was exactly what she needed to hear, exactly what needed to be said.

Pulling her rapidly thinning body closer still, he softly touched his lips to hers before wrapping the blanket over her shoulders to keep her from feeling a chill. The promise was more than mere words, more than a way of calming someone he loved so very deeply that also happened to be in desperate need of reassurance.

The promise was as genuine and heartfelt as any he'd ever made. Again the wind blew and again the chimes sang. Megan would remain wrapped in the arms of her husband for ten more minutes before the pair retreated into their home for the evening. After carrying her upstairs, Chris laid her on the bed and wrapped her tenderly in the covers. Almost instantly, she drifted into a deep sleep. Chris, however, would remain awake for hours, staring blankly at the bluish moonlight just outside their bedroom window and listening to her breathe beside him. Like life itself, promises can prove tricky business. Though mind-bogglingly intricate, they are often made on little more than a whim. However, like most things in life, promises rarely last forever.

36. THE DIFFERENCE BETWEEN UNICORNS AND PEGASI

"Holy crap, you've gotta be kidding me! I mean seriously, come on, you guys have got unicorns?"

Upon hearing the boy's words, the modest group of would-be rescuers turned in the direction of Donald Rondage with starkly similar expressions of confusion. Standing at the far end of a second, slightly larger hangar-like room, Donald now found himself gazing up at a creature greatly resembling a horse, yet was something else entirely. Covered in course, coal-black hair with an ivory colored horn between its eyes that looked like it had been shaved down to half a nub, the massive thing stared back at the boy with a pair of deep, soulful eyes. Though its basic features were strikingly similar to the horses Donald was accustomed, this creature was bigger than any he'd seen before. From head-to-toe, its body was layered with thick, sinewy muscles, a single one of the beast's enormous legs nearly wider than the length of his body from head to toe.

"Uni-what? What the hell is a unikron, kid?" Roustaf remarked from the opposite end of the room, his little body floating next to

Tahnja as she climbed onto the back of another one of the massive black-furred stallions.

"Unicorn, not kron, and this thing right here is one of them," Donald responded, hot breath pouring from the nearby creature's nostrils warming the flesh of his face like the heat from a flame.

"We call them Pegasi," Tahnja stated with a chirp as she strapped herself into a saddle attached firmly to the black beast's massive back. "Do you have them on your world too?"

Donald chuckled slightly. "Well, the D&D nerds spend an awful lot of time drawing pictures of them but no, not exactly."

Reaching up, Donald gently patted the thick side of the creature's neck. Its muscles were so tight and weighty that the action felt remarkably like slapping his hand against cement.

"Pegasi?" He muttered under his breath, his palm still stinging. "That's a pretty stupid name."

From either side of him, the two Tycarians hooked their meaty arms under his, lifted him into the air, and deposited him roughly in the leather saddle. Though annoyed and slightly embarrassed by the fact that the giant turtles picked him up like a sack of dirty laundry, Donald opted to remain silent. This was partially because he realized he very well might not have been able to get on top of the creature without them. Underneath him, the Pegasi stomped its enormous hoofed feet a few times in the soil, lifting its head into the air for an instant to shake the dark mane running along the back of its neck. From his new vantage point, Donald could more clearly recognize the fact that the horn on top of the creature's head had in fact been filed to nearly a nub. A series of deep, awkward looking grooves were scraped ragged and rough into the now flat tip of the sturdy grayish colored bone. Not only had the horn been filed away, it was filed sloppily. Scanning the area around him, Donald noticed the same feature present on each of the creatures scattered throughout the room.

"What happened to their horns?" He asked anyone willing to listen while reaching forward carefully to touch the calcified nub with the tip of his index finger.

"The Ochans file them down," Tahnja responded, while patting the massively muscled neck of the mostly harmless looking Pegasi she was seated on. "They're easier to domesticate like this. It's a shame really; when allowed to reach their full potential, the horns are quite beautiful. This is what the Ochans do best though: take what doesn't belong to them and distort it to suit their needs. It's what they've always done."

From the back of the dimly lit room, an enormous furry creature with dark, deep set eyes and a mouth full of two rows of sharp teeth punctuated by a pair of extremely dangerous looking fangs on either side rode from the shadows on the back of yet another black haired Pegasi. "We can make it to the doorway to Ocha by nightfall but we must get moving," he remarked assuredly, his monotone voice remarkably disguising whatever emotion he might have felt, if any at all.

"Don't worry, Brutus. We'll make it there in time, and once we do, you'll have more Ochans to slice open and gut then you'll know what to do with," Tahnja responded with subtle grin. Though it had only been a few months since she met him, Tahnja had already become accustomed to the vehemently time-oriented nature of her new friend. Though Brutus was the first and only of his kind she'd ever met, she often wondered whether this was a trait of his species as a whole, or a nugget of personality uniquely his own. To date, however, she hadn't yet worked up the courage to ask him.

"Wait a minute," Donald asked, struggling to maintain his balance on the massive, jerking beast heaving underneath him like a bull moments away from being released from its pen. "Are we supposed to ride these things all the way to Pleebo and *Slow*amennes? Here's a little nugget of information that might shock you, but I don't know how to ride a Unicorn. I don't even know how to ride a horse. I mean, is black beauty here safe? It's not going to toss me into a tree at thirty miles per hour or anything, is it?"

Fluttering across the room, Roustaf came to a stop near the Pegasi's massive ear, which was nearly large enough for him to walk inside without ever having to worry about hitting his head. Gently the little man ran his tiny hand across the space between the creature's eyes and just under its horn. Slowly the huffing beast relaxed, it's previously hurried breathing slowing to a steady pant.

"On foot it would take more than a few more days to get to Ocha, kid, and I'm talking ten or eleven, and that's if we ran the entire time at full speed without ever stopping. If we're lucky these guys can get us there before the sun goes down. Let me give you some advice about Pegasi, slick, and I've found this works for most things in life. Just think of them like a beautiful lady," Roustaf paused for a moment, glancing briefly between the creature's massively muscled legs. "In fact, as luck would have it, looks like yours *is* a lady. Listen, kid, just be gentle with her. Treat her right and she'll treat you right. Get a little out of hand, go and make a move you shouldn't be making quite so early in your relationship, and she'll send you airborne so quick you won't have time to apologize . . .just like a lady."

From the opposite side of the room, Tahnja flashed Roustaf a sly smile followed immediately by a wink. After meeting just six months ago, the pair had grown progressively closer. When fighting alongside someone, wading neck deep through the nearly overwhelming emotions brought on by battle, feelings such as these were not entirely uncommon. As it did to most, war had treated Tahnja harshly. When she first encountered Staci Alexander in the prisoner transport, years spent hiding in the Fillagrou forest had reduced her to little more than a babbling, incoherent flood of emotions. She was lost and alone, drowning in the demons of her past and unwilling to even attempt to fight the currents pulling her down. The budding relationship between her and Roustaf was more than simply a result of circumstance, however. It was more than the fact that that he had saved her from the axe of an Ochan soldier in the courtyard of Prince Valkea's castle, or the fact that they were, for all intents and purposes, the only two remaining of their respective species. There was a shared connection between them, more than friendship and entirely different from love. It was almost as if they were meant to be, two souls chipped into existence from the same block of marble. This was a feeling she had experienced only once before in her life. Simultaneously frightening and exhilarating, this was a feeling they were only just beginning to explore. Though they had been gone for some time, Tahnja could often see the face of her daughter when she closed her eyes, hear the voice of her husband dragging along the tail end of the wind. Exactly as it should be though, with time these visions and sounds were getting blurrier. At least in part, she attributed this to Roustaf. The strange children and the possibility of what they represented had allowed her to focus her mind for the first time in as many years as she could recall. There was the possibility of hope again, and hope was worth fighting for.

From the opposite end of the room, the Pegasi underneath Brutus leapt onto its hind legs, snorting angrily into the stuffy darkness. "The daylight wanes, Tahnja," Brutus stated without a hint of emotion from the mammoth back of the beast.

Again Tahnja chuckled, glancing at him briefly then turning her attention to Roustaf with a grin. "Well, big guy, ready to do the impossible?"

Leaving Donald's side, the little man floated over to her and came to a soft landing on the nape of her long, pink neck. Reaching up, he tightened the buckle on his dirty blue overalls.

"Six months ago I would've thought you and me would've been as impossible as impossible comes, doll. Now though, traveling to Ocha, sneaking into Kragamel's castle, and somehow fighting off a few thousand guards to rescue Pleebs and Walcott? Well, that's gonna seem like an absolute breeze."

37. A NOT SO FRIENDLY WELCOME

Moments after holding his breath and subsequently lowering himself into to the sticky-thick liquid, Tommy Jarvis found himself overcome with strange, yet altogether familiar sensations. It was at this point the ideas of gravity, form and shape again disappeared into the background, unceremoniously replaced by the absence of things common, understood and quantified. Immersed completely in the strange in-between, Tommy forgot about his father, his brother, his mother, Fillagrou, the Ochans and the war. He even forgot himself — if such a thing were possible. To call the act of traveling between worlds a unique experience is akin to referring to the sea as wet or the arctic cold. While both described the sensation adequately, neither came close to capturing the true nuances of the experience. Though his time spent in this void between universes was actually less than a fraction of a second, the fraction dragged like nails across a chalkboard, creating the illusion of time where none existed. At last the weightiness of gravity slid again sneakily underneath his feet, heralding the coming of a journey's end. The nothingness around him morphed quite dramatically into something gritty and grimy and thick. His lungs, flesh and lips were again given form; Tommy held his breath as a sandy glop melted around his skin like warm fudge over ice cream. Again he found himself fully submerged in the very same tepid glop he stepped into a moment prior, swimming toward what he believed to be up — or crawling, as the case might be — as "swimming" through a substance such as this was quite impossible. From somewhere above, a meaty green paw pierced the black-brown darkness, flailing wildly and searching for the boy in the lumpy sludge. Reaching upward, Tommy wrapped his hands around the three-fingered hand tightly, allowing it to pull him at last from the soundless depths and into the light. Free at last from the goopy slop, he breathed in the air around him as his body was deposited again on solid ground. After wiping a pile of thick gunk from his eyes, he flicked it away with a twist of his wrist. His eyes wiped clean, Tommy took the opportunity to examine the new surroundings.

Before he had a chance to fully absorb this new world, the same paw that pulled him from the brown sludge shoved him stiffly in the shoulder and slid his mud covered body across the soil. "Get behind me, child! Get behind me, now!" Heavy, gruff and serious, the voice belonged to Nestor Rockshell.

At this point, the world around him began to come rapidly into focus for Tommy Jarvis. Standing directly in front of him, sword at the ready, his free hand still shoving the boy behind his thick brownish-green shell, was Nestor. Next to Nestor stood another battle-ready Tycarian, and next to him, with a blade in each hand, was Krystoph. The massive wall of green alien flesh was preventing Tommy from seeing who or what the threesome was looking at, or exactly why they had their weapons drawn. Based on the intensity in Nestor's voice, however, there was no doubt it was something serious. Glancing briefly behind him, Tommy looked to the muddy liquid from which he was just yanked. Neither Staci, his brother nor the remainder of their group had yet made the journey through the doorway from Fillagrou and into this world. More than likely, it would be only a matter of moments before they did. Without warning, Krystoph broke away from the threesome, charging forward in a semi-crouched position, his jagged teeth clenched and muscles tight.

The instant the Ochan disappeared from Tommy's sight, Nestor turned hurriedly toward the boy, leaning his massive shell over of him like a great stone umbrella.

At the top of his lungs, Nestor screamed at the soldier to his right, "Incoming volley! Get down, Reginald!"

With the Tycarian's massive body covering him entirely and bathing him in deep shadow, Tommy heard an odd sound, similar to a whizzing or possibly a hum, getting louder and closer by the second. An instant later, three nearly two-foot long arrows sailed in from above, thrusting dangerously into the soil a few feet away. These three arrows were immediately followed by more—many more, in fact. While some of the steel tipped weapons missed Tommy and the Tycarians completely, sticking upright in the grass around them or sinking into the sandy liquid behind, others contacted the back of Nestor and Reginald's protective exteriors with sickening clanks. The sound of metal against shell proved terrifying: a hollow, painful, echoing crack that reverberated in every direction.

Grimacing, Nestor could feel each and every steel tip collide with his sturdy exterior, tearing away chunks of shell and leaving only rough, deep gashes in their place. When an arrow struck the ground mere inches from Tommy's face, the Tycarian pulled the squirming boy further underneath him, trying his best to keep him safe from harm. Unable to make out his attackers visually during the onslaught of arrows, Nestor could, however, hear them quite clearly in the distance. The feast of noise his ears were taking in was familiar and uplifting: Ochans choking and gagging as they swallowed their own blood. This was a sound he'd happily grown accustomed to. Defying the dictates of logic, Nestor assumed Krystoph had managed to somehow close the distance between the group and the attacking Ochan soldiers without being struck down. At this moment, he was undoubtedly doing what he did best: killing.

The heart inside his chest pounding, Tommy lifted his head slightly while lying in a fetal position beneath Nestor. Everything was happening so fast. One minute he was floating in a world of absolute nothingness, and the next he found himself smack dab in the middle of a war zone. Though this was something one might think he should have been accustomed to at this point, he unfortunately was not. With so many arrows sticking out of the soil around him and more still on the way, the ground had begun to resemble a bed of nails. As arrows continued to rain down around him by the dozens, Tommy wiped a rather large blob of sweat from his eye, then spotted Staci's mud covered locks ascending from the sandy drink less than ten feet away. Gasping for breath, the girl was understandably disoriented, her arms flailing wildly, hands opened wide as they grasped for something firm to hold onto to keep her from drowning. Simultaneously, a set of three or four arrows narrowly missed the young girl before being swallowed up by the thick slop.

"Tommy?" Staci yelped though a mouth half full of mud with her eyes shut tight, terrified and unsure of what was happening.

She's calling for me, Tommy remarked to himself with a hint of surprise, followed immediately by an awkward moment of happiness he was not entirely comfortable with. *She's calling for me and she needs my help.*

Choosing to ignore the dangers of his actions, Tommy began crawling toward her, his arms stretched as far as they would go. With the upper half of his body submerged in the sandy mud, he managed to snag her wrist at the exact moment an arrow whizzed by and removed a chunk of flesh the thickness of a pen from his forearm. Ignoring the searing pain, he forced his muscles to stretch further still. Grabbing Staci's wrist tightly, he began pulling her from the liquid, onto land and underneath Nestor's massive form. Though totally unaware of doing it, he tugged her shivering body close to his chest, mashing her frightened, mud covered form into the dirt under him. In much the way Nestor was looming over him, Tommy stretched himself protectively over her. A few moments later, the awful storm of arrows reached its conclusion, the final two swallowed whole by the muddy liquid. Off in the distance, away from the eyes of Tommy, Staci, Nestor or Reginald, the last of the Ochan archers screamed aloud before his breath caved in on itself and disappeared from existence. With his stomach sliced open, the soldier's innards slid to the soil with a disgusting splotchy splat, followed immediately by the remainder of his body.

For the children, again the world was silent . . .again they were safe.

To Nestor's right, the Tycarian soldier named Reginald cautiously rose to his feet. His legs were noticeably wobbly, his exterior shell awash in sharp tremors of pain. One by one, he carefully began removing the arrows still wedged between the plates of his shell before tossing them to the ground angrily then stomping them to splinters.

After quickly surveying the area, he turned to his commanding officer and added through gritted teeth, while poking annoyingly at a large section of his shell that had been chipped away, "It would appear the coast is clear."

Upon hearing this, Nestor too rose into a upright position. "It's all right, children; you may stand," he added, offering a paw to Tommy and Staci, both of whom remained curled in the grass near his massive flat feet.

Slowly Tommy peeled his arms from around Staci's waist. She was shivering beneath him, her breathing erratic and short. Touching her face, he tenderly pulled a few strands of clumpy mud-encrusted hair from her eyes. The tears streaming down her cheeks had left clean rivers across her otherwise filthy flesh.

"It's okay, it's over, " he whispered softly, staring into her jittery face.

Slowly beginning to regain some semblance of control over her emotions, Staci opened her eyes and smiled back. Tommy felt warm against her, and strong, despite his rather average size. He was covered in sticky-thick brown glop, wadded strands of his once blond hair clinging to his face in matted clumps.

"You look awful," she said breathily, with just the hint of a smile.

He, of course, smiled back. There was something about being wrapped in his arms, something she didn't hate.

Less than ten feet away, the dark-haired head of Nicky Jarvis broke the surface of the mud-water, arms flailing in every conceivable direction. Reginald quickly rushed to the child's aid. Grabbing hold of him tightly, he lifted the boy into the air and onto land.

Once he and Staci were again upright, Tommy turned his attention from her briefly. A little less than a hundred yards away, Krystoph stood motionless among the bodies of at least twenty Ochan soldiers. Breathing heavily, he wiped dark splatters of blood from his blades, random arrows still sticking from various points across his blood stained flesh. Though his face remained emotionless, there was something else going on beneath, something not as easily readable, yet undeniably present. It was an unending, unyielding, undeniable sadness. Holding back a torrent of emotions most could scarcely endeavor to contain, Krystoph closed his eyes and raised his head to the dense clouds above. The pains caused by the arrows still piercing his flesh had resulted in considerable pain. It was a pain he was not ready to be free of. It was a pain he needed desperately to hold onto. This was a pain he needed to experience fully.

Wiping the gunk from his eyes, Nicky paused in the massive shadow of Reginald, blobs of mud dripping from his soaked clothes.

Wide-eyed, he scanned the arrow-filled area around him before adding with a slightly worried whisper, "What did I miss?"

38. THE STORIES WERE REAL

For Chris Jarvis, the moment he at last lifted his head from the murky black water, the very act of inhaling deeply, proved to be a revelation. Moments afterward, he again opened his eyes, quickly realizing the world around him had drastically changed. Gone now was the tree fort built by his sons. Gone was the tiny stream he lowered himself into, and most notably absent was anything and everything he believed impossible in the universe. Wading in a puddle just barely big enough for his entire body to fit, surrounded by a forest of stark reds with various tints of gray, Chris realized that every irrational nonsensical thing Owen told him was indeed true. None of it made an ounce of sense, but it was true. Pulling himself onto land, he stood upright on a pair of unsure legs, every inch of him soaked and dripping and confused. Slowly spinning in place, he examined the strange red forest around him further. Though at its most basic this odd new place was similar to many of the forests he'd seen before in his life, it remained starkly different at the same time. The leaves were the color of blood, alive and vibrant, so deeply red that the hue transformed into something closer to purple in certain areas. The air was thick and heavy, with humidity so noticeable that it had already begun to make him sweat. For miles in every direction, he could see nothing but dense foliage. Above him, just barely peeking through the trees, was an almost white light of what looked like three suns. Save for the flutter of the leaves on the trees brought on by the occasional gust of wind, this weird forest seemed completely and totally devoid of sound. So eerily silent was it, in fact, that he believed he thought he might be able to hear a pin drop.

Gap-jawed, Chris timidly began to move away from the puddle and further into the trees when a voice cut through the silence like the flicker of light in a darkened room. "Look at that . . .you're right on time."

Spinning so quickly he nearly fell over, Chris turned to look behind him. Standing among the red bushes less than ten feet away was a tall, lanky feminine-looking creature with enormous red pupils and grayish-white skin pulled tightly over the musculature beneath.

"My name is Zanell, Christopher. I've been expecting you."

His heart pounding, a million ideas began trouncing through Chris' head, not a single one of them making any sense. Though unaware of it, his body began moving backward and away from Zanell. "H-how do you — how do you know my name?"

This couldn't be happening. This couldn't be happening, and yet it *was* happening.

Zanell took a single step toward the frightened man, cautious of her speed with her hands raised, hoping that it might calm him. "I imagine this is going to be a bit hard to accept, but I know everything one could possibly know about you, Christopher."

While moving backward, Chris tripped over a loose log and fell hard onto his rear in the dirt. On the brink of losing control, he instinctively lifted his hands into a defensive position while at the same time frantically searching the ground around him for a rock, stick or anything else he might be able to use as weapon.

The moment his hands raised, Zanell halted her movement. "It's okay, I'm not going to harm you," she said in her absolute most steady voice, deciding she might be better served taking a step backward and giving him his space. "This is Fillagrou, and this is my home. It isn't by mere chance that you've found this place; you're here for a reason, Christopher. You're here to make right those things you've done wrong. You're here to save the lives of your sons."

Almost instantly, the rabid thumping in Chris' chest slowed to a crawl. "My — my sons? W-what do you know about my sons?"

While still practicing extreme caution, Zanell opted to again take a step in the direction of the now motionless form of Chris Jarvis sprawled out in the dirt. "Like I stated before, I know everything," she added with a bit of a grin.

Slowly Zanell extended her hand in Chris' direction; opening her palm, she offered her long bony fingers to him.

The most obviously malnourished part of her body, Zanell's fingers were covered in strange winding veins with a slightly darker grayish tint than the rest of her skin. Staring up at her, Chris found himself lost in the redness of her eyes, moist and enormous, the light glared off her pupils in flashlight-sized circles. For reasons he couldn't fully explain, Chris reached forward and took her strange hand in his. Maybe it was the odd truthfulness in those bizarre looking eyes or the soothing patience of her voice. Whatever the reason, without knowing anything about who or what she was, he trusted her — maybe not completely, but enough — for the moment, anyway.

With a tug, Zanell lifted Chris to his feet once again, his backside caked in grayish-brown Fillagrou soil. "I would love nothing more than to fill you in on all the details," she added with a slightly wider grin than before. "At the moment, however, I need you to come with me. You see, a patrol of very large, very mean

Ochans will pass through this exact spot not too long from now, and it would be in our best interest to not be standing here when they do."

"Wait a minute, Ochan what? Where are you taking me? Can I see my boys?" Chris quickly shot back, now more confused than ever.

"All in good time, Christopher. I can't take you to see Tommy or Nicky right at this moment, I can, however, offer you something you desire just as badly, something that isn't often made available in life: a second chance."

Turning, Zanell took two steps in the opposite direction before again coming to a halt. "Oops, I almost forgot," She added while lifting a finger and pointing behind Chris.

His mouth hanging low, a look of utter confusion on his face, Chris glanced over his shoulder just in time to see Owen Little break the surface of the water. Gasping for air, the boy pulled himself onto land and buried his face in the mud while shaking it back and forth.

"What the heck am I doing here? This is so stupid, what am I doing here?" He mumbled to himself before looking up briefly to wipe the mud from the lenses of his glasses.

Zanell smiled brightly while chuckling just a bit. "Okay, now we're ready to go."

39. MODE OF TRANSPORTATION

Still brushing caked mud from his hair, Nicky Jarvis lifted his nose to the clouds and inhaled deeply the stark saltiness of the air around him. To his left, less than a mile away, he spotted a beach with a sandy shoreline extending for a few miles before turning back on itself and heading in the opposite direction. To his left there was much of the same. At first glance, it seemed that Aquari was little more than a rather small island with a mud pit leading to Fillagrou and a single, rather crude looking stone castle off in the distance. Built into the sandy beach at precisely mathematical intervals were long wooden piers—hundreds of them, maybe thousands—each leading maybe two hundred or so feet out over the water, then abruptly stopping. Beyond the sand and the piers, there lay only a crystal clear ocean with a subtle bluish hint not too dissimilar from those he'd seen back home. The ocean breeze was remarkably cold, causing Nicky to shiver and making his teeth chatter together loudly. Dropping his backpack to the ground, he opened it up and pulled out a sweater, pleased with himself for taking the time to pack earlier and come prepared.

From behind Nicky, Tommy patted loose the bits of remaining crud on his little brothers back. "Hey, you all right?"

"Yeah, I'm fine," Nicky responded from underneath his sweater as he struggled to work it over his head.

Tommy helped his younger brother get himself into the sleeves while keeping an eye on Nestor, Reginald and the third Tycarian soldier huddled ten feet away, whispering amongst themselves.

"What do you think they're talking about?" Staci asked, suddenly standing alongside the brothers still pulling chunks of mud from her long brown hair.

"I don't know," Tommy responded, his eyes unblinking, brow furrowed quizzically. "They don't look happy though."

With Tommy's response doing little to quell her growing uneasiness, Staci turned and looked out over the beach. Frothy white waves crashed with a violent gentleness against the shore. The sound created was unmistakable and familiar, and it was a sound she didn't particularly like. Staci hated swimming, she always had. She didn't like water and it was because of this very fact that she was finding herself significantly more nervous about this new world than any other she'd encountered thus far. Suddenly, staring down the gaping maw of a giant stampeding dinosaur with horns as long as her body didn't seem all that bad.

Biting down on her lower lip, she continued running her hands through her crusty hair. "What's with all the piers?"

"I don't know. I guess they're for boats," Tommy answered, his attention slowly moving from the Tycarians to Krystoph, who was standing a bit further down the shoreline with his back to the group.

"If all of those piers are for boats, then where the heck are the boats?" Staci responded while pulling her arms close to her chest in an attempt to keep from shivering.

Tommy made no attempt to answer, as he had no answer to offer. He didn't like this situation, not one bit. Near the opposite end of the island stood a fairly decent sized castle, as castles go, though it looked to have been built in a rush, and the only opposition they had encountered was a measly twenty or so Ochan soldiers. It didn't seem to make sense. Despite only being fourteen years old and not exactly well versed in the art of war, even Tommy understood there should have been more resistance — there should be a lot more. So where were they?

Not far from the children, the Tycarian contingent remained huddled together, their normally verbose voices purposefully reduced to hushed whispers.

"Every ship on the island has set sail? How can that be?" Reginald stated with some surprise and just a hint of worry.

"It would seem so, and I do not know." Nestor responded calmly.

"Realistically there could be a thousand ships on the ocean, maybe more," The third Tycarian added, his voice deeper than the others, more of a growl than a whisper.

"I am well aware of the situation, Tennission," Nestor remarked quickly, rubbing his hand across his sweaty, clammy scalp, "and yet this information changes nothing. Even with five thousand ships, finding a single artifact in all of Aquari while having no idea of where to look is a daunting task, to say the least. Unlike the rest of them, OUR Ochan knows exactly where he is going and because of this, the advantage remains with us."

After a brief pause, Nestor's facial features stiffened, twisting themselves into an expression that could only be described as steely determination. His deep green eyes moved from his fellow soldiers to the endless ocean behind them that stretched outward for as far as the eye could see. Reflections of the soft orange hue created by the Aquari sun sparkled atop the waves, shimmering like the leftover glow of stars resting somewhere on the sandy ocean floor. Without a doubt, Aquari was an astoundingly beautiful place. Discovered very early on by the Ochans, it had remained mostly untouched by the atrocities of war. A world made up almost entirely of water offered few resources and no real creatures of which to make slaves, thus it proved of little interest to King Kragamel. In fact, it was not until he discovered that this world was the hiding place of the Rongstag that the king even bothered to station a regiment or build a castle. Shortly after the first group of Ochan soldiers arrived an outpost was established, ships were constructed, and the scouring of the seas for the artifact began.

So achingly beautiful a world this was . . .so very dangerous as well.

Though Nestor expected there to be quite a few ships, never in his wildest dreams did he imagine the Ochans could have constructed so many in such a short amount of time. They had been working feverishly. This implied either that they were closer than ever to finding the Rongstag, or they were simply growing desperate. Never in his life did he remember desperation sounding so very enticing.

From behind the turtle man came the undeniable voice of Krystoph. "Where is this ship of yours, Tycarian?"

Turning to face the massive Ochan, Nestor glanced over the creature's muscled shoulder and across the blue sea. "I am unsure. We were late arriving. He should have been here by now."

Gritting his teeth, Krystoph cursed under his breath. "Hurm. Never should have come to you for help. Foolish mistake. Growing foolish with age."

With every passing hour, Krystoph was beginning more and more to question his choice to approach the Fillagrou female in the first place. After walking among the corpses at Prince Valkea's castle, he began to wonder if possibly the stories were true, if in fact the Fillagrou elder's prophecy — bizarre and nonsensical as it might have seemed — was somehow coming to pass. Since meeting the children rumored to have "incredible powers" though, he had seen no evidence of such things. Were it not for his last minute intervention on two occasions already, the useless pink-skinned creatures would be dead. The children were proving themselves worthless, the Tycarians were only slowing him down, and Kragamel was no doubt getting closer to the Rongstag with every hour. His patience was rapidly reaching its limit. Though unaware of it, Krystoph's fingers began tapping gently on the sturdy leather handle of the sword dangling at his side. Killing them and continuing without them would have made sense on many levels. The time may have arrived to do just that.

Cutting through the relative silence came the girlish voice of Staci Alexander. "Hey! What's that?"

All at once, the heads of Krystoph and the Tycarians looked in her direction. Less than ten feet away, Staci stood shivering, her finger outstretched and pointing across the beach and over the ocean. Next to her, the youngest Jarvis brother jumped excitedly, pointing as well. Following her finger, Krystoph gazed across the water, at last spotting a ship in the distance.

"Is that yours?" He asked Nestor sternly, choosing not to turn and face the turtle man.

Pulling a pair of binoculars from his belt, Nestor scanned the ship's hull. Constructed of a worn and aged timber, deep brownish-red in color, the ship looked old and in desperate need of repair. Carved into its bow was a skeleton quite similar proportionately to an Ochan. Though beaten and chipped in various spots, he could just barely make out two words cut into its side: "Briar Patch."

Pulling the binoculars from his face, Nestor grinned just enough to annoy the former Ochan general he was rapidly growing weary of. "Indeed, it is."

Never one for smugness, even he had to admit that on this occasion the satisfaction of being right was quite enjoyable.

40. A NEW PROBLEM

"Oh crap."

With every stride, the movement of the creature underneath Donald briefly sent the boy airborne before depositing him stiffly again onto its heavily muscled back. Using both hands, Donald gripped thick clumps of grayish fur belonging to one of Tahnja's friends sitting directly in front of him. Seeing as the boy had never ridden atop a Pegasus, she believed it was in his best interest to travel with a more experienced rider. Moving at mind-bogglingly incredible speeds through the forest, the Pegasus darted between trees both big and small with astounding precision. The unicorn-like creature was moving so fast, in fact, that from a distance it resembled barely more than a blur. Less than ten minutes into the trip, Donald instantly regretted gorging himself at the New Tipoloo feast two days prior. The odd looking, yet wonderfully juicy meat that tasted an awful lot like chicken had been slowly making its way from his stomach toward his mouth and threatening a second appearance. To top it all off, he had a pounding headache, was beginning to feel dizzy, and desperately needed to relieve himself. The revolting odor of the dusty, gray haired thing with a body like a bear and a snout like a pug dog seated in front of him wasn't helping matters any.

"Oh crap, oh crap, I'm gonna puke," Donald mumbled, his face mashed into the creatures stinky fur, his eyes rolling back in his head. "We need to stop. I'm gonna puke. I'm seriously gonna puke, we need to stop."

Feeling the boy's face pressed against his spine, the massive gray bear glanced over his shoulder. "Did you say something, kid?"

The sounds of heavy Pegasus hooves crushing leaves and plants alike, coupled with the roaring wind resistance created by its incredible speed, made hearing and understanding anything less than a scream an awfully difficult task.

Donald's stomach lurched, the bizarre alien food not yet digested in his belly again threatening to explode like a volcano of hot bile from between his lips.

"I said I'm gonna puke. I'm gonna–puke–if we don't stop," Donald gurgled, putting one hand over his mouth, his head rolling loosely atop his neck.

Above him, the trees were a blur, stretchy reds and grays starkly contrasted against the darkening sky. As the revolting baked potato rolled in street tar smell of the creature in front of him again snaked its way up his nose, he began to wish he had decided to remain with the Jarvis brothers and Staci, instead of following that little red jerk Roustaf. Wherever they were and whatever they were doing, it couldn't be as bad as this; it just couldn't.

"Please, stop, you damn gray haired Yogi! Please stop," Donald belted with a half scream, and half mumble.

"Yogi? What's a Yogi? You can call me Teek, kid! We can't stop though, big guy, not if we want to make it to Ocha by nightfall!"

Dropping his head into Teek's matted fur, Donald groaned deep and long.

"Listen, kid, if you've got some business to do, just do it over the side! Trust me, it wouldn't be the first time someone's lost their lunch while riding on the back of a Pegasus!"

The forest passing by at well over a hundred miles per hour, a heavy sheen of sweat pouring down his face and slimy lumps of disgusting mystery meat hammering at his insides like they were a punching bag, Donald found it impossible to hold back any longer. Removing his face from Teek's dry matted fur, he leaned his wobbly, pale white head over the side of the huge unicorn and let the sticky, lumpy glop inside his belly fly.

What resulted was quite messy to say the least, even by messy standards. Needless to say, for young Donald Rondage, the next few hours were mostly a blur.

When the boy next became aware of his surroundings, he noticed that the spinning, bouncing blurry world had finally come to a stop. With his stomach-churning having lessened, he lifted his head and wiped a slimy sheen of stingy sweat from his eyes. "Wh- where ar–"

Teek's gruff, old sounding voice interrupted his train of thought. "Shhhh. Quiet down, pally."

Breathing deeply, Donald steadied his head. Leaning to the left, he glanced around the massive mountain of fur blocking his view. About twenty feet ahead of the group, Tahnja and Brutus had dismounted from their Pegasi and were now huddled close together behind a rather bushy patch of red foliage. Hovering just over the pink woman's right shoulder was little Roustaf. Off in the distance, too far for Donald to see in any real detail, the forest opened up to an expansive grassy field. Near the center of the field was an enormous, frighteningly black hole dug into the earth. Extending for miles in every direction it eventually disappeared, transforming into something blurry and vague before folding into the horizon. One after another, massive beasts resembling long-necked dinosaurs larger than even the tallest of Fillagrou trees appeared from the blackness of the pit. One by one, the gargantuan creatures lifted themselves onto land with legs as thick as buildings and toe nails the size of trucks. So massive were the monsters that thirty or forty Ochan soldiers were able to stand easily on their gargantuan backs, with room still for twenty more. Now standing upright, the massive head attached to the end of a neck longer than three football fields, one of the monsters eclipsed one of the three Fillagrou's suns. Shaking its enormous dome from side-to-side, the great beast let out a roar that shook the ground underneath Donald and his Pegasus, nearly tossing the boy to the soil. The train of monsters emerging from the pit seemed endless. Donald watched as five emerged from the abyss, with still more on the way.

Eyes wide, the boy muttered through tight lips, "What the hell is going on?"

"They're Girafadons," Teek answered back, his gruff voice now just a whisper as he stared angrily at the grand spectacle before him with an ever-growing sense of fear. Unfortunately for Teek, this was not the first time he'd laid eyes on such a sight.

Cautiously, Tahnja, Brutus and Roustaf made their way back to the group, staying low enough to keep themselves from being spotted. Roustaf's tiny face wore an expression of complete and utter defeat, of hopelessness and loss. Reaching up, the little man pressed his fingers against his eyes with a significant amount of pressure, praying it might relieve the bit of the tension built up behind.

"Well, looks like we're gonna have to wait awhile before we get anywhere near the doorway," he added with a heavy sigh before coming to a hovering stop near the center of the group.

"Wait a minute," Donald peeked up from behind Teek, "are you telling me that hole all those dinosaurs are coming out of, that's the doorway to Ocha?"

"Yep, that's exactly what it is, slick."

"How the hell are we supposed to get into it with the cast of Jurassic Park coming out?"

Roustaf's head drooped, his shoulders slumping. His mind wandered momentarily to Walcott and Pleebo, suddenly doubting if they were even alive. He'd failed his friends. How foolish it was of him to think he could rescue them in the first place: how very, very foolish.

Absent-mindedly playing with the straps of his overalls, Roustaf glanced at Donald with a pair of somber, defeated eyes. "We aren't."

Donald's body froze. His rear end was sore and his stomach had tied itself into a hundred achy knots. He was dirty and grimy and hungry and smelled like the rear end of a billy goat with a bad case of diarrhea. As if all this wasn't enough, according to Roustaf, he, along with the rest of his group of would be rescuers, were apparently out of options.

Letting his suspenders flop against his chest with a heavy thwack, Roustaf looked at the boy again. "That's not even the worst of it, kid."

Slowly his tiny eyes moved from one member of the group to the next, each among them replicating his downtrodden expression on their own faces.

"What?" Donald asked, a bit annoyed that everyone but him seemed to know what the little man with the transparent wings was implying. "What? What is it?"

"Girafadons are diggers, kid, and there are an awful lot of them coming outta that hole from Ocha," Roustaf continued. "Those damn lizards would only get this many diggers together for one reason. They've located another doorway."

Donald's heart dropped from his chest and into his suddenly weak knees. Rolling from the leg of his pants, it tumbled to the ground.

"As far as we know, there was only one doorway they hadn't yet found, kiddo: yours."

41. SINS OF THE FATHER

Walking beside each other the entire time, their clothes drying significantly slower than either would have liked, Chris and Owen followed close behind Zanell and across the red forest. Eventually the threesome dropped into a camouflaged hatch in the ground and proceeded through a series of dark tunnels, at last arriving at the stone doorway leading into New Tipoloo. Chris spent the majority of the journey attempting to wrangle information from the strange, bony white creature leading the way. Her answers, however, were often vague and contradictory, leaving him more confused than he was prior to asking them.

Owen Little spent the trek staring at his feet, shaking his head and mumbling to himself, "I never should have come. I shouldn't be here. Never should have come, shouldn't be here, so stupid. Dad's going to kill me."

At one point, Chris awkwardly reached over and patted the boy on the shoulder. The gesture did very little to quell Owen's rapidly expanding disappointment in himself and his choices.

From the moment they entered the dimly lit underground city of New Tipoloo, Owen and Chris were greeted by a mass of jubilant creatures in every size, shape and color. For at least the fifteenth time since climbing from the puddle and into this bizarre world, Chris pinched the skin on his arm, half believing that he was dreaming. Once again, the pinch did nothing; he did not wake up. If, in fact, this was a dream, he was stuck in it.

Like a living, breathing sea of multi-colored flesh, the enormous group of creatures surrounded Owen lifted the boy into the air and began cheering so loudly that the noise of the many quickly drowned out the voices of the few. Simultaneously, a second group surrounded Chris, attempting to hoist him into the air as well.

"No! Wait a second! No!" Chris yelled above the roar of the crowd, his body suddenly airborne while gesturing with his arms that he would have preferred to remain with his feet firmly planted in the dirt.

"Leave this one for a moment! He and I have much to discuss!" Zanell bellowed above the excited voices while stepping between Chris and the city's citizens, convincing them to lower him.

His heart racing, Chris found himself unable to focus on just one thing. Dancing around him were creatures so bizarre they should have existed only in storybooks, movies, or the overactive imaginations of teenagers who play entirely too many video games. This simply couldn't be real. It just couldn't. It was impossible.

A seven-foot tall creature covered in orange and black feathers with a beak the shape of a football bumped stiffly into his side. Quickly, the massive bird-man snatched Chris' right hand with a pair of bony fingers stretching out from underneath one of its wings. "Welcome, my friend, welcome! The name is Alouicious, and I would just like to say what an absolute honor it is to meet the father of two of the five! Undoubtedly, this ranks as one of the highlights of my life, good sir! An honor, an absolute honor!" Its breath smelled like garbage, like an apple pie topped with cottage cheese and pickles. The sour odor causing his eyes to water, Chris recoiled a smidge and covered his nose with his hand.

Quickly replacing the winged hand of Alouicious with her own, Zanell began pulling Chris through the crowd and further down the street.

"An honor, I say! An honor like no other! I'd love to invite you to dinner, sir! We'll speak later and hash out the details!" The bird-man yelled from behind while waving his feathered wing happily.

Carefully maneuvering their way through cracks between the tightly packed bodies, the pair eventually ducked into the awkwardly shaped doorway of Zanell's dwelling. The light was dimmer here than in the street, and Chris' eyes required a moment to adjust. In the corner of the room, sitting on top of a sturdy looking, yet delicately crafted table looted from Prince Valkea's castle, was a candle with a single, hauntingly beautiful bluish colored flame.

Unable to avert his eyes from its unusual flicker, Chris muttered in a monotone voice, "It's blue. Why? How it is blue?"

It was a stupid question. Of all the questions he had concerning everything that had happened and everything he'd seen, it was the most obvious and simple he could possibly ask. With his brain going in so many directions, he was having trouble focusing, and unfortunately it was the first thought that popped from his mouth.

On the opposite end of the extremely tiny room, Zanell smiled, chuckling softly under her breath.

"It's blue because it's not a flame, Christopher; it's magic," She answered politely.

Lifting a second candle from a nearby dresser, Zanell ran her long, bony fingers over the wick at a medium pace. Instantly, another blue flame appeared from thin air.

Wearing a grin as wide as the entirety of her long face, Zanell looked again in Chris' direction. "Pretty amazing, no? It took me an annoyingly long time to figure out how to do that. You see, the powers I have weren't always mine. Not too long ago, they belonged to my grandfather, the same as they did to his grandfather before him. You know what is so frustratingly strange about knowing everything there is to know, something that no one else seems to understand? Knowing everything isn't the same as understanding everything. In fact, it's not even close. They're like night and day, like the ocean and the land, like this world and the universe in which it resides."

There she went again with the mysterious, confusing statements. Chris was getting tired of mysterious and confusing.

Reaching up, he applied some pressure to his temples. His head was hurting, his breathing irregular, and everything around him was getting wobbly, teetering on dizziness. He needed to sit down.

"Feel free to sit anywhere you desire, Christopher," Zanell offered softly, pointing toward an elaborately decorated chair also taken from Valkea's castle a few feet to the man's left as an option.

After dropping into the cushioned seat with a heavy plop, Chris' shoulders drooped as he inhaled deeply, trying to wrangle control of a breathing pattern as confused as his brain.

Taking a seat on the bed opposite him, Zanell's smile slowly faded, changing into something more closely resembling concern. In her head, she had seen Chris Jarvis a hundred times, maybe a thousand. She'd observed him during his highest of highs and, of course, his lowest of lows. She'd seen him do awful things, things even he barely remembered and things he no doubt wished he could forget. Looking at him now though, watching him struggling to gain control over his emotions from only a few feet away, the experience was proving remarkably more palpable and real and frightening than she imagined it would be.

Her voice turned flat and stern. "I won't ask you why you did it, because I know you don't have an answer — at least not one that makes any sense."

Chris' breathing halted, his jaw locking tight. Her words hit him in the chest like a baseball bat threatening to destroy what remained of the bandaged, partially healed heart hidden behind. There was no way she could know. There was no way she could possibly know, and yet he understood without an ounce of hesitation that she did. Even if he wanted to lift his head and look her in the eyes, he knew he couldn't.

"Christopher...long ago my world became the epicenter of a war that continues to this day. I like to think that I know a little something about your people, and I am fully aware of the fact that you are a race well versed in the concepts of war. Still, I guarantee you, this is bigger than anything even you can imagine. This is genocide, genocide on a scale that puts all possible meanings of the word to shame. I have seen the face of each and every life extinguished by this atrocity, and counting them would be impossible."

Standing, Zanell sighed deeply. "Your children—your children are very special, Christopher."

Hesitantly, Chris lifted his head to look in her direction, his expression shameful and lost. This was the look of a man who had reached the absolute bottom. This was the look of a man who could sink no further. The faint light of the dual blue candles in the room flickered off of Zanell's massive red pupils, turning them a color more akin to a smoky purple. The taut, tightly stretched skin on her face seemed so very fragile, like dried and crumbled paper, capable of transforming to dust with even the most gentle of touches. Her expression was somber, sad and remorseful, neither forgiving nor understanding, yet exactly the opposite all at once.

A few feet away from him, Zanell stopped; dropping to one knee, she put herself within inches of his face. "Your children—they can change all of this. They can erase all of this nonsense and make the wrong things right. They cannot, however, do it alone. They will need your help, Christopher. To you, time is linear, moving in a single, definable direction and never coming back around. To you, the past is the past, what's done is done, and can't be changed."

210

Reaching forward, she placed her hand gently on Chris' shoulder, her fingers so long that they extended halfway down his back. "I know better than that. Though I've only recently picked up the blue flame thing, I understand all too well that it's never too late to start again."

42. OF RAPSCALLIONS AND PIRATE CAPTAINS

The group consisting of Nicky, Staci, Tommy, Krystoph, Nestor and the Tycarian soldiers quickly made the transition from the small island to the deck of the Briar Patch, utilizing one of the long piers built into the shore by the Ochans. For a moment, Staci hesitated before stepping onto the ship, not only because she was terrified by the idea of being on the ocean, alone and surrounded by water, but also because the ship itself honestly didn't look seaworthy. Up close, it seemed even older and more poorly made than it had from a distance. The massive wooden planks making up the deck were warped, twisting and bending in ways wood shouldn't be capable of twisting or bending. The nails holding them together had long since rusted through, chips of crumpled steel scattered about like dandruff. Every inch of the huge, rickety structure was creaking and grinding, its joints worn to the nub like the bones of an old man suffering from severe arthritis. Looking up,

Staci stared at the odd design etched onto the worn blue fabric of one of the sails. At first glance, it seemed to be a very normal, very predictable skull and crossbones. The only difference was a pair of boney rabbit ears protruding from the top. Glancing to her left, she noticed that Nicky was staring strangely at the design as well. Turning toward her, the boy shrugged his shoulders, equally confused as she. The various creatures roaming the deck and tending to ropes, chains and various tattered tarps looked nearly as grimy, old and filthy as the ship itself. Their clothes were ripped and torn, seeming like they hadn't been washed in years and smelling much the same. A scruffy faced, four-foot tall pudgy gray thing, covered in roll-after-roll of excess skin, approached the children, sniffing the air in their general area with a moist black nose. Reaching up, he lifted a dangling flap of skin from over his eyes and smiled wide in Staci's direction. His mouth contained a total of three, maybe four, yellow tinted teeth just barely holding onto the binds keeping them tied to his gums. She could only assume that the rest had fallen out years ago due to some sort of decay.

Dropping the skin flap back over his eyes, he gave her an awkward salute. "Welcome to the Briar Patch, m'lady." His voice was like gravel and smelled like a garbage bag full of dirty diapers. Staci returned the smile awkwardly, slowly backing away until she bumped into Tommy's chest and could go no further.

At that exact moment, the door to an outhouse-sized box rising from the center of the deck swung suddenly open, and a plume of accumulated gray dust took to the air in the aftermath. "Get a move on, ya useless scallywags! If we aren't back to sea in five minutes, I'll start tossing yer filthy hides overboard one atta time!"

From the darkened doorway stepped what seemed, at first glance, to be a three-foot tall bunny rabbit. His fur was gray and crusty, matted together in thick clumps that were in desperate need of a thorough combing. His whiskers were bent at strange, almost painful looking angles. Like every other creature on the ship, his clothes were a disgusting, dirty-stained mess of mismatched fabrics scavenged and pieced together without rhyme or reason. On his head he wore a comically oversized pirate hat with two holes cut into it that allowed his equally filthy ears to poke through.

Near the bow of the ship, the scruffy bunny took note of the fact that one of the deckhands seemed a bit lost. Covered in dark brown fur, the creature was walking back and forth aimlessly, unsure of where he should be and what he should be doing. Rearing back, the rabbit captain tossed the empty bottle in his left paw at the confused deckhand's head, connecting with a deep echoing clank. "Get a move on, ya lousy rapscallion, or I promise you'll be swimmin' wit' the sea dragons quicker than you can say 'Please, oh please, don't make me swim wit' the sea dragons, Cap'n!'"

Afterward, the captain scanned the remainder of his ship, seeming eternally upset and occasionally grunting in dissatisfaction. Shaking his head, he turned his attention to his ship's newest passengers. His small round eyes came to an immediate stop on Krystoph, and it was there they lingered while he drank in every single solitary inch of the massive, stone-faced Ochan. For years he'd avoided Ochans whenever possible. For years he'd seen them as enemies and nothing more. To see one standing on the deck of his ship felt odd, just plain wrong.

Moving on, the captain glanced briefly at the children, his expression one of mild disgust coupled with a fair amount of confusion. It was when his eyes at last settled on Nestor that his appearance changed dramatically, and a wide smile instantly stretched out from under his puffy, fur-covered cheeks.

"Nestor Rockshell, ya ol' bottomfeeder! It's good to see ya again!" Anxiously closing the distance between the two, the captain smacked Nestor on the back of his shell playfully. "Sorry 'bout makin' ya sweat a bit, but these days ya can't sail more than an hour without running into one of those damn scalefaces! The seas are infested with 'em, I tell ya . . .infested!"

Nestor smiled back in the half-smile, half-growl sort of way he often did. "It is of no worry, old friend. Most important is that you arrived in one piece."

"Course I did, course I did. I'da never let ya down, pally! I still owe ya and the Fightin' Fifth for savin' my puffy gray keyster in Scarburough two years ago. Always do right by yer friends, I say; it's the pirate way."

With a long drawn out creak followed by a series of smaller clanks, grinds and thumps, the Briar Patch began to slowly pull away from the pier, swaying gently back and forth momentarily as it prepared to move to open sea. Losing her balance, Staci stumbled forward. Wrapping his arms around her, Tommy saved her once again from falling flat on her face.

He was making a habit of this.

The dirty bunny captain leaned in close to Nestor and whispered with a sigh, "Argh, that one's not whatcha might consider sea worthy, is she?"

Before Nestor could respond, the voice of Krystoph tore its way into the conversation. "Set your bearing north. Do not deviate from the heading."

The former Ochan general had grown weary of idle conversation and tired of pointless small talk. His focus remained on recovering the Rongstag, and the incredible distance they had yet to travel before reaching it. Everything else was a waste of time. Everything else was meaningless.

An instant scowl appeared on the face of the Briar Patch's captain. "Don't ya be thinkin' that ya got a right to tell me which direction my ship sails, ya limey green-skinned cancer." From his side he pulled a dagger about five inches long before using the dangerous looking tip to lift the brim of his hat from his marble-sized eyes. "If it weren't for ol' Nestor here, one the likes of you wouldn't be allowed to set foot on me ship. I'da slit yer throat the moment I caught a glimpse of yer green hide."

In direct response to the little captain's comment, Krystoph slowly removed one of his many blades from its sheath as well. Cold, black and dangerous, his eyes settled directly on the somewhat diminutive form of the dusty rabbit. Briefly his upper lip quivered, exposing the jagged teeth underneath. The hands of both creatures tightened the grip on their respective weapons, preparing themselves for what now seemed inevitable.

Sensing the situation was a moment away from getting out of hand, Nestor stepped between the snarling, posturing pair. "Enough of this nonsense; it solves nothing. We share the same goal and fighting amongst ourselves succeeds only in making the attainment of it less likely."

Both Krystoph and the captain reluctantly returned their weapons to their holsters. Not before shooting each other glances so sharply telling they could cut glass, of course.

Angrily Krystoph moved away from the group. Mumbling under his breath, he headed to the side of the ship, opting to calm his fiery temper by gazing over the endlessness of the water world known as Aquari. It had been so long since he was there. As a general rule, the Ochan race had never much cared for the ocean; in fact, most of them hated it with a passion. This was partly the reason Krystoph opted to hide the Rongstag beneath the tumultuous Aquari waves in the first place. Though Krystoph couldn't honestly say that he was "fond" of this world, he did not hate it either. There was cleanliness about it, a simplicity that he found not entirely unappealing. For a moment he allowed the salty-cool odor of the ocean fill his head, wipe his brain clean and remind him of why he was here, of why he made the decision to allow these useless creatures to join him in his cause in the first place. Partially frozen images of his wife and his family flashed like bizarre solar flares behind his eyes. He would never forget their faces. For as long as he breathed, he would never forget their faces. Nor did he harbor any desire to.

Having calmed himself somewhat, the raggedy rabbit captain turned again to face the children. Momentarily frozen in place, none had moved. Taking two steps forward, the scruffy captain came within inches of Tommy's face, sniffing at the air around the boy, then grimacing as if the child smelled awful.

"I ain't much for prophecies," The furry little creature stated plainly, poking Tommy's chest with a single stubby finger on his fat padded paw. "It all seems like a load of gobbeldy-gook if'n yer askin' me. I've learned over the years that ya can only believe what ya can see, and I ain't seein' much from you at the moment, mate."

Tommy chose not to respond, mostly because he couldn't think of a single thing to say.

"I owe that mound of shelled goop over there my life, though," the captain continued, now pointing toward Nestor. "For that reason alone, I'm willin' to take ya where it is yer headin'." Shaking his head again, he began moving away from the children and up a set of stairs to a slightly more elevated section of the ship.

Crossing his arms, he turned again to survey the entire group. "In case I didn't mention it, the name's Captain Jacques Fluuffytail. It'd be in yer best interest to keep in mind that it's pronounced Floo-fee-tall and *not* fluffy-tail. See that you get it right, cause friendship or not, you flub me name and I'll toss yer caboose right over the side! Welcome to the Briar Patch, kiddies. She's a dirty ol' bird, 'n she's got a wild temper, but she'll get ya where ya wanna go in one piece, if'n lady luck sees fit to shine a little bit of her goodness on us, of course. We got a long journey ahead of us, so I suggest ya settle in!"

Behind Staci another tattered dark blue sail dropped from high above, instantly catching the wind and ballooning. Caught off guard by the noise, her heart did a double-take and her body jumped slightly. Over the side of the creaky ship, thick waves smashed against the wood angrily. Cascades of water sprayed onto the deck in haphazard intervals, pooling under the soles of her shoes, instantly making her feel queasy and tying her mostly empty stomach into knots. Behind her, the beach seemed far away, getting further by the second. Ahead there lay only the ocean and its bizarre, untold dangers. To her left, she watched as the reddish colored sun began its long descent into night. It would be dark soon. From here on out, there would be only darkness and waves and the unknown.

More than ever, she wished she could go home.

43. HOLLOW SHELL

His wife was an exquisite creature. Sensual, defined, yet effortless, she had been gifted with features the vast majority of Ochan females would quite literally kill for. Stepping through the front door of the modest dwelling he called home, located within the safety of his king's castle, he was immediately greeted by her sly smile. Her sturdy form melted into his arms, resulting in a familiar oneness that felt comfortable, safe and warm. He had been away too long and he had missed this. While no doubt rewarding in ways that could not be matched, leading a war on so many fronts had proven superbly taxing, requiring him to dig deeper into the reserves of his strength than he had ever dug before. The fortitude of his enemies had surprised him. The Tycarians in particular fought with intelligence and fever neither he nor the king anticipated. The Tycarian leader was blessed with a warrior's spirit, crafty and flexible; when shoved, he often shoved back. Eventually though, he would misstep, as they all did. This Tycarian would succumb to the might of the Ochan race the same as the rest.

Gently, his wife touched her lips to his. The feeling was electric, instantly doing away with thoughts of bothersome Tycarian kings and wars that had not gone exactly as planned. Wrapping her arms around him, she unlatched his breastplate, lifting the weighty armor from his shoulders and allowing his tense muscles to at last relax. The familiar chill of her flesh was intoxicating, drawing him closer still as she wrapped herself again in his arms. This was the moment he longed for, the moment he dreamt of so often while wading in the throes of conquest. Were it physically possible, he would have bottled this exact instant, corked it and carried it around his neck, saving it for those instances when he needed it most.

This moment was beautiful and right and perfect; it was also, unfortunately, no longer real.

Now little more than a memory, the moment was fading, as all memories do. The reality of what was now and what was real collapsed inward, unceremoniously swallowing all things good and beautiful and simple. When the hungry beast at last had its fill, what remained was dark and frightening and confused. Engulfed in a smoky haze of agony, his body racked with such pain that pain had become the norm, his limp form was dragged miles below the surface of Ocha. Here his throat was slit and he was left to rot within the sweltering heat of the fire caves. This was the punishment for failing to satisfy the every desire of his king; this was the punishment for a lifetime of unwavering service. His wife was gone, as was his family, their tattered and torn bodies left on display in the king's courtyard, turned from living things into trophies and warning signs. What remained of his body now teetered on the edge of a massive chasm extending to the center of Ocha. At the bottom, there was only fire, fire and a heat so ungodly it could easily reduce his body to little more than ashes in a fraction of a second. Already the incredible heat from below had begun to sear his bruised and battered exterior, slowly cooking and charring his dark green skin a dirty, grayish brown. From a crack in the rock underneath him came a trail of combustion beetles. No bigger than a single fingernail, the hungry creatures could sense his presence from miles away. It had been months since they'd dined on tender, delicious Ochan flesh. Forced to live off much smaller, far less satisfying creatures, they were hungry and anxious to gorge themselves. Numbering in the thousands, the tiny coal black insects with their oversized jaws began pouring from various cracks in the stone cavern around him, their nimble legs hungrily propelling them forward. Though he could sense their presence, he was unable to move from their path or defend himself in any way. Too many beatings had been suffered, too many bones left broken and useless, too much blood lost to the sand underneath. He was helpless. He was worthless. He was food. Like a living black blanket, all at once the beetles converged on his fallen form, digging their way hungrily into his open sores, tearing at his flesh and peeling it from his body, eating him alive. Like the world in which they resided, the beetles were capable of producing small yet dangerous flames from an appendage attached to their heads. Much in the way one might utilize a blowtorch, the tiny creatures used this incredible burst of interior fire to slice into his flesh, opening wounds further and making it easier for them to crawl inside.

Defeated and hopeless, he chose simply to allow the scavengers their meal.

He was a failure. He had failed his wife, his family, and his king. Let these filthy things feast on what remained. Let them hollow him out. Let them transform him into the empty shell he had become. After all, this was exactly what he deserved. Closing his swollen eyes, he gritted his teeth, bearing the pain of their hungry, dirty business as best he could. The beetles would ensure his end came painfully and would not come quickly, exactly as it should be.

However, as suddenly as the feast began, it stopped. The blanket of combustion beetles retreated from his body, regurgitating that which they had partially digested and covering him in a layer of his own sticky, half-eaten flesh. Confused, he opened his weary eyes once more. The creatures had now formed an unmoving circle around him, their black, soulless eyes staring blankly into his.

"Finish me," He muttered to the collective, confused and annoyed with their curious inaction.

The two thousand or so beetles remained steady, their bodies covering the rock around him completely and transforming it from a dusty red to a shiny black.

"Damn you, finish me!" He growled again, blood seeping from his mouth and neck before pooling in the dirt beneath.

Again there was no response. Not a single beetle moved, the partially lit torches atop their tiny heads flickering among the super-heated shadows of cave.

"Finish me!" He roared as loudly as his sore, useless throat could manage.

His arm was broken in several places, the bones in his fingers shattered to dust, yet still he managed to raise his fist in anger and swat at the pathetic creatures. Moving as one, the combustion beetles stepped backward, dodging the blow with ease. Having wasted what remaining energy he had at his disposal, he lowered his head into the bloody dirt, mumbling in frustration with a mouth full of sticky-wet sand. Still the beetles stared, as if they were judging him, though he knew such a thing was impossible. Why did they continue to watch and refuse to end his suffering? Why were they doing this to him? All at once the beetles turned, slowly retreating to their homes inside the cave rock. Only a single one among them remained behind, its attention never waning. Despite the very real possibility of a broken spine, he lifted his head to look at the pathetic thing. The insect's inaction made no sense. Combustion beetles were hungry, mindless scavengers existing only to reproduce and eat. Why then had they chosen to ignore him? Was he too pathetic, too worthless and undesirable for even the lowest of the low? Had he fallen so far?

Without warning, he was suddenly again in his home, with his wife by his side and his children in the next room. Though he knew the image was fleeting, an illusion, he tried to hold onto it as long as he could, attempting to capture this moment, superheat it and brand it with an iron onto his brain where he could keep it forever. He would not succeed. A sudden flare of the flames boiling from the center of Ocha below dragged him to reality once more. Again it was gone. Again he was alone with the single, frustrating beetle; again he growled in its direction through a mouth coated in blood.

He had bled for his king more times than he dared count, pledged his life and soul to Kragamel in the name of his people, in the name of Ocha. For his hardship and suffering he had received nothing. For his pain he received exactly that. The king was a liar. The king had stolen his family, his country and his life. The king was a liar and a thief. Suddenly he understood why the beetles had chosen not to devour him. Suddenly, it seemed so obvious why a single one of the soulless, eating machines continued to watch him from the sand. He had become one of them. He had become one of them and there was no going back.

He had become one of them, and he, too, was hungry.

44. STORM ON THE HORIZON

Standing atop a wooden crate, Nicky leaned his head over the edge of the ship to better watch the waves crash violently against the side. Feeling a chill, he pulled the hood of his sweater over his head and tied the strings just below his chin. In the distance the sun had nearly set, the blue sky transformed into a series of lavish deep purples and brick reds. Never having been on a boat, let alone at sea, the boy was surprised at how remarkably quiet the ocean was. For as far as he could see in every direction there was nothing but water. As went the gentle sway of the waves below, the ship and he went. Behind him a few of the Briar Patch's more gnarly looking crew members mumbled to each other in a slightly incoherent gibberish while occasionally chugging back on an unmarked bottle full of a liquid that looked an awful lot like urine. The bubbly substance was causing them to burp sporadically, flinging particles of food and frothy golden bubbles from between their lips and onto their filthy clothes. Almost directly above him, the tattered sail flapped tightly as it caught the breeze. Leaning further over the edge of the ship, Nicky tried to gaze through the now nearly black water for signs of life, but saw none.

"Be careful, child. These waters are quite capable of swallowing you whole when you least expect it." The voice was familiar and quite welcome.

Looking up from the edge, Nicky glanced behind him just in time to see Nestor step alongside. The orange glow of descending sun cast deep shadows across the cavernous wrinkles and scars of his dark green face. Like an awning, his brow hung at least two inches over his eyes, which seemed both weary and intensely battle ready at the same time.

Breathing deeply, Nestor scanned the sea much the same as the boy to his left. It had been so long since he'd seen these waters. Quite at home in the ocean, there was a point during the war when his people considered retreating to the oceans of Aquari to escape the Ochan invasion. After further examination, however, the waters proved too dangerous. The Tycarians had spent entirely too many generations on land as well. Returning to the ocean after so many years away—a lifetime for most—would have proven disastrous.

Still, he could not deny the majesty and simplicity of this place. "There are legends claiming an entire race of creatures reside at the bottom of these waters. When I say creatures, I am not simply speaking of sea dragons and fluker fish, mind you, but of beings with great intelligence, beings capable of making choices—choices such as remaining neutral in the war raging above despite the fact that so many die."

Reaching up, Nestor ran his paw along the curve of his hairless head. His fingers lingered for a moment, absentmindedly tracing the length of a scar he received many years ago in battle. The Ochan who had cut him very nearly ended his life that day. In the end though, only one of the two remained standing; only one lived to fight again.

Choosing to instead focus on the here and the now, Nestor turned his attention from the water to the child at his side. "Ultimately, I believe submerging oneself in mere legend serves no purpose; better to exist in the reality of the moment. How are you faring, lad?"

"Alright, I guess," Nicky mumbled in response.

"Your feet—do they remain sore?"

"No, they're better."

"Very good, child, very good indeed. Your recovery was short. You heal with a warrior's spirit. For this you should be commended."

The absurdity of the statement caused Nicky to giggle for a moment. Behind him, two of the Briar Patch's deckhands burped simultaneously, turning his giggle into a full on laugh. It felt good to laugh again; laughter helped him forget, if only for a moment. Raising his hand to his face, he attempted to reign in the chuckles before they got too out of hand. Turning to the always proper, businesslike Nestor, he was about to apologize for the outburst when he noticed that the massive turtle man was smiling as well. Though Nicky hadn't known Nestor long, he had been around him long enough to understand all too well that he rarely smiled. Nicky appreciated the gesture.

Near the rear of the ship, Staci sat shivering atop a series of dusty crates holding rope as thick as her arm and as heavy as her body. Quietly she wished to herself that she'd been given the time to pack a sweater like Tommy's little brother. The sea breeze was remarkably cold, like a blustery fall back home, though carrying with it an odd humidity that left her skin moist, salty and shimmering. Pulling her knees to her chest, she sunk her head between her arms, trying desperately to capture some much-needed warmth.

From behind her came the familiar voice of Tommy Jarvis. "Hey, I have an extra sweater if you want it."

Looking up, she spotted the blond haired boy behind her holding a large hooded sweatshirt with a worn and dirty version of their school logo displayed on the back. Instantly she forgot about the cold; instantly she smiled.

Her cheeks flushing red, she reached up and took the piece of clothing from his hand. "Thanks. Are you sure you don't need it?"

"Nah, I'll be fine." Tommy responded, plopping himself onto the crate next to her.

Despite his bravado, in truth the cold was already beginning to bother him — even though he'd never let her know it.

Immediately after lifting the shirt over her head, Staci could feel the difference. The sweater was much too big for her, falling almost to her knees and encasing her in extra warmth. Reaching over, Tommy lifted the hood over her head as the pair exchanged a subtle, warm smile.

After a moment of only slightly awkward shared silence, Staci was the first to speak. "How do you think Donald and Roustaf are doing?"

"I don't know," Tommy responded, pausing momentarily to reminisce about Pleebo and Walcott, wondering once again if maybe he should have been looking for them rather than searching the ocean for some useless amulet. "I'm sure they're fine."

In his heart, he knew this was more than likely not the case. He was simply giving Staci what he believed she wanted to hear, even if she didn't necessarily think it true herself. Again there was a pause; again there was only the crashing of the waves. Somewhere behind him Tommy heard his little brother laugh, which in turn made him smile. Slipping her hand from underneath the sleeve of the oversized sweater, Staci let her fingers rest gently atop his. Though hesitant at first, eventually the digits of the children's hands intertwined and locked together tightly.

"I'm glad you came to get me," Staci whispered, her eyes glued to the light dancing on the waves in the distance.

"Yeah, well, that makes one of us," Tommy responded with a sigh. "I shouldn't have let Roustaf drag you into this, you or my brother. You aren't safe here. Heck, I don't even know what I was thinking when I agreed to come along. The only one of us with any brains is Owen."

"Well, he does get much better grades than you," Staci joked, trying her best to make the boy feel better. "Then again, so does pretty much everyone."

Tommy laughed subtly for a moment; his forlorn expression, however, never wavered.

"We'll be okay," Staci added as she turned toward him, her face wrapped snugly in the hooded sweatshirt, her ponytail causing it to bulge awkwardly in the rear like a pup tent.

Tommy, however, couldn't bring himself to return her glance. For some time now he had felt lost, tied in a knot he couldn't seem to work free no matter how hard he tried. It felt like so long since he'd had a real, deep, lasting rest, the kind of rest where you forget everything and everyone, maybe even yourself. For so long now, a wad of grayish brown festering guilt, anger, and shame had hung over him like a dark cloud torrentially raining atop his head.

When he at last chose to speak, his voice was barely a whisper, a remnant of something that once was and might never be again. "I hope so."

Sensing the faraway hopelessness in his voice, Staci was strangely overcome with a surge of confidence. She felt the need to say something she'd wanted to say to Tommy for a very long time, something she just couldn't keep locked inside any longer. Breathing in deeply, she tried to steady her emotions, her heart speeding and forehead perspiring.

"Tommy," She whispered, staring longingly at his profile, the orange setting sun behind blackening his boyish features, "Tommy, there's something I need to tell you; something—I don't know, something I wanted to tell you when we got back home. You were never around, though, and the time never felt quite right. I dunno, I just . . .there's something I need you to know . . ."

Though neither child was aware of it, as Staci struggled to make sense of the overflowing of emotions building inside, her chest began to glow. An odd warmness she hadn't felt since she brought Tommy back to life in Prince Valkea's castle moved briskly from her upper torso into her shoulder, down her arm, into her hand and toward the tips of her fingers. Moments later, a softball sized sphere of pure light had begun to form around their connected digits. Having engulfed their hands entirely, it abruptly halted its expansion and settled into a gentle, mid-air hover. The soft, white reflection rising up between them eventually managed to garner their attention, and both children looked down in unison.

"Tommy, I . . .think maybe I . . ." Stopping mid-sentence, Staci was caught off guard by the strange light, leaping to her feet while attempting to pull her hand free from his.

"No, wait," Tommy muttered, gripping her fingers tighter in order to maintain their connection as he rose to his feet as well.

Standing parallel to each other, Tommy lifted their glowing hands between them, staring with wide-eyed fascination at the ball of energy. Her pulse slowing, Staci too became entranced by the otherworldly display. Using his free hand, Tommy poked cautiously at the humming ball with the tip of his index finger. Like liquid lightning, the sphere sparked for an instant. When he pulled his finger back, the strange glow stuck to him like sticky-stretchy gum, pulling back with his finger before at last losing its grip on his flesh and bouncing into the wobbling orb once more.

"It's . . .amazing," Staci muttered through a wide smile, her face lit brightly in the hypnotic glow.

She was not, however, staring at the ball of light; she was staring at Tommy.

Less than twenty feet away, standing among a growing crowd, Krystoph watched the pair of them with a mixture of amazement and fear. For the first time since meeting these children of the prophecy, he was witnessing firsthand that there might be a sliver of truth to the stories of their power. Seeing the bizarre light show between them, his mind wandered back to Prince Valkea's castle, to the endless Ochan corpses littering the soil for miles in every direction. Though he tried denying it even to himself, for the first time since encountering these creatures, he was overcome with a subtle, barely there twinge of fear. While this may not sound like much, it was more fear than the Ochan had felt since he was a child. The earsplitting hum created by blowing into one end of an Aquari Concota shell, however, pulled his attentions away from the children and instantly back to reality.

Stationed in a lookout box high above the ship, one of the Brian Patch's crew bellowed at the top of his lungs to those below, "We've got company, Cap'n!"

Following his extended finger toward the ocean, the entire crew gazed out across the dark water in unison. The hands of Tommy and Staci at last came apart, the glow from her chest quickly evaporating into nothingness. Off in the distance, barely visible though the rapidly darkening sky, was another ship. Constructed of wood as black as the absolute blackest of ash, it looked sturdy, well-built, and dangerous. Despite being still so far away, the ship seemed quite massive as well. Like a great, snarling black beast, the enormous boat cut across the waters with ease on a direct course for the Brian Patch. Scurrying from his quarters below as fast as his furry legs and oversized feet would take him, Captain Fluuffytail ran to the side of his ship and hopped alongside Nicky on a set of crates near the edge. Immediately his brow lowered, his little gray nose twitching sporadically as if he had an itch.

Through the two massive buckteeth just underneath his furry lips, he growled only two words: "Battle stations!"

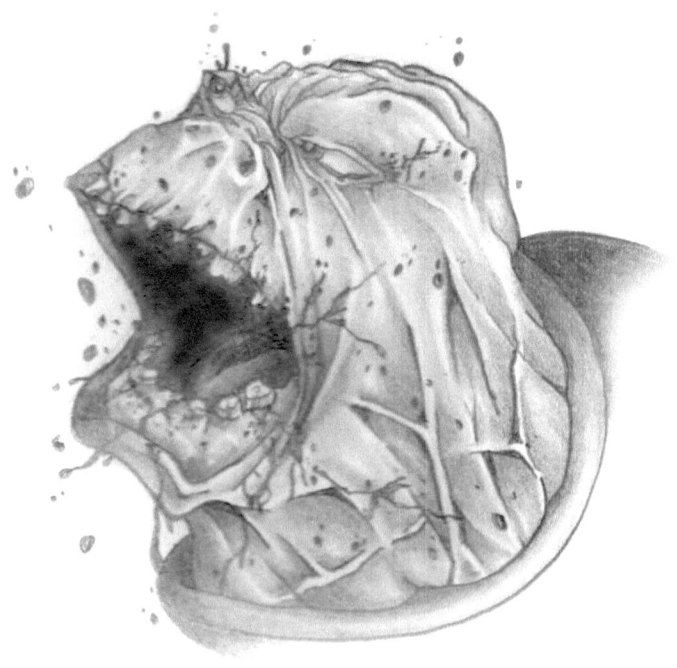

45. THE TYCARIAN SPIRIT

It had been some time since Walcott watched from behind weary, heavy eyelids as Pleebo was dragged back to his cell and chained into position on the wall again. Since that moment, the lanky Fillagrou had not moved; since that moment, there had been only silence and black. Was it not for the subtle rising and falling of Pleebo's chest, coupled with the fact that the Ochans bothered to drag him to the dungeon in the first place, Walcott might have believed his friend dead. The beatings Walcott had become so very accustomed to stopped coming at their regular intervals. In fact, he hadn't seen the scaly, dark green face of a single Ochan in hours. The fact that neither he nor Pleebo were dead, or getting interrogated anymore, led him to only one conclusion: they had finally gotten the information they were seeking. Somehow, after all this time, they managed to pry it from Pleebo. He supposed it was bound to happen sooner or later. One could only withstand so much. No one could hold out forever. Pleebo lasted longer than Walcott ever imaged he would, longer than he imagined any others of his peaceful, non-violent race could have hoped. The fact that Kragamel now had what he desired, however, added some urgency to their situation. With their usefulness having run its course, the king would see no reason to keep them alive. It was somewhat surprising they'd managed to remain breathing for as long as they had. Fate had made the decision that he and Pleebo had reached the end of their journey. Like a wall miles high, constructed of the thickest unbreakable stone, it now stood erect in front of them, preventing further travels.

Walcott, however, had no interest in fate or patience for its endless whims. Having never bent to the will of any creature in his many years, he would not bend for it.

If he and Pleebo hoped to survive another day, they had to do the absolute impossible: they had to escape this dungeon. Painfully, the Tycarian king pulled his mostly broken, bent and bloody fingers into something vaguely resembling a fist. Drawing from reserves of energy he believed age had wiped away, Walcott forced the tired, injured muscles in his neck back to life. From there he coaxed those in his arms, torso and legs to do the same. They must work. They had to work; there was no longer a choice. Breathing heavily, a thick sheen of sweat pouring down his wrinkled green flesh, he gritted what remained of his teeth, tugging on the chains binding his arms to cold stone. The steel links instantly pulled tight, the sound echoing throughout the endless, stuffy dank tunnels. Planting his feet firmly against the wall behind in order to use it for leverage, the full weight of his huge body ripped tighter still on the thick steel binds slicing grotesquely into his flesh. A low gurgle from his mouth quickly morphed into something grimier, more guttural and animalistic. Utilizing the very same spirit that had given the Ochan nation so much trouble over the course of the war, Walcott jerked forward with all of his might. The muscles in his arm had been useless for some time, his shell had been cracked repeatedly and he had lost more blood than he believed resided in the whole of his body. None of this mattered, though. He needed to pull, and he must continue pulling until he was free. If he ended up tearing his limbs from his torso, so be it. He was dead already; meeting his end a few hours earlier would be of no consequence. The chains were inches thick. It would take a number of blows from the most finely constructed Tycarian weapons to cut them, and even then there would be no guarantee of success. The stone to which they were attached was old but sturdy, showing very little wear. Where stone meets steel, however, there existed weakness. There had to be a crack hidden between the joining of materials; there needed to be a crack.

The idea that the Ochans could construct a substance more resilient than the Tycarian spirit was utter madness, and it simply could not be true.

Whipping his massive body forward violently once more, Walcott let out a pained scream, then quickly muffled it in an attempt to remain as quiet as possible, despite the fact that his muscles were being torn to shreds just beneath his skin. The king of Tycaria would not fold or bend. It is the steel and the stone that would crumble, this he promised himself. Again he whipped his arms forward and again the chains rattled, garnering the attention of the other malnourished, barely awake unfortunate souls hidden within the darkness of Kragamel's dungeon. His eyes closed, pulling so tightly that the color had drained from his hands, blood seeping from underneath his fingernails, and at last Walcott heard it: a crack. A piece of stone no larger than a grain of sand fell from the wall behind and to the floor below. The rock had faltered. It was a sign of its weakness. He was winning.

Beyond the dictates of logic, science and common sense, he was winning.

The rattling of chains four times the thickness of his arm woke Pleebo from a sleep that seemed to have lasted only hours, yet felt more like weeks. His head was throbbing, his skin cold and clammy. Like a frosty tattoo on the interior his eyeballs, the awful

image of the conjurers gazing down at him evilly remained
transparent and ghostly, overlaying everything in his field of vision.
Every muscle in his body felt useless and broken, as if they would
never work the same again. Remembering the moment when the
damned creatures pulled the location of the doorway to the
children's world from his brain, he lowered his head in shame as his
lanky body went limp. He'd failed them. He'd failed them all. He'd
failed them all and there was no going back. Again came the sound
of chains, this time followed by the ever so slight crack of stone and
a deep, angry, menacing grunt. Lifting his weary head, the world
still swirling as if gravity were somehow pulling downward and
emptying it into a drain, Pleebo glanced in the general direction of
the noise. The dungeon was dark, the blacks deep and unforgiving.
Barely visible among the shadows, tucked behind the bars of his
cell, was Walcott. With muscled, blood-covered arms jutting from
the sides of his enormous shell, the Tycarian thrust forward with an
enraged sort of violence Pleebo didn't believe possible in the aged
creature. Again the sound of cracking rock from somewhere behind
was swallowed whole by the monstrous shadows. Opening his eyes
wide, Walcott glanced at him through a set of animalistic, bloodshot
pupils, puddles of sweat having built up at his feet, more still
dripping off him with every passing moment.

"He's trying to pull himself free," Pleebo muttered to the air.
"That crazy old fool is seriously trying to pull himself free "

Again came the sound of cracking stone, followed by the echo
of chunks tumbling to the floor.

"He's trying to pull himself free...and he's actually doing it."

From his cell, Walcott continued to jerk with everything he had.
Long ago the feeling in his arms and legs drifted away and were
swept into the air by a breeze made up of only pain, carried from
him forever. His eyes made contact with the slowly waking form of
Pleebo in the cell across from him, and his body heaved tighter still.
Singularly focused on the task at hand, what remained of the
dungeon faded from view. Now there was only he and Pleebo. Now
there was only the promise of freedom. Kragamel, the war, his
comrades in the New Tipoloo rebellion, the agony overtaking his

body and the chains binding him tight from this point on ceased to exist. They would not defeat him; they could not defeat him. He would not allow it. Though his body was old and his muscles only half of what they once were, Walcott understood all too well that at its heart, escape was simply a matter of will, and age had no bearing on will.

I can do this for ages, you bastard, he growled to the stone and the steel. *It is you who will relent, not I.*

Snarling through a mouth of shattered teeth, the Tycarian king pulled once again with every single muscle in his body, fully functioning or otherwise. Able to withstand no more, the wall gave way. Tearing from the stone, a heavy chain whipped across the cell, the jagged, shattered hunk of rock at its end colliding with the bars. With one arm suddenly free, Walcott's body at last folded in half, going limp as he struggled to catch his breath. Wearily he glanced at Pleebo, a wide smile slowly spreading across the face of his battered and bruised friend.

Though the act itself caused him considerable discomfort, Walcott smiled back.

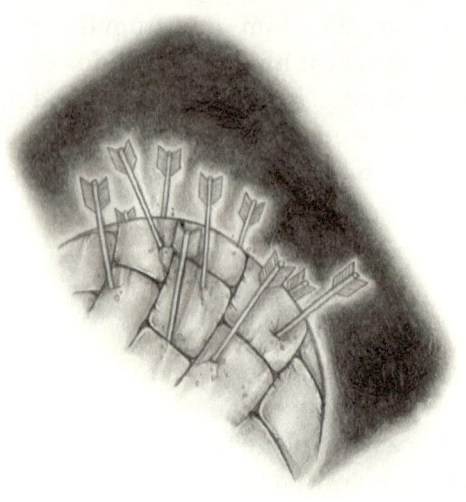

46. GREAT ANGER, GREAT POWER

"Get down, lad!" Nestor screamed, while expertly avoiding a slew of fire-tipped arrows puncturing the deck of the ship around him before throwing his body over a terrified Nicky Jarvis in a last ditch effort to protect the boy.

Though still some distance from the Briar Patch, the Ochan vessel—much larger, newer and significantly better-constructed—had rapidly closed the distance. Silhouetted in what remained of the setting sun, the forbidding ship sliced through the water with the deadliest of intentions. Lit up on its deck were pockets of orange red flame, casting a dangerous, eerie glow across the hellish form. One after another, like a finely tuned machine of war, the Ochans began sending over volleys of flame-tipped arrows numbering in the hundreds. The vicious assault created pockets of sporadic fire that soon began running rampant across the deck of the Briar Patch. As half of Fluuffytail's crew attempted to douse the flames, the other half began firing arrows of their own in retaliation. With so many creatures scurrying in so many directions at once, the ship had rapidly descended into a state of absolute chaos.

Removing a long curved sword from the sheath at his waist, Captain Fluuffytail raced to the highest point of the Briar Patch's deck and pointed his weapon angrily toward the Ochan vessel, flaming arrows cascading around him like acid rain.

"Return fire, ya useless Grazealumps! Deliver those lousy green-skins a first class ticket to the great beyond!" He screamed loud enough for his scattered and frustrated crew to hear over the madness. They needed his encouragement now more than ever.

Wrapping Nicky in his arms, Nestor rose into a crouched position, a flaming arrow ricocheting off his shell painfully before spinning like a top into the cool dark waters. Moving as quickly as his flat feet and massive oval shaped body would allow, he rushed to the opposite end of the ship near Tommy and Staci, who were coiled in the fetal position against a railing partially engulfed in flame.

"Get under me, children! We have to get you below!" Nestor screamed over the insanity while turning his back to the Ochan war ship as yet more arrows connected with his sturdy exterior, a few wedging their fiery tips between the plates of his shell.

Overcome with fear, Staci had long ago pulled the hood of her sweatshirt over her face. Sobbing uncontrollably into the fibers, her body trembling, she was finding it impossible to gain control over her emotions with so much lunacy brewing around her. Wrapping the girl in his arms, Tommy pulled her close to his chest. Forcefully dragging her to her feet, he managed to maneuver her shivering form behind the safety of Nestor's massive shell, using the Tycarian as a shield. Though his heart was racing, arrows blanketing the area around him in flames, Tommy attempted to keep some semblance of composure. He had to. For his brother and for Staci, he had to. In front of him, the deck of the Briar Patch was lit up like exploding fireflies across a blackened night. To his left, two of the crew's bodies were engulfed in flames, no less than three arrows protruding from what remained of their charred corpses. For every fire the crew was able to snuff, three more sprouted to life. It had become painfully obvious even to one as new to the concept of war as Tommy that they were losing the battle. Crouched over the children, Nestor began to slide along the deck while keeping them safely in front of him the entire time. Peeking around the massive Tycarian's shell, Tommy glanced quickly toward the Ochan ship in the distance. The enormous wooden structure was now less than two hundred feet away, bearing down on the Briar Patch with astounding speed. This close, it looked larger than anything he could scarcely imagine. Extending higher into the sky than some small buildings, the gargantuan sails alone seemed bigger than the whole of Captain Fluuffytail's pathetic looking vessel.

At last reaching the doorway to the lower deck, Nestor began shoving the children through, arrows exploding off his back like fireworks. "Inside now! All of you inside!"

Nicky stumbled through the doorway, followed closely behind by Staci. The pair began hurriedly descending a rotting, wobbly staircase leading into the dank, stuffy blackness below. A moment before Tommy followed them through, he overheard the voice of Fluuffytail buried amidst the craziness outside.

"Brace for impact, ya scoundrels!"

Glancing to his left, Tommy watched as the front of the monstrous Ochan vessel violently collided with the side of the Briar Patch. Wood splintered and cracked, straining and shattering to pieces. A low rumble shook the timbers of the Briar Patch to their core, unable to withstand the weight and construction of the Ochan ship. The sheer size and incredible speed of the Ochan vessel very nearly flipped the Briar Patch over and succeeded in lifting it out of the water for an instant. Defying gravity, Fluuffytail's ship was weightless for a moment, teetering perilously on the tightrope between remaining upright and spilling its contents into the sea. The collision whipped Tommy and Nestor across the deck, slamming the pair into the railing on the opposite side. Somewhere within the vessel's belly, Nicky and Staci lost their already shaky balance and tumbled forward roughly to the foot of the stairs. When the Briar Patch at last splashed back into the ocean, every board, nail and bolt holding the aged ship together elicited a deep, uncompromising moan, making its captain aware in no uncertain terms that the chances of it surviving a similar collision were unlikely. Within its dank underbelly, splinters in its already worn timbers split open wide, allowing the chilly Aquari sea to spray in. Their limbs sore from their fall, Nicky and Staci regained control over their senses only to discover they were partially submerged in no less than three inches of water that was rising quickly. All around them, random crewmembers scrambled wildly to close the leaks before they became too much for the ship to handle. The fact that the Briar Patch had managed to stay afloat this long despite the collision and the gallons of ocean pouring into its belly was nothing short of remarkable.

Slowly opening his eyes, the pain of a thousand needles pressing against a rapidly forming lump on his head, Tommy glanced wearily in the direction of the Ochan vessel now less than fifty feet from the Briar Patch. Beneath him, the momentum of the collision continued to cause the ship to wobble back and forth atop the tumultuous waves awkwardly. Attempting to balance himself and get to his feet, Tommy stumbled. Slipping on the water soaked deck, he landed hard on his rear. One after another, improbably thick ropes with enormous three-pronged anchors as large as the whole of Tommy's torso were tossed from the Ochan ship to the deck of the Briar Patch. Wrapping themselves around crates, wedging themselves between boards, or simply slicing into the partially rotted wood like scissors through paper, the anchors attached themselves to the soaked timbers and tied the vessels together. Like a tired old fly caught in a spider web, Captain Fluuffytail's ship had been captured. Using the ropes as a means of transportation, the Ochans began the process of boarding the now helpless vessel like a well-oiled machine of death. They had done this before and they would do it again. Warfare was commonplace to them, even on the high seas. It was in their blood. It defined them.

Within a matter of minutes Captain Fluuffytail's ship was infested with Ochan soldiers.

At last able to find secure footing, Nestor retrieved the sword from his back. Gritting his teeth, he swatted away the arrows jutting from his shell while tightening his muscles and preparing himself for the inevitability of battle. In every corner of the ship, hand-to-hand combat had begun. Steel clashed with steel. Steel sliced through flesh. Blood was sprayed in frighteningly copious amounts. Mixing with the half-inch of water now glistening in the light of the impending moon on the slippery deck, the multi-colored insides of those fighting for their lives coated the ship's floorboards a milky, cloudy rainbow of savagery.

Reaching to his side, Nestor snagged a handful of Tommy's shirt, lifting the boy into the air and pulling him close. "Stay behind me, lad!" He screamed angrily as an Ochan soldier barreled in his direction from ten feet away with a blood soaked weapon at his side.

Near the front of the ship, Krystoph was fending off a group of five Ochans. Each instantly recognized him as a traitor to his race, making the prospect of ending his life all the more enticing. The former general's movements were too fluid though, too precise and far too deadly. At every turn, Krystoph remained no less than three steps ahead of his countrymen-turned-bitter enemies. While they were still searching for ways to strike him down, he had already set forth the process inevitably leading to their deaths. He was the future and they were the past; no matter how quickly they moved, there was simply no catching up. Even Krystoph understood, however, that he could not stay ahead of the pack forever. As their numbers grew, so would their chances of catching him off guard. With every passing minute, more and more Ochans made their way from their massive ship to the fiery deck of the Briar Patch. Soon Fluuffytail's crew would be vastly outnumbered; soon they would be overrun. This, too, was inevitable.

Trying his best to keep Tommy out of harm's way, Nestor continued to fend off a pair of Ochan soldiers while keeping the boy behind him the entire time. He was able to strike one of the two down, but the second landed a stiff, echoing blow to the underside of his shell that nearly split it open. The strike dropped Nestor instantly to his knees. When the wild movement of the waves caused the sides of the two ships to again smash into each other, Tommy was sent airborne for the second time in less than ten minutes. Thrown clear across the deck, the world around him went blurry, painful and cold. His ribs slammed into the debris of a half-shattered wooden crate, bringing the wild spinning to an immediate halt while knocking the wind out of his lungs in the process. Glancing down at his knees in an attempt to regain his bearings and catch his breath, he noticed that he was partially submerged in a purplish colored substance that could only be blood. Seeping into the fabric of his sopping wet jeans, it stained the fibers to their very core. This was the kind of stain that wouldn't easily be washed away, the kind of stain that remained even when it was no longer visible to the naked eye. Every inch of his body was sore and aching, dipped in a boiling vat of confusion and pain. Beneath his chilled, jittery skin and the clumped strands of drenched dirty blond hair hanging in his eyes, his bones shivered. His ears felt sore, packed to the point of overflowing with the clashing of steel, the pained death cries and the thunderous booms of monstrous ocean waves. The sound of battle was attacking his every sense, and winning. His heart was racing, his mind swirling; the situation was quickly proving too much for him to absorb and far too much to make sense of.

Closing his eyes, Tommy held his breath, his body beginning to feel warm, and angry, and stuffed . . .in desperate need of release.

Pulling his hand from the puddle of warm purple-colored liquid, he lifted it to his face and peeked through a pair of squinting eyes. The tips of his fingers had begun to glow.

It was happening again.

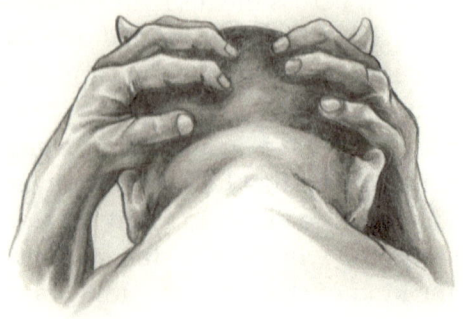

47. A CHOICE MUST BE MADE

"That's it. I can't sit here like some two-bit schlep while those damn Ochans tear into Pleebs and Walcott. I'm going in."

Lifting himself off a rock, Roustaf began hovering slowly toward the tree line. Off in the distance, Ochan workers and soldiers alike continued to exit the blackened hole leading from their home world into the sprawling night of the Fillagrou Forest. Roustaf and his group, consisting of his pink skinned love interest Tahnja and the rest of her traveling companions, as well as a pair of Tycarian soldiers and the burly bodied bully Donald Rondage, had remained hidden just inside the tree line for quite some time. The break they were waiting patiently for in the exodus of Ochans appearing from the doorway had yet to arrive. Sick of sitting around doing nothing, Roustaf made the decision to take matters into his own miniscule hands. Keenly aware of the fact that the longer his friends were captives of the tyrant king, the less likely they were to survive, he understood there simply was no other choice. No matter the danger, no matter the unlikelihood of success, he had to at least attempt to help Pleebo.

"Wait a minute!" Tahnja yelled as loudly as she could while still remaining low enough as to not be heard, "What do you think you're doing? That doorway is packed to the gills with Ochans. Trying to sneak through now is suicide!"

"I honestly don't give a crap, darlin'. My friend is in there. I gotta get him out. I gotta do something," Roustaf responded after licking his palm and using it to smooth down the loose hairs of his bushy mustache in preparation for high-speed flight.

He knew that if he turned to look at Tahnja and spotted the worry on her face, his heart would instantly melt like hot butter in a pan. He couldn't turn around. He couldn't think. The time for planning had come and gone, now there could be only action. He had to keep going. He couldn't look back.

Lunging forward, Tahnja snagged his left leg between her fingers, preventing him from zooming forward into the darkness. "Oh no, no, no, you're not going anywhere, mister."

Tugging wildly and trying to pull his leg free, Roustaf's body thrashed back and forth, his wings moving so fast they'd become invisible. "Will you let go, woman?" He grumbled while attempting to pry her fingers—which were nearly as long as his entire body—from his appendage with both of his arms.

Unable to shake himself loose, the little man relented with an angry growl. Throwing his hands into the air in frustration, he sighed deeply. The night air was abnormally sticky and warm, even for Fillagrou, and aided by his wild thrashing, it had left him covered in a thin sheen of extra salty sweat. Though Roustaf had lived within this forest for so many years and had come to think of it as home, the non-stop humidity was something he never became fully accustomed to. Nor did he really look forward to the day that he managed to. Tahnja's huge eyes, with her low-hanging pink eyelids, slowly morphed from annoyance to sympathy to at last pleading. As he predicted it would, the expression on her face began to open up the tiniest of stress fractures in his normally steel-coated resolve. She was playing dirty pool and she knew it. He had to help Pleebo though, no matter what look she was tossing his way. He simply had to. Roustaf's relationship with Pleebo began long before Tahnja was ever in the picture, and Pleebo had always been there for him, no matter what. When there was no one else, there was Pleebo and very often only Pleebo. Leaving his friend in the hands of the Ochans — leaving him to the whims of fate — Roustaf knew this was wrong by every possible definition of the word. It was something he just couldn't do.

His wings slowing to a flutter, he rested his free leg on Tahnja's closed fist, his tone suddenly soft and gentle. "Listen, beautiful, I understand that everyone trying to make it through the doorway right now just isn't gonna work. I get it. I have to go, though. It's night and I'm small enough to fit in one of those bastards' pockets; I can sneak right past them and into the castle before any of those bums even spots me."

Tahnja paused momentarily, shaking her head and doing her best to fight back the ever so subtle hint of a tear forming in the corner of her eye. "And then what? What do you plan on doing once you're through? Do you seriously think you can break them out all by yourself?"

"I don't know," Roustaf answered honestly. "I'll tell you this much though darlin', don't let the size of these meat hooks of mine fool you. Any one of them crumbs gets in my way and I guarantee you, they'll end up with a mouth full of broken teeth."

Tahnja rolled her eyes, giggling slightly against her better judgment at the outlandish statement while wiping the single tear from her cheek. Less than a few inches from her face, the pint-sized man who had unexpectedly come to mean so much to her was holding his fists in front of his tiny head, moving them back and forth and shadow boxing comically.

He was so very stupid . . .so very, very loveable, stupid and brave.

Dropping his hands, Roustaf smiled from underneath his furry mustache. "Look, I'm just going to sneak through, look around, get a lay of the land, and come back. It's better that we know what we're up against before charging in there with our guns blazing like a bunch of idiots anyway. Just keep everyone here until I get back. Can you do that for me, darlin'?"

Smiling subtly, though still shaking her head, Tahnja released her grip on his leg and whispered breathily, "Yeah, I can do that."

Just over her shoulder, the remaining group watched the exchange between the two closely. One of the two Tycarian soldiers in the back dipped his head and nodded in Roustaf's direction, impressed with the mettle of the little man.

Rising to his feet, Donald Rondage huffed, "I'm going with you."

The instant the words escaped his mouth, he wondered why in the world he was saying them. A large part of him wished he hadn't. Despite the fact that sneaking past the Ochans and into the doorway seemed, at first glance, to be an impossible task, and ignoring the fact that lizard men and their gargantuan dinosaurs were most likely headed to the doorway to his world, the only thing in the young boy's head seemed to be Walcott and his safety. If it hadn't been for that annoying old turtle, Donald knew full well that he wouldn't even be there. He owed it to the old coot to help him. He owed it to himself.

Closing the distance between himself and the headstrong boy, Roustaf came to a hovering stop a few inches from his chubby pink-skinned face. "Think again, slick. You're not going anywhere. You try to sneak past those goons and the only thing you'll accomplish is getting yourself hacked into bite-sized pieces. When they're done with you, they'll use whatever's left of me to pick their teeth."

Donald rolled his eyes, locked his jaw and gritted his teeth. "Oh gimme a break, you little turd, I ca—"

Roustaf interrupted him. "When I get back, and the minute there's an opening, you'll be going through with the rest of us at your side and not a minute before. That's all there is to it, kid! No more discussion!"

Turning, Donald stomped his foot in the dirt, cussing at the annoying little man beneath his breath.

Sensing the boy's frustration, Roustaf's tone once again changed. Gone was the hard edge and the gruffness, quickly replaced by something far more understanding. "Look kid, this doesn't work unless you help me out. I know you wanna get Walcott outta there, believe me, I do too. We can't pull it off if we don't work together, though. I need your help; I need you to stop being such a pain in the tush and go along with me on this one."

Something in the tone of Roustaf's voice calmed Donald a bit. Instead of ordering him around the way his brothers so often did, the little man was simply talking to him, treating him like an equal and like a friend. In his fourteen years, not once could Donald recall having been spoken to like that, like he was more than a number or an obstacle, like he mattered. He didn't hate it.

Though still slightly frustrated, he lifted his hand and waved the little man away while never turning around. "Yeah, yeah, yeah, whatever. Go on. See you when you get back."

Roustaf grinned slyly. "You can count on it, kid."

A moment later Roustaf's tiny body was slicing through the night air at blistering speeds while staying low enough to the ground to remain unnoticed. Using the darkness as a shroud, he managed to zip past the Ochans with relative ease. Reaching the edge of the massive pit leading to Ocha, he dove headfirst into the black without an ounce of hesitation. There was no time for second guessing, no time for pause. In fact, there was no time to waste at all. Never much of a math genius, the equation was so remarkably simple even Roustaf could make sense of it. Immediately after descending into the darkness of the doorway, a deep, penetrating cold folded over his body like gooey frozen sludge. Seeping into his every orifice, it melded with him at a microscopic level, chilling him to the core of the stuff from which he'd been made. Despite his bravado, despite his dedication and heroism, he was suddenly overcome with a profound feeling of fear. Only once before in his life had he dared venture into the miserable frozen world known as

Ocha. It was a journey he hoped he would never have to make again.

Unfortunately for Roustaf, it seemed that in this and every other world, one rarely gets what they hope for.

48. THE ENEMY WITHIN

His broad sword wedged in the belly of one Ochan soldier, while his dagger pressed against the throat of another, Krystoph heard an odd hum emanating from somewhere behind him. Though disguised by the sounds of war and the crash of waves, the hum was growing significantly with every passing moment. Steady and unending, it sounded almost mechanical in nature, yet there was something else beneath the rhythmic resonance, something alive, vibrant and deadly . . .something unlike anything the former Ochan general had ever heard. Sensing uncommon warmth on the scales of his back, he pulled his sword from the Ochan's belly and turned his head quickly in its direction. Some distance away from him, young Tommy Jarvis sat on his knees near the center of the ship. The boy's eyes were shut tight, his hands lifted to his face. This in itself would hardly be worth noting were it not for the incredible glow emanating from those very same hands. After using his blade to dispatch the second Ochan, Krystoph turned his attention fully to the incredible sight.

Tommy Jarvis squeezed his eyes closed as tightly as he could, his chest heaving underneath his soaked shirt. His mouth slammed shut, coiling into an angry grimace. Beneath his knees, the deck of the Briar Patch rumbled and swayed, water sloshing about, spraying around him wildly.

Krystoph's body froze in place as he stared at the boy, though the grip on his weapon tightened significantly. The sight unfolding before him was both astonishing and frightening, while scarcely seeming real. The invading horde of Ochan soldiers paused their assault as well, engrossed in the light show as much as he. Ever since the disaster at the castle of their prince, there had been no shortage of wild stories of the murderous walls of light, and magic unlike any magic that had come before. Very few of the soldiers, however, actually believed the ramblings of those claiming to have witnessed the murder of the prince firsthand. After all, how could such a thing be possible? It couldn't.

The two spheres of light encasing Tommy's hands began to grow; like bubbles floating underwater they eventually merged together and became one. The newly formed sphere spread outward as well, continuing until it had swallowed the whole of Tommy's body. Cackling and humming, it popped like electricity, if electricity were somehow a living, breathing thing. More than a little confused, the Ochan soldiers opted to do what they did best: fight. Those carrying bows immediately began firing arrows at the bizarre ball of translucent electricity. Their weapons, however, had no effect. The moment the arrows came into contact with the ominous light they evaporated to dust. His heart racing, Krystoph swallowed deeply, his muscles pulled tense and tight, unwilling or simply unable to move. It was true, all of it. Every single solitary rumor was true.

Whatever this thing kneeling before him was, it was indeed more than the simple useless child its outer flesh would have liked him to believe. The monster was hidden within, and the monster was angry.

The light surrounding Tommy halted for a moment, bulging inward then outward once more as if it were breathing. Scanning the area around him, Krystoph retrieved the remnants of a half shattered crate. Dropping to one knee, he lifted the dusty wood in front of his body and created a makeshift shield. Breathing deeply, he lowered his shoulder and steadied his position, preparing himself for whatever might come next. Peering through a crack between the shattered boards, he watched as Tommy opened his eyes and began to slowly scan the ship around him. Though barely noticeable, Krystoph took note of the fact that the child's grimace had transformed into something more resembling a smile. He had seen this expression before; it was one he knew all too well. Not only was the boy aware of what was happening, he was enjoying himself.

The powerful, airy electricity pouring throughout Tommy's body felt different this time than it had in the past. When the amazing sensations overtook him in Valkea's castle, it was the power pulling the strings, the power making the decisions. This was no longer the case. Tommy was fully aware of the burning, crackling power encasing him. He could feel the bizarre light coursing through his pores, sense it snapping angrily against his skin, and feel it causing every hair on his body to stand at attention. He was fully aware of it, just as it was fully aware of him. When he breathed, it breathed as well. When he moved, it moved with him. Similar to a shadow, it was a variation of his form, a connected distortion of the original that could never leave his side. Once a one-way street leading to a dead end, the lanes making up the whole of Tommy Jarvis had opened up and expanded to two. Not only did the traffic now move freely in both directions, but Tommy was the one moving it. To his left, he spotted an injured Nestor surrounded by gape-jawed Ochan lizard men, all staring blankly at the ball of living light he'd become. To his left, Captain Fluuffytail sat on his rear in the inch of water covering the deck of his ship. A few feet behind the dusty rabbit, the mysterious Ochan Krystoph was using a shattered crate for protection—protection from him. Behind Tommy, the massive Ochan war ship continued to occasionally crack against the side of the Briar Patch, threatening to tear the ship apart at its rusty seams. Tommy knew that he couldn't allow this to happen, not with his little brother and Staci on board. He couldn't allow this to happen and he wouldn't allow this to happen. When

Tommy stretched his hands from his sides, the ball of energy mirrored the movement, expanding again at an incredible rate. In an instant, it swallowed the entirety of the Briar Patch. Moving across the water, it required only a moment for it to encase the entirety of the Ochan ship as well. The Ochan warriors the glow came into contact with were instantaneously engulfed in something nearly the strength of the sun, frying them from the inside out and cooking their flesh to a blackened crisp in mere seconds. The rope that only moments ago tied the two ships together disintegrated as the Ochan vessel became engulfed in the bizarre white glow. Scorching, ripping, tearing and breaking the incredible structure all at once, the monstrous ship was reduced to mere timbers in an instant. The parts of the ship not transformed to dust were thrown violently for miles in every direction like fiery debris shot from a cannon. When the enemy had been dispatched, the light folded back into Tommy's body. Like boiling water, it evaporated to vapors that then rose from the boy like steam off the top of a lake. Feeling drained yet wildly energized, Tommy closed his eyes once again while attempting to catch his breath. Unable to hold his head up, it flopped forward. He suddenly felt empty and spent, like he could sleep for days.

The smile on his face widened.

Pulling the makeshift shield from his face, Krystoph patted the sides of his body, ensuring that everything was exactly as it should be. Scattered around him were a bevy of charred Ochan corpses, their skin pitch black and shiny with seawater, crispy and unrecognizable. Plumes of grayish smoke now rose in steady streams from their smoldering bodies. The stench was ungodly. Though enveloped in the light as much as any of his people, Krystoph had not suffered even a scratch; for that matter, neither had any of Fluuffytail's crew. Scattered around the ocean surrounding the Briar Patch floated the smoldering remains of the Ochan ship, slowly sinking below the dark waves. Bits of timber were scattered for miles in every direction, along with the corpses of yet more Ochan soldiers. The scene was grizzly, terrifying and undeniably impressive. In a moment, the pink skinned child had transformed himself in Krystoph's eyes from a weak and useless nothing to something else entirely, something demanding respect, something requiring his full attention. He would no longer take these children lightly.

"Such power," Krystoph muttered under his breath, the smell of freshly burnt Ochan flesh filling his nostrils and making his heart race. "Such incredible power."

As if awaking from a trance, Krystoph's mind snapped back to the reality of the situation. The impressive light show created by the boy momentarily lit the night sky as if a star had been pulled from the sky and dipped in the water. There was no doubt it had been visible for mile upon mile upon mile. There were hundreds of Ochan ships sailing the waves of Aquari; more than one of them had to have caught a glimpse. Flinging what remained of his broken crate to the ground, he stomped across the deck in the direction of Captain Fluuffytail. Like everyone on the ship, Jacques was staring wide-eyed at Tommy, still unsure if what he'd just seen had actually happened.

Grabbing the dusty wet rabbit by his protective chest plate, Krystoph lifted him into the air, their faces suddenly only inches apart. "Continue north, now!" He growled through a mouth full of razor sharp teeth, spittle spraying onto Jacques' face and making his broken whiskers twitch wildly.

"I don't take orders from the likes of you, ya green-skinned bastard!" Fluuffytail barked back, his little rabbit feet dangling mid air.

Reaching down, the captain retrieved a dagger from his belt. Krystoph quickly snagged his wrist, twisting it violently until the pain forced Jacques to drop the weapon. "Every Ochan vessel within a hundred miles will have seen the boy's magic," The Ochan stated sternly. "He has awakened a sleeping giant. The time for discussion has passed. We leave now, or we die."

Dropping Fluuffytail back to the deck, Krystoph stepped away, now glaring at Tommy near the center of the ship. For a moment, the two locked eyes, neither willing to blink.

From the center of the ship, Staci and Nicky hesitantly made their way from the watery interior of the ship and onto the deck. Sniffing the stinky humid air thick with the flavor of burnt flesh, Staci cringed, then pinched her nose and waved her hand back and forth in front of her face. Though careful not to slip on the wet timbers, Nicky instantly bolted across the deck and collided with his brother's chest. The two embraced. Staci was not far behind, wrapping her arms around Tommy as well, happy to see him uninjured.

His wrist aching, Captain Jacques Fluuffytail realized that the massive Ochan was indeed correct in his assumption, though he hardly agreed with the manner in which it was delivered. The way the boy lit up the night; someone would undoubtedly have seen it. There was absolutely no way they could have missed it. No doubt, Ochan ships were heading toward their position at this very moment. Rubbing his wrist, he told himself that he would remind the foul-mouthed Ochan calling himself Krystoph of just who was the captain of this vessel later. Things being as they were, however, time was short and vengeance would have to wait. After retrieving his dagger from the gently swaying deck, he inserted it back into its sheath.

Turning to his still confused crew, he screamed, "Get below and repair whatever damage those damn forked tongues caused! We're heading north, ya mangy seadogs! See to it that ya put some grease in yer gears while yer at it! I want us moving within the hour!"

Straightening the bent brim on his dusty sea-soaked hat, Jacques Fluuffytail came to the realization that this trip had suddenly gotten significantly more interesting, whether he liked it or not.

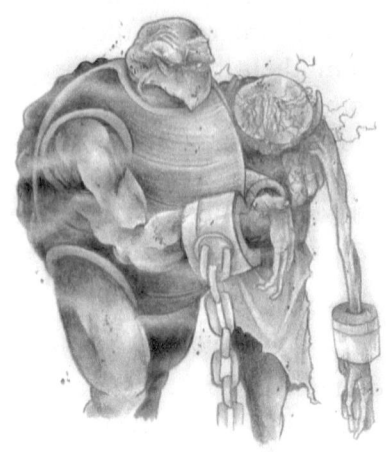

49. INCORRECT ASSUMPTIONS

Barely conscious, his long toenails dragging across the stone, arm draped over the thickly muscled neck of Walcott, Pleebo felt nearly weightless to the Tycarian King. Remarkably skinny before being captured and tossed in Kragamel's dungeon, the lack of sustenance during his imprisonment had left the Fillagrou citizen more malnourished than ever. The grayish white flesh covering his lanky skeleton was taut, dry and sickly looking, delicate like fine particles of dust in the breeze. Despite the fact that most of the bones in his legs were broken or severely fractured in multiple places, it was through sheer will alone that Walcott forced them to continue working. Just a little longer; they had to stay functional just a bit longer. When he and Pleebo had fully escaped from the castle of the tyrant king, then, and only then, would he allow them to bathe in the much-needed rest for which they so terribly ached. Not a moment before, and not a moment less.

The dungeon was a labyrinth of dimly lit, barely habitable tunnels extending for miles underneath the castle and its surrounding grounds. Attempting to navigate them with no prior knowledge of where he was going was proving a difficult task, to say the least. Walcott's head was pounding, his entire body on fire. Every corridor looked the same as the last, every cell as empty, desolate and dreary as the one before. Finding it difficult to focus, he realized that he was unsure of exactly where he was. Did he go down this tunnel before? He thought maybe he had—maybe? It seemed familiar for some reason. Under his arm, pulled close to his body, Pleebo continued to drift in and out of consciousness. His long gangly body had gone entirely limp, and Walcott was finding him more and more awkward to carry. Reaching a three-way junction, the Tycarian at last came to a stop. Each tunnel was lit up for just about fifteen feet before being swallowed by darkness once again. Which way should he go? Everywhere he looked, everything felt the same. The only difference from one corridor to the next was the prisoners locked behind the bars of the cells lining the walls. Unfortunately even they were obscured by shadows. The random parts remaining exposed were lifeless, bloody, unmoving and of little help. Ochan gnats circled the bodies of the captured and beaten like vultures, surviving on microscopic pieces of their rotting flesh. Closing his eyes, Walcott lowered his head. Every part of him hurt, hurt so very bad. Simply remaining upright was proving to be among the most challenging tasks he'd undertaken in his many years. It would have been so easy to lower Pleebo to the floor, drop to his knees, lie on his back, and give in to the agony spreading like wildfire across his body. There would be no honor lost in such an act. Not a single one of his fellow Tycarians would judge him harshly if he made such a decision, not after everything he'd suffered. For a single fleeting moment, Walcott actually considered the idea. For a barely existing instant in time, it became more than a simple, passing thought. For the briefest of seconds, it had substance, and it seemed almost logical in a strange, disturbing way. In this moment, his grip on Pleebo wavered, his knees wobbling as a defeated sigh slightly part his dry, cracked lips—for a moment.

From the darkness at the end of the hallway directly in front of him came the clank of heavy steel latches being unlocked. This was followed immediately by the sound of an ages-old knob turning, along with squeaky rusted hinges desperately in need of lubrication. The corridor filled with a light so bright it forced Walcott to squint and lift his thick forearm to his face to shade his eyes. Instinctively, he pulled tighter on Pleebo while ducking the both of them behind a nearby wall and out of sight. A second later he heard voices, two of them, possibly three: Ochan voices, the guards. As the door behind the Ochans closed, the corridors were again washed in deep black shadow. Realizing he would stand no chance in a hand-to-hand skirmish, Walcott opted instead to hold his breath, make as little noise as possible, and pray they chose a corridor other than his to venture down. Six feet stomped heavily on the stone floor, growing louder as they got closer. Their thick armor clanked and ground the steel of their various bladed weapons, creating long drawn-out rattles that reverberated throughout the darkness. Under his arm, only partially conscious, Pleebo mumbled something incoherent. Immediately Walcott's hand covered the wide mouth of his friend, muffling his faraway voice. From the blackened corridors, the sounds of walking Ochan feet stopped, the clank of metal weapons grinding to an immediate halt. Still pressing his massive flat paw over Pleebo's mouth, Walcott closed his eyes, a sheen of sweat building on his forehead and dripping over his wide brow. Locking his jaw, he held his breath. If they had heard him, he would be forced to fight. More than likely it would prove a battle he was destined to lose. He would fight nonetheless. If he was to die on this day, it should be a death worthy of a Tycarian; it should be on his feet. This could be the only way. In the back of his mind, he cursed himself for considering giving up a moment prior. The situation he found himself faced with resulted in a brief lapse of judgment; it would not happen again.

The Tycarians deserved more from their king, and he expected more from himself.

After mumbling to each other for a moment, one of the Ochan guards laughed boisterously, his gravelly voice bouncing off the walls. Seconds later, Walcott listened intently as the group moved off in another direction until at last the sounds of their steps faded away. Quickly adjusting his grip on Pleebo, Walcott hoisted the floppy, spindly limbs of his friend into the air once more.

Cautiously, he began moving toward the door the Ochans exited moments ago. Unable to see more than a few inches in front of his face, he extended his arm forward until eventually his palm came into contact with steel. Running his fingers over the metal blindly, he eventually discovered a lever and tugged downward. Pressing open the door just a crack, he peeked into a well-lit corridor on the other side. At first glance, this new area looked empty, quiet and surprisingly peaceful. Stained into the stone beneath his feet were various-colored bloods. Many creatures had been dragged through this hall kicking, screaming and begging for a mercy they likely never received. From the shadows of the dungeon behind him, Walcott again heard the distant chatter of the Ochan guards; they were moving in his direction. There was no time to waste. Again the dreary, only partially-conscious Pleebo could only mumble limply.

"Fear not my friend. Freedom is forthcoming," Walcott whispered in response.

Ignoring the crippling pain coursing throughout his body, the massive-bodied Tycarian pressed the door open and stepped through, quickly closing it behind. Though currently empty, the corridor was enormous, extending so far in either direction that Walcott guessed it might take him twenty minutes to walk from one end to the other. A number of other corridors branched out from it at fairly regular intervals, along with fifty or so closed doors lining the walls, each of them covered in a muted, barely noticeable red paint. The air was chilly, bordering on freezing. Walcott watched as a puff of warm steam exited his mouth with every breath. Though he had never set foot in Ocha, the Tycarian king had heard any number of stories concerning its unforgivable winters, winters that could often last the entire year. The Ochans loved the cold. No doubt this was one of the many reasons they so despised Fillagrou.

"Wha-what's going on?" Pleebo babbled sloppily as he was drawn briefly back into consciousness, his head flopping back and forth as if his neck were without muscles.

"Quiet, my friend," Walcott whispered shortly, dragging the woozy Pleebo away from the door to the dungeon and into the corridor. "There is much ground to cover if we're to escape this place." Ducking into the first hallway on the right, the pair found themselves faced with another endless corridor strikingly similar to the first. Gravity reasserting itself across his body, Pleebo's feet slowly progressed from dragging, to stumbling, to limping and something as closely resembling the act of walking as he was likely to manage in his current state.

"I've got it. I can walk, it's okay," He added through painfully dry lips while thankfully patting his burly protector on the rear of his shell.

Walcott cautiously allowed Pleebo to slide from his grip and soon the Fillagrou was again standing upright under his own power. His legs were wobbly though, bending back inward at awkward moments and very nearly causing him to stumble forward. Through bloodshot eyes, the world around Pleebo began sharpening. What had been little more than a fuzzy abstraction moments ago now looked solid, familiar and quite terrifying. Every part of his body was sore, every muscle transformed into a bundle of nearly useless pain receptors. Reaching up, he inserted one of his fingers into his mouth. Where once there had been teeth, there were now only gums. The Ochan interrogators had taken the rest. His pale flesh was covered in disgusting lumps, welts and scars. A few of his wounds remained open, dried and caked blood sticking to the ripped flesh.

"How did you get us out?" Pleebo asked as his memories were reduced to disjointed puzzle pieces that might never again fit perfectly.

After a brief pause Walcott answered, "The chains believed they could defeat me. They were mistaken."

Stopping for a moment, Walcott sniffed the chilly air around him, surprised to discoverer there was no discernable scent of life. What he smelled was old and dusty, as if only a few creatures had traversed the corridors in quite some time.

"What? What's wrong?" Pleebo asked, keeping his weary eyes peeled for Ochans, despite the fact that alertness was not easily accomplished through only one fully functioning eye.

"Nothing," Walcott whispered, "I smell nothing. It is too clean, too clean and empty."

Lifting his head, Pleebo scanned the area around him, for the first time realizing the obvious: they hadn't encountered a single Ochan over the course of their escape. Unsure of what this meant, he decided instead to ignore it.

"Who cares? Consider it a blessing in disguise. Keep moving."

Walcott grumbled, coming to the decision that Pleebo was right; it was best to ignore such things for the time being. If they wished to escape, they had to continue moving forward. This was all that mattered. After making their way down two more equally empty corridors, the pair arrived at a sturdily constructed steel door at least ten inches thick and built into the end of the hall rather than on the side like all that had come before it. Unlocking the exceptionally large latch, Walcott pushed the door open slowly. Immediately a cold breeze smacked his face, freezing the sweat running down his forehead and pushing the heavy steel backward. Lowering his shoulder, both he and Pleebo shoved the full weight of their bodies against the powerful winds outside until the door at last swung open and smacked against the exterior stone with a heavy thud.

Instantly Pleebo and Walcott froze in place.

The pair now found themselves staring out across an impossibly large yard surrounded by walls so high they disappeared into the heavy gray clouds blanketing the night sky. The sand in the yard was dark brown and frozen solid, without an ounce of vegetation. Scattered about the frozen tundra were creatures of every race imaginable, each with a pickaxe or a shovel dangling between their frostbitten fingers. They looked as if they were just barely clinging to life. Covered in a layer of filth and dressed in crinkly, partially frozen rags, the creatures mindlessly broke piles of stone beneath their unprotected, frostbitten feet.

Though the facial features of each were remarkably different, their expressions remained startling similar. They were the walking dead. There was no sign of life behind their eyes, no hope and no dreams. They were lost, holding onto snippets of a past they'd likely forgotten and would never find again.

"It would seem this is not Kragamel's castle, my friend," Walcott mumbled as the icy wind stung at the flesh of his beaten, defeated face. "This is a work camp."

50. THE CALVARY HAS ARRIVED

Sneaking into the Kragamel's castle proved remarkably easy for tiny Roustaf. Locating his friends, however, was another matter entirely. Using the darkness to his advantage, the little man had zipped from one end of the castle to the other over the course of the long, cold evening. In the dungeon, he found nothing, and in the courtyard, even less. The endless rows of prisoner barracks near the rear of the fortress offered no signs of hope either. Either Pleebo and Walcott weren't there or they were already dead. Realizing that there was a very real possibility that he'd arrived too late, that his friends were gone, Roustaf came close to breaking down. Diving headfirst into a pile of stiff half-frozen hay for cover, he buried his head in his hands, fighting back a torrent of tears. Absent-mindedly, his fingers traced the contours of the stubby horns on his head. Though he'd managed to ignore it until this point, suddenly Ocha's bitter cold seemed remarkably colder and insurmountably bitterer. From the points of the calcified bone protruding from his scalp to the tips of his frozen toes, the extreme weather had begun to have

261

an effect on him, not only physically, but mentally. Every muscle in his body felt tired, drained and worn, as if he were twice his age and his body working at half its strength. Pulled tightly together, his wings were overly sensitive and brittle; they had been for hours. Even the briefest of touches from something as delicate as the straw surrounding him now resulted in a nearly incomprehensible amount of pain.

Wrapping his arms around his knees in an attempt to take advantage of what little body heat he had remaining, Roustaf mumbled under his breath, "You blew it, you stupid schmuck." The thick whiskers of his mustache were frozen stiff, poking against the flesh of his forearm and adding to his overall state of discomfort. "They needed your help and you blew it."

Berating himself in this fashion did little to improve his mood. Through slight openings in his house of straw, he watched intently as the Ochan sun began to peek just above the outer wall of the castle in the distance. So far away, the star seemed tiny in the sky, only slightly larger than the points of light surrounding it and hanging perilously onto the night beyond the heavy cloud cover. It would be daylight soon, or as close to daylight as it got in this awful dark place. Sneaking around the castle would soon become remarkably more difficult, if not impossible. If his friends were still alive, the chances of him finding, releasing and rescuing them without the aid of a shadowy night were almost nonexistent. For the time being anyway, Roustaf had come to the difficult decision that he needed to stop looking. Since the outset of the war, he'd seen so many he'd cared about die. Try as he might to hide the pain, with each and every one he lost a piece of himself, a piece he would likely never get back.

After so many years and so many pieces, it was astounding that there was anything left.

Breathing in, he sucked back the pain once more and swallowed it whole, allowing the awful disgusting feeling to sink heavily into the pit of his stomach. He needed to head back into Fillagrou, back to Tahnja and the rest of the group. Spending the day hiding out in Kragamel's fortress would accomplish nothing.

Not only was freezing to death a legitimate concern, but he would likely be discovered as well. There was no other choice; he needed to leave now, before dawn. Crawling on all fours through the mound of grayish-brown hay, Roustaf used his hands to dig away an opening just large enough to scan the courtyard. In the immediate vicinity, there were only a few guards visible. In an hour's time, this would no longer be the case. In two hours' time, the fortress would be filled to the brim with angry, well-armed, sharp-toothed and green-skinned lizards.

The soldier nearest Roustaf checked briefly to see if any of his comrades happened to be glancing in his direction. Realizing there were no prying eyes upon him, he opened his mouth wide and yawned deeply while stretching his muscular arms. Twenty feet from the sleepy lizard man, a pair of guards exited a large doorway on the fortress wall, dragging the body of an unconscious and possibly dead prisoner across the frozen soil. Initially Roustaf didn't recognize the creature's species. Its pale orange-purple flesh had been so badly disfigured that it might be unrecognizable even if he did. If Pleebo was alive, he was no doubt in just as terrible a condition as that unfortunate soul. The mere suggestion sent a shiver of fear up the ridges of Roustaf's spine. Rubbing his hands together for warmth, the tiny red man examined the movements of the guard closest to him carefully. The instant the Ochan turned his back, he would make his break for the outer fortress wall. It would be his only chance. Attempting to get some blood pumping to his sore wings, he fluttered them back and forth quickly, which in turn caused the hay above his head to scatter just a bit. He would need to get as high as he could as fast as possible, and over the wall quickly. From there, it would be a short flight to the doorway and Tahnja. What would happen after that wasn't quite as clear. Plans would have to be made. There were difficult decisions ahead.

Again the guard closest to him lifted his arms and yawned, this time turning his back to Roustaf's hay pile hiding place. The moment the burly Ochan closed his eyes and opened his mouth, the tiny winged man fluttered his wings at incredible speeds and blasted into the air. Within the blink of an eye, he'd flown nearly twenty feet straight up. A moment later and he was closer to forty. Once high enough, Roustaf changed his direction, now zooming toward the enormous outer wall of Kragamel's castle. After clearing the wall, he again shot toward the ground where he changed direction once more, this time heading for the black hole in the Ochan soil that was the doorway to Fillagrou. Of all the doorways in all the worlds Roustaf had visited, this was the largest. So massive was it, in fact, that he believed his entire home world might actually be capable of fitting inside. Without a doubt, the concept was terrifying. Maneuvering just inches above the ground, the little man was making incredible time. He'd closed the distance between himself and the doorway in a matter of minutes. Moments before descending into the darkened pit, he noticed something out of the corner of his eye, something that forced him to dig his heels into the hard dirt and come to a sliding stop amidst a cloud of uprooted soil.

It was Tahnja, Donald and the rest of the group, less than two or three hundred yards away.

Having exited the doorway, they seemed to be on a direct course for Kragamel's fortress with weapons at the ready. What they didn't see, however, and Roustaf could, was the fact that a rather large, nasty looking regiment of Ochan soldiers had spotted them from a lookout post near the north end of the pit. Unsheathing their weapons, the Ochan contingent began moving in the direction of the group. In a matter of minutes they would be on top of them.

In a matter of minutes, even more of Roustaf's friends would be dead.

51. MISTAKES AND REGRETS

While Owen lay curled on his side in the tiny dwelling, asleep and snoring louder than one might imagine possible based on his diminutive size, Chris Jarvis stared with some regret at the boy from the opposite end of the room. He looked so young, so innocent. He imagined what the boy's father must have been thinking at that moment, wondering where his son was, wondering if he was okay. He wished Owen hadn't followed him into the stream. There was no reason he needed to be there. The absolute silence in this place was unlike anything Chris had ever experienced. There were no crickets down here or bugs or anything creaking, crawling or chirping, and there was no breeze. In this bizarre city below the ground, there was nothing except quiet stacked on top of quiet and lathered with a thick, gooey layer of even more quiet on top of that. Though the strange skinny thing calling herself Zanell suggested he try and get some sleep, and claimed repeatedly that she would take him to his children in the morning, Chris had found sleeping impossible. There was simply too much going on, too much to think about, worry about and fret over. In the matter of a day, he'd been transported to another world, met creatures so bizarre they shouldn't have existed, and learned that those very same creatures believed Tommy and Nicky were the realization of an ancient, rather confusing prophecy. Replaying the day's events in his head, Chris chuckled to himself at the absurdity of it all. It was the plot of a poorly written story, the synopsis of a "B" grade late night movie. It was nonsense, and yet it was real, every bit of it.

From the other end of the room, little Owen settled into a snoring fit so violent that it knocked the thick glasses from his face and into the dirt. Realizing there was no possible way he was going to get to sleep, Chris stood and dusted the sand off the rear of his khakis. Careful not to wake Owen, he tiptoed through the awkwardly constructed doorway and into the tunnels of New Tipoloo. The air was a bit less stuffy out there, though only a bit. The doorways dug into the soil on either side of the street were silent and unmoving, entire families of odd monsters residing sleepily behind. The light was dim, lit sparsely by torches hanging from the high ceiling above. Near the end of the street, partially obscured in shadow, Chris noticed a fairly average sized creature with an appearance slightly reminiscent of an upright walking fish. His body was covered in fine scales of varying blue hues creating striped patterns across whatever wasn't obscured by clothing. The fish man was sitting on a massive grey rock that looked noticeably out of place among the surprisingly smooth and level streets. No doubt at some point during the construction of the city, it was decided that the stone was much too large to move or break apart, therefore it was left alone. Turning his head toward Chris, the fish man nodded; his face was noticeably sad, distant and forlorn. It was the face of someone who had lost and would lose again. It was a face Chris could instantly relate to. Breathing deeply, Chris mustered up some courage and began walking in the creature's direction.

Fellow Undergotten listened to the man's every step as he approached from the other end of the dimly lit street. Like Chris, he too had found sleep to be an impossible dream. Though neither was aware as of yet, the reasons for their current case of insomnia were strikingly similar.

"It's a pleasure to finally meet you, Mr. Jarvis," Fellow stated calmly, his voice just barely a notch above a whisper despite the fact that Chris was more than ten feet away. "I guess you're having trouble sleeping too? You know, for the life of me, I'll never figure out how everyone else around here manages to do it: sleep, I mean. Even with all this craziness going on around them, every night they drop their heads to the ground and drift away. It's pretty remarkable when you think about it. Between you and me, though, it doesn't make a whole heck of a lot of sense."

Coming to a stop a few feet from the fish man, Chris found himself unable come up with anything he considered appropriate from the wide variety of responses tumbling around in his head. In the end, he chose to not respond at all. Staring back at Fellow through a pair of unbelieving eyes, he was having problems dealing with the fact that a six foot tall fish was speaking to him as if there was absolutely nothing strange about the situation, as if this kind of thing happened every day.

"The name's Fellow Undergotten, by the way," Fellow added with a half-hearted grin while extending his webbed hand in Chris' direction.

After another moment of hesitation, Chris reached forward, grasping the slightly slimy fish paw and shaking it gently.

"I always wondered what you'd look like," Fellow continued. "The kids and I never had much of an opportunity to talk about you, or their parents in general I guess."

Immediately Chris perked up. "The kids? Wait, you've met my boys?"

"Sure. In fact, I wouldn't be sitting here right now, working on only a few hours sleep, if it wasn't for them."

Chris paused for a moment, his attention piqued. "What do you mean?"

"Your kids saved my life, Mr. Jarvis, saved my life a couple of times in fact, along with the lives of a number of others around here."

His heart pounding and his legs wobbly, Chris suddenly found himself overcome with the need to sit on something solid, stable and familiar. Plopping himself into the dirt with his back against a nearby wall, he breathed deeply while trying to corral the chaos of emotions threatening to overtake him like an invading army.

"Amazing children you've got there, very special . . .important too. You must have done something right to raise a couple boys like that."

The comment was like a dagger smashing through Chris' ribcage and sinking into his heart. Whatever this six foot tall fish believed Tommy and Nicky were, whatever they'd accomplished, there was no doubt in Chris' mind that it had very little to do with him. As far as fathers went, he was keenly aware that he had not been the best.

Lowering his head, Chris sighed and briefly closed his eyes. "No, not me. Think maybe they got it from their mother."

"Well, where ever it came from," Fellow responded politely, "They're incredible creatures, your children. The things they can do. Well, they're unbelievable."

The pair paused. From behind a nearby doorway wafted the soft hum of labored breathing, followed by a throaty garbled mumble. The creature passed out inside switched its position in mid-sleep, trying to get comfortable. When the breathing had disappeared, again came the silence.

"I was a terrible father," Chris stated plainly, staring at the fine grains of dirt beneath his feet. "When their mother passed — my wife — it hurt, hurt a lot. I was so damn caught up in myself that I didn't stop to think about what they were going through. It was stupid, really damn stupid. I was . . .stupid."

The moment he finished the sentence, Chris wished he could take it back, wished he could wipe it from existence along with the last three or so years of his life. Why did he even say it? More importantly, why now? Of all the places and all the times, why did he choose this one to say the things it took him a month with a trained therapist to blurt out? A human sized fish in an underground tunnel filled with a bunch of characters from science-fiction comic books? It was idiotic. Suddenly he wanted to be somewhere else, anywhere other than there.

Using the wall to brace himself, he rose to his feet while shaking his head. "You know what, I'm gonna get going. Getting tired. Need some sleep."

Chris managed to get only a few feet before he again heard the voice of Fellow Undergotten waft up behind him. "You remind me of Leeko."

Despite a mountain-sized lump of judgment telling him to ignore the comment and keep walking, Chris stopped. Not only did he stop, but he chose to speak, knowing full well that it would serve only to drag the uncomfortable conversation on longer. "Who's Leeko?"

"My brother—or at least he was my brother. Leeko was killed within a few days of the Ochan's invasion of my world. I loved him. He was my best friend. You know, in that weird way only brothers can ever really understand."

Standing motionless a few feet away from Fellow, Chris now found himself listening as intently to the fish man as he'd ever listened to anyone in his life. Maybe it was the silence of the strange underground city, maybe it was the fact that the fish man seemed so incredibly bizarre he barely seemed real, or maybe it was simply that this was the exact opportunity Chris had been waiting for. Before him now, in a form he could never have imagined, was the chance to confess the things he'd done. This was an opportunity to free himself of burden.

Fellow's head drooped, his wide mouth coiling into a frown as he spoke. "Leeko never felt he was a very good father. He could be

269

a little too harsh sometimes, a little too honest, distant and quiet, sometimes hard to read, and even harder to get a reaction from. It was just his way, though. He never really opened up to anyone but me and on the rare occasion he did, even then he was always guarded with his feelings. Everyone always thought he was rude and standoffish. I knew better though. He was as confused and insecure as any of us, he just expressed it differently. I remember one evening though; Nell and the children were asleep and we were sitting on his porch looking out over the lake. He was a little tipsy on Secardin Vino and he started to open up. He told me how much he wished things could have been different, how he had never been able relate to his children or to get close to them, and how much it bothered him. I could tell by the look on his face that he was ashamed. He tried to hide it, but we could never hide anything from each other, not since we were kids. He hated the way things turned out."

Sighing deeply, Chris lowered his head. The already stuffy air around him suddenly felt stuffier, thick and chunky. His lungs seemed to be having trouble making proper use of it. Still seated on the rock a few feet away, Fellow Undergotten looked up at him with a pair of large moist blue eyes, his expression remaining introspective and somber.

"I'll tell you what though, in the end, when the Ochans broke down the door to his house and grabbed his wife and kids, none of that mattered. The quiet, subdued Leeko I grew up with and watched grow into an adult was wiped from existence. My brother fought with everything he had to save his family. He loved his children more than anything in the world, and he wasn't going to let those damn Ochan bastards hurt them. The soldiers cut my brother open at least a hundred times. They stabbed him, ripped him and tore him to shreds, hacked him to bits on the floor of his own home, and he never stopped fighting. After twenty minutes of working him over, there wasn't any blood left in his body. He should have died ten times, and still he kept on swinging. He had to. They were his children. He loved them and he owed them."

Realizing that his mouth was hanging open, Chris quickly closed it. Realizing he hadn't blinked in over two minutes, he decided to do that as well. The knot in his stomach had swelled to epic proportions and was now pressing against his interior lining painfully. Across from him, Fellow Undergotten wiped a barely noticeable stream of tears from the side of his face before reaching up with his webbed fingers to rub a pesky knot in the muscles of his neck. Chris noticed that the creature's lower lip was quivering ever so slightly. He then realized his was doing the same. The once merely interesting silence of New Tipoloo had transformed into something dangerous, deafening and uncomfortable. Chris' skin felt a size too small, as if he'd outgrown it somehow. More than ever, he wanted to get away. More than ever, he knew he couldn't.

Before either of the pair was given the opportunity to speak, the ground beneath their feet began to rumble violently, shattering the quiet veneer of the city into a million tiny jagged pieces. Fellow's muscles stiffened, his body going rigid and straight. Again the ground shook, roaring angrily. Clumps of dirt tumbled from the ceiling, creating brownish puffs of supremely fine sand that had begun blanketing the tunnels of New Tipoloo. Rising from his rock, Fellow moved to Chris' side. Reaching forward, he helped the man remain upright as another jolt nearly tossed the duo to the floor. From the doors lining the city streets, creatures of every shape and size emerged with a weapon in hand, expressions of confusion and anger sprawled upon their radically different faces. The rumbling was a sound most had heard before, caused by the gargantuan feet of Ochan digging beasts trouncing through the forest above. Immediately those calling New Tipoloo home assumed that like its predecessor, its location had been discovered. Gripping their weapons, they prepared for the inevitable battle. The steady rumbling knocked loose the candles dangling from the ceiling. Falling to the ground, they were snuffed out by the soil, bathing the entire city in the unknown of a terrifying blackness.

"What the hell's going on?" Chris Jarvis screamed, his breathing speedy and uneven as sweat poured down his face. Fellow's response was steady calm. "I don't know." Moving toward the crowd while pulling Chris along with him, Fellow began shoving his way through the mass of anxious creatures, vibrations bouncing off the city walls.

His head moving back and forth in small, quick jerks, the Chintaran raised his hand to the worried mass of alien flesh as their fear continued to mount. "Hold on a minute! Settle down! If they knew we were down here, we'd have digger heads crashing through the ceiling already!"

Understanding that Fellow's statement was most likely correct, the worried yelps of the group slowly reduced to mumbles and then eventually whispers.

Rising from within the voices came a single recognizable question: "If they aren't looking for us, what are they doing out here?"

Almost instantly, Fellow knew the answer. To shake New Tipoloo the way it was currently shaking, the Ochans would have had to amass an absolutely massive group of soldiers, workers and slaves. Groups of this magnitude were generally assembled for one reason and one reason only: to invade. Turning his head slowly, Fellow stared at the frightened face of Chris Jarvis alongside him. Gazing up at the shaking ceiling, clouds of loose dirt dropping onto his head, the man seemed to have progressed beyond mere confusion and was now petrified with fear. The news that the Ochan convoy above was most likely headed in the direction of the last world left undiscovered—Chris' world—wasn't going to ease his worry.

"I don't know," Fellow answered to the faceless voice among the crowd, though his gaze never moved from Chris. "I don't know."

Though Fellow Undergotten had never much cared for lies, in this moment the lie made sense. In this instant the lie was the only choice.

52. ONE MUST ESCAPE

Lifting one of the flat, oversized fingers on his paw to the crest of his lips, Walcott whispered, "Keep quiet and stay low, my friend."

Crouched beside him just outside the massive steel doorway leading to the work yard, and barely able to walk under his own power, was Pleebo. Scattered throughout the frozen area around them, creatures of every shape and size hammered mindlessly at the solid Ochan soil. Lit only by what remained of the descending sun and the luminescent moonlight only now beginning to take its place in the sky, the slaves were soulless husks of their former selves, barely there things tortured so badly they were no longer aware of their own existence. To these poor souls the world had long since faded away, replaced by pain: endless, unyielding pain, and nothing more. Strewn among the mass of zombies, Walcott spotted a few Tycarians, and his blood began to boil. Swallowing an overflowing of emotion, he fought the urge to charge to their aid, knowing full well that such an act would ultimately prove pointless.

The things hacking mindlessly at the Ochan earth bore resemblance to no Tycarians he had ever encountered. Normally proud muscular legs had been reduced to gaunt, ghastly sticks, barely able to support the weight of their chipped and worn shells. The expressions hidden beneath the mass of scars and welts were blank, their faces a mass of wrinkles, drawn and crumpled like dirty-burnt paper. Though it pained him to the point of tears to admit it, at this point there was nothing he could do to save them. These hapless souls were no longer Tycarians; they hadn't been for some time. The same as they had everything else, the Ochans had stolen this too. For him and Pleebo, however, there remained at the very least a glimmer of hope, a nugget of possibility vaguely reminiscent of a future. Beside him, his Fillagrou friend stumbled forward on wobbly uneven legs, his muscles struggling to remain in a partially crouched position. Walcott knew he needed to remain focused on Pleebo. There was hope for Pleebo. He would return for his brethren when the opportunity presented itself. He would not leave them to rot in this place.

Wrapping his muscular green arm around Pleebo's waist, Walcott hoisted his companion into an upright position yet again. "I understand all too well the difficulty of the situation, but I must insist we keep moving, my friend. I swear to you that I will get you to safety. I shall allow no more to die in this icy pit."

With the Tycarian king leading the way, the pair carefully moved along the outside of the building while keeping to the shadows and scanning the yard for anything resembling an exit point. Though Walcott had never seen an Ochan work camp for himself, he had heard the grizzly, terrifying stories, stories he now realized were unfortunately true. Normally located just outside the walls of the main castle, it was here that many interrogations were conducted, and it was here that survivors of those interrogations toiled the remainder of their days. In this place, freedom walked hand and hand with death. Of course, there was no real "work" being done. The act of breaking rock was quite meaningless, as the Ochans had no real use for shattered stone bits. This was busy work, intended only for the perverse amusement of the king's soldiers. This was extended torture and nothing more. Coming to a stop behind a pile of unbroken boulders at least fifteen feet high, Walcott and Pleebo dropped to their knees and peered through the tiny spaces between the stone. Two hundred yards away, a group of Ochan soldiers were huddled together, engaged in idle chatter beside a massive steel gate. Walcott found the smiles slicing across their faces beyond revolting, especially considering the massive amounts of death and despair surrounding them. Just beyond the gate there was an open field of frozen dirt littered occasionally by spiny sharp foliage. Even the plants had teeth in this world. Beyond the field lay a row of densely packed, though mostly leafless trees. Further still there was freedom, at least comparatively. Giving his full attention to the guards and the gate, Walcott began to formulate a plan of escape. Years spent attending to the dead and dying had left the guards stationed here complacent. They had lost their edge and weren't the least bit prepared to deal with an enemy willing or able to fight back. Walcott immediately saw this as an advantage, maybe their only advantage.

"If we move quickly, I believe we can make it," The turtle man stated through tight lips, his eyes narrow and focused as the pain crippling his body slowly faded to the background, exactly where he needed it to be.

Unsure if Walcott was seeing the same thing he was, Pleebo stated with some surprise, "No offense, but are you nuts? Even if we somehow manage to get past the guards, how are we supposed to get through the gate?"

"Leave the useless piece of Ochan steel to me, my friend," Walcott replied sternly.

Reaching between the pile of stone and the wall, the Tycarian retrieved the remnants of a rusted and broken pickaxe with a snapped wooden handle. Bouncing it in the palm of his hand, he tested its weight, finding the tool sufficient to meet his needs.

"No matter what may occur," Walcott continued, "You are to run and continue running, Mr. Pleebo. Do not stop until you have entered the tree line. Once there, I suggest you hide for only a moment, then run some more."

With his bones cracking and an expression of absolute rage on his face, Walcott Shellamennes rose to his feet. Gripping tighter on the broken handle of the pickaxe, his knuckles popped, crunched and ground against each other.

Reaching up, Pleebo tried in vain to pull the massive Tycarian into a crouched position once more. "Wait a minute. What do you mean me? What are you going to do?"

Walcott shrugged away the arm of his friend as his heart began to race, the adrenaline of battle now coursing through his veins like molten steel. "I regret there is currently no time for discussion, my friend. Our talks have proven enlightening in the past. I shall miss them. You have been given your orders. I expect you to follow them. Do not stop running until you are safely hidden among the trees."

Again Pleebo tugged at the burly arm of the Tycarian; again Walcott wiggled free. "Hold on a minute, you nutcase!"

Unwilling to allow Pleebo further protest, Walcott breathed deeply of the chilly Ochan air and exhaled. Ignoring the fact that the majority of his bones were broken and his body was overrun with ungodly pain, he barreled forward in the direction of the Ochan guards and the enormous steel gate. Realizing he suddenly had no real choice in the matter, Pleebo forced his tired and mostly useless muscles to do the same.

The frozen soil shattered like broken glass beneath Walcott's massive flat feet. The sound resulting from his every lumbering step resonated throughout the yard. With every second he picked up speed, his resolve expanding and mutating, boiling red with anger and popping when reaching its crest. In perfect health, Pleebo could have easily outrun the Tycarian; things being as they were, however, he found himself struggling to keep pace. For one so large, old and injured, Walcott was moving with impressive speed. Less than a hundred feet from the gate, the guards first took note of the heavy thumps of Walcott's feet over the cool breeze and turned in his direction. Caught off guard, they hurriedly retrieved their weapons, instantly moving toward the charging Tycarian.

As the guards turned to face him, Walcott screamed through a mouthful of shattered teeth. There were four of them and one of him. In his condition, with little more than a digging tool for a weapon, he had no hope of putting the entire group down for good. He understood, however, that he needed only to stop them , to remove them from the equation long enough for Pleebo to escape. This much he could do. This much he was capable of. This much he had to do.

Moments later, Walcott and the guards clashed violently. Despite the fact that even walking should have been impossible when considering the extent of his injuries, it was Walcott and his sad excuse for a weapon that somehow gained the upper hand. Born from years of experience in battle, his every step was measured, precise and deadly. The massive Tycarian slid under the blades of two guards while tripping one to the ground with his shattered forearm and sinking the pickaxe into the belly of the other. Leaping straight into the air with his feet leading the way, he slammed the full weight of his body into the remaining two. The force of the blow dented the armor into their chests, collapsing bone underneath and cracking the back of their heads against the frozen ground with sickening thuds. Intent on maintaining his speed, Walcott lowered his shoulder and tucked his head into the top of his shell just enough to keep it safe while in no way obscuring his vision. The steel gate was less than fifty feet away, its bars nearly the thickness of his leg and considerably more sturdy. The Ochan construction was solid and built to last, much the same as the chains that formally bound him to the wall of the dungeon below. It remained, however, old, its best days having come and long since gone. Over many years, the harsh Ochan weather had eaten away at the once robust connections binding steel to steel leaving it vulnerable.

With age, all things lose their durability. In time, all things become useless. As it is a foe that has no equal, only the truly foolhardy challenge time. It is an enemy that's never tasted defeat.

Possibly more than most, of this fact King Walcott Shellamennes was keenly aware.

A low, grimy, guttural growl bellowed from between the Tycarian's lips once again, his black-green eyes focusing on the bars and the bars alone. The muscles in his aching legs worked double-time, kicking clumps of loose soil into the air as he barreled forward. Never slowing, Walcott slammed the entire weight of his body into the steel, tearing away a chunk of his already battered shell in the process and racking the entirety of his body in searing pain. As he knew it would, as if super-heated and pliable, the steel miraculously bent, tore, and gave way. Of course, the collision and subsequent pain caused Walcott's legs to give way as well. Stumbling forward, he slammed into the ground while spinning wildly, tossing chunks of frozen sand in every direction as he was engulfed in a cloud of debris. Quickly moving through the bent steel opening, Pleebo came to an awkward sliding stop alongside the body of his fallen friend. Not far behind the pair, the Ochan guards not mortally wounded had already begun to recover as more still poured from the doorway to the building further away.

Wrapping his arms underneath Walcott's body, Pleebo attempted to pull the Tycarian to his feet. "Come on! Get up! We've got to keep moving!"

Walcott, however, had reached his limit. There would be no more moving. Drowning in pain and unable to speak, the Tycarian growled something incoherent, a frothy liquid seeping from between his lips. His body was gargantuan, even his arm alone weighed more than Pleebo could lift in his current state of health. Despite his tugging, Pleebo was accomplishing nothing. The Ochan guards were getting closer with every passing moment.

"Come on! Please! Move!" Pleebo's voice cracked as he screamed, cursing every muscle in his body for being so sore and useless.

Passing through the blinding pain overtaking him for the briefest of instances, Walcott pried the bony finger of his friend from his wrist. "Go . . .to the trees. Go now. I cannot follow."

"No! That is not an option! I'm not leaving you here!"

Reaching up, Walcott grabbed the filthy, tattered fabric adorning Pleebo's body and pulled his Fillagrou companion close to his face. His lips quivered as he whispered sternly, "If you do not escape, it was all for nothing. Go now, my friend. Go and hide. Prove to me that this old shell of a king is still worth a damn."

Pleebo's grip loosened, Walcott's beefy wrist sliding from between his sweaty, broken fingers. Within moments the guards would be on top of them both. Within moments it would have been all for nothing.

Struggling to breathe, his eyes floated to the back of his head as unconsciousness overtook him, Walcott whispered pleadingly, "Go my friend. Go now, please . . .."

Pleebo leaned in close enough to catch the salty smell of Walcott's sweat in his nose. Wiping a single tear from the corner of his eye he sputtered, "I'll come back for you, I swear it."

Forcing himself to a standing position, Pleebo sprinted toward the tree line. Ochan arrows whizzed past his head, ricocheting off the frozen soil and bouncing back up like springs. Never once did he glance behind him. Walcott wouldn't have wanted that. Soon the pain in his legs drifted away. He was running for his friend now. Pain was no longer an option. After entering the trees, Pleebo continued running until the Ochan guards had broken chase and he could run no more, until the night had strangled the life from the day and the darkness enveloped him completely. Running and hiding was what the Fillagrou did best. In this instance, Pleebo proved to be no exception.

53. OF BEST LAID PLANS

From Roustaf's perspective, it happened so fast, too fast for him to begin forming an appropriate response. One minute he was about to dive headfirst into the black abyss of the Ochan doorway leading to the Red Forest, and the next he was watching as his friends were ambushed by a regiment of Ochan soldiers just outside the king's fortress. As he watched Tahnja get knocked violently from the back of her coal black Pegasus, the initial shock of the situation evaporated and was replaced by rage. The wings of the tiny man responded before his brain even gave them an order. Pulling his tiny hands into only slightly less tiny fists, Roustaf's body blasted forward at a blistering speed. Forming a loose circle around his friends, the Ochan soldiers had managed to erase any possible means of escape. With this entire situation taking place just outside the castle, the group would no doubt be surrounded by hundreds of additional soldiers in a matter of minutes. The plan to rescue Walcott and Pleebo had gone to complete and absolute hell. Nearly halfway to his fallen Tahnja, icy wind cracking painfully against his frozen face, Roustaf cursed her for coming through the doorway at this hour of the day. He then cursed himself for not getting back to her sooner. She should have listened to him! Why didn't she listen to him?

Roustaf suddenly knew he should have listened to Zanell. He should have never gone on this wild goose chase in the first place, and he definitely shouldn't have included Tahnja. Had he thought with his head instead of his heart, all of this could have been avoided.

Tossed from her perch atop the muscular back of the Pegasus by a rather stiff blow to the center of her back, Tahnja landed hard on the frozen Ochan soil. Before she could even retrieve a dagger from her waist, she was kicked stiffly in the stomach. The blow made her eyes bulge and knocked the air from her lungs, leaving her gasping for breath as it scurried away. On either side of her, the remainder of the group now found themselves in equally precarious positions. Leaping from his Pegasus, Brutus pulled a pair of axes from his back, each nearly the length of his body. A pair of Ochan soldiers was rapidly closing on his position, sharp, dangerous smiles spread across their enraged faces. With weapons at the ready, the Tycarians ushered young Donald Rondage into a small space between them in order to protect the boy. Each was fully prepared to die to save him. Two more of Tahnja's group, both friends of hers for many months, had already been struck down. Their bodies now lay prone in the partially frozen soil, blood pouring copiously from their wounds. Again the foot of the massive bodied Ochan guard hovering over Tahnja collided with her torso, sending a blood-curdling twinge of pain across her upper body. Something in her chest was broken, fractured, or possibly both. Trying to ignore the pain, she cursed herself for making the decision to leave their hiding place and come through the doorway. It was dumb, stupid and childish. It was the decision of a love struck fool rather than a soldier. She let her fear for Roustaf's safety cloud her common sense. Those she vowed to protect were now paying for her mistake.

Sandwiched between a set of incredibly thick turtle shells, Donald tried his best to regain some control over his emotions.

After everything he'd been through, everything he'd seen, everything he'd done and had done to him, he imagined situations such as this would have become easier to deal with. This, however, was proving not to be the case. In truth, facing the possibility of death is easy for no one, least of all a fourteen-year-old boy. Realizing his hands were shaking, Donald squeezed them into fists in a vain attempt to halt the wild jitters.

"No matter what happens, see to it that you remain between us, lad!" One of the Tycarians snarled from above while swinging his weapon in the direction of an advancing enemy.

A group of four Ochan soldiers had surrounded the trio and the Tycarians were using all of their nearly seven foot frames to keep the hungry predators at bay. The heavy blades of the combatants clashed violently, the sound of steel on steel ringing in Donald's ears. Somewhere behind the boy, a terrified Pegasus broke through the Ochan defense, kicking its legs wildly, then instinctively bolting in the direction of the doorway to Fillagrou. Moments before reaching the enormous black pit, an arrow sliced through its neck. Howling wildly, the creature stumbled face first to the soil. Legs still twitching as it gasped for air, Donald watched the beautiful black creature as it swallowed its last chilly breath. With a final defiant and ultimately useless heave, it died. Dropping to his knees between the walls of Tycarian muscle on either side, Donald could no longer control the shaking of his hands, nor did he desire to. A feeling he'd felt before had begun spreading across his body, feeding off the jumbled mess of emotions making up the vast majority of his headspace and growing stronger as it devoured his fear, resentment and rage. Though his shaking had yet to stop, Donald Rondage suddenly felt stronger, and more alive than he had in quite some time. He felt different, bigger than himself, more than himself. Behind him, one of his Tycarian protectors hit the ground with a heavy thud as the dangerous blade of an Ochan sliced open its lower leg, making it impossible for the heavy-bodied turtle to remain upright. With half of Donald's protective walls collapsed, he had become easy prey for the energized Ochans nearby — or so they believed.

Squeezing his fists tighter still, Donald's jitters at last came to a screeching halt. For the briefest of moments, the world around him went silent and hollow. The sound of battle stretched, twisting and dragging into blurry disjointed echoes. Every muscle in his pudgy body was on fire, tingling with something similar to electricity, only more. Above him an Ochan coiled his broadsword back, intent on lopping the boy's head from his shoulders. Lifting his fists into the air, Donald smiled. He knew this feeling well. He'd felt this before.

Roustaf was less than ten feet from Tahnja and her attacker when he spotted the expression on Donald's face. He too had seen this before. The moment the boy lifted his hands into the air, Roustaf pulled his wings straight and his body vertical. Still airborne, his body slid to an immediate hovering stop.

Covering his face, he turned his back to Donald Rondage and muttered to himself, "Awww crap."

In one quick movement Donald dropped his fists, slamming them into the ground with every ounce of the incredible strength suddenly electrifying his body. The frozen Ochan soil proved no match for the blow. The boy's fists shattered the jagged clumpy soil to bits, tearing it to shreds and sending debris sailing in every direction. Cracks as wide as twelve inches extended from the center of his arms, which were now buried at least that many inches into the ground. The smashing of fist to dirt caused the ground to rumble so violently that the attacking Ochans lost their balance and stumbled forward. A mound of fine dust and rocky pebbles rose up in a mushroom-shaped cloud from the area surrounding Donald. Quickly, it spread outward and over the still rumbling ground, engulfing everyone in the immediate area, snaking its way into their lungs and sending many of them into uncontrollable coughing fits. The warrior instinct of the Ochan soldiers instantly clicked on. Though they could hardly believe what they'd witnessed, the well-trained creatures chose to ignore the child's ungodly feat of strength for the moment and simply retaliate. In a matter of seconds, the entire regiment was on their feet with weapons in hand, carefully making their way in Donald's direction through the smoky debris cloud. Though Donald couldn't see them through the brownish haze, he could hear their coughing hacks as they approached. His breathing was ragged and excited, his heart pumping double time, mounds of dirt sticking to the sweat on his grimy face. Fervent, terrified and entirely energized, he angrily spit a clump of sand from his mouth. Despite the horror of the situation and despite the fact that he was surrounded by lizard men with muscles on top of muscles carrying weapons that could easily slice him as fine as sushi, only one thing popped into Donald's head: it was good to be back.

His hands still buried in the ground, Donald opened his fists and grabbed hold of large clumps of icy soil just below the surface. As he stood, he ripped a chunk of rock at least a hundred, maybe two hundred, times the size of his entire body from the ground and hoisted it above his head. When an Ochan soldier emerged from the smoky cloud in front of him, Donald swung the sandy boulder at the creature, smacking it directly in the chest with such force that the lizard man was instantly sent airborne. The creature landed with a thump over fifty feet away, its ribs shattered to jagged particles of bone. Another soldier leapt at Donald from behind, trying to catch the child off guard. Twisting with surprising speed to meet him, Donald used the enormous rock as a club once again, cracking this Ochan square in the chest as well. Donald used his gargantuan boulder to launch soldiers into the air, one after another, denting their armor and breaking various important bones in the process.

Carefully navigating the debris cloud as rocks continued to rain down from above and the body of an Ochan sailed past, Roustaf called to his pink-skinned infatuation, "Tahnja! Where are you, you damn crazy broad? Where are you, baby?"

Vision beyond a few feet had been reduced to nothing. From somewhere within the cloud of dust, the little man heard the sound of snapping bone combined with the high-pitched yelp of yet another mortally wounded soldier. A moment afterward, an airborne green-skinned Ochan parted the dust cloud above him momentarily. Soaring backward at an incredible speed, the soldier's legs flopped loose in the wind like the wobbly, shapeless limbs of a marionette. Clutching the inverted steel of his chest plate, the screaming Ochan was quickly swallowed by the mist, sailing forth to an unknown destination. Coughing loose a mouth full of sand, Roustaf gazed to his right and spotted what he believed to be the blurry outline of Tahnja lying face down in the dirt ten feet away. Sailing over to her, he came to a sliding stop on her shoulder.

Pulling forcefully at the fleshy loop rising up from her ears, he tried frantically to wake her. "Come on, come on, come on, get up, you're not hurt, you're not hurt, you can't be hurt!"

His voice was hoarse, sore and coated with a layer of dust so thick it had added an inch to the interior of his throat. "Come on, please, please, please, come on, get the hell up. Please get up . . ."

Again the sound of cracking bone and bending steel sliced through the dust. With the cloud of dirt beginning to slowly settle, Roustaf watched as pudgy little Donald Rondage threw his massive stone at the last of the attacking soldiers. The rock collided with the creature, carried him well over a hundred yards, then squashed him against the outer wall of the king's castle. Though Roustaf had seen the boy's unbelievable feats of strength before, he couldn't help but be amazed and horrified.

"Rou–Roustaf?" Tahnja whispered between coughs, her eyes slowly fluttering open.

Rolling onto her back, she hacked a wad of dirt from her lungs, at last noticing the tiny body of her tiny love standing on her collarbone just a few inches from her face. Her pale pink skin was covered in a thin layer of dust, transforming it into something more sandy and brown.

"Welcome back, cutie. You scared the beejeezus outta me for a minute there," Roustaf added playfully, breathing a sigh of relief.

Initially overcome with joy just to see the little man alive, Tahnja's exuberance transformed quickly to shame. "Shouldn't have come through. Sorry. Thought you were caught. Worried you were dead."

Roustaf patted her on the cheek tenderly, his entire hand smaller than the tip of her nose. Leaning down, he planted a loving kiss on the crest of her sand coated lips. "You should have known better. Kill me? These jerks have been trying to pull off that feat for years now with no success whatsoever. Long story short, it just ain't gonna happen."

The shared moment between the two was shattered by the anxious voice of young Donald Rondage from behind, "Uh, I hate to break up your little make out session, but I think maybe you should turn around."

Simultaneously Tahnja and Roustaf craned their heads in the direction of the boy's voice. With the dust continuing to clear, the pair was now able to see far beyond the few feet they were allotted only a moment prior. Just beyond Donald, Kragamel's castle had become frighteningly clear and visible. Perched atop its walls were hundreds upon hundreds of Ochan archers, every last one with an arrow pointed in their direction. Hundreds more soldiers began pouring from the doorways near the base, each one angry and ready to fight, a deadly weapon in hand. The sheer volume of the advancing force was staggeringly heartbreaking. Like a tidal wave, the mountain of green flesh surrounded them entirely. The excitement coursing through Donald's veins moments ago instantly washed away, leaving barely a shadow behind. His strength, no matter how amazing, wasn't going to do him much good against so many. Walking slowly across Tahnja's chest, over her stomach and up her leg, Roustaf came to a stop on the tip of her bony knee. Placing one hand on his hip, he reached up with the other and began twiddling his bushy beard nervously.

Breathing deeply, he slumped his shoulders, threw his hands into the air and mumbled, "Ah yeah, this is gonna suck."

54. MR. BUTTON IS DEAD

"Your dog's dead. Get your ass out back and do something with it."

His father's voice was ragged, garbled and twisted, slathered in the sour, tangy wetness of a night spent drowning sorrows with drink. At first, young Tommy Jarvis scarcely believed what had just come from the old man's mouth. Whether intentional or otherwise, so very often his father had lied to him. As if greased, the lies tended to slide easily from him in this state. Though only eleven years old, Tommy already understood the fact that lies should never come easily. They should be rough, they should require thought, and they should never come without regret. The act of passing them through your lips should be a painful, painful experience. Starting up the darkened stairway leading to his bedroom, Tommy's father came to a wobbly stop barely three steps into the journey. When he turned to look at his son, his face was distorted, a mass of awkwardly angled wrinkles and two-day-old stubble.

Faraway his eyes wandered and dipped, struggling to remain focused. "I said, clean up your damn dog! If that thing is still out back tomorrow morning, I swear to God, you'll regret it."

It was at that instant Tommy knew the words were more than the ramblings of a mind only half there. No matter how horrifying the idea might have been, no matter how badly he wished it weren't the case, his father was telling the truth. Tommy's lower lip began to jitter as warm, salty puddles of emotions given birth in the corners of his eyes.

Though his body was loopy and uncoordinated, the voice of his father remained monotone and serious, glaring at his elder son under the hood of heavy eyelids. "Do we understand each other?"

More of a reaction than a choice, Tommy nodded. He wasn't sure why. Content that he'd made his point, the awkward, foul-breathed thing the boy's father often transformed into hobbled upstairs like a scarecrow on legs of straw. A single tear rolled from Tommy's right eye and down his cheek. Quickly he wiped it away.

Crying would do him no good. It never had.

His little brother was upstairs asleep, and Tommy figured it best to leave him that way. Nicky did not need to know about or see this. Things like this weren't meant for his eyes. It would only hurt him. When he woke tomorrow morning, Tommy would lie to his brother, convince him that their dog hopped the fence and ran away. The story might leave Nicky heartbroken, though not nearly as heartbroken as the truth. Lying to his brother's innocent, round little face wouldn't be easy, which is exactly as it should be. With some hesitation, Tommy slowly made his way from the living room, into the kitchen, through the creaky screen door with its torn mesh, and onto the porch. The entire journey took only a few minutes. To the shaky boy overcome with even shakier emotions, it felt like so much more.

Time is little more than a matter of perception, after all; time is strange that way.

The night air was chilly. Winter had yet to fade away entirely, and spring yet to take hold. Across the cold wood of the porch, Tommy's bare feet shuffled. At the base of the stairs leading into the darkened backyard lay a coiled ball of matted fur. Only occasionally did a jagged-stiff angle protrude awkwardly from the oval-shaped mound of brownish-black hair. Even in the subtle starlight, Tommy instantly recognized the patterns of color. He'd seen them hundreds of times before, ran his hand across them lovingly, and often felt them against his face. They were undeniably familiar; they could belong to no other. Curled up in the dry grass was his lifelong friend. The ugly, deformed thing sprawled among a bed of crinkly paper-like fallen leaves was Mr. Button.

When Tommy was only still in diapers, Mr. Button was barely more than a puffball from which extended four stubby, mostly useless legs that would wiggle comically when rolled onto his back. As Tommy's limbs stretched, so did Button's. The pair crawled together and grew side by side, laughing and playing the same as any brothers or the best of friends might. Though Tommy's parents strictly forbade Button to sleep on his bed, when they retired for the night, the fluffy-haired rapscallion would immediately sneak into the boy's room and curl up beside his pal. At the break of day, he would hop to the floor once more, leaving none the wiser. Mr. Button was smart; he was always so smart. On Tommy's first day of school, Button walked with him to the bus stop. As it drove his friend away, Button chased the massive yellow vehicle for an entire block before relenting. He waited on the porch for hours until Tommy returned. On the day Megan Jarvis passed away, Button was there too, lying between both the Jarvis brothers underneath the stars well into the night as they stroked his furry back for comfort. Button's offer of solace was his presence. It was more appreciated than he could ever comprehend.

Moving alongside his fallen friend, Tommy scooped up his awkward, cold body and hoisted Button onto his shoulder with a grunt. Mr. Button had grown significantly since he was a pup. His body was heavy. Making matters worse, his limbs had already begun to stiffen; carrying him would prove a difficult task. Already the boy's shoulder was sore and his legs wobbly as he struggled with everything he had in him to avoid ending up face down in the grass. With Button's fur pressed firmly against the side of his face, Tommy set forth into the night to bury his friend and say goodbye. His progress was slow, every step bringing with it an agony born of both the physical and the emotional—yet another burden to add to the ever-growing list. Like all those that had come before, Tommy would not stumble, because he couldn't. The option no longer existed. Mr. Button's familiar scent snaked its way into his nostrils, thick brown hair tickling the tip of his nose and causing him to sneeze. High above, the glow of a full moon in the cloudless sky provided all the light he would require for the journey ahead. Tommy had made this trip before, many times in fact. Since the death of his mother, spending time at home had transformed into a mostly frightening experience. Scary, misshapen and wrong, it is now ranked among the very last places in the world he wanted to be.

Even here with Button, even under these circumstances . . .even this was strangely preferable.

Moving slowly, sweat pouring down his face as he struggled to carry Button's limp, dangling weight, Tommy made his way through the space between the Parkers' and the Thompsons' houses and into the tree line adjoining their backyards. After ten long minutes of trudging through the forest, he exited the trees, lumbering his way up and over a large grassy field. The trip upward proved the most difficult of all. No less than three times did he drop to one knee, questioning whether or not he should continue his journey. Each and every time, he rose more dedicated than before. Having reached the crest of the hill, Tommy continued down the other side and toward another thin line of trees near the bottom. Arriving at the bank of a small stream, at last he stopped. The pain in his shoulder had crept its way into his back and was now progressing toward his legs, leaving the majority of his body inflamed and sore. The bones in his neck cracked, popping like the final few kernels of un-popped popcorn. Dropping to his knees in the mud, Tommy gently lowered Button's stiff body to the dirt. Patting the belly of his friend tenderly, he ran the palm of his hand along Mr. Button's side. His fur was clumped, matted and twisted, half frozen stiff by the chilly late winter air. Occasionally the light of a firefly would pop into existence above the slow moving waters of the stream not far from the pair. A moment later, as if the tiny insect never existed in the first place, the yellow dot disappeared again, swallowed by the dark sky and the even darker silhouettes of surrounding foliage. Free of their summer bloom, the limbs of the trees above resembled the fingers of the elderly; bent and knotted, the bark encrusted digits reached to the stars, aching to touch the sporadic points of light hanging stationary in the sky. Planks of wood were awkwardly nailed to the top of the larger branches directly above Tommy's head, the humble beginnings of a tree fort he'd been working on since his mother's death. Directly below his fort, at the bank of the stream: this was the perfect place for Button, the only place.

Again a tear leaked from Tommy's eye. Again he wiped it away. The instant his lower lip began to quiver, he bit down hard, clamping the soft flesh between his teeth so tight it split and began to bleed. The ground was cold and thick, solid with the stiffness of winter's remains. Digging would be difficult. Tommy didn't care. He should have brought a shovel, but he forgot to, and in the end it really didn't matter. He wouldn't need a shovel to dig. Fingers would do just fine. Breathing deeply, Tommy leaned forward, tearing into the soil with his bare hands. Tossed over his shoulder, the handfuls of frosty mud and sand began piling up near the base of the home of his future fort. With time, the pile grew. Lying beside Tommy, Mr. Button remained exactly as he had been when the boy first discovered him at the foot of the stairs, exactly how he would remain from this point forward. Tommy noticed, however, that his friend's nose looked dry and crinkly, riddled with deep, painful cracks. It had never looked so dry.

His wide eyes appeared sad. Even in his most joyous of moments, Button had always had sad eyes.

After ten minutes of furious digging, the muscles in Tommy's arms were on fire, his fingers frozen and sore. Every scrape of his nails into the stiff dirt sent a ripple of pain along the contours of his hand, into his forearm and across his shoulders. Despite the pain and the numbness, never once did he stop digging. He couldn't and wouldn't stop. If the roles were reversed, Button wouldn't stop.

After twenty minutes, Tommy's face was lathered in a sheen of moist sweat. The disgusting wetness glimmered occasionally in the moonlight. Tired, sore and confused, Tommy had begun to break down. He didn't want to do this, and knew he shouldn't be doing this. Things like this were meant for people bigger and older than he. This shouldn't be happening. He wanted to be strong, ached to be tough, and wished he could find the strength hidden within to simply brush the entire situation away and treat it as no big deal. In the end, as he did so very often, he asked too much of himself. Despite his attempts to the contrary, Tommy began to cry. Pointless or not, he simply could no longer hold back. Under his breath, he chastised himself for being so childish, chastised his father for putting him in this situation, and chastised his mother for getting sick and going away. The lie he would tell Nicky is the exact lie his father should have told him. As the sweat dripped from his face and splashed into the hole his frozen hands had created, so did his tears, one liquid indistinguishable from the next. After half an hour, covered in splotches of black dirt, Tommy Jarvis relented. The hole was deep enough. Mr. Button could rest comfortably here. Grabbing the cold paws of his friend, he slid Button into the newly dug hole, closed his furry eyelids, and rolled his dry, rubbery tongue back into his mouth. Standing up, Tommy twiddled the filthy frozen toes of his shoeless feet in the dirt, sandwiching the gritty coldness between them. Staring lovingly at his friend, he wiped the runny snot from his nose and tears from his face. Unsure of what to say, he chose instead to say nothing. Button couldn't hear him anymore than his mother, his grandmother or anyone else that had left him over the past year. Though less messy, in the end words were as pointless as tears, meant solely for those grieving rather than those gone. Tommy was done with grieving. He'd had his fill. Mr. Button had gone, and he wasn't coming back. Once done, things could not be undone. Once stuck, there was no getting unstuck. Nothing could change this. These were the harsh realities of life that should never enter the mind of twelve-year-old boys, the harsh realities Tommy Jarvis had come to know all too well. Dropping to his knees, he covered the body of his friend with the black-brown soil. What took nearly a half an hour to dig was filled in less than five. When the ground had again taken something resembling its original shape, Mr. Button was gone. Choosing not to return home for the night, Tommy instead slept alongside his lifelong pal beneath the stars. The air was cold, the ground colder still, and yet again none of this mattered. He would enjoy this final night with Button.

At daybreak he'd start home, sneak into his room and into his bed, leaving none the wiser.

Fireflies popped in and out of existence around the pair, circling the area where Button now lay, the only attendees of the funeral. It was at least an hour before Tommy fell asleep. At some point during the night he believed he could hear Mr. Button breathing just below the dirt underneath his head. This, however, was only a dream, and dreams are, unfortunately, not real. Mr. Button was no different than anyone else. Mr. Button could not speak to those living anymore than Tommy could to those dead. These were constants that could in no way be altered, despite the best of intentions of scared young boys. Mr. Button was dead, and Mr. Button was not coming back; this was absolute and this was forever.

So be it.

55. THE ARTIFACT

From the bow of the Briar Patch, Krystoph screamed at the top of his lungs, "We have arrived!"

Stepping alongside the burly Ochan, Nestor scanned the surrounding waters with an obvious confusion. At first glance, the area seemed no different than any of the miles upon miles of water they'd sailed to that point. Krystoph's arbitrary announcement made little sense.

Rubbing his chin, Nestor turned to the scowl-faced Ochan beside him. "Might I inquire as to how exactly you've arrived at this conclusion?"

Krystoph's response was monotone and deliberate, soaked in a hint of anger. "Hurm. We are here. Nothing more need be said. Question me again, Tycarian, and I promise it will be the last thing you do."

Never once did Krystoph's black gaze stray from the froth-tipped waves ahead. Shaking his head while rolling his eyes, Nestor opted to end the conversation.

From the door leading to the lower decks, the children emerged one by one, with Tommy Jarvis leading the way. As a group, they had spent the night asleep on a dusty bed in the quarters of Captain Fluuffytail himself. Just outside, the crew worked tirelessly throughout the night patching leaks and draining ocean water in a desperate effort to keep the ship afloat. Despite the noise, and the fact that they were lying on top of a smelly, dust covered mattress barely large enough for one rather than three, each of the children managed to sleep at some point, including Tommy. The eruption of power earlier in the night had left him drained and tired, making the act of simply keeping his eyes open difficult, bordering on impossible. After running his hand through his stiff morning hair, Nicky stretched his arms and yawned. Standing beside him, Staci did the same, though she believed this was more of a reaction to the boy's yawn rather than a general feeling of tiredness.

"I'll be going down with you," Nestor stated in a matter of fact tone, passing by the sleepy-eyed children and in hot pursuit of the muscular Ochan on a direct course with the rear of the ship.

Lifting the heavy metal breastplate over his head, Krystoph tossed it to the deck with a clank. "Hurm. Did not ask for your help Tycarian. Do not require it."

"It only makes sense for me to accompany you, as I am the superior swimmer," Nestor responded, kicking the heavy armor from his path with his flat foot.

Instead of responding, Krystoph shook his head, growling in annoyance under his breath. After unlocking the belt from his waist, he dropped it to the deck of the Briar Patch as well. Placing a single dagger between his razor sharp teeth, he stepped onto the railing overlooking the water. The early morning light exposed the scars covering his dark green flesh in frightening detail. Nestor stopped moving forward, momentarily taken aback by the self-inflicted wounds, each of which represented a dead Ochan. There were so many. Reaching forward, the turtle man grabbed hold of Krystoph's leg moments before he could leap headfirst into the calm waters.

The Ochan scowled, biting on the steel between his teeth harder and growling through tight lips, "It would be in your best interest to remove your hand."

Nestor squeezed tighter, "These waters are dangerous. You will need help."

"Hurm. Rest assured, I am fully capable of taking care of myself."

Nestor's brow lowered angrily. With his free hand, he reached down and unlocked the belt from around his waist, letting it fall to the aged wood below. "If you truly believe my desire to accompany you is due to the fact that I fear for your safety, I regret to inform you that you are sadly mistaken. I simply refuse to have traveled all this way only to return empty handed. If you fail, I will not."

Showcasing remarkable balance for one so large, Krystoph remained motionless, perched atop the thin wood railing. Looking behind him, he glared down at Nestor. His expression was petrifying, cold and undeniably annoyed. A semi-circle of crewmembers had formed around the pair, every last one of them unsure of exactly how to respond to the standoff. Gnawing on a moldy piece of food somewhat similar to a carrot, though more purple in color, Captain Fluuffytail chuckled softly from underneath his dusty, oversized hat.

Nudging Nicky in the ribs playfully, he whispered, "Hehehe. I'll bet ya fifty doubloons the shellhead wins this one, boy."

As he chomped away, the bent whiskers extending from his cheeks flapped in the breeze, his gray nose twitching. Nicky couldn't help but chuckle. The rest of the ship, however, remained silent. Staring at one another, neither Nestor nor Krystoph blinked, both unwilling to budge even an inch.

Having grown tired of the pointless standoff, Krystoph at last turned away. "I have no interest in rescuing you, Tycarian, nor do I have an interest in carrying your excess weight. If trouble arises, you are on your own." A second later he dove headfirst into the frothy waves.

After a brief glance in the direction of the children, Nestor slid a dagger between his lips, took a deep breath, and splashed into the cool waters as well. Once submerged, the Tycarian spotted the vague, dark outline of Krystoph twenty feet below. Despite belonging to a race with such disgust for water, the Ochan was moving quite fast, making remarkable time. Nestor, however, was as at home among the waves as on land, and he quickly closed the gap. As the pair sank deeper, visibility reduced. What seemed crystal-clear, blue and inviting above twisted into something with a hint of green, black and mysterious below. Instantly Nestor's senses heightened; at this depth, things became infinitely more dangerous. Nonchalance would cost him his life.

Descending into the murky blackness, the water growing significantly colder the further down he swam; Krystoph found himself relying more heavily on senses other than sight. Visibility was near zero. Shapes had been reduced to blurs, and those blurs reduced to something even less recognizable. Reaching an underwater cliff with a ninety-degree drop into a realm even he was incapable of treading, the Ochan pawed his way across the sandy soil and into an alcove twenty feet away. Once inside, he shoved aside a rock nearly half his weight, dug into the ground underneath, and retrieved a piece of brown fabric tightly wrapped with rope at the top.

The Rongstag, exactly where he'd left it.

Placing the bag between his teeth alongside the dagger, Krystoph immediately began swimming toward the Briar Patch. A brief glance of the surrounding water revealed that Nestor was nowhere to be found. The ocean, however, remained as black as coal at this depth and almost impossible to see through. Theoretically, the Tycarian could be swimming alongside Krystoph at that very moment and he might not have been aware. The dense cloud of darkness encasing him, molded into a grayish mist which shifted again into something slightly more greenish blue. Suddenly able to see more than a few inches in front of his face, it was at this point Krystoph realized without a shadow of a doubt that Nestor was no longer following him. In a rare, uncharacteristic moment of weakness, he allowed the idea of searching for the frustrating Tycarian to slide its way into his brain. As quickly as it arrived, however, he pushed it away. The fool had been warned. His fate was his and his alone; let him sink in it.

Above Krystoph, the tattered, deep brown underside of the Briar Patch faded hazily into view. The waters were slowly warming at the same time, transforming soft and crystal clear with a hint of blue once again. Already Krystoph missed the cold. If there was anything he ached to feel again, it was the icy chill of an Ochan winter, the kind of cold that would seep into your muscles, make them ache and leave them sore for months. He'd spent too many years in the humid Fillagrou forest; he longed for the cold of his home world.

Less than a hundred feet from the surface, something massive sliced though the water alongside him. So large and moving so fast, the shape created a tornado-like ripple effect in the tide that caused Krystoph to spin wildly to the right and launched the dagger from between his teeth. Quick to regain his bearings, the Ochan snagged the bag containing the Rongstag from his mouth and gripped it tightly between his fingers, intent on not losing it the same way as his weapon. Again the gargantuan shape emerged and whizzed past, turning him upside down and spinning him awkwardly. Normally able to hold his breath for an astounding amount of time, being tossed about had caused the Ochan's concentration to slip, allowing tiny amounts of warm sea water to seep into his lungs. He needed to breathe, and he needed to do it quickly. Less than a hundred yards above, the underside of the Briar Patch continued to ride the ebb and flow of the waves expertly, unaware of everything taking place below. Again the dark green shape whipped past. This time Krystoph managed to avoid being spun, and at the same time got his first good look at the thing tormenting him. It was a sea dragon. Of all the known dangers in Aquari waters, sea dragons sat atop of the list. At nearly sixty feet long and weighting upwards of fifty tons, the long-bodied creatures held their spot at the apex of the food chain for as long as the Ochans had known of their existence. So massive were the jaws of these incredible eating machines that even an adolescent was fully capable of swallowing Krystoph, or any Ochan for that matter, in a single gulp. Usually the beasts tended to keep to deeper, darker, significantly colder waters. Unfortunately for Krystoph, it appeared this one in particular preferred its dinner warm. Having swum by three times already, the Ochan realized that the beast was circling him, sizing him up as they did all their prey, and patiently awaiting the opportunity to strike. It was exactly what he would do in the same situation. It was exactly what he'd done for years. Even with a full arsenal of weapons, Krystoph understood he would stand little chance against the monster one on one, especially on its turf. He stood absolutely none without a weapon. His only hope was to reach the Briar Patch. Hopefully the Sea Dragon would taper off as they ascended into warmer waters . . .hopefully.

Pulling from the sparse reserves of oxygen stored in his lungs, Krystoph resumed his upward swim with renewed vigor. He managed to make it only a few feet before the Sea Dragon again whizzed past. This time, the enormous creature nudged him stiffly with its massive head. Nearly the size of Krystoph's entire body, what was a simple bump to the dragon was a stiff blow to the Ochan. The fifty or so horns on the creature's head slammed into Krystoph's side and knocked the wind from his chest. More liquid seeped between his tightly drawn lips. The Sea Dragon twisted its gargantuan body in the water, dragging a tail twice the length of its torso behind before swimming in the direction of its prey yet again. The top of its skull smashed into Krystoph's spine, turning cartilage to dust and sending shivers of pain across his muscled back. Grunting through gritted teeth, he expelled yet more precious oxygen. There was very little left. With every pass, the beast was becoming more aggressive. Mostly unfamiliar with Ochans, it was testing him, unsure if the muscular lizard man posed any sort of threat. With every pass, it was getting closer to discovering that the answer was a resounding no. The pain in his lower back traveled to his legs, and now a little less than fifty feet from the surface, Krystoph suddenly came to a stop. From the corner of his eye, he spotted the Sea Dragon moving toward him at an incredible speed.

This time its massive mouth was opened wide, teeth as long as Krystoph's arm and as thick as his leg anxious to tear hungrily into his flesh. Realizing there was no hope of out-maneuvering the beast, the Ochan gripped the bag containing the Rongstag tighter, determined to not let go as he braced himself for impact. Through a pair of enormous milky eyes with even milkier pupils set on either end of its long snout, the Sea Dragon never averted its gaze. It was intrigued, it was hungry, and it would not be deterred. With the speed of a creature half its size, the gargantuan crocodile-like jaws of the dragon snapped around Krystoph's midsection. Somehow the Ochan managed to not only avoid the dangerous teeth, but wedge his body in the mouth of the great beast as well, thus preventing it from biting down. Immediately the Sea Dragon shook its head violently from side to side in response, attempting to whip its wedged food loose. When this didn't succeed, it started thrashing the whole of its body, coiling and spinning in every conceivable direction. Wedged between the jaws of the monster while struggling to hold his breath and maintain his grip on the Rongstag, Krystoph could tell his muscles were close to giving way. The Sea Dragon's fourteen-foot long tongue rose from the abyss of its throat and wrapped around his waist, attempting to tug him into its belly. Krystoph's collarbone snapped, chunks of bone slicing into the muscle underneath his skin and pressing against the fleshly exterior. Three fingers in his right hand broke. One of the massive ebony teeth near his left leg sliced through his deep green scales, leaving a cloud of blood spewing into the ocean. The strength of the Sea Dragon's jaw was simply too much and he was too weak. It was winning.

Their complete attention on one another, unbeknownst to both Krystoph and the Sea Dragon was the fact that Nestor Rockshell was currently gripping tightly to a row of pointy, bony fins lining the creature's spine. Despite the dragon's wild flailing, Nestor maintained his grip and his position, a dagger sandwiched between his flat edged teeth. Carefully, the Tycarian began clawing his way toward the beast's head. If he were to be tossed off, he might not be able to get back on. His grip meant everything; his grip meant life. Furious with the fact that it was unable to swallow its prey, quite suddenly the Sea Dragon dove downward and headed for the darker, cooler, more familiar surroundings of deep sea. Using the row of fins as a ladder, Nestor at last reached the top of the beast's skull. The ocean had again begun to change from blue to black, the temperature dropping noticeably. Nestor understood that the deeper the monster carried them, the more the pressure would build. If they were pulled too deep, it would crush both he and Krystoph like cans. Collapsing bone and muscle with ease, the depths of the sea would leave little more than a disgusting blob of goop behind. He had to act and he had to act now, before it was too late.

Pulling the knife from his teeth, Nestor muscled himself forward and drove the weapon directly into the Sea Dragon's exposed eye. Gummy streams of egg colored liquid spurted from the wound, spreading out across the surrounding water in grotesque cantaloupe-size clumps. Whipping its head violently, the Dragon managed to not only shake Nestor from its back, but Krystoph from its mouth as well. Spinning in circles as its tail thrashed haphazardly, the monster released a horrifying yelp accompanied by a wall of air bubbles so immense they engulfed the bodies of Nestor and Krystoph entirely. Through the bubbles, blackness and pained cries of the Sea Dragon, Nestor spotted Krystoph's body floating limply a few feet away. The Ochan's eyes were closed, his expression blank. Streams of blood poured not only from his leg, but a few nasty looking wounds along his back as well. Still gripped tightly between Krystoph's fingers, however, was the Rongstag. Snagging Krystoph's wrist, Nestor swam for the surface as fast as his sore muscles would allow while dragging the burly, lifeless body of the Ochan behind. From somewhere below came the angry roar of the Sea Dragon. More frightening than the howl was the fact that it was getting closer. Instead of stopping to look behind him, Nestor chose to swim faster. Nearly matching the speed of the dragon below, he could say without a moment's hesitation that it had been years since he'd moved so fast. The underside of the Briar

Patch again became visible, now barely a hundred yards away. Again the great beast screamed from the depths as a bed of bubbles rose up around Nestor and the partially unconscious Ochan in tow. Moving at such an incredible speed, the moment Nestor reached the surface he shot at least twenty feet into the air as water sprayed in every direction around him. With his free hand he grabbed the railing of the ship and held tight. Using his momentum, he tossed Krystoph and the Rongstag onto the deck. The Ochan's body hit the wood with a thud and slid across the soaked beams toward the center of the ship.

A moment later the Sea Dragon exploded from the surface of the water as well. Its massive jaws attempted to clamp down on Nestor. Narrowly missing, the beast instead took a bite out of the side of the ship, ripping a huge chunk of the wood away with ease. After spitting the rotted timber aside, it lunged at Nestor once more as he dangled perilously from the side of the Briar Patch. The Sea Dragon's jaws were only a few inches from his shell when a bevy of arrows begin to pierce the flesh of its head and snout; a few found their way into its already injured eye. Howling in pain, the dragon dove below the water once again. With the aid of the crew, Nestor was hoisted onto the ocean-soaked deck a moment later. Never in his life had he been happier to feel the familiar hardness of solid ground. Rushing to his side, young Nicky Jarvis did his best to help the turtle man to his feet.

"Thank you, lad," Nestor said with a thankful sigh, mussing the boy's dark brown hair with his flat paw while trying to corral his hurried breath.

Less than ten feet away, Krystoph slowly rose to his feet. He hacked and spit a disgusting, slimy mix of ocean water, saliva and blood from his mouth.

"Glad ya made it back in one piece, ya green-skinned scallywag!" Captain Fluuffytail commented to Nestor with a smile, shoving a bow and several arrows into the hard shell of the Tycarian's chest. "I hate to put ya back to work the moment ya return, but we got ourselves bigger problems than a teenage Sea Dragon with an eye-ache!"

Following the furry little creature's extended finger, Nestor glanced over his shoulder. What he saw in the distance caused his heart to sink. Extending as far as the eye could see in nearly every direction was an armada of Ochan ships that blanketed the horizon entirely. Hundreds of them. Maybe a thousand. So many, in fact, Nestor dared not count for fear the exact number would cause him to break down emotionally. Every last one looked to be on a direct course with Briar Patch, and at the speeds they seemed to be progressing, they would arrive within the hour.

Out of the frying pan and into the fire.

56. FALSE TRUTHS AND NECESSARY LIES

After shoving his way through the crowd of worried creatures stuffed into the streets of New Tipoloo, Chris Jarvis stormed into Zanell's modest dwelling and slammed the door against the interior dirt wall with a bang. High above, an army of Ochan soldiers, workers, and bizarre beasts of burden continued their march toward the doorway leading to the hundredth world. Every single footstep of the enormous digging monsters resulted in a series of tremors that cascaded across the city below, shaking clumps of dirt loose from the ceiling and filling the streets with a dusty fog of uncertainty. Seated on the edge of her bed, Zanell stared wide-eyed into the simple blue flame of a candle in her lap. Lost in the endless variations of hue and the mysteries residing within, she seemed indifferent to everything happening around her. Keenly aware of all that had occurred before and would occur again, the expression had become more the norm than otherwise. On the opposite end of the spectrum, a confused and angry Chris stared at her from the doorway.

The ground beneath his feet shook again, filling the tiny room once more with a fine layer of dust. "I'm sorry, but I can't just sit around here doing nothing anymore!" he snarled, his chest heaving.

"You've told me more than once that you would take me to my kids. I've waited patiently, and I can't wait anymore. I need you to tell me where they are, now!"

Pushing his way through the crowd, Fellow Undergotten stepped into the room behind Chris. Wrapping his arms under the man's armpits, Fellow tried to gently nudge the angry human into the street, apologizing for the interruption. "I'm sorry, Zanell. He got away from me in the commotion."

Whipping his arm free with a snap, Chris took two large steps in Zanell's direction. He was sick of being calm, he was sick of waiting, and he was sick of all the weirdness going on around him. He wanted to find Nicky and Tommy and get out of this place. The problems of these creatures were theirs alone; he had enough to deal with as it was.

Breathing heavily, Chris tried valiantly to lower his voice and steady his emotions. Every part of his body felt annoyingly itchy, covered in a fine layer of dirt that only added to his feeling of general unease. "Look, it's obvious you people have a lot on your plate right now. I get it. I'm sorry for that, but it's really not my problem. I just want to find my kids. If you can't help me, great. I don't care either way. I'll do it on my own. I just need to know one way or the other because I can't just sit here anymore. I can't. I won't."

Looking up from her flame, Zanell gazed wearily in Chris' direction. The man's face was sweaty, his hair an awful matted mess of stiff unwashed follicles and clumps of perspiration. The cloud of dust filling the room obscured his sharp features and naturally sad eyes. Even if she hadn't known absolutely everything about his past, it would have been painfully obvious that he was walking a tightrope, struggling to maintain his balance with every ounce of remaining strength . . .moments from falling to his doom.

Staring at him from behind the ghostly flame, Zanell's eyes turned soulful, her lids as heavy as her heart. Softly she whispered, "I'm sorry Christopher. We can't go, not yet."

Chris Jarvis threw his hands in the air. "God damn it! I could have been out there already! I could have been looking! I could have been doing anything other than sitting here on my ass doing nothing!"

Running his hand through his sticky-crisp hair, he managed to once again just barely wrangle his anger back under control. The bonds he used to momentarily tie it were weak, however, and they would not last long. Staring at Zanell sternly, chest heaving, he pointed his index finger in her direction, stating through gritted teeth, "You lied to me."

Turning quickly, Chris shoved his way past Fellow Undergotten and back into the crowded street. Through it all, Zanell remained expressionless. Again the city shook. Nearly losing his balance, Fellow braced himself on a nearby wall in order to remain upright. On some level, he understood Chris' frustration because he was feeling it himself. For so long he'd followed the word of Zanell to the letter, even when that word seemed to make little sense, if any at all. Leaving the children in the care of a former Ochan general . . .he still believed that was a mistake, no matter how hard he tried to convince himself otherwise. Standing beside the door with his head hanging low, Fellow turned to Zanell and shook his head. Immediately she looked away, gazing into the candle gripped between her long, bony fingers once again.

"I can't do this anymore," Fellow whispered softly, rubbing his eyes in a vain attempt to alleviate the pressure rapidly building up behind.

"Can't do what?" Zanell responded, her attention remaining on the flicker of light.

"This, Zanell. I'm sorry, I just can't."

Again the city shook; again a cloud obscured the pair.

"Those kids — they saved my life, saved the lives of a lot of us. I know you told me I needed to stay here, but what exactly is it I'm supposed to be doing here? Nothing. I'm not doing anything. I don't think I can leave this all in the hands of the gods or fate or whatever magic you can see that no one else can; I just can't. I'm not wired that way. I'm sorry."

Staring at her from across the room, Fellow waited patiently for a response. None came. Again the city rumbled, a much larger mass of dirt descending from the ceiling and drowning the room in the largest cloud of dust yet, completely obscuring everything residing inside. Outside Zanell's door, more than a few of the city's inhabitants shrieked in fear, scurrying to their living quarters in hope of finding safety. Safety, however, was only an illusion in this world. A large part of Fellow Undergotten was beginning to believe the same could be said for the words of the newly appointed Fillagrou elder. He had grown weary of illusions. When the dust at last cleared, Fellow noticed that the candle previously held between Zanell's fingers has fallen to the dirt, its magical blue flame was now buried under a mound of fallen soil — extinguished.

Through the remnants of the smoke, at last Zanell gazed in his direction.

Fellow breathed deeply, paused to locate some much-needed courage, and said, "I'm going after them."

Though barely a moment in actual time, the instance of quiet between the two seemed an eternity. Again Zanell looked away; again New Tipoloo was rocked by the weight of the enormous beasts above. Reaching down, she scooped her candle from the dirt beside her feet and blew the excess dust from the wick.

"Well? Do you have anything to say? Give me a reason, Zanell; convince me that staying here is the right thing to do. Give me something, anything."

Waving her hand gently over the dusty candle, the blue flame spurted to life once more. Turquoise shadows cascading across her wrinkled face, Zanell glanced momentarily in Fellow's direction before offering to him only two words: "Be careful."

The Chintaran grit his teeth and mumbled in frustration, "Fine."

A moment later, Fellow had left the room and was swallowed by the growing mass of creatures coalescing outside Zanell's dwelling in search of spiritual guidance. Inside, Zanell cursed the universe for giving her none to offer them. Sighing deeply, she turned her attention from the flame. She hated having to treat Fellow that way, hated having to lie to him. He was her friend and he didn't deserve it. If things were to progress as they should, however, the moment was unavoidable. Zanell understood all too well that what she had said was exactly what needed to be said, exactly what had been said before, and would be said again. The time was approaching when many sacrifices would be made. By compression, hers was tiny, almost pointless. Fate could be a generous mistress at times, but she was equally harsh. In the end, that which had been written would not be denied, no matter how badly one might hope to do exactly that.

Dreamily, Zanell gave herself to the hypnotic flicker of the blue magic once more.

Gazing into the vastness of the universe can be an awesome, life altering revelation that will change one for the remainder of their days. There comes a moment for all, however, when the universe gazes back.

Zanell was no exception.

57. RESCUE MISSION

Awkwardly shoving his way through the crowd of worried New Tipoloo citizens, Fellow Undergotten screamed across the dust filled city, "Wait a minute! Hold on a second! You don't even know where you're going!"

Ten feet ahead of him, an infuriated Chris Jarvis wormed his way past one bizarre creature after another, mumbling angrily beneath his breath the entire time. The city continued to shake under his feet as loose dirt piles plumed sporadically from the ceiling. Maneuvering himself in between something vaguely resembling a Sasquatch with fingernails nearly three feet long, and a creature sporting a pair of ears so floppy they were dragging in the dirt near its feet, Chris approached the stone doorway he used to enter the city a couple days prior. Pressing against the massive boulder with his back, he tried to muscle the rock aside and accomplished nothing. Digging his feet into the sand for extra leverage, he tried again; it did not budge an inch. Exiting the crowd at last, Fellow spotted the man attempting in vain to pry open the massive stone, his face a sweaty grimace of frustration.

"That's not going to work," Fellow offered with a sigh.

Chris Jarvis heard the fish man and chose to ignore him . His skin felt itchy, his pulse much too quick. Emotions he'd struggled to keep in check since releasing himself from the iron grip of the drink began bubbling dangerously to the surface. The strength he only recently discovered inside himself was cracking and splitting, perilously close to shattering to pieces. The scariest part of the entire situation was the fact that Chris knew there wasn't a single solitary thing he could do about it. For the moment, it would seem that he was the one being controlled, and not the other way around.

Turning from the huffing, sweat-covered man, Fellow looked across the sea of worried creatures huddled together in the crowded city street. A few among the group had been reduced to tears; others now teetered on the brink of a terrifying, all-encompassing rage. More still were simply confused, wishing beyond hope they could somehow return to their lives as they were before the onset of the war. Fellow understood better than most that this was an impossible dream. Things would never go back to the way they were; it simply wasn't possible. The awfulness the tyrant King had laid at their doorstep had changed them all in ways many of those residing in New Tipoloo weren't yet fully aware, and might never be.

There was no coming back from this.

Turning back to Chris, Fellow watched as the man continued to struggle against the weighty stone, ultimately gaining no ground.

"Even if you did somehow manage to get it open, this tunnel isn't going to take us where we need to go. In fact, if we tried to use it to get into the forest, more likely we'd end up squashed between the toes of a digger."

Chris stopped shoving and wiped the sweat from his forehead, flicking it to the soil. "What do you mean, *we*?"
"I mean we, as in you and me."

"Since when?"

"Since about five minutes ago, when I decided to tell the spiritual leader of the rebellion, who also happens to know everything there is to possibly know in the whole of the universe, that she has no idea what she's talking about when it comes to your kids."

Though he found the fish man's attempt at humor not entirely appropriate considering the situation, Chris grinned.

Fellow, of course, grinned back with a breathy sigh, rolling his massive blue eyes. "Yeah, you know what? Now that I've said it aloud like that, it doesn't seem like such a smart move on my part, does it?"

The city shook once more. Over Fellow's shoulder, Chris noticed that the mass of creatures outside Zanell's dwelling near the end of the block had swelled, tripling in size. Every one of them seemed anxious for her to emerge and remind them that everything would be okay. It was at times like this that they needed her more than ever.

Turning his attention to Fellow, Chris scanned the blue-skinned fish man from top to bottom, unsure of what to make of his offer. He'd grown tired of these creatures and their promises. He was wary to take another at their word.

Dusting the caked dirt off his shirt, he took a few steps forward as another tremor rumbled the city. "Why do you want to help me?"

"Honestly, don't take this the wrong way, but it doesn't have too much to do with you specifically. Your boys and their friends. They saved my life. Plain and simple, I owe them. I owe them big, and I can't sit here any longer while they fight for their lives out there without at least trying to help them, no matter what Zanell says. I have to be better than that."

For reasons Chris Jarvis didn't fully understand, it was at this moment he decided to trust the blue-scaled fish man. For the second time today, he was allowing himself to trust Fellow Undergotten, a fact he wasn't fully comfortable with, yet a fact nonetheless.

Brushing a mound of soil from his hair, Chris stepped away from the massive stone door and closer to Fellow. "So if we can't go through here, how the hell are we supposed to get out of this place?"

"We'll use the Western passage," Fellow responded quickly. "It'll add just a little time to the trip. At the same time, though, it'll keep us from getting captured by any patrols wandering about. I can tell you from experience that getting tossed in an Ochan dungeon isn't exactly high on the list of things either of us should want to do."

"Fine. Which way, then?" Chris asked while rolling his sleeves, anxious to proceed, his forearms covered in a thin layer of grainy dirt.

"Not so fast. We can't go charging into the forest like a couple of idiots. We'll need weapons, a plan, and some backup. Long story short, we're going to need some help."

Chris followed Fellow through the crowds filling the streets of the ever-rumbling city. Slowly the fear of those calling New Tipoloo home, brought on by the Ochan army above, had settled into a quiet uneasiness. The city hadn't been located and wasn't going to be invaded. If the opposite was true, they would have been dead already. Whatever was going on above didn't directly involve them. While this could hardly be considered good news, it was considerably better news, and in this situation, considerably better had to be enough. It took very little discussion on Fellow's part to convince others to join him and Chris in search of the children. Many of them were saved by Tommy or returned to the realm of the living by Staci's healing touch, facts they had not forgotten. In no time at all, the group of two expanded to fourteen. Each new creature brought with them a wide anxious smile and an eagerness to shake Chris' hand, or simply touch his skin.

He was the father of the gods, after all.

A massive creature more round than tall, covered in bumpy, bright red skin and sporting a gray goatee nearly a foot long, stood on the tip of its dirty toes and planted a sloppy kiss on either side of Chris' face. With a gumball-sized blob of spittle leaking down his cheek, Chris smiled at the weird looking thing awkwardly. The moment it turned, he wiped the sticky substance away and smeared it onto the fabric of his jeans. Every addition to the group brought more of the same. Stories of the things Tommy, Nicky, Donald, Owen and Staci had done or were prophesized to do got wilder and more unbelievable. Blasts of energy blowing castles to pieces while searing the flesh of lizard men black, the dead being brought back to life, and balls of light capable of blasting apart the clouds — it was all so unbelievable, every last word. Even taking into consideration everything he'd seen since sinking into the stream near the boys' tree fort, Chris couldn't help but find the wild tales difficult to believe. They couldn't be true, they just couldn't. Could they?

With the group having ballooned to nearly thirty, Fellow began handing out only the weapons he believed New Tipoloo could spare. Taking any more would have put the city in grave danger, leaving them helpless if the army above managed to stumble onto its location. This was something Fellow could not allow. Gathered around another stone doorway on the opposite end of the city, Chris found himself awestruck at the willingness of these bizarre creatures to help his children. Despite the living conditions and the awful stench of death surrounding them, the strange beasts were willing to put their lives on the line to rescue the kids. They were willing to kill or die, or possibly both, simply to ensure their safety. He found the gesture touching, confusing and strangely horrifying. Putting so much faith in children seemed fundamentally wrong, a mistake waiting to happen.

Standing atop a rock to the left of the Western Passage doorway, Fellow Undergotten called out loud enough for the gathered mass of would be rescuers to hear: "The plan is to take the tunnels as far as we can. Above ground we'll do our traveling at night. No doubt the forest is fairly packed with Ochans at the moment, so the chances of us running into a regiment or two are good."

With the group staring back at him, Fellow paused. The vast majority agreeing to come along had experience in battle on some level; more than a few, however, did not, including Chris Jarvis. For them, the journey would be the most dangerous. It was them who would be changed the most by the situations they were bound to encounter, and whom he now chose to address specifically.

The volume of his voice dropping drastically, Fellow scanned the eyes of the inexperienced somberly. "You should be aware that in all likelihood, many of us will not return. We have all lost someone we love over the course of this war, myself included. I can't honestly say if these children are really the culmination of the Fillagrou prophecy. I'm not sure anyone can. I'm not even sure if I believe in prophecies. What I can say without a moment's hesitation is that I'm sick of watching innocents die. I've buried too many bodies. I can't to do it anymore. I refuse to add these kids to the list. Maybe it means something to you, but whether or not these kids can change the course of the war doesn't really make a difference to me. Without them, none of us would be standing here today. None of us would be breathing the air we breathe or eating the food we eat. Prophets or not, if these children need our help, we owe it to them to try. They've given us too much not to."

The instant Fellow stopped speaking, a cheer rose from the crowd. Though the Chintaran's speech was inspiring to say the least, none among the rescue party needed it. Every one of them understood quite well exactly what the children had given them, and was as anxious to give something back, no matter the danger.

While failure did indeed seem a likely outcome, failure would not come lightly.

As the stone doorway to the passage slid open, the large group began to filter in. Anxiously chatting amongst themselves, the rescuers had prepared themselves for every possible outcome as well as they could, even those difficult to face. Not a single one among the group dwelled on the idea of failure, however. Dedication and hope remained the emotions of the day. If the children were alive, they would be found. When found, they would be rescued.

As the group continued piling single-file into the dank, claustrophobic tunnel, Fellow and Chris spotted Owen Little standing alone in the slowly emptying street.

His hands buried in the pockets of his jeans, the boy sighed deeply, his eyelids heavy behind his thick-rimmed glasses. Once again Owen was finding himself entirely unsure of why he was doing exactly what he seemed to be doing. He'd always prided himself on logic. His recent inability to follow through on the suggestions of logic, however, was frustrating and confusing with a heaping spoonful of frosty annoyance on top. It had become painfully obvious that he shouldn't have led Mr. Jarvis to the tree fort. Most definitely, he shouldn't have followed the man into the stream shortly afterward. Now he found himself staring at Tommy's father once again as he stood alongside a six-foot tall fish man in leather pants, about to inform the both of them that he would be joining the group in the search.

If his father were there, he would have grounded Owen so many times that the boy wouldn't have left the house until his sophomore year in college.

"Owen?" Fellow asked quizzically, staring in the direction of the diminutive, floppy auburn-haired boy. "Go to Zanell's, Owen; you should be safe there until we get back."

Lifting the glasses from his head, Owen rubbed his eyes and shook his head back and forth, not believing the reality of the words about to spring from his mouth. "I'm going with you."

"Oh no, you're not." Fellow answered quickly, leaping from his rock and stepping toward the boy.

"Yes, I am. Believe me, I don't want to, seriously. I don't at all. It's the last thing I want to do actually. I have to go, though. Don't ask me why, because I've got no idea. I think I'm supposed to go with you, though. I know I'm supposed to go with you."

Now just a few feet from the boy, Fellow gently placed the webbed fingers of his hand on Owen's shoulder. "No, you're not. I'm sorry, kiddo. There's no way I'm going to be the guy that puts the life of another kid on the line. There's been enough of that going around lately. I don't care what kind of powers everyone seems to think you have, I can't do it and I'm not going to do it, end of story. Go back to Zanell's. If everything goes well, we'll only be gone a few days."

Staring down at the dirt while still shaking his head, Owen placed his hand on top of Fellow's, the fish man's scales like sandpaper against his palm. "Look, I have a feeling you're going to need my help. I can get you through the forest without anyone noticing you."

Though impressed with his eagerness to help the other children, Fellow chuckled at the childlike innocence in Owen's statement. "Listen, kiddo. I'm sorry, but it's just not going to happen, so stop trying to make it happen. I don't know what we're going to come up against out there. No matter what, I have to imagine it's going to get ugly. You won't be safe, and if something does go wrong, I can't promise that I'll be able to help you. The best thing you can do to help is stay here and stay alive."

Looking up from the dirt, Owen gazed into the enormous blue-gray eyes of Fellow Undergotten. In his heart the boy understood that he shouldn't be there. He wasn't a hero. The idea of him actually "rescuing" someone was ludicrous, the kind of thing that would send anyone he'd ever met into a fit of uncontrollable laughter. At the same time, though, something buried deep inside — something he was incapable of ignoring — was telling him that more than any of the creatures that had agreed to go along, he was the one that needed to be there. Still resting on top of Fellow's scaly hand, Owen's fingers began to tingle. The sensation arrived quickly, carrying with it a sense of familiarity. In a matter of moments, it had spread across the entirety of his body. Quite strangely, like electricity jumping from one conduit to the next, Fellow Undergotten's hand began tingling as well. Less than ten feet away, eyes wide and jaw hanging low, Chris Jarvis watched as the pair disappeared into thin air.

Looking down at the empty space where Owen stood only moments prior, Fellow realized that not only has Owen vanished, but his own hand, arm and body were gone as well.

From the empty space in front of him came Owen's familiar voice. "See? I told you I could help."

58. FATES REVEALED

Surrender proved a simple, painfully obvious choice for Roustaf. In fact, there really was no other. Surrounded by a castle full of Ochan soldiers, the plan to rescue Walcott and Pleebo was no longer an option. Donald Rondage could throw as many boulders in as many directions as he wanted, or create earthquakes by slamming his fists into the ground until he opened up a crater to the center of Ocha, and none of it would make a difference. The boy was strong; he wasn't invincible. If even one of the hundreds upon hundreds of arrows pointed directly at the child's chest hit their mark, like everything else in the universe, he too would die. Surrender extended the length of their lives, and extending the length of their lives brought with it a chance for further survival. Tahnja, Donald and the rest of the group still alive were quickly shackled as a small army of Ochans kept their weapons pointed at Donald the entire time. Roustaf was tossed into a tiny metal cage normally used to capture HonduBirds, a sight that garnered snickers from many of the Ochan soldiers.

Once within the walls of Kragamel's massive castle, the group of would-be rescuers was taken below the castle and into the dungeon, where they were tossed behind the thick bars of their very own cells. Kragamel's dungeon was quite different from that of his recently deceased son Valkea. For instance, buried just beneath the Frosty Ochan tundra, the air here was bitterly cold, the kind of cold that paralyzed the muscles, a cold so awful it made the flesh burn. Lowering herself to the floor, Tahnja curled into a corner and breathed into knees pulled close to her chest. The dungeon was silent and dark. Swallowed by the shadows came the sound of dripping water in the distance, and behind it the low moan of prisoners aching for the sweet release that only death could bring. Across from her, partially obscured by a frighteningly endless shadow, puffs of steam rising from her mouth with every breath, Tahnja noticed icicles glittering off the steel bars. Cutting through the agonizing hums of the dying from the next cell over, Tahnja could clearly hear Brutus' enormous sharp teeth chatter. Despite his layers of thick fur, he too was feeling the chill. Across from her, just beyond the bars, Roustaf's tiny box dangled from a hook on the ceiling, swaying ever so slightly in a cold breeze emanating from an unknown source.

In the cell opposite her, obscured by the black abyss, she recognized the muffled sobs of Donald Rondage. Intent on ensuring that no one heard him, Donald cried into the fabric of his filthy shirt, icy tears freezing the instant they seeped from his eyes. Peering above the pink flesh of her bony knees, Tahnja stared at Roustaf with sad, apologetic eyes. This was all her fault. She should have stayed put like he told her. She should have listened to him. If she had, they'd be back in the Fillagrou forest right now, planning their next move. If she had listened, no one would be dead.

From his tiny cage, Roustaf glanced briefly in her direction and shook his head. He knew he would forgive her eventually. Though they had only known each other a short time, he realized some time ago that staying angry with Tahnja for any significant amount of time would be entirely impossible. What she had done was stupid, but she was only trying to help. A lifetime of thick-headedness, however, made forgiving her just yet equally impossible. He needed to be mad a little longer, and he needed for her to know that he was mad.

In the cell to Roustaf's right, Donald Rondage snorted into his shirt, fighting back shameful tears with every ounce of strength. "It'll be okay, slick. There was nothing you could've done," Roustaf whispered in the boy's general direction, doing his best to assure the child that he did nothing wrong. "We'll get out of here, kid, we aren't done just yet. You can count on that."

The gesture did little to stymie Donald's emotions. A deep, uncontrollable fear had settled into the back of his mind. Like the stifling cold of the dungeon, it left him paralyzed, unable to halt the chattering of his teeth or the leaking of his eyes. Thankfully, the shadows kept him hidden; thankfully, no one could see his personal disgrace.

A bright light emerged from the darkness behind Roustaf, accompanied by the squeak of a heavy steel door. Turning in its direction, the little man spotted the silhouette of a figure so massive in stature it barely fit in the oversized doorway. As the enormous shape moved closer, it got somehow larger, blurry dark details growing crisp and sharp. Squinting with his head wedged through the tiny bars of his dangling cage, Roustaf realized that the shape in question was actually the tyrant king himself, Kragamel. Ducking his head, the enormous, white-bearded Ochan stepped under Roustaf and came to a stop in front of Donald's cell. Having never seen the king face-to-face, Roustaf marveled at the size of the creature from above, realizing most of the stories he'd heard were in fact true. Monstrous in stature, every ounce of Kragamel's body was layered in thick, beefy, well-aged muscle. His skin was darker than most Ochans, closer to a smoky gray than green. The gold-encrusted armor adorning his body was intricately detailed, polished free of anything even faintly resembling an imperfection. Beneath his chest plate, the king's heart beat so loudly it echoed throughout the dungeon, bouncing off the walls and back again. A pair of soldiers stepped to either side of Kragamel. Pulling back on their bows, they trained their weapons at the sobbing child hidden behind the bars. His black eyes unblinking, Kragamel directed his stare in Donald's direction.

When at last he spoke, his tone was as cold as the surrounding air, calculated and devoid of the slightest bit of emotion. "I find you to be an intriguing anomaly, child."

Unable to answer or even look up, Donald Rondage pulled the shirt tighter against the soaking flesh of his face.

"Leave the kid alone, you bastard!" Roustaf screamed with his hands wrapped tightly around the bars of his swaying prison.

Turning his head, Kragamel glanced in the direction of the tiny man. His face remained expressionless, his voice a steady unchanging growl. "Do you sincerely believe your threats are of the slightest concern to me, mongrel? Have you already forgotten how easily your kind was slaughtered? I can count the Ochan warriors lost in the invasion of your world on one hand." Reaching up, the king wrapped the fingers of his massive gloved hand around Roustaf's cage, encasing the little man in a tomb of darkness. "A single squeeze and you are gone. One squeeze, and you're transformed into nothing more than a smear for the servants to clean from my glove. One squeeze, and I successfully put the period on the sentence that is the obliteration of your race. Your threats are as hollow as the bones of a Scarbeak; they, like you, mean nothing to me."

"Leave him alone." The voice came from the shadows. Falsely heroic in tone, it belonged to Donald Rondage.

Releasing Roustaf's cage from his grasp, the king turned his attention to the child's cell once more. The archers on either side pulled tighter on their bows, aiming their weapons at the puffy-faced boy slowly emerging from the darkness with his hands pulled into shaky unreliable fists. Wiping the final remnants of the tears on his face with his forearm, Donald approached the bars. His heart was pounding, his lip quivering. Looking up at the massive Ochan with the gray beard as long as he was tall, Donald was frightened beyond words. Mashing his tongue between his teeth, he tried his best to quell his growing fear and to give the impression of confidence where there was none to speak of.

"Welcome, child," Kragamel grumbled through tight lips. "I have been anxious to meet you for so very long now. We have much to discuss. I believe you knew my son, yes?"

His body shaking, Donald's throat squeezed shut and left him unable to respond. His legs had gone stiff and straight, worthless. Realizing his hands were shaking uncontrollably, he dug them deep into the denim of his jean pockets. His face was smeared and filthy, glistening with a layer of salty, partially frozen tears.

Staring down at the child, the tyrant king smiled wide with a mouth full of yellow teeth built over generations of evolution specifically for ripping and tearing. "As I was saying: you have within your pathetic body something that interests me greatly, something I would like very much to have for myself. One way or another, I shall have it. My only hope is that you prove less hard-headed than the Tycarian king. He has left me with little time, and sparse remainders of patience."

Upon the mention of Walcott, Roustaf slammed the whole of his body violently against his little cage, causing it to whip back and forth. "Where is he? What did you do with him?"

Turning in the little man's direction once more, Kragamel smiled wide. "Fret not. You shall see him soon, little one. I have taken the liberty of arranging a demonstration for the boy. My aim, of course, is to prove to the child the seriousness of his situation."

Looking away from Roustaf, the king stepped closer to the cage holding Donald once again. As he moved, so did the archers at his side, their eyes glued to the boy's every gesture. Reaching up, the king wrapped his fingers around the cold steel, leaning in the direction of the frightened child. Despite every part of him wanting to maintain his position and show his confidence, Donald could not help but take a step back.

"During his interrogations, the Tycarian spoke of you and your cohorts often. Despite our best attempts, the fool proved a difficult puzzle to solve. No matter the pain he suffered, and I assure you, he suffered quite a lot, he continually refused to reveal the location of the doorway to your world. In the end I retrieved the information from his Fillagrou friend, of course. Still, I must admit, the Tycarian's willpower impressed me. They are strong creatures; otherwise worthless, yes, but strong, much stronger than you could ever hope to be. It is this point I want to stress to you, boy. It is this I want you to keep in the forefront of your mind as you watch him die."

59. IMPOSSIBLE ODDS

Previously blue, the sea had turned a frightening wooden black. Where once there was ocean, there now was only an endless blanket of Ochan warships. Packed tightly together in every conceivable direction, numbering well into the hundreds, and possibly even thousands, the awful mass converged on the Briar Patch like a swarm of vultures on slowly dying prey. The lone defender in a sea of enemies, Captain Fluuffytail's warped, barnacle-encrusted collection of scavenged items and hastily made repairs had no real chance of survival. The situation was hopeless and the odds, quite honestly, impossible. Ignoring the inevitability of the situation, the grizzled ship's captain climbed atop a set of dusty crates, retrieved the blade hanging from his belt, and lifted it defiantly into the air.

Through his puffy gray cheeks and slightly off-color buckteeth, Fluuffytail screamed at the top of his lungs, "Get to yer battle stations, ya useless lumps of dragon plop! Today's as good as any to die, and I don't plan on goin' out without puttin' up a fight that'll make em remember our names!"

It was not simply by luck alone that the Briar Patch and its crew were among the few ships to have avoided destruction at the hands of the Ochans, though luck had assuredly played a role. Jacques Fluuffytail was born on the water; it was all he knew, and it was his home. His crew was also his family, and despite his often-gruff tone when dealing with them, they were by far the most important things in his life. He refused to simply roll over and let the Ochans take them from him. More times than he was capable of counting — mostly on account of nonexistent schooling and an inability to count — his crew had spat in the face of the odds and prevailed. This time would be no different. If there were indeed a way to escape this situation with their lives, those calling the Briar Patch home would discover it.

Huddled close to Nestor, Tommy, Staci and Nicky began moving toward the rear of the ship, doing their best to stay out of the way of the determined crew. The deck was buzzing with nervous, angry energy. Ropes were being pulled, sails raised, and weapons readied. Sailing in from every direction, the wall of black ships continued to steadily advance. Simply outrunning their aggressors was no longer an option as the Briar Patch and its crew had been thoroughly surrounded. Escape, like victory, was impossible. The only choice remaining was to fight, and this choice didn't seem very promising. Emerging from the patches of excited movement near the rear of the ship with a bladed weapon in each hand, Krystoph approached the children and Nestor. The Ochan's face was a mask of steely seriousness. Fear had ceased to exist for some time as far as Krystoph was concerned. Twisting underneath and into itself, it had long since transformed into something abstract, more idea than reality, an emotion better observed than experienced. Before him now lay the promise of battle. This was where he excelled; this was where he'd spent the majority of his life. This was home.

Staring into Nestor's green eyes, he stated with obvious sarcasm, "Suggest you take your precious cargo below."

For the first time since their meeting, Nestor found himself in complete agreement with the Ochan murderer. Quickly wrapping his outstretched arms around the group of children, Nestor began nudging them toward the doorway leading to the lower deck. They would be safer below, at least for the time being. Considering the size of the Ochan fleet sounding them, however, Nestor believed the word "safe" had no real place here.

Standing beside the muscular leg of the turtle man, Nicky Jarvis pointed to the ships in the distance and stuttered breathlessly, "Um, oh my God."

Turning, Nestor saw exactly what had the boy so spooked. All at once, a mountain of arrows from the surrounding ships took to the air, so many that they blocked out the light of the sun and blanketed the Briar Patch in the shadow of darkness.

From the opposite end of the ship Fluuffytail bellowed, "Incoming!"

Immediately the crew dropped what they were doing and scurried for cover. Some took refuge under nearby crates, while others lifted shards of wood and hastily constructed shields in the air for protection. A few ripped away patches of the recently repaired deck and dove headfirst into the lower levels. Flipping over a partially constructed escape raft, Krystoph hid what he could of his overly muscled body underneath. Pulling the children close together, Nestor leaned over the top of the group, using his already battered shell as an umbrella once more. For a moment, as the wall of arrows approach the ship, everything went quiet. Only the awful hum of thousands of steel tipped weapons cutting across the sky and the crash of the waves on the side of the ship could be heard. In a hurricane-like flurry, the arrows struck all at once, contacting with nearly every area of the ship and its crew instantaneously, slicing through wood and flesh alike with bitter-stunning ease. While the cover of some provided ample protection against the Ochan's initial onslaught, others among the crew did not fare so well. Pained screams rose up from every corner of the ship's deck as arrows sliced through muscle and bone, leaving many seriously injured and a few others dead. The ship's already tattered sail was chopped to pieces and reduced to a dilapidated, useless piece of fabric. Cut loose from its cable, the frayed material floated worthlessly to the deck, covering those below. Lifting himself off the children, Nestor stumbled awkwardly to the deck, his face a grimace of absolute pain. A number of arrows now jutted from ugly, bloody wounds on his shoulders and arms, a few more from the back of his legs. Causing him the biggest problem, however, was the arrow protruding from the side of his neck. Leaning against the side of the ship, he reached up and pulled the stick of wood free. A stream of thick blood squirted from the open wound, and he quickly applied pressure with his paw.

With the sobbing heads of Nicky and Staci buried against his chest, Tommy opened his eyes. Around him, the ship had been tossed into a state of disarray. The deck was littered with stiffly standing arrows, the tips of which had sunk deep into the aged, water-soaked wood. Moaning in agony, arrows sticking grotesquely from various parts of their bodies, random crewmembers scratched their way across the deck, leaving trails of blood in every color of the rainbow sprayed behind. Pulling away from his older brother's body with his face drenched in tears, Nicky ran to Nestor's side.

Through a mouth filled with blood, Nestor shoved the boy in the direction of the doorway to the lower deck and gurgled, "Get below. Go now."

Sobbing uncontrollably, the tiny boy wrapped his arms around the underside of Nestor's shell as best he could, shaking his head and refusing to leave.

Warm blood seeping between his fat fingers, the Tycarian pried Nicky loose, angrily shoving him in the direction of his older sibling. "Take your brother, lad! Get below before it is too late!"

Grabbing Nicky by the wrist, Tommy forcefully tugged his little brother in the opposite direction with Staci still clinging to the fabric of his shirt, both awash in a torrent of tears. Hearing the suddenly familiar, utterly terrifying hum of incoming arrows, Tommy glanced toward the sky. Like a great, hungry black beast, again the wall of pointed weapons blocked out the light of the

Aquari sun and replaced it with something entirely different. This time the arrows tips were on fire, leaving trails of crackling orange and red behind like fireworks as they tore across the sky. Looking in the direction of the doorway to the lower decks, Tommy realized it was still too far away; they would never make it.

A few feet behind the children, Nestor tried rising to his feet, using the edge of the ship as a brace. Having lost far too much blood, he awkwardly stumbled to the slippery deck below, squealing in pain as the fall drove an arrow further into the back of his leg. Similar situations were playing themselves out across the whole of the ship. The crew was injured, disoriented and unorganized, in no way prepared for a second volley. Peering through a hole in the underside of the boat he was using for cover, Krystoph growled angrily at the inferno of fiery arrows filling the sky. When he was the leader of the armies of Ocha, he secretly despised this type of warfare, finding it entirely too impersonal for his tastes. War should be waged in close, close enough to stare into the eyes of the enemy and watch as death wrapped its bony fingers around their necks and choked the remaining bits of life from their bodies.

As the pained moans of the dead and dying stabbed their way into Tommy Jarvis' ears, the swarm of flaming arrows continued to sail forward, now only moments from scorching what remained of the already battered Briar Patch. Less than thirty feet from the doorway to the lower decks, Tommy came to a sudden, surprising stop. His fingers had begun to tingle. His head felt fuzzy and warm, smothered by a blanket of static. Prying Staci from his chest, he shoved her to the deck beside his younger brother. The situation was beyond words, overwhelming, the pressure incredible. Unsure of exactly what he planned to do, Tommy understood he needed to do something. If he didn't, Nicky would die, Staci would die, he would die—everyone would die. Clamping his teeth together so hard it hurt, he raised his hands above his head and pressed the otherworldly pressure building up in his fingertips toward the sky. A beam of miraculous, crackling energy shot from his hands, quickly climbing higher than the ship's highest point. Once there, it spread out like a translucent umbrella, and back down into the ocean with a splash, encasing the Briar Patch in a protective bubble. The instant the fiery arrows came into contact with the crackling energy, they were reduced to cinders. What remained caught the breeze and floated away, tiny particles of charred black wafting upward into the dark clouds. Immediately, the surrounding Ochan ships fired a third volley. With Tommy maintaining his protective bubble, these new arrows suffered the same fate.

Violently tossing the shell of the escape boat from his head, Krystoph stared at the amazing sight above with terrified wonder. Less than ten feet away, the bizarre glow continued to pour from Tommy's fingertips. The astonishing light above hummed softly as if somehow alive, its shape melted and thick like hot wax, a perfect half-sphere. Gripping the weapons in his hands tighter, Krystoph stared at the boy carefully, taking special note of the angry grimace on his young face.

"Staci, get up!" Tommy yelled as he looked down at the teary-eyed girl crouched at his feet.

Hesitantly, Staci glanced in his direction. Her hair was a disheveled, matted mess, her eyes puffy-red, glassy with tears. Above her, with his arms stretched high over his head as glowing light pouring from his fingers, Tommy stared at her sternly. Slowly the boy's blue eyes were devoured by the incredible energy emanating from within, shooting tiny streams of power like beams from a flashlight in her direction.

As he spoke, his mouth too was awash in the incredible glow. "You have to help them, Stace."

Shaking uncontrollably, Staci spotted Nestor through the crook of Tommy's legs. The Tycarian was bleeding to death near the railing of the ship, struggling to breathe as blood continued to spurt from the gaping hole in his neck. All around her much of the crew shared his grizzly fate. They were dying, all of them — dying. It was at this point Staci realized exactly what Tommy was asking of her.

"You have to help them," The boy stated seriously from above.

"What? I–I can't. I mean, I don't know —"

"Yes, you do! You have to help them! I've seen you do it, and you have to do it now!"

High above, a fourth volley of Ochan arrows slammed against Tommy's protective bubble, each arrow turned instantly to dust as if fried by a jolt of electricity. The bizarre situation had become too much for Staci to bear. Her mind was drowning in a sea of ideas and emotions, ranging from the startling to the utterly horrifying, and her body had responded the only way it knew how, by freezing. She wanted to help, she knew she needed to help, but she couldn't bring herself to help. Even if she wanted to, she wouldn't have known how. The task was too daunting.

Burying her head in her hands, Staci returned to sobbing wildly, shaking her head back and forth as she screamed, "I can't, Tommy! I can't! I can't do it! I don't know how!"

Lowering one of the hands over his head in Staci's direction, Tommy opened his palm. "Yes, you can, Stace." The bubble encasing the ship wobbled momentarily like the surface of water broken by a falling stone. Remaining intact, the energy continued to pour from the boy's remaining fingers.

The tear-soaked wetness covering Staci's face glimmered with a trillion tiny reflections brought on by Tommy's light show. Hesitantly reaching up, she placed her hand in his. With the boy's help, she crawled to her feet. Upright on spaghetti legs, Staci stared lovingly into the incredible glow of her friend's eyes. They looked understanding and safe, calming in a way she'd never known.

Drastically, Tommy's voice softened, suddenly filled with longing, pleading and understanding. "Please, Stace, you have to help them. I know you can do it."

Staring into the glowing eyes of Tommy Jarvis and feeling the crackling warmth of his hand in hers, Staci's heart began to expand and change, growing larger and fuller than she believed possible. The sensation was beyond explanation, indescribable in fact. Passing through the microscopic pores of her skin, the energy created by her heart cascaded across her exterior. Within moments, it had engulfed her in pure, undiluted crystalline light. Moving to her toes, it spread in every direction at once across the deck of the ship, enveloping everything in its path. Every injured crewmember touched by the living heart-light was instantly healed. The energy repaired and closed their wounds, turning the arrows protruding from their bodies to dust. Those already taken by the hand of death were miraculously given life. Everything done was undone, the impossible, made possible. Through the ball of energy encasing her body, Staci gripped Tommy's hand tighter, smiling in his direction as the power continued to erupt from beneath her skin.

Through the haze of humming white, Tommy smiled back.

When every member of the crew had been healed, the light retreated back across the deck of the ship, seeping into Staci's body and disappearing from existence once more. With some reluctance, Tommy allowed her hand to slide from his. It took less than a second for him to miss her touch. Looking in the direction of his wide-eyed little brother now sitting on his knees at his feet, Tommy's expression turned serious once more.

With a sly, slightly undiscerning grin, the eldest Jarvis boy stated in a very matter of fact tone, "If we want to get out of here alive, I'm going to need your help, bro."

While looking at his brother, Nicky's throat began to warm. Something foreign and itchy was building, something uncanny, fantastic, and beyond-words-powerful beginning to boil and rise to a violent crescendo within.

Closer than ever, the first fleet of Ochan ships was now mere moments away from crashing headlong into the protective bubble surrounding the once helpless Briar Patch. On the decks of the dark-wooded war vessels, Ochan soldiers readied a full arsenal of weapons, including cannons so large they required five of the massive creatures to properly fire. As if aware of what was to come next, the tide cracked violently, turning dark, foamy and angry.

Real or imagined, the afterlife prepared itself for a plethora of new tenants.

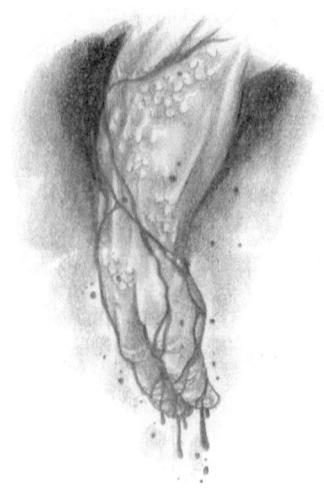

60. THE RAIN SHALL TELL HIS TALE

Despite its lack of teeth or arsenal of bladed weapons, even the air in Ocha could be a painful, dangerous enemy. Stiff and sharp, the bitter cold nibbled at the flesh of those unaccustomed to its harshness like a million hungry mouths feeding simultaneously. Led from the dungeon below into the massive courtyard of King Kragamel's castle, Donald Rondage gazed wearily into the gray, cloud-covered sky. A substance resembling snow in form, function, and texture, though as black as the darkest of dark coals, began to flutter gently from above. Landing in Donald's hair, the odd substance leaked down the front of his face, staining his skin black like mascara running from his mother's eyes on the nights when she cried alone in the kitchen. Lead by a massive chain attached to a steel collar around his neck, Donald turned away from the clouds and the awful black snow. Shamed, he lowered his head, watching as his feet shuffled across the small piles of charcoal snow and frozen dirt. Spaced evenly around him, six archers pointed the tips of their arrows in the direction of his heart, head and other vital organs likely to produce instant death. An attempt to escape, or even the slightest movement in any direction, and they would cut him down. Incredible strength was of no use here. He was helpless and he was worthless. His fate was in their hands. Dangling from a belt loop on his pants hung the cage containing the shivering form of little Roustaf. As the pair was led across the icy soil, large groups of Ochans began to form on either side, many among them women and children. Every single one of the creatures sported an angry, disgusted scowl across their face. They hated the boy because he was different. They hated the boy because they were told to. A rock tossed by an Ochan child barely older than Donald hit him in the center of his back. Stumbling forward, Donald managed to remain upright due mostly to the massive Ochan guard pulling him forward like a dog on a chain.

"You little putz!" Roustaf screamed at the Ochan child while beating his fists against the bars encasing him, "If I wasn't in this cage, I'd come over there and tan your hide, you little brat!"

The courtyard was absurdly large, and the journey across took nearly ten minutes. Eventually the soldier pulling the pair forward came to a stop at the base of a rather rudimentary looking stone altar. Unlike many of the finely detailed artifacts within the castle walls, the altar was little more than two stone blocks piled on top of one another, the bottom significantly wider than the top, creating a tiered effect. Rusty chains of old, stained steel dangled loosely over the edge on either side. The crowd surrounding the stone altar quickly ballooned, and the entire courtyard was soon filled with green-scaled Ochan citizens. Loaded to the brim with anxiousness and disgust, they stared at Donald and Roustaf angrily while pointing, snarling and shaking their heads. Gatherings such as this were not an uncommon aspect of life within these walls. Intended for those of all ages to enjoy, they were meant to lift the spirits of the community as a whole and to reinforce undying faith in the king. One of the archers behind Donald lifted his foot into the air and kicked the boy in the back, knocking him to his knees. The blow sent a jolt of pain down Donald's spine, flinging Roustaf against the bars of his cage violently as well and creating a sizeable welt on the side of his red face.

Many among the crowd chuckled at the boy's pain; a few applauded. Indeed, the show had officially begun. These theatrics were only the prelims, however; the main event was soon to come.

Peering through the bars while rubbing the throbbing lump on the side of his head, Roustaf watched as a door along the exterior wall of a medium-sized tower not too far behind the stone altar opened. In unison, every head in the crowd turned in its direction.

A pair of burly Ochan soldiers emerged from the darkened doorway, dragging behind them the limp, filthy body of Walcott Shellamennes. The appendages of the Tycarian king were bruised beyond recognition, his shell a mass of partially chipped fragments and cracks just barely managing to hold together. As if the muscles in his neck were nonexistent or simply nonfunctional, Walcott's bulbous head drooped heavily, bouncing back and forth as he was pulled across the dirt, hoisted into the air, and deposited onto the massive gray altar. After carefully securing him to the stone, the guards stepped away, disappearing again into a sea of green flesh. Random pockets of cheers immediately rose from the younger members of the tightly packed crowd. Those having observed this ceremony many times over the course of their lives, however, managed to contain their emotions for the moment. They understood all too well that the show was only just getting under way. The moment to give themselves freely into jubilation would arrive in due time, and patience was virtue. From the very same doorway from which Walcott was dragged, King Kragamel himself stepped into the hazy, mid-day light. Approaching the altar, he stood above the body of the fallen Tycarian king, staring past his rotund shell and into the brown eyes of Donald Rondage kneeling in the dirt not too far away.

"Behold!" the king bellowed deeply, lifting his hands triumphantly to the heavens in a quite uncommon display of exuberance. "At long last, the Tycarian king belongs to the citizens of Ocha!"

Those who previously managed to stifle their emotions now screamed aloud, pumping their fists angrily as thick strands of spittle shot from between their chilly lips. Another rock slammed into Donald's back just below his neck; a smaller stone hit him in the shoulder. The expressions of the archers surrounding the boy remained steady, calm and entirely dangerous. Though they were under the strictest of orders not to kill the child unless totally necessary, many among them hoped beyond hope that he attempted some sort of escape. Killing a creature with such power would be both an honor and a pleasure, a story to tell their grandchildren.

Sprawled across the cold stone, Walcott's eyes began to flutter. What had been black only moments before transformed into a wobbly mass of blurry grays and blues. Slowly the formless shapes sharpened; given form, they were brought forth into the crispness of day. The first thing Walcott noticed in this new world was the round, pink-skinned face of young Donald Rondage. Not yet fully aware of his surroundings, Walcott smiled softly, simply happy to see the face of the smart-mouthed child again. He'd missed Donald. He'd missed all the children. It was good to see him again.

Gazing across the sea of Ochans gathered in the courtyard, the king momentarily ignored the woozy Tycarian and the somber-faced boy, choosing instead to address the masses. "For years, this mongrel, this affront to the very laws of nature, has proven itself an enemy of the Ochan race. The blood of endless Ochans is stained into the contours of its paws: the blood of your children, and the blood of mine! Long overdue, the time has arrived for this awful thing to pay for its misdeeds! Today it learns the true meaning of power! Today it is reminded just who is master and who is slave!"

The roar of the crowd reverberated in Donald's ears; a few more stones hit him in the back, and one whizzed past his head. The raucous, blood-curdling cheers succeeded in jolting Walcott from his pain-induced haze. All at once, the reality of the current situation settled like the weight of the universe on his chest. Wrapped tightly around his wrists, heavy chains as thick as his legs bound him to the cold stone beneath his shell. Every muscle in his body was inflamed and torn, sore in ways neither he nor they ever thought possible. Above him, soaking in the admiration of the screaming horde, stood the ghastly tyrant king himself. On the ground below, Donald Rondage lowered his head to the dirt as he attempted to dodge an onslaught of stones being tossed in his direction. Hanging from the boy's waist, cursing at anyone and everything within earshot, was little Roustaf. Though the bones in his hands had been broken for some time, Walcott achingly pulled them into fists. Shattered cartilage audibly cracked and popped, a flash of pain shooting up his forearm. Taking note of the Tycarian's feeble gesture, Kragamel looked down and smiled.

Ignoring the pain coursing through his body, Walcott tugged at the chains binding him. "Let the child alone, you bastard!" The rattling of steel against stone succeeded in drawing the crowd's attention from Donald and Roustaf to the action on the main stage once more.

Welts just now beginning to form across his body, Donald peeked through his fingers in Walcott's direction. Puddles of warm, salty tears had begun to form in the corners of his eyes. He didn't want to cry. He wanted to do anything but cry, or let anyone see him cry. Try as he might to hold back his emotions, he was failing.

The sight of Walcott whipping like a wild, angry beast at his chains only made things more difficult.

Realizing the struggling was getting him nowhere, and suddenly finding it remarkably difficult to breathe, Walcott relented in his assault against the steel. He needed time to recover, time to think. Breathing heavily, he stared angrily into the black eyes of the tyrant king. "Have you no morals, fiend? He is just a boy; he need not see this."

Kragamel leaned close enough to Walcott that the Tycarian could feel the warmth of his acrid breath across his flesh. "You dare to speak of the dictates of morals to me, mongrel? We are in this together, you and I, just as we have been from the start. Do not think for a second that your hands are not as stained as mine. How many have you killed in the name of your country? How many of your race has killed in the name of their king?"

Still struggling with his breath, Walcott gritted what remained of his teeth, a low growl seeping through the cracks in his blood-caked lips. "In *defense* of my country."

The king's voice dropped to a whisper. "Call it what you may. Words change nothing. We are not so different, you and I. You feel just in lecturing me due exclusively to the situation in which you currently find yourself. Were the tables suddenly turned, I have no doubt you would chirp a different tune entirely."

"We are *nothing* alike," Walcott growled, trying his best to ignore the pain caused merely by the act of keeping his paws pulled into fists.

The tyrant king immediately smiled. "In this statement you are correct. We are nothing alike. You are dead, and I am alive."

Jerking upright, the king threw his hands into the air and gazed over the sea of Ochans filling the courtyard of his castle for at least a mile in every direction. With a half-smile, half-snarl he screamed at the top of his lungs, "We shall afford this atrocity no more of our precious time! Split the scum and be done with it!"

Louder than any of the previous eruptions, the crowd burst into a wild frenzy. So raucous were their voices that the ground literally shook beneath their feet, causing Donald to lose his balance and stumble forward. His shoulder crashed to the ground with a thump, Roustaf's steel cage digging painfully into his kidney. As the tyrant king stepped back from the altar, six Ochan soldiers wielding long steel rods bent at one end similar to a crowbar surrounded the Tycarian.

Walcott knew what was coming.

The grizzly, awful practice of splitting a Tycarian from his shell began early in the conflict between the two worlds. To this very day the landscape of Tycaria remained littered with the empty, hollow shells of the dead.

Of all the things one could do to a Tycarian, this was the most painful; this was the worst.

His heart beating wildly, Walcott's body tensed and his muscles pulled taut. His limbs began suddenly shaking uncontrollably. His breaths were out of sync, too short and moving too fast for him to ever really fill his lungs. Rolling his head to the side, he stared at Donald in the dirt at the foot of the stone altar. The boy looked feral and disheveled, an absolute mess. Fountains of tears poured from his wide eyes as he sobbed passionately, his frostbitten fingers digging into the frozen dirt beneath his knees. Dangling beside him, a crazy-eyed Roustaf pounded on the bars of his cage screaming, his little voice drowned out by the roar of the crowd. Despite the overwhelming fear coursing through the boy's form, Walcott noticed Donald's body begin to jerk upward. The child wanted to help him, even if the muscles in his body had other ideas entirely. Sensing the slight movement as well, the soldiers behind Donald pulled tighter on the taut strings of their bows. If Donald moved again, he would die.

"Stay where you are, lad!" Walcott screamed over the noise. "No matter what happens, you are not to move a muscle! Do you understand me?"

Tears seeping into his mouth, Donald shook his head, unsure of what to say, unsure of anything.

Walcott steadied his voice, trying his best to stifle the anxiety rapidly taking control of his body. No matter what, he needed to ensure the child's safety. This was priority number one. "You have been given your orders, young Mr. Donald. I expect you to follow them!"

Despite his situation, Walcott's face was the absolute pillar of strength as he spoke. Donald's knees immediately halted their shuffling.

All at once, the Ochan soldiers stiffly wedged their steel bars between the connection points of the Tycarian's shell. The movement sent an immediate, blinding wave of pain shooting through Walcott's body. His paws opened wide as his fingers coiled themselves into awful, open-palmed death grips. His flat toes pulled tight and wide as his feet began to shake uncontrollably. To keep from crying out, he bit the tongue in his mouth so hard it nearly split in two. Weeding through flashes of searing pain, he noticed that Donald now seemed unable to look away. The boy was utterly terrified, confused and emotional in ways one so young could never hope to fully comprehend.

Donald shouldn't be seeing this. He didn't need to see this.

As the steel dug further into his side, Walcott cried through a mouth full of blood in the terrified child's direction, "This is not meant for the eyes of children, boy! Turn your head!"

One after another, the Ochan guards pushed down on the steel bars. Slowly and yet oh, so violently, they had begun to peel the Tycarian king's shell apart. The process was more a marathon rather than a sprint, every moment agonizingly drawn out, every second bringing with it a world of untold horrors. Behind Donald, the archers pulled tighter on the bows pointed in his direction. Overcome with emotions, he was finding himself unable to look away, despite wanting more than anything to do exactly that. Walcott's body began to thrash wildly, pulling into ugly contorted angles as he was literally ripped in two, slimy discharge spurting from the newly formed cracks in the sides of his shell. Fighting with every ounce of energy he had, Walcott refused to scream. He was unwilling to give Kragamel the satisfaction. The king would indeed beat him this day, but he would not see him beaten. As one half of his shell began to peel away from the other, however, remaining silent became impossible. The pain was simply too blinding, too incredible, and far too much to bear, even for a king.

Thrashing his head from side to side, Walcott's eyes opened wide, his face an angry grimace of emotions so ravenous and untamed words could never truly do them justice. Donald was still watching him, watching, and crying, and seeing things he'd never forget. Donald needed to look away.

"Close your damn eyes, boy!" Walcott's voice was husky and crunchy, as if his throat was filled with gravel and shattered glass.

Horrified, Donald immediately dropped his head to the dirt. Placing his hands over his ears, he pressed with all of his incredible strength against his skull, hoping beyond hope to snuff out the horrifying sounds. Below him, the frozen soil was stained with his tears and sweat. Around him, the crowd continued to roar, getting louder by the moment. Beside him, Roustaf dropped to his knees, defeated. The little man's fists were bloody from beating on the steel containing him. Deep crimson purple welts had already begun to form. Unable to bear seeing anymore, he, too, looked away.

For the king of Tycaria, the world slowed to a crawl. The ungodly pain had reached its apex; from this point on, thankfully, it could get no worse. One by one, various parts of his body slowly slipped into a wonderful, relieving numbness. Warm liquid now flowed openly from the split in his shell, bathing the stone underneath in a warm, sticky green, the only warmth in this entire awful world. His head and arms went limp. Fighting was pointless now. The soldiers tearing him apart had gone too far, and there was no coming back. The world around folded into something softer and whiter, more blurry and manageable, something he could hold onto and something he could make sense of. Perched atop this strange new bridge between the living and the dead, the cold gray Ochan clouds suddenly resembled those commonly filling the Tycarian sky. He recalled his youth and fondly remembered his childhood love, smiled as he was returned to the day he was crowned king of his people. His mother was so proud of him, so confident he would grow to be the king all of Tycaria deserved. In this instance, Ocha and its king, and the madness Kragamel brought to his race, ceased to exist. Years spent fighting a war that claimed those he had loved and the place he called home, split into particles too small for the eye to capture and disappeared. What remained was something entirely different, something warm and comforting and familiar. What remained was the end, and the beginning, and whatever might come next.

What remained was a revelation.

Lifting from the empty husk of his shell, these newly-formed unseen particles that once made up the creature calling itself

Walcott Shellamennes caught the breeze and rose softly into the clouds above. Absorbed into the atmosphere, they again changed shape, transforming into something entirely different and wholly unexplainable. With time, they would return as a cold Tycarian rain, drenching a world unaccustomed to anything other than black snow.

Walcott had missed the rain. Oh, how wonderful it would be, to feel it one last time.

In the end, the moisture would tell his story; the rain would deliver his message. On this day, the universe bid adieu to a king among kings and returned him to his rightful place among the clouds. This was the unalterable cycle of things. This was the beginning, the end and the often-bashful, bittersweet beauty hiding between the cracks.

Walcott Shellamennes, King of the Tycarian people, the holder of the sacred cup of Peladrov, the keeper of the great Mud Chalice and the leader of the New Tipoloo rebellion, was dead.

So be it.

61. SLIDE

Tommy Jarvis had always loved the cold. In winter everything became smooth, clean and sterile. There was a beautiful slickness to freshly fallen snow and frozen ice, something slippery and sparkling and concentrated. Molded by the winds, when untouched by the hand of man, winter was pure, honest and real.

The snow did not lie, the snow simply was.

The previous night brought much of what the young boy had come to love so dearly, so much in fact that it caught the quiet little town he called home unprepared. With school closed for the day, Tommy and his little brother bundled themselves into thick winter jackets, snagged the flat circular sleds from the shed behind the house, and headed to the hill by the Fergusons' near the end of the block. With snow came sledding, and Tommy liked that too. Though she was feeling both nauseated and sleepy on account of the medication, Megan Jarvis followed close behind her children. In a few days she would be admitting herself into the hospital for an extended stay; her doctors believed she couldn't afford to wait any longer. She had delayed the inevitable long enough. Megan needed simple moments such as these now more than ever. Far too many times in her life she'd let them pass without fully acknowledging their importance. While she regretted many things, this stood alone atop the list. Moments were like snowflakes, so plentiful, it was easy to take them for granted. No two were exactly the same however, and missing just one meant missing it forever.

Snowflakes offered no second chances.

Pulling the hood of her jacket over her head for warmth, Megan smiled brightly as she watched Tommy push his younger brother down the modest-sized hill on a circular sled. Spinning like a top, Nicky lost his grip near the bottom and was thrown into the fluffy whiteness face first. Despite the awkward fall, she knew her son wasn't hurt. Though his head was half buried, she could hear his muffled laughter from beneath the drift. Rushing to his brother's aid, Tommy hoisted the smaller boy into the air, both children giggling wildly as flakes of white continued to fall around them.

Nicky turned toward his mother, his face soaking wet and red, his smile wider than she'd seen it in some time. "Mom! Mom! Did you see me? Oh my God, Mom, did you see that wipe out?"

Lifting her hand to her mouth, Megan laughed into the fabric of her wool mitten and nodded her head in the direction of her younger child. He looked so much like his father, more so with every passing year. Many times since his birth, she'd seen glimmers of her husband in his eyes, a child-like reflection of the things she had come to love so much about Chris. This made her happy.

Starting up the hill once more, Nicky yelled in her direction, "Mom! Mom! Watch me! Watch me, I'm going again!"

"I see you, bubby! I'm watching yo—" An uncontrollable coughing fit stopped Megan mid-sentence.

At times, it seemed all she did was cough anymore. Her throat had been raw for months; the pounding in her head was so constant it had become the norm. Every day she grew weaker. With each passing hour, even the simplest of things seemed worlds harder. Just living was rapidly becoming an obstacle. She wasn't sure how much longer she could go on this way, and there were times she wondered if she even wanted to.

As Nicky trudged carefully up the hill, buried to his waist in snow, Megan's elder son approached her timidly. Unlike Nicky, Tommy had taken note of every aspect of his mother's physical deterioration. Like the wood on the deck in the back yard, or the rusted tricycle by the shed that hadn't been used for years, she was falling apart. Every day she seemed different: smaller. Everyday her smile faded just a bit, replaced by something false, something pretend.

"Are you all right, mom?" Tommy asked, his face sticky-wet and bright red, pillars of hot breath puffing from his mouth with every word.

"Yeah, I'm fine, hunny, totally fine. Go play with your brother, I'll be right here watching."

Looking in Nicky's direction, Tommy noticed that his little brother was only halfway up the hill, struggling with the mounds of snow as he lugged the oversized sled behind with one gloved hand. Turning his attention back to his mother, he watched as a jittery smile crept its way across her face. In stark contrast to her happy grin, beads of moisture had begun to pool in the corner of her eyes. Her skin had grown so pale in the last few months, now nearly the tone of the cascading snow above her head. Reaching up, she used her mitten to wipe away the tears. She wasn't sure why she was crying. Realistically it could have been any one of a million reasons, maybe all of them.

Biting her lower lip, she smiled down at her son, nudging him gently in the direction of the snowy hill. "Go on, Tommy. Go help your brother. I'll be fine."

Tommy held his position. Something was scratching at the inside of his skull, begging and pleading on bended knee to be asked, something he'd avoided until this very moment.

"Mom . . .I don't want you to go away."

He was never sure why he said it or what it was even supposed to mean. The question was less a conscious decision than a reaction, and it caught Megan off guard.

"What? What — what are you talking about? I'm not going anywhere. I'm just going to be in the hospital for a little while, remember? We talked about this the other day."

Despite the feeble attempt at reassurance, Megan's eleven-year old son remained unsatisfied. He didn't believe her. He could see right through her answer, and knew she was lying.

Having successfully trekked his way to the top of the hill, Nicky yelled happily in the direction of his mother, "Mommy! Hey, mom! Watch this!" Leaping onto the plastic sled, the little boy slid down and collapsed into a frenzied heap at the bottom once more, laughing the entire time. Megan chuckled at his innocence, happy she still had it in her life. Beside her, Tommy continued to stare, his beautiful blue eyes — so achingly similar to hers — pleading for an answer she wasn't prepared to give. A part of her wished he was younger. Just a few years and he'd be seeing the entire situation through very different eyes, through his brother's eyes. He was not younger, though. He was older, and he had questions — questions she knew as a mother she needed to answer. Lying to him would only make things worse as the years went by. Lying to him would only leave the boy resenting her, and she wouldn't be around to pick up the pieces. He deserved the truth, no matter how badly it might hurt or how unprepared he might be to deal with it. When she was a little girl, Megan's mother once told her that pain was like a Band-Aid, always better to get it over with quickly. With Nicky starting up the hill again, yelling for his older brother to join him, Megan turned to Tommy and placed her hands on his shoulders. He was growing up so quickly, getting so tall, turning into a little man. Despite his size, at the core his features remained much the same as those of the infant that required so very much of her attention in order to survive. No matter how old he got, at least from her perspective, this much would never change.

Reaching up, she placed her hand against the side of his cold face. "Everyone goes away when it's their time, hunny. Unfortunately, we don't get to choose; it just happens and we have to accept it."

Whether due to the cold, his emotions, or a combination of the two, Tommy's expression remained frozen. His response was so simple it tore at the very fibers making up Megan's heart: "But I don't want you to."

Lowering to one knee, Megan put herself at the same level as her son, staring into his confused yet strangely expressionless face. "I know you don't, baby. I know you don't. I don't want to go either. When our time comes, we go. It's the way it's always been, the way it'll always be."

Tommy's expression went sour, his chilly blue tinted lips pulling tight. "No."

"Sweetie it's all right. Everything will be okay, I swear. You may not understand right now, but you will one day, I promise."

"I can change it. You'll see. I'll change it. I can do it mom, I really can."

"Tommy, listen to me —"

"NO! I'm not letting you go!" Her son's expression changed dramatically, his voice rising in volume as puddles of warm liquid began to spout from the corners of his eyes. "I'm not letting them take you! I won't let you go! I can fight! I can fight, and I'll fight them all! You don't have to go! You don't!"

At the top of the hill, Nicky Jarvis now stood frozen in place with the sled pulled tightly to his chest as he listened to his brother screaming. Wrapping her son in her arms, Megan pulled Tommy close to her chest, allowing his tears to fall into the nape of her neck as he sobbed.

Patting him gently on the back, she whispered, "It's okay. It'll be okay, I promise," over and over again, struggling to fight back her own tears and remain strong for her child. When his mother's neck was thoroughly soaked and Tommy had nothing left with which to cry, he stopped trying to wiggle loose from her grip. The familiar scent of her hair and the warmth of her body succeeded in calming him much the same it always had. The cool breeze freezing his tears to her flesh, Megan pushed her son away once more, cupping his cheeks in her gloved hands. He looked so lost, so hurt, alone, and confused. It would have been so simple to lie to him, to tell him something she didn't believe simply because it would likely make him feel better. In her heart though, she knew she couldn't do that; she wouldn't do that. He deserved more than lies, false hopes and nonsense. He deserved what all children deserved, despite the fact that so many believed they were unable to process it: he deserved the truth.

Placing her hand under his chin, Megan lifted his face to hers, hardened tears glistening off the pink of his cheeks. "Tommy, look at me."

Fighting back his emotions, Tommy breathed deeply and gazed into the eyes of his mother. Just over the crest of her soft, flowing hair, the sun had begun to peek through the dense clouds. It looked whiter than it did yellow, an explosion of light.

"I promise you it'll be okay, sweetie. You know I would never lie to you, and I promise it's going to be all right. Everything's connected, and no matter what, Mommy will always be with you. No matter where you go or what you do, I'll be watching you the entire time. I'll be in the stars or the trees or the snow or even the air. I'm never going to be out of reach, sweetie. I want to see you grow up; I want to see you turn into a handsome young man, and do everything you've ever dreamed, and you're going to do great things, Thomas Charles Jarvis. I know you are."

Though the sound of his mother's words were comforting in a way only a mother's could be, their meanings did little to mend the awful aching of Tommy's heart. The same as most children, he preferred the answers to questions simple, black and white without the gray, yes or no. This was anything but. He didn't care what his mother said; he was not going to let her go away. She didn't have to go, and he could stop it. He would stop it.

From the corner of her eye, Megan spotted Nicky still standing motionless atop the hill, staring blankly at her and Tommy, his fingers drumming nervously on the plastic sled.

"Now go play with your brother, Tommy. Go slide," She said with a whisper and a somber smile to her eldest child before planting a kiss on his cold cheek. "Go ahead, he's waiting for you up there. Go take care of him."

With his head hanging low, Tommy turned and shuffled in the direction of Nicky, the hill and the sled. He would pretend to have fun because he knew he had to, because it was what his mom wanted and needed him to do. Sliding was simple and fun and as white as the fallen snow. Sliding came free of confusing, difficult-to-deal-with grays.

Megan watched as Tommy quickly scaled the mountain of snow and greeted his younger brother with a playful, though somewhat half-hearted shove at the top. For the next thirty minutes, she breathed in the chilly-fresh air, smiling and chuckling at the brotherly bond shared between her children. She was happy they were so close, and wished it might last forever. The snow continued to fall well into the evening, covering the sleepy little town even deeper in a blanket of white. The first snowfall of the season was always the most memorable, and memories were what Megan Jarvis needed most.

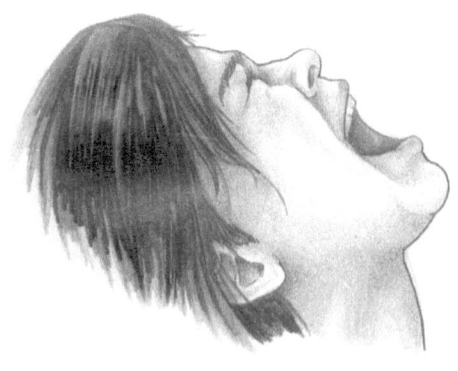

62. BROTHERS IN ARMS

As the Briar Patch wobbled drastically atop the cresting waves, Captain Fluuffytail was tossed violently to the deck. Spinning across the old, splintered wood, he slammed into the ship's railing and came to an immediate, painful stop, grunting deeply as a wave of pain coursed through his midsection. Above him, the crackling translucent bubble rising from Tommy Jarvis's hand continued to encapsulate his ship. Constantly bombarded by a barrage of arrows and cannon fire, the bubble wobbled like gelatin, reducing everything coming into contact with it into little more than puffs of grayish-black smoke. As Tommy struggled to maintain the bubble's integrity against the onslaught of Ochan weapons, his younger brother charged to the front of the ship, leaned over the railing, and screamed as loudly as his little body could muster. What came from his mouth, however, were anything but mere words. The instant the boy opened his mouth, the words built up inside transformed into something quite different, something massive and dangerous, something of weight and matter and speed, something that passed with ease through Tommy's protective bubble on a collision course with a patch of Ochan warships. This incredible new thing, no longer resembling a word like any word the universe had come to know, slammed into the dark ships, ripping them to pieces in the blink of an eye. Sturdy blackened wood, coarse bone, hardened steel and sinewy flesh were scattered for miles in every direction in a cacophony of destruction. Having destroyed one ship, the incredible force moved onward to another and another after that. By the time the energy dissipated, it had reduced at least ten warships to flaming pieces of floating rubble. The force of the boy's word was terrifying. The strength of his word was awe-inspiring. The fleet of Ochan warships was massive, however, and the obliteration of ten ships barely made a dent in the overall force. With ten ships gone, ten more immediately cut through the debris field to take their place. Sprinting full speed to the opposite end of the Briar Patch, Nicky leaned over the railing once again and fired another blast of his astounding word power, reducing still more ships to worthless husks.

Near the center of the Fluuffytail's ship, Krystoph watched the boy with unbelieving eyes. These children were more powerful than he could ever have imagined, and more dangerous than they had any right to be. To put such power in the hands of children—this was the plan of a fool, a recipe for destruction. There could be no other outcome. Above him, enormous cannon balls and arrows continued to slam into the slightly bluish, humming bubble of energy. The sounds resulting from the collisions were remarkable. Having more in common with a burst of electricity than an explosion, the bubble of light hummed, popped and crackled angrily, flashing and glowing like the surface of the sun. Following the glow to its source, Krystoph took careful note of the peculiar expression on the face of Tommy Jarvis. The boy was in obvious pain; maintaining the integrity of the sphere seemed to be requiring his complete physical energy and mental focus. Tommy's entire body was shaking, a thick sheen of sweat pouring down his face. Despite the obvious discomfort, however, the child refused to relent. He was determined, steely and hardheaded, traits inspiring feelings of both admiration and caution in the former Ochan general.

Running from one end of the ship to the other was quickly wearing on young Nicky Jarvis. His legs were on fire, the bottoms of his feet more sore than he remembered them being at any point in the whole of his young life. His throat was sore, scratchy like sandpaper, and getting significantly sorer with every blast of energy. Around him, the crew of the Briar Patch watched in awe, confused as to exactly what was happening or how they could help.

While cautiously weaving through a patch of arrows protruding from the deck, Nicky's feet slid out from underneath him and he tumbled forward. Landing hard on his chest, the air was forced from his lungs, small gashes opening immediately on both his elbows. Tired and on the verge of tears, Nicky tried to pull himself to his feet only to stumble again. He should have listened to his brother. He should have listened to his brother and stayed with Ed and Edna. He shouldn't be doing this. Everything was spinning out of control, and he wasn't cut out for this. Not too far away, he watched as his brother dropped to one knee, the bubble encasing the ship slowly shrinking, dwindling in tune with Tommy's strength. Despite having destroyed so many ships, Nicky could scarcely see anything other than the black beasts on the water, each rapidly closing in on the Briar Patch. Trying again to crawl to his feet, he stumbled forward once more and began to sob into his cupped hands. He couldn't do this. He couldn't do this and he shouldn't have been asked to do this.

He wanted to go home.

From across the deck, Nestor spotted the flattened out, teary-eyed boy and understood immediately that he was incapable or unwilling to rise. With the remainder of the crew too confused to act, Nestor took a deep breath and hopped to his feet. Thanks to Staci, his muscles felt energized and full, every nagging pain and life-threatening injury healed completely. He vowed not to let her aid go to waste.

Charging in Nicky's direction, he snagged the child in mid-stride, quickly carried him to the opposite end of the ship, then held his tiny body over the tumultuous waters. "Go lad! Fire, now!"

Weightless in Nestor's gargantuan paws, Nicky could only shake his head, unable to gain control over the flood of emotions strangling his ability to act.

The ships were getting closer, and the closer they got the more destructive the force of their cannons. Glancing over his shoulder, Nestor noticed that Tommy was now on both knees, his face an ugly grimace of tightly drawn muscles. Kneeling beside him, a terrified Staci Alexander continued to encourage the boy, pleading for him to find a way to work through the pain.

Pulling Nicky close to his face, Nestor stared into the weary, tear soaked eyes of the child. "You must continue, lad. I am sorry but there is no other choice."

He hated having to say it, to push the terrified boy further and demand so much of one so very little. He hated it more than anything he'd been forced to do in recent memory. Nicky remained the only chance they had for survival. For this singular moment, the child would have to become more than the sum of his parts, more than even he might believe he was capable. For this singular moment, he would have to be a hero.

"Believe me, I know how hard it is, lad. I understand how terribly it must hurt." Nestor continued. "You must not stop, Nicholas. You cannot stop. I swear to you, I shall not leave your side. I will remain here with you the entire time, but you must act now."

Despite the pain and the frustration, despite the fact that his body was urging him to lie down and call it quits, Nicky Jarvis opened his eyes, took a deep breath, and nodded in the direction of the green skinned turtle man. Nestor smiled wide. He was growing more and more impressed with these strange children every day. He once believed the Fillagrou prophecy to be nonsense, wishful thinking at best. He was not so sure anymore.

With Tommy's bubble continuing its gradual implosion and Nestor running from one side of the ship to the other lugging the weary-faced Nicky as he blasted Ochan ships to oblivion, Krystoph realized neither child would last long enough to destroy the entire fleet. There were simply too many ships, and they were far too tired. When at last the Tommy's protective bubble gave way and fell, the Briar Patch would be ripped to pieces. They could not win this battle. If the Briar Patch was destroyed, he would be as well, and so would the Rongstag. Krystoph could not allow this. If he was to have his vengeance, both he and the Rongstag needed to survive the day.

There was no other choice. He had to find a way off the ship.

63. REMOVE THE FEMALE

The orders of his king were clear, concise and simple. "Remove the female child from the situation, and retrieve the artifact." The reality of bringing this order to life, however, was proving significantly more difficult than General Thrax envisioned. Though more than a few miles and hundreds of warships separated him from Captain Fluuffytail's pathetic vessel, the general could clearly distinguish the ominous glow of young Tommy Jarvis' protective bubble. He'd seen this magic before. He was there when the child laid waste to a castle full of well-trained Ochan warriors, just barely escaping with his own life. Emerging from somewhere within the glowing sphere, destructive waves of a force that warped and distorted the sky as they moved slammed into the nearest Ochan ships and reduced them to explosive cinders in the blink of an eye. For a moment Thrax considered calling for a retreat. In truth, however, he knew that retreat was not a viable option. He had retreated once already, leaving the body of the prince to rot among the shattered bricks of his demolished Fillagrou castle. Leaving without accomplishing his mission a second time might mean saving the life of his soldiers. It would also mean ending his. The king would not accept another failure. There was no backing down, not until the meddlesome pirate's ship had been destroyed, the girl captured, and the artifact recovered. Hearing the familiar squawk of Scarbeaks, Thrax quickly made his way to the rear of his ship as three of the massive winged creatures were led from the lower decks and into the open air. Whipping their heads back and forth while cawing wildly, the winged beasts stumbled awkwardly across the slippery wood as three burly Ochans held them in place with impossibly thick leather leashes. Behind him, Thrax could clearly make out the sounds of yet more vessels meeting their gruesome, untimely demise. Muffled Ochan screams sliced through the air as more of the fleet was obliterated and scattered across the water.

"I need the female child," Thrax said sternly to the Scarbeak riders. "Your king believes she is the key; she must be removed from the situation, and she must be kept alive."

The trio of Ochans nodded sternly, though they were more than a little disappointed with the "must be kept alive" part.

"If need be, we can retrieve the artifact from the bottom of the ocean after their ship has sunk. The child, however, is the priority. Do not return without her. Failure is unacceptable."

After nodding again, the Ochans hopped onto the backs of the squealing Scarbeaks, the creatures cawing angrily through their hideously curved beaks. Receiving a stiff kick in the side from the Ochans, the monsters flapped their enormous wings and took instantly to the air.

Turning again to the battle ahead, Thrax watched as the protective bubble surrounding Fluuffytail's sad excuse for a ship began to flounder. It was slowly shrinking. Like all things, it seemed even the incredible powers of these children had their limits. With persistence and time they too would fail and fall, as all that had threatened the Ochan nation in the past. On the east end of the incredible bubble, ten more warships were reduced to flaming timbers, hundreds of soldiers killed in the process. Thankfully, General Thrax had thousands of anxious warriors at his disposal, and all the time in the world.

Tommy Jarvis was tired, every part of him drained, sleepy and sore. Even the simple act of breathing had become difficult and labored, as if there was a plastic bag over his head. From the corner of his eye, he watched as Nestor sprinted past with Nicky tucked tight to his chest. His little brother's face was pale, tears seeping slowly down his drawn cheeks while one of his hands massaged an unbearable wad of pain wedged firmly in his throat. High above, the cannons and arrows continued to batter his rapidly shrinking protective bubble. Tommy could feel the collision of every single piece of sharpened wood and tempered steel rattling in his bones, each bringing with it a force comparable to a punch in the stomach. As the pain continued to pour over him, Tommy eventually found himself unable to keep both hands above his head and dropped one to the water-soaked deck with a splash. Everything hurt; everything was cold, stiff and foggy. He couldn't keep this up much longer.

Kneeling less than a foot away from the boy, Staci could see the strain on his face. His eyes had gone glassy; his body was covered in a layer of sweat so thick it had soaked through his clothes. The weaker Tommy got, the faster the protective bubble he'd created shrank. Having fallen well below the Briar Patch's sails, the newly exposed sections of the ship were immediately hammered with Ochan cannon fire. Enormous balls of iron tore the massive wooden polls to pieces, jerking the entire ship back and forth atop the crashing waves. Dropping flat to her stomach and digging her fingers between awkwardly constructed panels of wood making up the deck, Staci managed just barely to keep from sliding across the ship. Above his head, Tommy's remaining hand wobbled, his mouth hanging open and face dropping low. His head was throbbing, the space behind his eyeballs were on fire. Like a deflating balloon, the bubble above continued to shrivel.

Lifting herself to her hands and knees, Staci whispered in his direction, "Tommy?"

Half awake and half somewhere else, Tommy directed his weary, far away glance in the direction of her voice. She looked so blurry, fading in and out of the background as if he were seeing her through the lens of a camera that was unable to focus.

More similar to an echo of the original rather than the source, again her soft voice slipped its way into his ears, "Tommy. *Pleasetommyplease* . . .Tommy, are you okay?"

Tommy believed that he responded to her with a nod. In his current state, however, he wasn't entirely sure. His arm weighed so much, as if the combined mass of the universe now rested on the tender flesh of his palm. Keeping it upright and allowing the energy to continually pour form his fingers suddenly seemed like an impossible task.

"Tommy, please, please tell me you're okay!"

Staci was yelling now, her voice dragging like the concussion blast immediately after an explosion. Tommy tried to open his mouth, tried telling her that he was okay, that he'd keep the bubble going no matter what, that he wouldn't let her down. Instead of words, only puffs of air escaped. His intentions betrayed his body, however. He was fighting a losing battle and stepping slowly into a world where intent ceased to have meaning and meanings were pointless. Everything was going black, fading into an untold future similar to the end of a movie. Despite his best efforts, unconsciousness swooped in, wrapped its ghastly arms around his neck, and began to choke. Tommy's arm dropped to the deck with a thunk as his body went limp. Immediately the bubble protecting the Briar Patch from the onslaught of Ochan weapons dropped away, fizzling into nothing.

Lunging forward, Staci caught her falling friend in her arms and screamed.

What would come next would undoubtedly hurt a good deal.

64. THE FIRST SNOWFALL

Ocha knew winter and only winter, only gray clouds and bitter cold. However, it was not until the first snow began to fall that those calling it home understood without an ounce of uncertainty that the true Ochan winter had begun. Sobbing into the frozen dirt, black snowflakes layering his body like rolled dandruff, Donald Rondage found that his limbs had gone stiff and uncooperative. He wanted to lift his head but he couldn't; it was too heavy and too thick for the muscles in his neck to properly maneuver. The snarling crowd of Ochans that had come to see Walcott's death began to peel away some time ago, their desire for blood temporarily satiated. As the last of them returned to the uneventful tasks of their daily lives inside the walls of Kragamel's castle, the courtyard became transformed, eerily silent. Trapped behind the steel bars of his tiny cage, Roustaf stared in the direction of the stone altar on which his friend had been tortured and killed, an angry grimace forever etched into the deep red of his face. Sprawled atop the stone, one half of Walcott's shell wobbled ever so subtly in the winter's breeze.

The limbs of the Tycarian king hung loosely over the edges, unmoving, limp and leathery. Walcott's massive fingers, once seeming so powerful, had gone stiff and crumply. Suddenly they looked so very breakable, like bent icicles slowly melting away. A garish thick liquid seeped through the spaces between them and over the cavernous wrinkles of his knuckles, dripping from his cracked fingertips to the chilly stone below. Standing above his lifeless corpse, the tyrant king stared in the direction of Donald, Roustaf and the Ochan archers whose weapons remained pointed dangerously in the boy's direction. Though his face was mostly expressionless, there was an undeniable smugness just below the surface, a feeling of pride and accomplishment the king was trying his best to disguise. Walcott Shellamennes, the king of Tycaria, a constant thorn in his side for more years than he cared to admit, was at last dead.

Feeling absolutely no pride whatsoever in this moment would be impossible, even for an Ochan, and even for a king.

Placing a single gloved finger along the rim of Walcott's shell, the king pushed downward gently, causing it to wobble like a marble. The sight elicited a chuckle from Kragamel as a toothy grin burst to life across his dark green face. Turning away from what remained of his fallen enemy, the tyrant king then gazed in the direction of the enemy still breathing less than ten feet away.

"It is difficult to explain fully, but I suddenly find myself overcome with a wholly uncommon sense of generosity," He said in what was no doubt his closest approximation of cheerfulness while wiping trace amounts of Walcott's blood from the tip of his finger. "So much in fact, child, that I am going to offer you a chance to say goodbye to your Tycarian friend."

Donald didn't answer. He wanted to, but he couldn't. Like the black snow continuing to pile onto his back, he was frozen. No longer in control of his emotions, the boy found himself at the whim of outside forces: a black snowflake caught in an updraft, utterly helpless.

Kragamel smiled slyly, realizing the Tycarian's death had accomplished exactly what he hoped it would. The child was broken and unwilling. Any fight that might have swelled within had been obliterated.

"I shall not make this offer again, boy. What remains of this pathetic creature is mine to do with as I please, and soon his worthless mound of flesh will hardly be recognizable. If you wish to say goodbye to this foul creature, I suggest you take this opportunity to do so, lest you lose it forever."

"Leave him alone, you son of a bitch," Roustaf mumbled angrily from behind his bars, throwing an icy stare in the king's direction.

Kragamel's grin disappeared. "Stay your tongue, mongrel. I can assure you from years of experience that Tycarians are not the only creatures capable of being split in two."

Grabbing hold of the bars so roughly his knuckles turned white, Roustaf slammed the weight of his tiny body against them, thick wads of foam flinging from between his lips. "I'll kill you! Do you hear me? You're dead, you son of a bitch! I'll kill every single one of you lousy bastards!"

Lifting one foot into the air, Kragamel kicked the side of Walcott's shell, tipping it over and spilling what remained of his floppy, blood-soaked body onto the altar. Bouncing off the stone, limbs flailing wildly, Walcott's corpse spilled into the freshly fallen dirty-black snow less than a few feet from Donald and Walcott.

With a clawed finger pointing in Roustaf's direction, the tyrant king snarled, "You will do nothing! Are you so oblivious to the world around you that you cannot see you and your kind have lost, creature? Surely even you cannot be so dense!" Breathing deeply, the king attempted to corral his anger. Lifting his chin into the air, he cracked the vertebrae in his neck and gritted his pointed teeth. If his years as the king of Ocha had taught him anything, it was that anger accomplished nothing. His father was prone to anger, his son as well, and both paid dearly for this flaw.

Slightly ashamed of himself for allowing the little red man to rile him up in such a manner, the king steadied his emotions before continuing. "There are no happy endings for you, mongrel, no last minute heroics and no victory celebration. You foolishly presume yourself on the side of the righteous, little one, yet in this belief you are sadly mistaken. The just cause belongs to us, to the Ochan race. For every prophecy made by a pathetic Fillagrou elder foretelling your eventual success, there are fifty made by my conjurers proclaiming the exact opposite. Prophecies are lies, nonsense and illusion. The victor and the victor alone are the true tellers of history, and it is history that shall carefully recall the story of murderers and thieves that attempted, quite unsuccessfully, to destroy the great Ochan nation. History is a matter of perspective, and history shall regale the circumstances leading to your vainglorious defeat. History shall be written by me."

Roustaf was barely listening to the king anymore. Instead he found himself unable to look away from the limp, shell-less body of Walcott spread across the dirt in front of him. The entire time Walcott's wide, glassy-dead green eyes remained open, staring back.

With a slightly frustrated huff, the tyrant king turned toward a group of soldiers standing patiently alongside the altar. "Return them the dungeon. Rotate guards. Keep at least six of you on the child at all times."

"What of the Tycarian, sire?" A single soldier chirped from behind his bulky black helmet.

Already on his way to the doorway leading into the castle, Kragamel stopped, momentarily gazing at the sloppy mass of sloppy flesh sprawled in the soil at the foot of the blood-drenched altar.

"Put what remains of him on display inside the doorway to Tycaria. Let his corpse remind the rebels that their cause is hopeless. However, remove his head first. I would rather enjoy keeping it for myself."

Grabbing hold of his arms, a pair of guards lifted the zombie-like Donald Rondage to his wobbly, useless feet. For the very first time the boy noticed Walcott's lifeless body stretched out in front of him. Barely recognizable without his shell, at first Donald scarcely believed it was he. This was not the king of Tycaria. This was a replica, a fake, a wax statue melting in the sun. Only there was no sun over Ocha. In this place there was only cold and black. Devoid of justice, forgiveness and the dictates of reason, this world offered only loss and pain to those daring to walk its soil. Here, the good guys did not always win; here the good guys did not even exist. Donald's eyes had ceased their crying some time ago, as he had no tears remaining. What the boy now found himself left with was nothing even remotely resembling an emotion. Like Walcott, he had been split open, hollowed out and left an empty shell. High above, the dark snow continued to fall and would continue doing so well into the evening before eventually covering even this horrible world in a blanket of slick, disgusting black. The Ochan winter had indeed officially begun. As had been said before and would undoubtedly be said again, the first snowfall of the season was always the most memorable.

65. VANTAGE POINTS

From the perspective of Captain Jacques Fluuffytail, what happened next happened very quickly. The moment Tommy Jarvis dropped unconscious to the deck, the protective bubble sprouting from his glowing hand vanished. As the ship's only line of defense faded into nothingness, Captain Fluuffytail found himself and his crew instantly engulfed in a maelstrom of destruction. A rather large cannonball slammed into the front of the Briar Patch, lifting the rear of the ship clear out of the water for a moment and tossing shards of dangerous debris in every conceivable direction. Another hammered through the deck not far from Jacques, into the lower levels, and through the bottom of the hull. With the blue ocean water pouring in by the gallon, the ship shuddered and began to sink. As flaming arrows pounded into the deck around him, Captain Fluuffytail dove for cover, narrowly avoiding another cannonball as it whizzed past and tore yet more of his ship away. Peering from under the brim of his oversized hat, he was horrified by what his dark eyes saw. His ship, his only ship, the ship that had kept him safe and alive over the course of this awful war, was being destroyed. The few parts of the Briar Patch not yet on fire had been ripped to shreds and scattered among the tepid Aquari waters. While some of his crew had also managed to find temporary cover, the vast majority of them were either dead or dying. Their lifeless, bent corpses were now bathing the deck in the slick, multi-colored blood of friends and family. It wasn't supposed to happen this way, not like this — anything but this. He promised them, time and time again, that he would keep them safe, that the Briar Patch, much like its captain, was an omen of luck or an invincible force, something the Ochan army could never hope to destroy. For years it had proved to be exactly that.

As a spattering of flaming arrows sank into the aged wood of the deck a few feet away, Fluuffytail leapt from his stomach and began crawling, frantically searching for cover among the patches of fire and debris. Hit with another cannonball, the Briar Patch lurched and moaned. The ship was in pain; she was crying. Reaching up, Jacques pulled his ears down against the sides of his furry face. He couldn't listen to this. He couldn't stand to hear her suffer, to listen to her die. Still shuffling awkwardly across the slick deck, he managed to only make it a few feet before another cannonball hit and launched thick slivers of shrapnel into the fuzzy gray flesh of his back. Jacques leapt to his feet in pain, his upper body on fire, plumes of black smoke rising up around him and seeping into his lungs. With half of its base shattered, one of the massive poles jutting upwards from the ship's deck gave way, narrowly missing Jacques as it smashed to the flaming wood below. The deck collapsed instantly under its weight and tossed the ship's Captain into the air thirty feet before depositing him into the ocean with a splash. For a moment, everything went silent. The awful moaning of his ship and the horrible cries of its crew faded into the smoky blue background. Submerged in the tides of the chilly drink, blood pouring from his back in cloudy trails, Captain Jacques Fluuffytail wondered if he should bother attempting to swim for the surface. The world above had nothing more to offer. Everything in his life, everything significant, or important, or holding any meaning, had been taken from him, taken by the Ochans. All he would have had to do was open his mouth, open his mouth and let the sea fill his lungs. It would be so painless. Many of his crew had shared the same fate over the years, and there would have been no honor lost in dying this way, in going down with his ship, beside her. In the distance, he spotted the forward portion of the Briar Patch tear away and dip below the surface. Surrounded by a cloud of smoky, broken timbers, it began slowly sinking downward. The bizarre, horrifying sight seemed strangely serene, quiet and peaceful. Under the water, everything was a whisper and a secret. As the dark ocean below at last swallowed the final chunk of his ship, Jacques said his final goodbyes. She was a fine lady and a sturdy, faithful companion. She had done her absolute best to keep him and his crew alive for many years. She was ugly and she was beautiful and he would miss her.

The instant Tommy Jarvis's world went black and his protective bubble evaporated, Nestor Shellamennes instinctively pulled the shivering form of Nicky closer to his chest. With nothing keeping the Briar Patch safe, the Tycarian knew all too well what would come next. Though Nicky's amazing abilities had managed to sink an incredible number of Ochan vessels, the sheer size of their force was astounding, and hundreds more remained. Captain Fluuffytail's ship stood no chance. Surrounded by the dark-wooded warships, there was no point of retreat and no hope of escape. Now there existed only an ending, and most likely a nasty, painful one at that.

Beyond-words tired, Nicky Jarvis was only half awake in his arms when the first cannon strike rocked Fluuffytail's old vessel, tearing chunks of wood away and tossing them violently into the ocean. Three arrows slammed into the rear of his shell, a fourth slicing through the recently repaired muscles of his shoulder and popping out the other side. Ignoring the pain, Nestor hunched forward, doing his best to keep the little boy from harm's way as arrows continued to pummel his rocky exterior. Less than five feet to his right, a stack of crates were suddenly engulfed in flames; to his left, another cannonball smashed into the deck. The collision shook the sopping wet floorboards, and Nestor struggled to maintain his balance. A monstrous wave, nearly twenty feet high, spilled over the railing as the ship lurched forward with a pained grunt. With incredible force, the chilly ocean water splashed into Nestor's back, snatching his feet from underneath him and tossing them into the air. Gripping Nicky tightly, the pair slid across the tattered wood, slipping through walls of smoke and flame before crashing through tattered debris and bloody bodies. The entire time, Nestor was spinning like a top on the rear of his shell, grimacing in pain as the world around him was reduced to a cloudy, confusing chaos. The boy in his arms had become slippery, and maintaining his grip increasingly difficult. He wrapped the sopping wet shirt of Nicky twice around his wrist in order to get a better grip, praying the fabric could withstand the pressure.

Dangling somewhere between the conscious and unconscious world, Nicky whispered through jittery lips, "Tommy? Wh– where's–where's my bro-brother?"

Though partially obscured by a thick layer of hazy madness, Nestor spotted a shape vaguely reminiscent of Tommy Jarvis near what little remained of the rear of the Briar Patch. The boy seemed woozy, not fully aware of where he was or what was happening. His body, however, was lit up like a candle in a darkened room. Flashes of blue lightning popped occasionally from his hunched shoulders and tightly closed fists. A familiar white light crackled and hummed off his skin, rising and falling in time with the boy's rapidly increasing breaths. To Nestor's surprise, he noticed that Staci was nowhere to be found. Smack dab in the middle of the thirty or so feet separating the Tycarian from Tommy's glowing form, another cannonball collapsed the deck of the ship, ripping it into smoking cinders. In its wake, a mountain of smoke immediately billowed twenty feet into the air. The violent collision of steel and wood lifted the deck beneath Nestor's feet and threw the Tycarian and Nicky backward through a wall of flames, over what remained of the ships railing and into the frothy drink. With the freezing water rushing up around him, Nicky Jarvis at last dropped fully into unconsciousness.

Having already made his decision to leave the ship, witnessing Tommy's Jarvis's protective shield disappear succeeded only in furthering the resolve of Krystoph. The Rongstag could not be allowed to return to the hands of the king. Without it, Krystoph's plan and his work meant nothing; without it, there would be no revenge. Less than a second after the boy's bubble dropped away, the deck of the Briar Patch was bombarded by enemy fire. As cannonballs began to tear the ship to pieces, the deck beneath Krystoph's feet snapped in two down the middle, and shattered, and broken boards flipped upward violently and smacked him in the face. A moment later, much of the ship was engulfed in flames. Monstrous plumes of black smoke and ash flashed into the sky and blocked out the clouds and the sun.

With a hailstorm of arrows raining down around him, Krystoph grabbed the still flaming corpse of a crewmember and hoisted it high above his head. Using the creature's body as a shield, he quickly made his way across the battered ship. Walls of black smoke and airborne debris had drastically reduced visibility, even for a pair of eyes as trained and capable as his. Darting through the smoke as another cannonball laid waste to the deck nearby, the former Ochan general gazed out across the Aquari sea. The Ochan fleet had momentarily halted its advance, choosing instead to pelt the suddenly helpless ship from afar. While it was a coward's maneuver, it was also an intelligent maneuver. Smoking hunks of wood and steel had transformed the ocean into an awful, lumpy flaming stew. Frothing angrily, the waves lashed at the busted remains of the Briar Patch, aiding the Ochan vessels in their cause. It would seem the universe had grown weary of the scuffle. It too wanted the battle to end, and it wanted it to end now.

Behind Krystoph, the familiar squawk of a Scarbeak managed to somehow slice through the crazed nastiness. Though obscured by a wall of flames, it was obvious by the sound that it was indeed close by; the creature was somewhere on the deck of the ship. After tossing the arrow-riddled corpse above his head into the water, Krystoph dropped to a crouched position and leapt through a wall of crackling orange-red fire. Sliding across the slippery deck on the other side, portions of his pants now ablaze, he looked up just in time to spot the enormous winged monster lift off the tattered remains of the deck and take to the sky. Gripped between its gangly toenails was the human female, Staci Alexander. Screaming at the top of her lungs, limbs flailing wildly as tears poured down her filthy soot-covered face, Staci was carried upward and into the billowing smoke, where she eventually disappeared from view.

Remaining on the deck below, Tommy Jarvis screamed, pounding his clenched fists into the puddles beneath his knees, an ominous, familiar and exceptionally dangerous light beginning to rapidly spread across his body. Again the boy screamed, and again he slammed his fists into the broken husk beneath his knees. Instantly Krystoph recognized the expression on Tommy's face. It was the look created when loss and frustration had become entirely too much to bear, the look created at the moment when an absolute, unending rage snagged whatever good might remain and strangled it from existence. Krystoph so easily recognized the expression because he had been wearing it himself for some time. Lurching forward, Tommy buried his head between his tightly drawn fists, breathing heavily as the light covering his body began to convulse and spew flashes of shaky, angry electricity.

He was losing control of his powers. That much was obvious.

Now more than ever, Krystoph knew he needed to get off the ship. Directly across from Tommy, the front of the Briar Patch was hammered with a series of violent cannon blasts. The heavy weapons ripped away a gargantuan chunk of Fluuffytail's ship and sent it spiraling to the depths of the ocean below. Through the dusty insanity, Krystoph noticed a second Scarbeak circling the area of the dying ship much the way a vulture might its prey. The rear section of the Briar Patch lifted into the air, beginning its slow slide forward into the cool churning waters. The black waters were hungry, and they would not be denied their meal. At no point did Krystoph allow the airborne Scarbeak to leave his line of sight. Eyeing it carefully, he watched it circle the ship's broken husk, a heavily armored Ochan soldier planted firmly at the center of its impressive wingspan. When the beast was moments from completing its rotation, Krystoph charged full speed toward the shattered, sinking front hull. Passing by Tommy Jarvis at full speed, he glanced momentarily in the child's direction. The electric light encasing Tommy was growing darker with every passing second, morphing into frighteningly deep purples, blues and blacks. This was a very different kind of magic than Krystoph had seen before. This magic was ugly. This magic was angry. Tommy's eyes went dark and empty, tears like scalding hot lava seeping from the black caverns where his pupils once rested. Though the sight was undeniably amazing, Krystoph could afford to stare at the boy no longer. The pink-skinned child's fate was his own, and maybe it was better that way. Krystoph understood he had only one shot to make this work, one shot to escape. Fail, and he'd be forced to face the wrath of the Ochan armada, or whatever dark thing Tommy Jarvis was becoming.

At the exact moment the Scarbeak completed its circle, Krystoph leapt through a cloud of black smoke from the sinking ship and in its direction, as arrows and cannonballs whizzed past his airborne form. His body slammed full force into the Ochan seated on the back of the beast. The strength of the blow knocked the soldier from his perch and set him spinning into the shadowy waters below. Hoisting himself into the Scarbeak's saddle, Krystoph kicked the creature stiffly in the side and tugged back on its reins. Altering the angle of its wings slightly, the monster immediately swung upward, heading full speed into the clouds above. It took only an instant for the beast to adapt to its new master.

Far below, Captain Fluuffytail's ship was barely recognizable. What little remained of the Briar Patch was hammered by an onslaught of cannon fire that instantly reduced the ship to barely more than a plume of awful black soot and wild fiery debris. From this cloud of craziness, however, something stirred, something black, and ugly and uncontrolled, something hungry for vengeance in a way to which only Krystoph could fully relate. The former Ochan general pulled tighter on the Scarbeak's reins, and the creature's wings began to pump double time. Soon the thick cloud cover overhead would engulf the pair completely. Krystoph understood just how important it was to get as high and far away from the battle below as possible. That was the only way he'd survive what came next.

66. BREAKING POINT

For Tommy Jarvis, in the beginning there were only sounds. No longer able to sustain the copious amounts of energy flowing from his fingertips, a foggy, out of focus darkness settled in and he dropped to the sloppy-wet deck of the Briar Patch with a thump. With unconsciousness beginning to grab hold of his senses and tug him downward, his brain pleaded for his body to continue fighting. Tommy knew he shouldn't stop, understood full well that he couldn't stop and exactly what would happen if he did. In reality, though, none of this mattered. He was simply too weak, and fighting the inevitable proved to be a pointless endeavor. Though visually the world around had faded into something dark, blurry and unrecognizable, Tommy's other senses remained mostly sharp. The sound of snapping wood and the pained, helpless yelps of the ship's crew pounded an awful out-of-tune beat against the interior of his skull and the exterior of his screaming brain. Perhaps not so surprisingly, the soft, familiar sobs of Staci managed to float just above the madness of the dying ship and the awful battle. She was whimpering, squeaking his name through cracked lips and dripping tears. He could feel the softness of her skin and the warmth of her chest as she hoisted his limp body closer, running her fingers through his hair and rocking him back and forth like a baby. In his mind, Tommy told her that it would be okay, that he wouldn't let anyone hurt her. In his head, he convinced her that he just needed a little rest, just a moment of silence before he saved her and everyone else on the ship. His body, however, didn't believe a word of this and ignored his brain, choosing instead to remain thoroughly unresponsive. Though only fourteen years of age, Tommy Jarvis had spent the majority of those years attempting to save everyone else in his life, often at the expense of his own well-being. For Tommy, the idea of something resembling a childhood had become an abstract, a concept devoid of meaning, a flawed hypothesis that would never truly be realized. For Tommy, there had always been and would always be only fighting, lies and sadness. What he was left with, in the aftermath of his youth, was an ugly, unending repetition without hope of parole.

As one might imagine, he was tired of it.

Sobbing wildly, Staci pulled her friend closer to her chest and dug her nose into the soft fibers of his sweat-soaked blond hair. Around her, the ship continued to be torn to pieces. Her world had quickly morphed into a jumbled mess of smoke, shrapnel and all the awful sounds accompanying them. The shabby, beaten remains of the Briar Patch squealed in agony as they were reduced to little more than flaming piles of waste. Closing her eyes, Staci's body began to settle into a gentle sway, almost as if she were rocking her injured friend to sleep, yet praying beyond all hope that this didn't happen. Most alarming to the young girl was the fact that in this single instant, quite possibly moments from her death, her mind had not wandered to her childhood or her friends or even her parents. Instead she could think of only one thing: Tommy Jarvis. More than anything in the universe, Staci didn't want him to go and couldn't imagine a world without him in it. Though she was uncertain at exactly which point over the last six months Tommy came to mean so much to her, the fact that he did was not only astounding, but terrifying.

Squeezing his limp body tighter, she pulled him to her chest and buried her face in the crook of his neck while mumbling, "Please Tommy, please, not like this. Wake up, please, wake up." His skin was cold and wet, sweating profusely like a chilly drink on a warm summer day.

From somewhere behind, a cloud of soot rolled in like fog, engulfing the pair of sopping children. It was in this moment that Staci's heart began to warm once again, and she smiled. The familiar feeling was a welcome one. She'd experienced it enough already to know what would come next. A wonderfully sweet tingling sensation spread quickly across her chest, into her shoulder, down her arms and into her hands. From there it squeezed through the tips of her fingers and into the flesh of Tommy's back. Where moments before there was only emptiness, there was now fullness. Where there had only been sadness, now there were smiles. Staci was repairing him, filing his aching muscles with a renewed vigor the same as she'd done before. Breathing into Tommy's neck, she bit her lower lip and closed her eyes and smiled.

Everything would be better now. It had to be.

Before the tingly glow could move outside of Tommy and to the remainder of Fluuffytail's crew, however, thick leathery claws grabbed hold of Staci's shoulders and lifted her into the air. As a set of horribly bent, painfully sharp fingernails dug nearly a quarter inch into her tender flesh, Staci screamed out loud and lurched her body forward, reaching for assistance from her sleepy-eyed friend. Unfortunately for her, Tommy was only partially aware of what was occurring, and unable to offer any assistance. The light from Staci's heart tapered away, folded back into her hands, shot up her arms, across her shoulders, and returned at last to her chest. The wonderful, life-giving warmth had vanished entirely. As yet another cloud of smoke swallowed both she and the massive beast hauling her upward, she made one final bit of eye contact with the partially awake Tommy Jarvis before he and the ship and the madness of the battle were gone. Within a matter of seconds, she found herself high above, looking down on what little of the ship remained intact below. It was from this vantage point that she would witness the end game. It was from here she would watch her friend die.

Not fully aware of what was happening, Tommy opened his eyes just in time to see Staci engulfed by a cloud of grayish smoke with tears pouring from her eyes as she reached for him. It was in this singular moment that everything changed.

This was the precise instant that young Tommy Jarvis snapped.

Something cold, dark and nasty, something hidden away, churning and bubbling and suppressed for years, began to boil to life deep within the core of the boy's stomach. Like a bizarre eight-legged cancer advancing across the delicate filaments of a spider web, the awfulness spread across the interior of his body and into his fists. Slamming his knuckles into the charred remains of wood beneath his knees, Tommy screamed aloud as the crackling electricity from within began to spread into every hidden crevice of his body. Clouding his brain, the disgusting thing advanced into the spaces behind his eyes and pressed forward, instantly transforming them into something entirely different, a pit without a bottom, a hole with no end. To his left, Tommy watched blankly as the Ochan Krystoph ran past at full speed before disappearing into a cloud of smoke. He was running away. He was a coward. Behind Tommy, the remains of the Briar Patch lifted into the air as chilly sea water began to rush onto the utterly demolished deck. They had lost. The Ochans had won. They'd lost and the ship was sinking. Despite the victory, the Ochan armada continued its relentless assault on the defenseless vessel. Arrows and cannon fire pounded violently into the rotted and broken timbers beneath Tommy's knees. They were breaking what had already been broken and beating what had been thoroughly beaten. This was an insult added to injury, the overkill of war at its absolute most pointless and ugly. Watching as the hungry water slowly swallowed the Briar Patch, Tommy understood its frustration and related to its pain. Not only did the Ochan vessels intend on sinking the ship, they hoped to wipe it from existence and erase it from memory. They'd won, and still they refused to relent. No one ever stopped. Nothing ever stopped. He wanted it to stop. He'd had enough of this and he wanted it to stop now.

He wanted it to stop and he would make it stop.

Rising slowly to his feet, Tommy suddenly realized that nothing mattered anymore. He had long forgotten about his brother, Staci, Pleebo and Walcott, the war and even his father. He simply wanted it all to end, to go away and never come back. He was tired of lying, tired of keeping things inside, and sick of being the sounding rod for the emotions of the emotionally unstable. He was sick of everything.

As the last of the Briar Patch sank into the abyss, Tommy Jarvis and his awful black glow remained atop the water. Standing effortlessly on the surface, the boy bobbed in tune with the waves. Surrounding him were hundreds of ships as dark and foreboding as the nasty electricity crackling and popping off his salty-soaked flesh. For the first time in his life, Tommy understood without a shadow of a doubt what needed to be done, what he believed should have been done long ago. He had reached the point of no return. Not only had he crossed the line in the sand, he'd wiped it from existence. From this point on, there would be no excuses and no forgiveness. From here on out, there would be no coming back. Life offered no second chances and neither would he.

This was his breaking point.

67. ANOTHER DEAD GENERAL

From his vessel miles away, General Thrax watched expressionless as a monstrous black void spread from the alien child's body and began moving forward at a blistering pace while swallowing hundreds upon hundreds of his ships and wiping them from existence with horrifying ease.

He had been lucky enough to survive this magic once. His luck, however, had run out.

68. FAMILIAR FEELING

At some point, the pain of the Scarbeak's claws digging into her flesh, not to mention the fact that she was sailing hundreds of feet above a vast endless ocean, became too much for Staci to bear, and she passed out. Time passed, though there was no way of telling exactly how much. Eventually, as all things did, Staci's hibernation came to an end. The darkness began to patiently twist, mold and pop, like a lump of sparkly modeling clay in a darkened room. Empty cavernous blacks were given form, depth, and weight as the world sharpened slightly and stumbled awkwardly into focus.

The muscles in her back and legs were sore. Having gone untreated, the wounds on her shoulder were throbbing significantly, caked in a crusty layer of dried blood. She was lying on something that felt like ice, though as hard as stone and equally uncomfortable. Her lower back ached, and her legs were tingling as if the blood had been drained from them. Her head seemed to weigh a thousand pounds, and when she attempted to lift it, her skull throbbed painfully. Every joint in her body felt stiff, as if they hadn't moved in decades; ancient, delicate and brittle, they felt in danger of crumbling to dust at any given moment.

Through a pair of still sleepily fluttering eyelids, Staci scanned the area around her. Wherever she was, it was dark. This much went without saying. The air was thick, heavy and so incredibly cold that her every breath came to life in smoky puffs from between her cracked lips. Though much of the strange new world remained foggy, Staci instantly recognized thick vertical strips of black less than ten feet away; they were iron, steel or some sort of metal. They were bars. Grunting deeply, she forced herself into something slightly resembling a sitting position. Scooting on her rear across the cold stone, she propped her body against the back wall and relaxed for a moment, attempting to let the pain in her torso subside a bit.

Closing her eyes, she tried her best to recall the moments leading up to the moment she awoke in this foul smelling place. Though it should have been simple, the act proved remarkably difficult. Everything was fuzzy, out of focus and jumbled like puzzle pieces scattered in tall grass. She could vaguely recall Aquari, the Briar Patch, the explosions, and Tommy pressed to her chest, unconscious—wait. Where was Tommy? There was also something black - something ugly and dark. Though it was difficult to nail down the awful thing's exact shape, she vaguely recalled an expanding void of some sort, something she noticed from miles above.

What happened to Tommy? Where was Tommy? As her eyes began slowly adjusting to the low light, Staci took note of a familiar shape in the cell across from her. Sprawled on the floor of the dreary, ten-by-ten enclosure opposite her own was none other than Donald Rondage. The same hair, the same ugly green shirt; it had to be Donald. Crawling across the floor on her hands and knees, Staci pressed her head between the bars anxiously, happy to see a familiar face, even if it was Donald's.

Wary of her surroundings and who might be listening, her voice remained a cautious whisper. "Donald? Donald, is that you?"

The Donald shape didn't move. In fact, the boy's face remained smashed against the freezing stone the entire time, offering no acknowledgement whatsoever of her frantic whispers.

Reaching up, Staci wrapped her frozen hands around the ice cold steel and called to his motionless body once more. "Donald, wake up."

Though much of the boy was obscured by the shadows, she was sure it was him. It had to be him; who else could it be? It couldn't be anyone else.

"Donald, it's Staci. Please, wake up, please!" The volume of her voice rose significantly, teetering perilously on the thin line separating a whisper from a full on scream.

Still there was no movement. If, in fact, the prone figure locked behind the bars on the opposite end of the dark hallway was Donald Rondage, he was either unconscious or dead. Staci's body shuddered at the possibility of the second option being true.

From the shadows to her left, something chuckled. Startled, she immediately slid away from the bars to the rear of the cell until she was unable to move further. From the shadows of the darkened hallway stepped a pair of muscled Ochans holding bows nearly the length of their bodies. From the blackness to the right of them stepped two more. Wide, disgusting smiles were spread across each of the soldiers' dark green faces as they cackled slyly in her direction. The previously motionless body of Donald Rondage wearily looked up and stared at her with a set of sad, defeated eyes. This was not the Donald Rondage she'd known all her life. This was someone else. They'd done something to him. They'd changed him. Seconds later, the boy lowered his head to the floor again with a breathy sigh. From somewhere further down the hall came the sound of a massive steel lock and the creak of a door swinging open. A pair of thunderous echoing footsteps followed immediately. Something large was coming her way.

When at last the footsteps stopped, the shadows began to speak, the voice more frightening than anything Staci had heard over the course of her young life: "Escort the boy to his permanent cell."

After unlocking Donald's cell, two of the Ochans lifted him into a standing position while the remaining two kept their weapons trained on his every subtle movement. The weapons, however, proved unnecessary. At no point did Donald fight, fuss, or even make a sound. His limbs had gone loose, wobbly, and ultimately useless. His head hung shamefully low as the massive creatures dragged him further down the hall and out of sight. At no point did he even glance in Staci's direction. He acted as if she was already dead, and maybe it was the truth.

When they had gone, the frightening voice rose from the shadows once more. "Fret not, little one. I have not forgotten about you."

Stepping into the light, the tyrant king of Ocha at last exposed himself to the shivering girl. He was a massive creature, larger than any of the Ochans Staci had the unpleasantness of meeting thus far. His beard was long and gray, his eyes containing the absence of anything calling itself color. Though the enormous creature had yet to formally introduce himself as the Ochan king, somehow Staci understood this was the case. In truth, he could have been no other.

"There will be ample time for you and me to become better acquainted over the course of the next few weeks, little one. You see, there is something locked inside of you that I would very much like to have for myself, and I will have it, no matter what. Even if it requires me to slice you open and rip it out with my bare hands."

Staci's body instantly froze.

This had absolutely nothing to do with the temperature.

69. CASTAWAY

Time passed, as time tends to do. When Tommy Jarvis at last opened his eyes, he found himself staring at a sky filled with clouds, stars, and the yellow-red glow of a sinking sun on the horizon. In this briefest of instants, both night and day were as one, harmoniously sharing the heavens and morphing into a glorious amalgamation of the two, which resulted in something unique, beautiful and astoundingly different. In a universe priding itself on repetition, different is often a welcome distraction from the norm.

Every square inch of Tommy's body felt drained and worthless, as if he'd been sliced open and emptied out. His stomach gurgled while his head throbbed, the sensations competing for his attention. The violent sounds of battle had faded away some time ago. All that remained were the waves, the breeze, and his uneven breath. Tommy enjoyed the familiarity of each sound individually, but appreciated them considerably more as a set. The silence was a welcome guest, and the hush of near-nothingness a comforting ally.

Though every inch of his body ached to continue his simple slumber, he sensed the presence of the frustrating necessity to wake.

Wearily flopping his head to the side, Tommy spotted only ocean: water, more water and still more after that, crystal blue for as far as he could see. Resting comfortably on the sea shelf in the distance was the Aquari sun. More crimson red than yellow in hue, it had only recently begun to dip below the horizon. Beyond it, the outlines of the pastel-colored moons had begun to fade into the purple-blue sky. Despite the obvious differences, for the most part the sky in this world was remarkably similar to the place he called home. Tommy found this fact oddly comforting in a strange, slightly unsettling sort of way.

Allowing his loose head to flop to the left, he spotted yet more water. Over the tips of his dirty shoes, more still. Everything was gone. The Briar Patch, the Ochan vessels, Nestor, Captain Fluuffytail, his brother — gone without a trace, as if they never existed. Slowly Tommy's fingers began to creep to life, lightly tracing the finely sculpted contours of the solid object on which he currently floated. The details felt familiar. He'd seen them before. They were letters, letters that once spelled the words Briar Patch.

He was floating on what little remained of Fluuffytail's ship.

Unable to maneuver his extremities further than a few inches in any direction, Tommy dropped his head to the floating timber beneath him and sighed deeply. While he appreciated the fact that his memories were crystal clear, they were almost too crystal and too clear. It was as if he was seeing them through the eyes of another, observing rather than participating. He could recall everything, every detail to its absolute fullest. Every excruciating second of every unbearable minute began replaying in his head.

He knew exactly what he'd done.

The instant Staci was captured, lifted into the air and taken away from him, something inside him tore in two. The concepts of rescuing and helping, or simply preserving, no longer mattered. Revenge instead became the priority. It suddenly wasn't enough for the Ochans to go away or even just die. For the briefest of moments, Tommy wanted much more than that; he wanted to be the one to kill them. He wanted to see their faces and watch them scream, to bathe in the dusty cloud created by their charred corpses. As the awful blackness began pouring from his fingertips, he knew exactly what would happen, how it would happen, and what would likely be the end result. What he did, he did of sound mind and without a moment's hesitation. What he did, he enjoyed doing. The realization of this sent an immediate, horrifying chill down his spine. The fact that he could not only entertain such ideas, but carry them out, was beyond words terrifying for the fourteen-year old boy.

It made no sense, and yet it made perfect sense.

What had he done? Nicky, Staci and Nestor: they were all gone and it was his fault. They were all gone and they weren't coming back. In the end, it wasn't the muscle-bound lizards with the teeth for days, and weapons larger than the whole of his young body that did them in; it was he and he alone. Coaxing his aching, useless muscles to life, Tommy managed to awkwardly prop himself onto his elbows with a pained grunt. His skin felt salty and damp, sticky with the dew of the ocean breeze. Gazing over the waters surrounding him, he could see nothing but an endless sea seeming to stretch on forever. How long had he been out here? How long had he been unconscious? How long had he been at the mercy of the tides? His clothes were shredded and filthy, his hair a sticky-stiff mess of dirty blond fibers. His mouth felt as dry as his stomach did empty. When was the last time he ate? He couldn't remember. Save for the single piece of wood he was currently lying on, there were no other signs of the battle that raged atop these waters: no fabric, or steel, or flesh, not even a splinter of wood. Everything was gone. He and the ocean had taken it all.

Dropping his head to the lumber, Tommy buried his face in his hands. It didn't make any sense. Nothing made any sense. His chest felt heavy and his ribs sore. In spite of the incredibly open space in which he found himself, the world felt as if it was closing in. Lifting his legs to his chest, he coiled into the fetal position as his body began to shake uncontrollably, the shattered wood beneath wobbling atop the uneven waves. Tommy Jarvis was alone with nowhere to go and no one to turn to, alone again. He'd lost everything he cared about, everyone who meant anything at all to him. He'd lost them all and they weren't coming back. He'd lost them and it was his fault.

Shivering atop the thick, slippery wood and the gently rolling waves, something quite uncommon happened to young Tommy Jarvis. For the first time in a very long time, he began to cry. Eventually the crying transformed into a lingering sob, drenching his face in tears, eyes suddenly afire with molten lava. In time, the sobs stretched angrily into frustrated, shamed screams. It had been so long since he'd cried, screamed or allowed himself to feel anything at all—so very long, much too long. Despite the pain and the sadness, it felt good.

Tommy cried for hours, emptying himself of everything he'd built up inside and cursing himself for the things he'd done. When there were no more tears left to shed, he fell back into sleep. It was here he planned to spend what remained of his life. He would just go to sleep and stay asleep. Like an insect, hunger would pick away at him in small bites until there was nothing left. He was content to die here, to pass willingly into the unconscious world, never wake up, and eventually draw to a close. This was where it would end for him, alone among the waves of this faraway place. A part of him doubted he deserved even this, after all he'd done. He was worse than his father ever was. He was worse than Krystoph or the king of Ocha or all of them combined. He had become a killer. A quiet end among the gentle waters was far more than he deserved. Due to a lack of options, however, it would have to do. Inhaling deeply, Tommy closed his eyes and rested his heavy head roughly on the tear-stained wood. In the end, he believed dying would be easy, much easier than living ever was.

Tommy's sleep proved to be a deeper, more relaxing sleep than he'd had in years, the kind of sleep that could only come when one finds themselves having reached the end, where nothing was left and nothing mattered. A dreamless sleep in which there was only silence and darkness, and the all too quick passing of time.

His sleep did not last forever, no matter how much he wished it could. When Tommy next opened his weary eyes, the sky above was black, punctuated by a vast array of stars and ghostly space gasses thinly connecting them somewhere deep in the void. It was an incredible sight, a fantasy almost too beautiful to exist in the real world. He'd never seen anything like it.

Never had he wanted to see anything less.

On the brink of tears once again, Tommy glanced in the direction of his feet. Though everything around him was dark, there was something oddly darker protruding from the waters ahead, something his floating piece of debris was gradually moving toward. The closer he got to the ominous black shape, the more it came into focus. Land. He was floating toward land. Barely more than a hundred yards across, this bit of solid ground among the vast Aquari ocean looked at first glance to be little more than a massive grayish-black stone. At its apex, the dark rock came to a terrifyingly pointed tip rising at least fifty yards above sea level. Dark, slimy, and covered sporadically in a disgusting green-blue moss, the patch of land looked lifeless and dead.

Drifting ever closer to the jagged stones, Tommy's floating debris was pulled toward a cave cut into the side that vaguely resembled the mouth of an enormous, toothy beast anxious to gobble him up. The dead rock was swallowing him whole. Still incredibly weak, he managed to prop himself onto his elbows once again. The act left him surprisingly winded and sore. From there, he gritted his teeth, winced, and found the energy to crawl to his knees. The moment he drifted into the cave, the stars disappeared and everything went black. Unable to see beyond a few inches, the cave's interior offered nothing, and yet somehow even less than that. This was the absence of nothing; this was a void and the absence of a void.

The breezy sea air suddenly turned sharp, stiff and cold, as the winds disappeared completely. Intent on devouring everything in its path, the darkness took even the sounds of the waves and replaced them with the whispers and echoes of what they once were. Careful not to lose his balance, Tommy's muscles tightened as he leaned forward into the nothingness. Squinting his eyes, he tried his best to locate something solid, anything at all that might give him a sense of where he was and what was around him. The void offered nothing in return. With his breath becoming more ragged, Tommy realized that even it sounded noticeably different now, lagging and distant, the wheeze of a tired old man who had lost the ability to properly breathe, and the willingness to try. With a sudden jerk, the floating wood beneath Tommy's knees came to an abrupt stop that tossed him violently forward. Rolling head-over-heels, he somersaulted onto something slippery, solid, and cold as ice. The movement sent a shock of pain across the whole of his already sore back. Arms outstretched, breathing heavily while trying to ignore this new twinge of pain, Tommy cautiously attempted to stand. The ground felt as if it had been greased, which forced him to be extra careful so that his feet didn't slide out from underneath him. The air was different here than it had been a moment ago, colder and clingier. It latched to his skin and drenched him in a slimy, sticky, entirely uncomfortable wetness.

Quite suddenly, from the darkness came a sound: footsteps. Immediately following the footsteps, a whisper floated in from all directions at once, bouncing back and forth off the hidden cave walls. The sound caught Tommy off guard; both his heart and his body jumped. As he took a step backward, he lost his balance and crashed to his rear on the slippery stiffness beneath. Again came the whisper, only this time it was not one, but two. The words were garbled, too dreamy and distant for him to make sense of.

Before Tommy's brain could convince him otherwise, his mouth muttered the word, "Hello?"

He didn't know why he said it. In fact, it seemed quite a stupid thing to do. If there was something hidden among the shadows and whispering from the void, informing it of his location was probably not the wisest decision. In the end, however, what difference did it make? If the whispers ultimately led to a monster and resulted in his being gobbled up, so be it. This was what he wanted anyway. It was what he deserved. He had screwed up, he had failed, and he was done. He was tired, and he didn't want to play anymore. Enough was enough.

A part of him hoped the end would be painless, while another still wished for the exact opposite.

Closing his eyes, Tommy took a deep breath and dug his nails into the slippery cold ground before stating sternly to the shadows, "I'm over here."

At first his voice was barely above a whisper. The volume, however, rose in conjunction with his growing anxiousness and fear. "I'm over here! I'm right here!"

Again came the whispers, this time in closer succession, a million tiny voices from a million tiny people calling to him from throughout the endless black.

Taking less care than before, Tommy stood once again, his frozen hands pulled into icy fists, his face contorting into a jumble of sharp angles. "I'm right here! Come and get me!"

The sound of his voice echoed across the dark expanse, mixing with the whispers rapidly turning into something better described as chatter. Surrounded entirely by the bizarre sounds, Tommy took a step forward angrily, anxious to put an end to this nonsense, anxious to put an end to himself.

"Come on, already! I'm right here! Come get me!"

All at once, the voices stopped. The moment they'd disappeared, a blinding ball of light erupted from directly in front of him. Swallowing the darkness entirely, the incredible glow replaced the black void with yet another made entirely of white. Carrying with it an odd heat, the light instantly turned the slippery dry, and the cold, warm. Using his forearms to shield his eyes, Tommy peeked cautiously through the cracks between his fingers and into the light with squinted eyes. From the whiteness came another whisper. Condensed, this time it was a single voice, feminine, soft, and familiar.

Dreamily it whispered his name. "Tommy?"

Lowering his hands from his face, Tommy watched as a ghostly, bluish figure emerged from the glow; its edges were blurry and stretched, extending backward to an epicenter of warm, white oblivion. The figure seemed to be barely more than an outline; without form or volume, it was two dimensions given shape in a three-dimensional world. Despite the oddness of the bizarre thing, almost immediately Tommy Jarvis recognized something within the odd play of sparkling and bending lights.

Confused and unable to move, he watched as the wiry figure of bent light approached and came to a stop less than ten feet away. Reaching forward, it extended its twisted, glowing arms in his direction. A shape on the area slightly resembling its face curved gently into a smile.

In a shaky, confused voice, Tommy uttered a single, unbelievable word: "Mom?"

70. DAY DREAMING ON THE EDGE OF FOREVER

The crowd outside Zanell's modest underground dwelling continued to grow for days. Since the rumbling of the dark army above began to shake the city, she had yet to address them. Her reluctance had not stopped the crowds from slowly swelling. The most devout of followers chose to set up camps outside her door, waiting patiently with their families for whatever words of guidance she might choose to offer. From the perspective of the citizens of New Tipoloo, it was Zanell who had brought the children of the prophecy into this war, and it was the children who had rescued many of them from the clutches of Prince Valkea and guaranteed death. The Fillagrou prophecy was the truth, and its speaker the truth teller. They would wait as long as necessary to hear her words, and they would wait with baited breath. They had been saved, and being saved is among the most life-changing of all life-changing experiences.

Zanell, of course, found the whole thing rather silly.

She was no savior. She wielded no magic powers, and her words or actions would in no way alter the course of things to come. She was as much at the mercy of the tides of the universe as they. The only real difference was that she was aware of this fact. There was no such thing as hope. Hope implied possibility, and possibility was simply an illusion. Sprawled out on the fabric of her dusty cot, Zanell stared at the ceiling with her enormous sleepy eyes. In New Tipoloo, hidden hundreds of feet below the surface of the forest above, the days often blended together. Night came only when the candles had been dimmed. Day emerged once again when they were relit. While life here had proven itself often dreary, it was her life and it would continue to be her life for some time more.

The day was rapidly approaching when this would change. The crowds outside her door remained mostly silent, showing a remarkable amount of patience and consideration despite the fact that she was essentially ignoring their desire for words of hope. A part of Zanell wished she could offer them something, anything at all to let them know she cared and that she hadn't forgotten, because she did, and she had not. The reality was she knew she couldn't. It was not her place to do so; it never had been. The end game grew nearer with every passing hour, and this was simply the way things needed to play out. This was the way they had always played out.

Sitting up, she grabbed hold of the blue candle flickering on the table near the foot of her bed and gazed into the flame for a moment. By the time this tiny flame had burned the wax of the candle to a nub, everything would have changed. The families gathered outside would have long since given up on her, and shortly after that, the city of New Tipoloo would be little more than a memory. Lost, its inhabitants would instead choose to dedicate themselves to a different cause entirely. New players would have reluctantly joined the fray, and a war that would shake the whole of the universe begun. All that had come before would pale in comparison to what came next. Many would die, and those who did not would suffer greatly. Though Zanell understood happy endings were as much an illusion as possibilities, all too often even the illusion could prove difficult to attain.

Things were only going to get worse before they got better, as things tended to do.

Leaning forward, Zanell pursed her lips together and softly blew the flame from existence, immediately bathing the room in darkness. Lowering her head to the cot below, she rolled to her side and away from the dim lights of the city streets peeking through the cracks in her door, then closed her eyes. Right now she wanted simply to sleep, to sleep and forget about everything that had happened and even those things yet to occur. Unfortunately for Zanell, the concept of sleep was little more than a vague remembrance. These days, her life had become a rambled mess of jumbled, nonsensical dreams. Whether she was awake or otherwise made no difference; the dreams did not stop. Even now, from the safety of her tiny dwelling, curled on her side with throngs of believers teetering on the brink of a wonderful sleepy oblivion just beyond her doorway, Zanell's mind drifted from one end of the universe to the other. The distance traversed proved much too much for any single being to fully comprehend, including her. Much of what she witnessed was familiar, while more yet proved so strange and unexplainable she'd never understand its purpose and wasn't likely meant to.

She could see her brother Pleebo, shivering among the dying trees of the freezing Ochan forest. His pale, wiry body was racked by indescribable pain. Lifting his forearm to his mouth, he bit down on his bruised flesh to keep from screaming as a regiment of Ochan soldiers searched for him in a chilly, cascading fog and enormous mounds of black snow. He was alone and frightened and dying, wondering how much longer he could survive in that awful, hellish place. Sobbing into his icy flesh, his mind wandered to his little sister, Zanell, completely unaware that she could see him and was doing the same.

In the dungeon of the tyrant king, Zanell watched as Roustaf dangled from the ceiling in his tiny cage. The incredible pain brought to life by the loss of his friend had transformed into anger the likes of which the little man hadn't felt in years. Before the night was through, it would have consumed him entirely, changing him into someone else, changing him into someone he didn't necessarily want to be.

Across from Roustaf, helpless behind her own set of steel bars, the pink-skinned body of Tahnja shook wildly, due mostly to the incredible, biting Ochan cold. Her people were not accustomed to temperatures such as this, and she feared she would not last much longer. The sound created by the chattering of her teeth echoed across the dank, lifeless hallways. Gazing in the direction of Roustaf, she noticed that the little man was still sitting with his back to her. He'd been this way for hours and hadn't spoken a word since returning to the dungeon with Donald. He looked lost, lost and unwilling to find his way back. This hurt her far more than the cold.

Far away from the terrifying chill of Ocha, Zanell spotted a massive group of determined rescuers, including Fellow Undergotten, Christopher Jarvis, and Owen Little emerging from the underground tunnels of New Tipoloo and venturing forth cautiously into the humid night. As the Red Forest would become more and more crowded with Ochan soldiers and beasts of burden, their journey would prove considerably more dangerous than they originally planned, and their chances of survival slimmer than they hoped. Each was aware of this fact, and it ultimately made no difference. Fellow Undergotten patted Chris Jarvis reassuringly on the shoulder. Though it did little to change their situation, the tiny gesture proved exactly what Chris needed.

Oftentimes, it's the simplest of things that prove the most profound.

Blasting from one world to the next in a fraction of a fraction of a second, Zanell neared the doorway to Aquari. A squawking, tired Scarbeak came to a sliding stop in the sand, kicking clumps of soil into the air and encasing it in a cloud of dust. Leaping from its feathered back among the cloud, the scarred Ochan Krystoph gazed briefly over the relatively still waters behind and the twirling, glassy-black night sky above. This place was a paradise; this place was a war zone. Recalling the incredible black light he watched pour from the pink-skinned child and devour hundreds of Ochan ships and thousands of soldiers with indescribable ease, for an instant Krystoph wondered if any of Fluuffytail's crew could possibly have survived the attack. Lowering his head, he looked away. It didn't matter. All that mattered now was the artifact dangling from a piece of twine wrapped around his muscled neck. He had his reasons for stealing it from the king originally, and his reasons for hiding it. He too had his reasons for wanting it back. Kragamel would pay for what he'd done. This was Krystoph's mission. This was the reason he continued to breathe, the only reason.

At the doorway to the world of man, Zanell watched as an indescribably large force of Ochans continued to gather. Monsters with necks reaching higher than the trees leaned forward and tore away chunks of earth surrounding the puddle leading to the hundredth world, then tossed them aside with frightening ease. In time, what was once a puddle would become a lake, a vast lake large enough for an army of snarling, angry creatures to pass through. This would be their greatest and their final conquest. For those who called the world on the other side home, the invasion would come quickly and violently.

History had shown all too often that this is a trait endings generally share.

In that strange, still-undiscovered world, bathed in sweat as the aches in his back continued to cause him a considerable amount of discomfort, Zanell watched as Ed Williamson stood in his modest backyard, blissfully unaware of the storm on the horizon. His wife hadn't spoken in days. She missed the children, and she was worried for their safety. Ed feared this would happen the moment she announced her desire to become a foster family. Worried for the feelings of the woman he'd spent the majority of his life with, he had warned her repeatedly not to get too close to Nicky and Tommy. Edna attempted to listen to her husband, understanding full well that there was, in fact, some common sense in his words. Ultimately, though, she failed, and she was heartbroken because of it. High above Ed, clouds of foreboding had begun to gather in the grayish sky. Within the hour, the downpour would begin. The rain would continue falling for weeks, well into the start of the invasion.

Sometimes the universe knows, and sometimes the universe cries.

Somewhere clean, white and eerily silent, Zanell caught an ever-so-brief glimpse of a weary eyed Nicky Jarvis as he opened his eyes. As quickly as it arrived, however, it faded away.

Eventually Zanell knew she would manage to wrangle something resembling sleep from the turmoil of her mind. She knew this because it had already happened, the same as everything else. When she first inherited her powers, she was intent on somehow making sense of them, on finding some sort of meaning hidden among the madness. Now she had begun to realize how incredibly foolish an idea this was. She was searching for what couldn't be found, for significance in places significance simply could not exist, nor should. The universe is far too complex and layered for such a simple, trivial, biological concept. The universe is endless. The universe is infinity. Infinity has no desire to be categorized, studied or made sense of. For infinity, endings and beginnings and answers mean nothing. For infinity the equation is thus: Why would one ever hope to find an answer, when questions alone are far more interesting?

ABOUT THE AUTHOR

Steven Novak is a writer, illustrator, graphic designer, podcaster, and lover of all things full-blown nerdy and vaguely nerd-related. He currently resides in southern California, where he lives with his wife of over ten years, Tami. Sometimes he forgets to shave and because of this he often sports a rather shaggy beard. Liars and Thieves is the second novel in a the Forts trilogy with the final installment due later this year. His work can be found at **www.novakillustration.com**